The Top of the World

By

Ethel M. Dell

Author of
"The Way of an Eagle," "The Lamp in the Desert," etc.

G. P. Putnam's Sons
New York and London
The Knickerbocker Press
1920

I DEDICATE THIS BOOK
TO THE PRECIOUS MEMORY
OF MY MOTHER

"The years shall not outgo my thinking of thee"

When you have reached the top of the world
    And only the stars remain,
Where there is never the sound of storm
    And neither cold nor rain,
Will it be by wealth, success, or fame
    That you mounted to your goal?
Nay, I mount only by faith and love
    And God's goodness to my soul.

When you have reached the top of the world
    And the higher stars grow near,
When greater dreams succeed our dreams
    And the lesser disappear,
Will the world at your feet seem good to you,
    A vision fair to see?
Nay, I look upward for one I love
    Who has promised to wait for me.

For to those who reach the top of the world
    The things of the world seem less
Than the rungs of the ladder by which they climbed
    To their place of happiness.
And I think that success and wealth and fame
    Will be the first to pall,
For they reach their goal but by faith and love
    And God's goodness over all.

CONTENTS

PART I

PART II

Contents

Contents

The Top of the World

——

PART I

CHAPTER I

ADVICE

"You ought to get married, Miss Sylvia," said old Jeffcott, the head gardener, with a wag of his hoary beard. "You'll need to be your own mistress now."

"I should hope I am that anyway," said Sylvia with a little laugh.

She stood in the great vinery—a vivid picture against a background of clustering purple fruit. The sunset glinted on her tawny hair. Her red-brown eyes, set wide apart, held a curious look, half indignant, half appealing.

Old Jeffcott surveyed her with loving admiration. There was no one in the world to compare with Miss Sylvia in his opinion. He loved the open, English courage of her, the high, inborn pride of race. Yet at the end of the survey he shook his head.

"There's not room for two mistresses in this establishment, Miss Sylvia," he said wisely. "Three years to have been on your own, so to speak, is too long. You did ought to get married, Miss Sylvia. You'll find it's the only way."

His voice took on almost a pleading note. He knew it was possible to go too far.

But the girl facing him was still laughing. She evidently felt no resentment.

"You see, Jeffcott," she said, "there's only one man in the world I could marry. And he's not ready for me yet."

Jeffcott wagged his beard again commiseratingly. "So you've never got over it, Miss Sylvia? Your feelings is still the same—after five years?"

"Still the same," said Sylvia. There was a momentary challenge in her bright eyes, but it passed. "It couldn't be any different," she said softly. "No one else could ever come anywhere near him."

Jeffcott sighed aloud. "I know he were a nice young gentleman," he conceded. "But I've seen lots as good before and since. He weren't nothing so very extraordinary, Miss Sylvia."

Sylvia's look went beyond him, seeming to rest upon something very far away. "He was to me, Jeffcott," she said. "We just—fitted each other, he and I."

"And you was only eighteen," pleaded Jeffcott. "You wasn't full-grown in those days."

"No?" A quick sigh escaped her; her look came back to him, and she smiled. "Well, I am now anyway; and that's the one thing that hasn't altered or grown old—the one thing that never could."

"Ah, dear!" said old Jeffcott. "What a pity now as you couldn't take up with young Mr. Eversley or that Mr. Preston over the way, or—or—any of them young gents with a bit of property as might be judged suitable!"

Sylvia's laugh rang through the vinery, a gay, infectious laugh.

"Oh, really, Jeffcott! You talk as if I had only got to drop my handkerchief for the whole countryside to rush to pick it up! I'm not going to take up with anyone, unless it's Mr. Guy Ranger. You don't seem to realize that we've been engaged all this time."

"Ah!" said old Jeffcott, looking sardonic. "And you not met for five years! Do you ever wonder to yourself what sort of a man he may be after five years, Miss Sylvia? It's a long time for a young man to keep in love at a distance. It's a very long time."

"It's a long time for both of us," said Sylvia. "But it hasn't altered us in that respect."

"It's been a longer time for him than it has for you," said Jeffcott shrewdly. "I'll warrant he's lived every minute of it. He's the sort that would."

Sylvia's wide brows drew together in a little frown. She had caught the note of warning in the old man's words, and she did not understand it.

"What do you mean, Jeffcott?" she said, with a touch of sharpness.

But Jeffcott backed out of the vinery and out of the discussion at the same moment. "You'll know what I mean one day, Miss Sylvia," he said darkly, "when you're married."

"Silly old man!" said Sylvia, taking up the cluster of grapes for which she had come and departing in the opposite direction. Jeffcott was a faithful old servant, but he could be very exasperating when he liked.

The gardens were bathed in the evening sunlight as she passed through them on her way to the house. The old Manor stood out grey and ancient against an opal sky. She looked up at it with

loving eyes. Her home meant very much to
Sylvia Ingleton. Until the last six months she
had always regarded it as her own life-long possession. For she was an only child, and for the
past three years she had been its actual mistress,
though virtually she had held the reins of government longer than that. Her mother had been
delicate for as long as she could remember, and it
was on account of her failing health that Sylvia
had left school earlier than had been intended,
that she might be with her. Since Mrs. Ingleton's
death, three years before, she and her father had
lived alone together at the old Manor in complete
accord. They had always been close friends, the
only dissension that had ever arisen between them
having been laid aside by mutual consent.

That dissension had been caused by Guy
Ranger. Five years before, when Sylvia had been
only eighteen, he had flashed like a meteor through
her sky, and no other star had ever shone for her
again. Though seven years older than herself,
he was little more than a boy, full of gaiety and
life, possessing an extraordinary fascination, but
wholly lacking in prospects, being no more than
the son of Squire Ingleton's bailiff.

The Rangers were people of good yeoman ex-
traction, and Guy himself had had a public school

education, but the fact of their position was an
obstacle which the squire had found insuperable.
Only his love for his daughter had restrained him
from violent measures. But Sylvia had somehow
managed to hold him, how no one ever knew,
for he was a man of fiery temper. And the end
of if it had been that Guy had been banished to
join a cousin farming in South Africa on the understanding that if he made a success of it he might
eventually return and ask Sylvia to be his wife.
There was to be no engagement between them,
and if she elected to marry in the meantime so
much the better, in the squire's opinion. He had
had little doubt that Sylvia would marry when
she had had time to forget some of the poignancy
of first love. But in this he had been mistaken.
Sylvia had steadfastly refused every lover who had
come her way.

He had found another billet for old Ranger, and
had installed a dour Scotchman in his place. But
Sylvia still corresponded with young Guy, still
spoke of him as the man she meant to marry. It
was true she did not often speak of him, but that
might have been through lack of sympathetic
listeners. There was, moreover, about her an
innate reserve which held her back where her deep-
est feelings were concerned. But her father knew,

and she meant him to know, that neither time nor distance had eradicated the image of the man she loved from her heart. The days on which his letters reached her were always marked with a secret gladness, albeit the letters themselves held sometimes little more than affectionate commentary upon her own.

That Guy was making his way and that he would eventually return to her were practical certainties in her young mind. If his letters contained little to support this belief, she yet never questioned it for a moment. Guy was the sort to get on. She was sure of it. And he was worth waiting for. Oh, she could afford to be patient for Guy. She did not, moreover, believe that her father would hold out for ever. Also, and secretly this thought buoyed her up in rare moments of depression, in another two years—when she was twenty-five—she would inherit some money from her mother. It was not a very large sum, but it would be enough to render her independent. It would very greatly increase her liberty of action. She had little doubt that the very fact of it would help to overcome her father's prejudices and very considerably modify his attitude.

So, in a fashion, she had during the past three years come to regard her twenty-fifth birthday as a milestone in her life. She would be patient till it came, but then—at last—if circumstances permitted, she would take her fate into her own hands. She would—at last—assume the direction of her own life.

So she had planned, but so it was not to be. Her fate had already begun to shape itself in a fashion that was little to her liking. Travelling with her father in the North earlier in the summer, she had met with a slight accident which had compelled her to make the acquaintance of a lady staying at the same hotel whom she had disliked at the outset and always sought to avoid. This lady, Mrs. Emmott, was a widow with no settled home. Profiting by circumstances she had attached herself to Sylvia and her father, and now she was the latter's wife.

How it had come about, even now Sylvia scarcely realized. The woman's intentions had barely begun to dawn upon her before they had become accomplished fact. Her father's attitude throughout had amazed her, so astoundingly easy had been his capture. He was infatuated, possibly for the first time in his life, and no influence of hers could remove the spell.

Sylvia's feelings for Mrs. Emmott passed very rapidly from dislike to active detestation. Her iron strength of will, combined with an almost blatant vulgarity, gave the girl a sense of being borne down by an irresistible weight. Very soon her aversion became such that it was impossible to conceal it. And Mrs. Emmott laughed in her face. She hated Sylvia too, but she looked forward to subduing the unbending pride that so coldly withstood her, and for the sake of that she kept her animosity in check. She knew her turn would come.

Meantime, she concentrated all her energies upon the father, and with such marked success that within two months of their meeting they were married. Sylvia had gone to that wedding in such bitterness of soul and seething inward revolt as she had never experienced before. She did not know how she had come through it, so great had been her disgust. But that was nearly six weeks ago, and she had had time to recover. She had spent part of that period very peacefully and happily at the seaside with a young married cousin and her babies, and it had rested and refreshed her. She had come back with a calm resolve to endure what had to be endured in a philosophical spirit, to face the inevitable without futile rebellion.

Girt in an impenetrable armour of reserve, she

braced herself to bear her burdens unflinching, so that none might ever guess how it galled her. And on that golden evening in September she prepared herself with a smiling countenance to meet her enemy in the gate.

They were returning from a prolonged honeymoon among the Italian lakes, and she had made everything ready for their coming. The great west-facing bedroom, which her father had never occupied since her mother's death, had been redecorated and prepared as for a bride. Sylvia had changed it completely, so that it might never again look as it had looked in the old days. She had hated doing it, but it had been in a measure a relief to her torn heart. It was thus she rendered inviolate that inner sanctuary of memory which none might enter.

As she passed along the terrace in the golden glow, the slight frown was still upon her brow. It had been such a difficult time. Her one ray of comfort had been the thought of Guy, dear, faithful lover working for her far away. And now old Jeffcott had cast a shade even upon that. But then he did not really know Guy. No one knew him as she knew him. She quickened her steps a little. Possibly there might be a letter from him that evening.

There was. She spied it lying on the hall table as she entered. Eagerly she went forward and picked it up. But as she did so there came the sound of a car in the drive before the open front door, and quickly she thrust it away in the folds of her dress. The travellers had returned.

With a resolutely smiling face she went to meet them.

CHAPTER II

THE NEW MISTRESS

"HERE is our dear Sylvia!" said Mrs. Ingleton.

She embraced the girl with much *empressement*, and then, before Sylvia could reach her father, turned and embraced him herself.

"So very nice to he home, dear!" she said effusively. "We shall be very happy here."

Gilbert Ingleton bestowed a somewhat embarrassed salute upon her, one eye on his daughter. She greeted him sedately the next moment, and though her face was smiling, her welcome seemed to be frozen at its source; it held no warmth.

Mrs. Ingleton, tall, handsome, assertive, cast an appraising eye around the oak-panelled hall. "Dear me! What severe splendour!" she commented. "I have a great love for cosiness myself. We must scatter some of those sweet little Italian ornaments about, Gilbert. "You won't know the place when I have done with it. I am going to take you all in hand and bring you up-to-date."

Her keen dark eyes rested upon her step-daughter with a smile of peculiar meaning. Sylvia met them with the utmost directness.

"We like simplicity," she said.

Mrs. Ingleton pursed her lips. "Oh, but there is simplicity *and* simplicity! Give me warmth, homeliness, and *plenty* of pretty things. This place is archaically cold—quite like a convent. And you, my dear, might be the Sister Superior from your air. Now, Gilbert darling, you and I are going to be very firm with this child. I can plainly see she needs a guiding hand. She has had *much* too much responsibility for so young a girl. We are going to alter all that. We are going to make her very happy—as well as good."

She tapped Sylvia's shoulder with smiling significance, looking at her husband to set his seal to the declaration.

Mr. Ingleton was obviously feeling very uncomfortable. He glanced at Sylvia almost appealingly.

"I hope we are all going to be happy," he said rather gruffly. "Don't see why we shouldn't be, I'm sure. I like a quiet life myself. Got some tea for us, Sylvia?"

Sylvia turned, stiffly unresponsive to her stepmother's blandishments. "This way," she said, and crossed the hall to the drawing-room.

It was a beautiful room aglow just then with

the rays of the western sun. Mrs. Ingleton looked all around her with smiling criticism, and nodded to herself as if seeing her way to many improvements. She walked to the windows.

"What a funny, old-fashioned garden! Quite mediæval! I foresee a very busy time in store. Who lives on the other side of this property?"

"Preston—George Preston, the M.F.H., said her husband, lounging up behind her. "About the richest man about here. Made his money on the Turf."

She gave him a quick look. "Is he young?" she asked.

He hesitated. "Not very."

"Married?" questioned Mrs. Ingleton, with the air of a ferret pursuing its quarry down a hole.

"No," said the squire, somewhat reluctantly.

"Ah!" said Mrs. Ingleton, in a tone of satisfaction.

"Won't you have some tea?" said Sylvia's grave voice behind them.

Mrs. Ingleton wheeled. "Bless the child!" she exclaimed. "She has a face as long as a fiddle. Let us have tea by all means. I am as hungry as a hunter. I hope there is something really substantial for us."

"It is less than an hour to dinner," said Sylvia.

She hardly looked at her father. Somehow she had a feeling that he did not want to meet her eyes.

He sat in almost unbroken silence while she poured out the tea, "for the last time, dear," as her step-mother jocosely remarked, and for his sake alone she exerted herself to make polite conversation with this new mistress of the Manor.

It was not easy, for Mrs. Ingleton did not want to talk upon indifferent subjects. Her whole attitude was one of unconcealed triumph. It was obvious that she meant to enjoy her conquest to the utmost. She was not in the least tired after her journey; she was one of those people who never tire. And as soon as she had refreshed herself with tea she announced her intention of going round the house.

Her husband, however, intervened upon this point, assuring her that there would be ample time in the morning, and Mrs. Ingleton yielded it not very gracefully.

She was placed at the head of the table at dinner, but she could not accept the position without comment.

"Poor little Sylvia! We shall have to make up for this, or I shall never be forgiven," with an arch look at the squire which completely missed its mark.

There were no subtleties about Gilbert Ingleton. He was thoroughly uncomfortable, and his manner proclaimed the fact aloud. If he were happy with his enchantress away from home, the home atmosphere completely dispelled all enchantment. Was it the fault of the slim, erect girl with the red-brown eyes who sat so gravely silent on his right hand?

He could not in justice accuse her, and yet the strong sense of her disapproval irritated him. What right had she, his daughter, to sit in judgment upon him? Surely he was entitled to act for himself—choose his own course—make his own hell if he wished! It was all quite unanswerable. He knew she would not have attempted to answer if he had put it to her, but that very fact made him the more sore. He hated to feel himself at variance with Sylvia.

"Can't you play something?" he said to her in desperation as they entered the drawing-room after dinner.

She looked at him, her wide brows slightly raised.

"Well?" he questioned impatiently.

"Ask—Mrs. Ingleton first!" she said in a rapid whisper.

Mrs. Ingleton caught it, however. She had

the keen senses of a lynx. "Now, Sylvia, my child, come here!" she commanded playfully. "I can't have you calling me that, you know. If we are going to live together, we must have absolutely clear understanding between us on all points. Don't you agree with me, Gilbert?"

Ingleton growled something unintelligible, and made for the open window.

"Don't go!" said his wife with a touch of peremptoriness. "I want you here. Tell this dear child that as I have determined to be a mother to her she is to address me as such!"

Ingleton barely paused. "You must settle that between yourselves," he said gruffly. "And for heaven's sake, don't fight over it!"

He passed heavily forth, and Sylvia, after a very brief hesitation, sat down in a chair facing her step-mother.

"I am sorry," she said quietly. "But I can't call you Mother. Anything else you like to suggest, but not that."

Mrs. Ingleton uttered an unpleasant laugh. "I hope you are going to try and be sensible, my dear," she said, "for I assure you high-flown sentiment does not appeal to me in the very least. As head of your father's house, I must insist upon being treated with due respect. Let me warn you at the outset, though quite willing to befriend you, I am not a very patient woman. I am not prepared to put up with any slights."

Her voice lifted gradually as she proceeded till she ended upon a note that was almost shrill.

Sylvia sat very still. Her hands were clasped tightly about her knee. Her face was pale, and the red-brown eyes glittered a little, but she betrayed no other signs of emotion.

"I quite understand," she said after a moment. "But that doesn't solve the present difficulty, does it? I cannot possibly call you by a name that is sacred to someone else."

She spoke very quietly, but there was indomitable resolution in her very calm—a resolution that exasperated Mrs. Ingleton almost beyond endurance.

She arose with a sweeping gesture. "Oh, very well then," she said. "You shall call me Madam!"

Sylvia looked up at her. "I think that is quite a good idea," she said in a tone that somehow stung her hearer, unbearably. "I will do that."

"And don't be impertinent!" she said, beginning to pace to and fro like an angry tigress. "I will not put up with it, Sylvia. I warn you. You have been thoroughly spoilt all your life. I know the signs quite well. And you have come to think that you can do anything you like. But that is not so any longer. I am mistress here, and I mean to maintain my position. Any hint of rebellion from you or anyone else I shall punish with the utmost severity. So now you understand."

"I do indeed," said Sylvia.

She had not stirred from her chair, but sat watching her step-mother's agitated pacing with grim attention. It was her first acquaintance with the most violent temper she had ever encountered in a woman, and it interested her. She was no longer conscious of being angry herself. The whole affair had become a sort of bitter comedy. She looked upon it with a species of impersonal scorn.

Mrs. Ingleton was obviously lashing herself to fury. She could not imagine why, not realizing at that stage that she was the victim of a jealousy so fierce as to amount almost to a mania. She wondered if her father were watching them from the terrace, and contemplated getting up to join him, but hesitated to do so, reflecting that it might appear like flight. At the same time she did not see why she should remain as a target for her step-mother's invective, and she had just decided upon departure when Bliss, the butler, opened the door with his own peculiarly quiet flourish and announced, "Captain Preston!"

A clean-shaven little man, with a horsey appearance about the legs which evening-dress wholly failed to conceal, entered, and instinctively Sylvia rose to receive him.

Mrs. Ingleton stopped short and stared as they met in the middle of the room.

"Hullo, Sylvia!" said the little man, and stamped forward as if he had just dismounted after a long ride. He had a loud voice and an assertive manner, and Mrs. Ingleton gazed at him in frozen surprise.

Sylvia turned towards her. "May I introduce Mr. Preston—the M.F.H.?" Her tone was cold. If the newcomer's advent had been a welcome diversion it obviously gave her no pleasure.

Preston, however, plainly did not stand in need of any encouragement. He strode up to Mrs. Ingleton, confronting her with aggressive self-assurance. "Delighted to meet you, madam. You are Sylvia's step-mother, I presume? I hope we shall be more nearly connected before long. Anyone belongin' to Sylvia has my highest esteem. She has the straightest seat on a horse of any woman I know. Ingleton and I between us taught her all she knows about huntin', and she does us credit, by gad!"

He winked at Mrs. Ingleton as he ended, and Sylvia bit her lip. Mrs. Ingleton, however, held out her hand.

"Pray sit down, Mr. Preston! You are most welcome. Sylvia, my dear, will you find the cigarettes?"

Sylvia took a box from the table and handed it to him. He took it from her, openly pinching her fingers as he did so, and offered it to her instead.

"After you, Cherry-ripe! You're lookin' spiffin' to-night, hey, Mrs. Ingleton? What do you think of your new daughter?"

Mrs. Ingleton was smiling. "I am only wondering what all you young men can be about," she said. "I should have thought one of you would have captured her long ago."

Sylvia turned round, disgust in every line, and walked to the window. "I will find Dad," she said.

Preston looked after her, standing with legs wide apart on the hearth-rug. "It's none of my fault, I assure you," he said. "I've been tryin' to rope her for the last two years. But she's so damn' shy. Can't get near her, by George."

"Really?" smiled Mrs. Ingleton. "Perhaps you have not gone quite the right way to work. I think

I shall have to take a hand in the game and see what I can do."

Preston bowed with his hand on his heart. "I always like to get the fair sex on my side whenever possible. If you can put the halter on her, you've only to name your price, madam, and it's yours."

"Dear me!" said Mrs. Ingleton. "You're very generous."

"I can afford to be," declared Preston. "She's a decent bit of goods—the only one I've ever wanted and couldn't get. If you can get the whip-hand of her and drive her my way—well, it'll be pretty good business for all concerned. You like diamonds, hey, madam?"

"Very much," laughed Mrs. Ingleton coquettishly. "But you mustn't make my husband jealous. Remember that now!"

Preston closed one eye deliberately and poked his tongue into his cheek. "You leave that to me, my good madam. Anythin' of that sort would be the gift of the bridegroom. See?"

"Oh, quite," said Mrs. Ingleton. "I shall certainly do my best for you, Mr. Preston."

"Good for you!" said Preston jocularly. It's a deal then. And you play every trump you've got!"

"You may depend upon me," said Mrs. Ingleton.

CHAPTER III

THE WHIP-HAND

"Why isn't Mr. Preston engaged to Sylvia?" demanded Mrs. Ingleton of her husband as she faced him across the breakfast-table on the following morning.

"He'd like to be," said Ingleton with his face bent over the morning paper.

"Then why isn't he?" demanded Mrs. Ingleton with asperity. "He is a rich country gentleman, and he has a position in the County. What more could you possibly want for her?"

Reluctantly the squire made answer. "Oh, I'm willing enough. He's quite a decent chap so far as I know. I dare say he'd make her quite a good husband if she'd have him. But she won't. So there's an end of that."

"Ridiculous!" exclaimed Mrs. Ingleton. "And, pray, why won't she?"

"Why? Oh, because there's another fellow, of course. There always is," growled Ingleton.

"Girls never fall in love with the right man. Haven't you found that out yet?"

"I have found out," said Mrs. Ingleton tartly, "that Sylvia is a most wilful and perverse girl, and I think you are very unwise to put up with her whims. I should be ashamed to have a girl of that age still on my hands."

"I'd like to know how you'd have managed her any differently," muttered the squire, without looking up.

Mrs. Ingleton laughed unpleasantly. "You don't know much about women, do you, my dear? Of course I could have managed her differently. She'd have been comfortably married for the past two years at least if I had been in command."

Ingleton looked sourly incredulous. "You don't know Sylvia," he observed. "She has a will like cast-iron. You'd never move her."

Mrs. Ingleton tossed her head. "Never? Well, look here! If you want the girl to marry that really charming Mr. Preston, I'll undertake that she shall—and that within a year. How is that?"

Ingleton stared a little, then slowly shook his head. "You'll never do it, my dear Caroline."

"I will do it if it is your wish," said Mrs. Ingleton firmly.

He looked at her with a touch of uneasiness. "I don't want the child coerced."

She laughed again. "What an idea! Are children ever coerced in these days? It's usually the parents who have to put up with that sort of treatment. Now tell me about the other man. What and where is he?"

Ingleton told her with surly reluctance. "Oh, he was a handsome young beggar she met five years ago—the son of my then bailiff, as a matter of fact. The boy had had a fairly decent education; he was a gentleman, but he wasn't good enough for my Sylvia, had no prospects of any sort. And so I put my foot down."

Mrs. Ingleton smiled with her thin, hard lips, but no gleam of humour reached her eyes. "With the result, I suppose, that she has been carrying on with him ever since."

Ingleton stirred uneasily in his chair. "Well, she hasn't given him up. They correspond, I believe. But he is far enough away at present. He is in South Africa. She'll never marry him with my approval. I'm pretty certain now that the fellow is a rotter."

"She probably deems herself very heroic for sticking to him in spite of opposition," observed Mrs. Ingleton.

"Very likely," he conceded. "But I think she genuinely cares for him. That's just the mischief of it. And, unfortunately, in another couple of years she'll be in a position to please herself. She inherits a little money from her mother then."

Mrs. Ingleton's smile became more pronounced, revealing her strong white teeth behind. "You need not look forward so far as that, my love," she said. "Leave Sylvia entirely to me! I will undertake, as I said, to have her married to Mr. Preston well within a year. So you may set your mind at rest on that point."

"He is certainly fond of her," said the squire. "And they both have sporting tastes. He ought to have a very good chance with her if only the other fellow could be wiped out."

"Then leave her to me!" said Mrs. Ingleton, rising. "And mind, dear"—she paused behind her husband's chair and placed large white hands upon his shoulders—"whatever I do, you are not to interfere. Is that a bargain?"

Ingleton moved again uncomfortably. "You won't be unkind to the child?" he said.

"My dear Gilbert, don't you realize that the young lady is more than capable of holding her own against me or anyone else?" protested Mrs. Ingleton.

"And yet you say you can manage her?" he said.

"Well, so I can, if you will only trust to my discretion. What she needs is a little judicious treatment, and that is what I intend to give her. Come, that is understood, isn't it? It is perfectly outrageous that she should have ridden roughshod over you so long. A chit like that! And think how pleasant it will be for everyone when she is settled and provided for. Dear me! I shall feel as if a great weight has been lifted from my shoulders. We shall really enjoy ourselves then."

She smiled down into her husband's dubious face, and after a moment with a curt sigh he pulled her down and kissed her. "Well, you're a woman, you ought to know how to manage your own kind," he said. "Sylvia's mother was an invalid for so long that I expect the child did grow a bit out of hand. I'll leave her to you then, Caroline. If you can manage to marry her to Preston I believe you'll do her the biggest service possible."

"Of course I should like to do that!" said Mrs. Ingleton, kissing him loudly. "Ah! Here she comes! She mustn't catch us love-making at this hour. Good morning, my dear child! What roses to be sure! No need to ask where you have been."

Sylvia came in, riding-whip in hand. Her face was flushed and her eyes shining.

"Had a ripping run, Dad. You ought to have been there," she said. "Good morning!" She paused and kissed him, then turned to her stepmother. "Good morning, Madam! I hope the keys have been duly handed over. I told Mrs. Hadlow to see to it."

Mrs. Ingleton kissed her effusively. "You poor child! I am afraid it is a very sore point with you to part with your authority to me. The only thing for you to do is to be quick and get a home of your own."

Sylvia laughed. "Breakfast is my most pressing need at the present moment. Winnie carried me beautifully, Dad. George says she is a positive marvel for her years, dear little soul."

"George—George!" repeated Mrs. Ingleton with playful surprise. "I presume that is the estimable young man who called upon me last night. Well, well, if you are so intimate, I suppose I shall have to be too. He was in a great hurry to pay his respects, was he not?"

Sylvia was staring at her from the other side of the table. "I meant George the groom," she said coldly after a moment. "Is there any news, Dad?"

She turned deliberately to him, but before he could speak in answer Mrs. Ingleton intervened.

"Now, Sylvia, my love, I have something really rather serious to say to you. Of course, I fully realize that you are very young and inexperienced and not likely to think of these things for yourself. But I must tell you that it is very bad for the servants to have meals going in the dining-room at all hours. Therefore, my child, I must ask you to make a point of being punctual—always. Breakfast is at eight-thirty. Please bear that in mind for the future!"

Again Sylvia's wide eyes were upon her. They looked her straight in the face. "Dad and I are never back by eight-thirty when we go cubbing, are we, Dad?" she said.

The squire cleared his throat, and did not respond.

Mrs. Ingleton smiled. "But we are changing all that," she said. "At my particular request your dear father has promised me to give up hunting."

"What?" said Sylvia, and turned upon her father with a red flash in her eyes. "Dad, is that true?"

He looked at her unwillingly. "Oh, don't make a scene!" he said irritably. "Your mother is nervous, so I have given it up for the present, that's all."

"Please don't call Mrs. Ingleton my mother!" said Sylvia, suddenly deadly calm. "Am I always to hunt alone, then, for the future?"

"You have got—George," smiled Mrs. Ingleton.

Sylvia's eyes fell abruptly from her father's face, but they did not return to her step-mother. She turned away to the sideboard, and helped herself from a dish that stood there. In absolute silence she sat down at the table and began to eat.

Her father sat in uncomfortable silence for a moment or two, then got up with a non-committal, "Well!" gathered up his letters, and tramped from the room.

Mrs. Ingleton took up the paper and perused it, humming. Sylvia ate her breakfast in dead silence.

She rose finally to pour herself out some coffee, and at the movement her step-mother looked up. There was a glitter in her hard grey eyes that somewhat belied the smile she sought to assume. "Now, my dear," she said, in the tone of one lecturing a refractory child, "you were a very wilful and impertinent girl last night. I told you I should punish you, and I have kept my word. I do not advise you to aggravate the offence by sulking."

"Will you tell me what you mean?" said Sylvia, standing stiff and straight before her.

Mrs. Ingleton slightly shrugged her shoulders. "You are behaving like a child of six, and really, if you go on, you will provoke me into treating you as such. The attitude you have chosen to adopt is neither sensible nor dignified, let me tell you. You resent my presence here. Very well; but you cannot prevent it. Would it not be much wiser of you either to submit to my authority or——"

"Or?" repeated Sylvia icily.

"Or take the obvious course of providing yourself with a home elsewhere," said Mrs. Ingleton.

Sylvia put up a quick hand to her throat. She was breathing very quickly. "You wish to force me to marry that horrible Preston man?" she said.

"By no means, my dear," smiled Mrs. Ingleton. "But you might do a good deal worse. I tell you frankly, you will be very much underdog as long as you elect to remain in this establishment. Oh yes!" She suddenly rose to her full majestic height, dwarfing the girl before her with conscious triumph. "I may have some trouble with

you, but conquer you I will.   Your father will not
interfere between us.   You have seen that for
yourself.   In fact, he has just told me that he
leaves the management of you entirely to me.
He has given me an absolutely free hand—very
wisely.   If I choose to lock you in your room for
the rest of the day he will not interfere.   And as
I am quite capable of doing so, I warn you to be
very careful."

Sylvia stood as if turned to stone.   She was
white to the lips, but she confronted her step-
mother wholly without fear.

"Do you really think I would submit to that?"
she said.   "I am not a child, I assure you, whatever I may appear to you.   You will certainly
never manage me by that sort of means."

Her clear, emphatic voice fell without agitation.   Now that the first shock of the encounter
was past she had herself quite firmly in hand.

But Mrs. Ingleton took her up swiftly, realizing possibly that a moment's delay would mean
the yielding of the ground she had so arrogantly
claimed.

"I shall manage you exactly as I choose," she
said, raising her voice with abrupt violence.   "I
know very well your position in this house.   You
are absolutely dependent, and—unless you marry

—you will remain so, being quite unqualified to earn your own living. Therefore the whip-hand is mine, and if I find you insolent or intractable I shall use it without mercy. How dare you set yourself against me in this way?" She stamped with sudden fury upon the ground. "No, not a word! Leave the room instantly—I will have no more of it! Do you hear me, Sylvia? Do you hear me?"

She raised a menacing hand, but the fearless eyes never flinched.

"I think you must be mad," Sylvia said.

"Mad!" raved Mrs. Ingleton. "Mad because I refuse to be dictated to by an impertinent girl? Mad because I insist upon being mistress in my own house? You—you little viper—how dare you stand there defying me? Do you want to be turned out into the street?"

She had worked herself up into unreasoning rage again. Sylvia saw that further argument would be worse than useless. Very quietly, without another word, she turned, gathered up riding-whip and gloves, and went from the room. She heard Mrs. Ingleton utter a fierce, malignant laugh as she went.

3

CHAPTER IV

THE VICTORY

THE commencement of the fox-hunting season was always celebrated by a dance at the Town Hall—a dance which Sylvia had never failed to attend during the five years that she had been in society and had been a member of the Hunt.

It was at her first Hunt Ball, on the occasion of her *début*, that she had met young Guy Ranger, and she looked back to that ball with all its tender reminiscences as the beginning of all things.

How superlatively happy she had been that night! Not for anything that life could offer would she have parted with that one precious romance of her girlhood. She clung to the memory of it as to a priceless possession. And year after year she had gone to the Hunt Ball with that memory close in her heart.

It was at the last of these that George Preston had asked her to be his wife. She had made every effort to avoid him, but he had mercilessly

34

tracked her down; and though she had refused him with great emphasis she had never really felt that he had taken her seriously. He was always seeking her out, always making excuses to be alone with her. It was growing increasingly difficult to evade him. She had never liked the man, but Fate or his own contrivance was continually throwing him in her way. If she hunted, he invariably rode home with her. If she remained away, he invariably came upon her somehow, and wanted to know wherefore.

She strongly suspected that her step-mother was in league with him, though she had no direct proof of this. Preston was being constantly asked to the house, and whenever they went out to dine they almost invariably met him. She had begun to have a feeling that people eyed them covertly, with significant glances, that they were thrown together by design. Wherever they met, he always fell to her lot as dinner-partner, and he had begun to affect an attitude of proprietorship towards her which was yet too indefinite for her actively to resent.

She felt as if a net were closing around her from which, despite her utmost effort, she was powerless to escape. Also, for weeks now she had received no letter from Guy, and that fact disheartened her more than any other. She had never before had to wait so long for word from him. Very brief, often unsatisfying, as his letters had been, at least they had never failed to arrive. And she counted upon them so. Without them, she felt bereft of her mainstay. Without them, the almost daily, nerve-shattering scenes which her step-mother somehow managed to enact, however discreet her attitude, became an infliction hardly to be borne. She might have left her home for a visit among friends, but something held her back from this. Something warned her that if she went her place would be instantly filled up, and she would never return. And very bitterly she realized the fact that for the next two years she was dependent. She had not been trained to earn her own living, and she lacked the means to obtain a training. Her father, she knew, would not hear of such a thing, nor would he relinquish the only means he possessed of controlling her actions. She believed that privately he did not wish to part with her, though her presence was a very obvious drawback to his comfort. He never took her part, but also he never threw his weight into the balance against her. He merely, with considerable surliness, looked on.

And so the cruel struggle went on till it seemed

to Sylvia that her physical strength was ultimately beginning to fail. She came to dread her step-mother's presence with a feeling akin to nausea, to shrink in every nerve from the constant ordeals so ruthlessly thrust upon her.

So far she had never faltered or shown any sign of weakness under the long-drawn-out persecution, but she was becoming aware that, strive as she might, her endurance had its limits. She was but human, and she was intensely sensitive to unkindness. Her nerves were beginning to give way under the strain. There were even times when she felt a breakdown to be inevitable, and only the thought of her step-mother's triumph warded it off. Once down, and she knew she would be a slave, broken beyond redemption to the most pitiless tyranny. And so, though her strength was worn threadbare through perpetual strain, she clung to it still. If only—oh, if only—Guy would write! If he should be ill—if he should fail her— she felt that it would be the end of everything. For nothing else mattered.

She did not greatly wish to go to the Hunt Ball that year. She felt utterly out of tune with all gaiety. But she could think of no decent excuse for remaining away. And she was still buoying herself up with the thought that Guy's silence could not last much longer. She was bound to hear from him soon.

She went to the Ball, therefore, feeling tired and dispirited, and looking quite *passée*, as her stepmother several times assured her.

She had endured a long harangue upon jealousy that evening, which vice Mrs. Ingleton declared she was allowing to embitter her whole life, and she was weary to death of the subject and the penetrating voice that had discoursed upon it. Once or twice she had been stung into some biting rejoinder, but for the most part she had borne the lecture in silence. After all, what did it matter? What *did* it matter?

They reached the Town Hall and went up the carpeted steps. Preston, in hunting pink, received them. He captured Sylvia's hand and pressed it tight against his heart.

She stared at him with wide unsmiling eyes. "Seen the local rag?" he asked, as he grinned amorously into them. "There's something to interest you in it. Our local prophet has been at work."

She did not know what he meant, or feel sufficiently interested to inquire. She pulled her hand free, and passed on. His familiarity became more marked and more insufferable every time she encountered him. But still she asked herself again, what did it matter?

He laughed and let her go.

In the cloak-room people looked at her oddly, but beyond ordinary greetings no one spoke to her. She did not know that it was solely her utter wretchedness that kept them at a distance.

She entered the ballroom behind Mrs. Ingleton, and at once Preston descended upon her again. He had scrawled his name against half a dozen dances on her card before she realized what he was doing. She began to protest, but again that deadly feeling of apathy overcame her. She was worn out—worn out. What did it matter whether she danced with the man or not?

Young Vernon Eversley, a friendly boy whom she had always liked, pursed his lips when he saw her programme.

"It's true then, is it?" he said.

"What is true?" She looked at him questioningly, not feeling greatly interested in his answer.

He met her look with straight, honest eyes. "I saw the announcement of your engagement in the paper this morning; but somehow I didn't believe it. He's a dashed lucky man."

That startled her out of her lethargy. She began a quick disclaimer, but they were interrupted.

One of the stewards came up and swept young
Eversley away.

The next moment Preston came and took possession of her.   He was laughing still as he whirled
her in among the dancers, refusing to give her any
breathing-space.

"I want to see a little colour in those cheeks of
yours, Cherry-ripe," he said.   "What's the Ingleton dragon been doin' to you, my pretty?"

She danced with him with a feeling that the net
was drawn close about her, and she was powerless
to struggle any longer.   When he suffered her to
stand at last, her head was whirling so that she had
to cling to him for support.

He led her to a secluded corner and put her into
a chair.   Then he bent over her and spoke into
her ear.   "Look here!   I'm not such a bad sort.
They've coupled our names together in the local
rag.   Why not let 'em?"

She looked up at him, summoning her strength
with a great effort.   "So it was your doing!"
she said.

"No, it wasn't!" he declared.   "I swear it
wasn't!   I'm not such a fool as that.   But see
here, Sylvia!   Where's the use of holdin' out any
longer?   You know I want you, and there's no
sense in goin' on pinin' for a fellow in South Africa

who's probably married a dozen blacks already. It isn't like you to cry for the moon. Put up with me instead! You might do worse, and anyone can see you're havin' a dog's time at the Manor now. You'll be your own boss anyway if you come to me."

She heard him with her eyes fixed before her. Her brief energy had gone. Her life seemed to stretch before her in a long, dreary waste. His arguments were unanswerable. Physical weariness, combined with the despair which till then she had refused to acknowledge, overwhelmed her. She was down.

He put his hand upon her. "Come, I say! Is it a bargain? I swear I won't bully you. I'm awfully fond of you, Cherry-ripe."

She raised herself slowly. It was her last effort. "One thing first," she said, and put his hand away from her. "I must—cable to Guy, and get an answer."

"Oh, rot!" he said. "What for?"

"Because I haven't heard from him lately, and I must know—I must know"—she spoke with rising agitation—"the reason why. He might be—I don't say it is likely, but he might be—on his way home to me. I can't—I can't give him up without knowing."

Preston grimaced wryly, but he was shrewd enough to grasp and hold such advantage as was his. "Well, failing him, you'll have me, what? That's a promise, is it?"

She looked at him again. "If you want me under those conditions."

He put his arms about her. "Of course I want you, Cherry-ripe! We'd be awfully happy together, you and I. I'll soon make you forget him, if that's all. You can't be very deeply in love with the fellow after all this time. I don't suppose he's in the least the sort of person you take him for. You're wastin' your time over a myth. Come, it's settled, isn't it? We're engaged."

He pressed her closer. He bent to kiss her, but she turned her face away. His lips only found her neck, but he made the most of that. She had to exert her strength to free herself.

"No," she said. "We're not engaged. We can't be engaged—until I have heard from Guy."

He suppressed a short word of impatience. "And suppose you don't hear?" he asked.

She made a blind movement with her hands. "Then—I give in."

"You will marry me?" he insisted.

"If you like," she answered drearily. "I expect you will very soon get tired of me."

"There's a remedy for everything," he answered jauntily. "But we needn't consider that. I'm just mad to get you, you poor little icicle. I'll warm you up, never fear. When you've been married to me a week, you won't know yourself."

She shivered and was silent.

He turned in his tracks, perceiving he was making no headway. "Then we're engaged provisionally anyway," he insisted. "There's no need to contradict the general impression—unless we're obliged. We'll behave like lovers—till further notice."

She got to her feet. Her knees were trembling. The net was close at last. She seemed to feel it pressing on her throat. "You are not—to kiss me," she managed to say.

He frowned at the condition, but he conceded it. The game was so nearly his that he could afford to be generous. Besides, he would exact payment in full later for any little concessions she wrung from him now.

"I'm bein' awfully patient," he said pathetically. "I hope you'll take that into account. You really might just as well give in first as last."

But Sylvia had given in, and she knew it. Nothing but a miracle could save her now. The only loophole she had for herself was one which she realized already was highly unlikely to serve her. She had been practically forced into submission, and she did not attempt to disguise the fact from herself.

Yet if only Guy had not failed her, she knew that no power on earth would have sufficed to move her, no clamour of battle could ever have made her quail. That had been the chink in her armour, and through that she had been pierced again and again till she was vanquished at last.

She felt too weary now, too utterly overwhelmed by circumstances, to care what happened. Yes, she would cable to Guy as she had said. But her confidence was gone. She was convinced already that no word would come back in answer out of the void that had swallowed him.

She went through the evening as one in a dream. People offered her laughing congratulations, and she never knew how she received them. She seemed to be groping her way through an all-enveloping mist of despair.

One episode only stood out clearly from all the rest, and that was when all were assembled at supper and out of the gay hubbub she caught the sound of her own name. Then for a few intolerable moments she became vividly alive to that which was passing around her. She knew that

George Preston's arm encircled her, and that everyone present had risen to drink to their happiness.

As soon as it was over she crept away like a wounded thing and hid herself. Only a miracle could save her now.

CHAPTER V

THE MIRACLE

"WELL, my dear," said Mrs. Ingleton, rising to kiss her step-daughter on the following morning, "I consider you are a very—lucky—girl."

Sylvia received the kiss and passed on without reply. She was very pale, but the awful inertia of the previous night had left her. She was in full command of herself. She took up some letters from a side table, and sat down with them.

Her step-mother eyed her for a moment or two in silence. Then: "Well, my dear?" she said. "Have you nothing to say for yourself?"

"Nothing particular," said Sylvia.

The letters were chiefly letters of congratulation. She read them with that composure which Mrs. Ingleton most detested, and put them aside.

"Am I to have no share in the general rejoicing?" she asked at length, in a voice that trembled with indignation.

Sylvia recognized the tremor. It had been the prelude to many a storm. She got up and turned to the window. "You can read them all if you like," she said. "I see Dad on the terrace. I am just going to speak to him."

She passed out swiftly with the words before her step-mother's gathering wrath could descend upon her. One of Mrs. Ingleton's main grievances was that it was so difficult to corner Sylvia when she wanted to give free vent to her violence.

She watched the girl's slim figure pass out into the pale November sunshine, and her frown turned to a very bitter smile.

"Ah, my girl, you wait a bit!" she murmured. "You've met your match, or I'm much mistaken."

The squire was smoking his morning pipe in a sheltered corner. He looked round with his usual half-surly expression as his daughter joined him. She came to him very quietly and put her hand on his arm.

"Well?" he said gruffly.

She stood for a moment or two in silence, then: "Dad," she said very quietly, "I am going to cable to Guy. I haven't heard from him lately. I must know the reason why before—before——"
A quiver of agitation sounded in her voice and she stopped.

"If you've made up your mind to marry Pres-

ton, I don't see why you want to do that," said
the squire curtly.

"I am going to do it," she answered steadily.
"I only wish I had done it sooner."

Ingleton burrowed into his paper. "All right,"
he growled.

Sylvia stood for a few seconds longer, but he
did not look up at her, and at length, with a sharp
sigh, she turned and left him.

She did not return to her step-mother, however.
She went to her room to write her message.

A little later she passed down the garden on her
way to the village. A great restlessness was upon
her, and she thought the walk to the post-office
would do her good.

She came upon Jeffcott in one of the shrub-
beries, and he stopped her with the freedom of an
old servant.

"Beggin' your pardon, missie, but you'll let me
wish you joy?" he said. "I heard the good news
this morning."

She stood still. His friendly look went straight
to her heart, stirring in her an urgent need for
sympathy.

"Oh, Jeffcott," she said, "I'd never have given
in if Mr. Ranger hadn't stopped writing."

"Lor!" said Jeffcott. "Did he now?" He

frowned for an instant. "But—didn't you have a letter from him last week?" he questioned. "Friday morning it were. I see Evans, the postman, and he said as there were a South African letter for you. Weren't that from Mr. Ranger, missie?"

"What?" said Sylvia sharply.

"Last Friday it were," the old man repeated firmly. "Why, I see the letter in his hand top of the pile when he stopped in the drive to speak to me. We both of us passed a remark on it."

Sylvia was staring at him. "Jeffcott, are you sure?" she said.

"Sure as I stand here, Miss Sylvia," he returned. "I couldn't have made no mistake. Didn't you have it then, missie? I'll swear to heaven it were there."

"No," Sylvia said, "I didn't have it." She paused a moment; then very slowly, "The last letter I had from Guy Ranger," she said, "was more than six weeks ago—the day that the squire brought Madam to the Manor."

"Lor!" ejaculated old Jeffcott again. "But wherever could they have got to, Miss Sylvia? Don't Bliss have the sortin' of the letters?"

"I—don't—know." Sylvia was gazing straight before her with that in her face which frightened

4

the old man. "Those letters have been—kept back."

She turned from him with the words, and suddenly she was running, running swiftly up the path.

Like a young animal released from bondage she darted out of his sight, and Jeffcott returned to his hedge-trimming with pursed lips. That last glimpse of Miss Sylvia's face had—to express it in his own language—given him something of a turn.

It had precisely the same effect upon Sylvia's step-mother a little later, when the girl burst in upon her as she sat writing letters in her boudoir.

She looked round at her in amazement, but she had no time to ask for an explanation, for Sylvia, white to the lips, with eyes of flame, went straight to the attack. She was in such a whirlwind of passion as had never before possessed her.

She was panting, yet she spoke with absolute distinctness. "I have just found out," she said, "how it is that I have had no letters from Guy during the past six weeks. They have been—stolen."

"Really, Sylvia!" said Mrs. Ingleton.

She arose in wrath, but no wrath had any effect upon Sylvia at that moment. She was girt for battle—the deadliest battle she had ever known.

"You took them!" she said, pointing an accusing finger full at her step-mother. "You kept them back! Deny it as much as you like—as much as you dare! None but you would have stooped to do such a thing. And it has been done. The letters have been delivered—and I have not received them. I have suffered—horribly—because of it. You meant me to suffer!"

"You are wrong, Sylvia! You are wrong!" Shrilly Mrs. Ingleton broke in upon her, for there was something awful in the girl's eyes—they had a red-hot look. "Whatever I have done has been for your good always. Your father will testify to that. Go and ask him if you don't believe me!"

"My father had nothing to do with this!" said Sylvia in tones of withering scorn. "Whatever else he lacks, he has a sense of honour. But you—you are a wicked woman, unprincipled, cruel, venomous. It may be my father's duty to live with you, but—thank heaven—it is not mine. You have come into my home and cursed it. I will never sleep under the same roof with you again."

She turned with the words to leave the room, and found her father and George Preston just coming out of the library on the other side of the hall. Fearlessly she swung round and confronted them. The utter freedom of her at that moment made her superb. The miracle had happened. She had rent the net that entangled her to shreds.

Mrs. Ingleton was beginning to clamour in the room behind her. She turned swiftly and shut and locked the door. Then she faced the two men with magnificent courage.

"I have to tell you," she said, addressing them both impersonally, "that my engagement to Guy Ranger is unbroken. I have just found out that my step-mother has been suppressing his letters to me. That, of course, alters everything. And —also of course—it makes it impossible for me to stay here any longer. I am going to him—at once."

Her eyes went rapidly from her father's face to Preston's. It was he who came forward and answered her. The squire seemed struck dumb.

"Egad!" he said. "I've never seen you look so rippin' in all my life! That's how you look when you're angry, is it? Now I shall know what to watch out for when we're married."

She answered him with a quiver of scorn. "We never shall be married, Mr. Preston. You may put that out of your mind for ever. I am going to Guy by the next boat."

"Not you!" laughed Preston. "You're in a

paddy just now, my dear, but when you've thought it over soberly you'll find there are a good many little obstacles in the way of that. You haven't been brought up to rough it for one. And Guy Ranger, as I think we settled last night, has probably married half a dozen blacks already. It's too great a risk, Cherry-ripe! And—if I know you —you won't take it."

"You don't know me," said Sylvia. She turned from him and went to her father. "Have you nothing to say," she asked, "about this vile and hateful plot? But I suppose you can't. She is your wife. However much you despise her, you have got to endure her. But I have not. And so I am going—to-day!"

Her voice rang clear and unfaltering. She looked him straight in the eyes. He made a sharp movement, almost as if that full regard pierced him.

He spoke with manifest effort. "You won't go with my consent."

"No?" said Sylvia. "Yet—you would never respect me again if I stayed. I could never respect myself." She glanced over her shoulder at the door which Mrs. Ingleton was violently shaking. "You can let her out," she said contemptuously. "I have had my turn. I leave her—in possession." She turned to go to the stairs, then abruptly checked herself, stepped up to her father, put her hands on his shoulders and kissed him. The anger had gone out of her eyes. "Good-bye, Dad! Think of me sometimes!" she said.

And with that she was gone, passing Preston by as though she saw him not, and ascending the stairs quickly, but wholly without agitation. They heard her firm, light tread along the corridor above. Then with a hunch of the shoulders the squire turned and unlocked the boudoir door.

Mrs. Ingleton burst forth in a fury. "You cad to keep me boxed up here with that little serpent pouring all sorts of poison into your ears! Where is she? Where is she? I'll give her such a trouncing as she's never had before!"

But Ingleton stretched an arm in front of her, barring the way. His face was grim and unyielding. "No, you won't!" he said. "You'll leave her alone. She's my daughter—not yours. And you'll not interfere with her any further."

There was a finality in his tone. Mrs. Ingleton stopped short, glaring at him.

"You take her part, do you?" she demanded.

"On this occasion—yes, I do," said the squire.

"And what about me?" said Preston.

Ingleton looked at him—still barring his wife's progress—with a faint, sardonic smile. "Well, she seems to have given you the boot, anyway. If I were in your place, I should—quit."

"She'll repent it!" raved Mrs. Ingleton. "Oh, she will repent it bitterly!"

"Very likely," conceded Ingleton. "But she's kicked over the traces now, and that fact won't pull her up—anyhow, at present."

Mrs. Ingleton's look held fierce resentment. "Are you going to let her go?" she said.

He shrugged his shoulders. "Seeing I can't help myself, I suppose I shall. There's no sense in making a fuss now. It's done, so you leave her alone!"

Mrs. Ingleton turned upon Preston. "You can bring an action for breach of promise!" she said. "I'll support you."

He made her an ironical bow. "You are more than kind," he said. "But—I think I shall get on better for the future without your support."

And with the words he turned on his heel and went out.

"Hateful person!" cried Mrs. Ingleton. "Gilbert, he has insulted me! Go after him and kick him! Gilbert! How dare you?"

Ingleton was quietly but firmly impelling her

back into the boudoir. "You go and sit down!"
he said. "Sit down and be quiet! There's been
enough of this."

It was the first time in her knowledge that he
had ever asserted himself. Mrs. Ingleton stared
at him wildly for a second or two, then, seeing
that he was in earnest, subsided into a chair with
a burst of hysterical weeping, declaring that no
one ever treated her so brutally before.

She expected to be soothed, comforted, pro-
pitiated, but no word of solace came. Finally
she looked round with an indignant dabbing of
her tears. How dare he treat her thus? Was
he quite heartless? She began to utter a stream
of reproaches, but stopped short and gasped in
incredulous disgust. He had actually—he had
actually—gone, and left her to wear her emotion
out in solitude.

So overwhelming was the result of this piece
of neglect, combined with the failure of all her
plans, that Mrs. Ingleton retired forwith to bed,
and remained there for the rest of the day.

CHAPTER VI

THE LAND OF STRANGERS

IT had been a day of intense and brooding heat.
Black clouds hung sullenly low in the sky, and
a heavy gloom obscured the face of the earth.
On each side of the railway the *veldt* stretched for
miles, vivid green, yet strangely desolate to unaccustomed eyes. The moving train seemed the
only sign of life in all that wilderness.

Sylvia leaned from the carriage window and
gazed blankly forth. She had hoped that Guy
would meet her at Cape Town, but he had not
been there. She had come unwelcomed into this
land of strangers. But he would be at Ritzen.
He had cabled a month before that he would meet
her there if he could not get to Cape Town.

And now she was nearing Ritzen. Across the
mysterious desolation she discerned its many
lights. It was a city in a plain, and the far hills
mounted guard around it, but she saw them only
dimly in the failing light.

Ritzen was the nearest railway station to the

farm on which Guy worked. From here she
would have to travel twenty miles across country. But that would not be yet. Guy and she
would be married first. There would be a little
breathing-space at Ritzen before she went into
that new life that awaited her beyond the hills.
Somehow she felt as if those hills guarded her
destiny. She did not fear the future, but she
looked forward to it with a certain awe.

Paramount within her, was the desire for Guy,
the sight of his handsome, debonair countenance,
the ring of his careless laugh. As soon as she saw
Guy she knew she would be at home, even in the
land of strangers, as she had never been at the
Manor since the advent of her father's second
wife. She had no misgivings on that point, or
she had never come across the world to him thus,
making all return impossible. For there could be
be no going back for her. She had taken a definite and irrevocable step. There could be no turning back upon this road that she had chosen.

It might not be an easy road. She was prepared for obstacles. But with Guy she was ready
to face anything. The adversity through which
she had come had made the thought of physical
hardship of very small account. And deep in her
innermost soul she had a strong belief in her own

ultimate welfare. She was sure that she had done the right thing in thus striking out for herself, and she was equally sure that, whatever it might entail, she would not regret it in the end.

The lights were growing nearer. She discerned the brick building of the station. Over the wide stretch of land that yet intervened there came to her the smell of smoke and human habitation. A warm thrill went through her. In two minutes now—in less—the long five years' separation would be over, and she would be clasping Guy's hand again.

She leaned from the window, scanning the few outstanding houses of the town as the train ran past. Then they were in the station, and a glare of light received them.

A crowd of unfamiliar faces swam before her eyes, and then—she saw him. He stood on the platform awaiting her, distinct from all the rest to her eager gaze—a man of medium height, broader than she remembered, with a keen, bronzed face and eagle eyes that caught and held her own.

She sprang form the train almost before it stopped. She held out both her hands to him.

"Guy! Guy!"

Her voice came sobbingly. He gripped the hands hard and close.

"So you've got here!" he said.

She was staring at him, her face upraised. What was there about him that did not somehow tally with the Guy of her memory and her dreams? He was older, of course; he was more mature, bigger in every way. But she missed something. There was no kindling of pleasure in his eyes. They looked upon her kindly. Ah, yes; but the rapture—where was the rapture of greeting?

A sense of coldness went through her. Her hands fell from his. He had changed—he had changed indeed! His eyes were too keen. She thought they held a calculating expression. And the South African sun had tanned him almost bronze. His chin had a stubbly look. The Guy she had known had been perfectly smooth of skin.

She looked at him with a rather piteous attempt to laugh. "I wonder I knew you at all," she said, "with that hideous embryo beard. I'm sure you haven't shaved to-day."

He put up a hand and felt his chin. "No, I shaved yesterday," he said, and laughed. "I've been too busy to-day."

That reassured her. The laugh at least was like Guy, brief though it was. "Horrid boy!"

she said. "Well, help me collect my things. We'll talk afterwards."

He helped her. He went into the carriage she had just left and pulled out all her belongings. These he dumped on the platform and told her to wait while he collected the rest.

She stood obediently in the turmoil of Britons, Boers, and Kaffirs, that surged around. She felt bewildered, strung up, unlike herself. It was a land of strangers, indeed, and she felt forlorn and rather frightened. Why had Guy looked at her so oddly? Why had his welcome been so cold? Could it be—could it be—that he was not pleased to see her, that—that—possibly he did not want her? The dreadful chill went through her again like a sword thrusting at her heart, and with it went old Jeffcott's warning words: "Do you ever ask yourself what sort of man he may be after five years? I'll warrant he's lived every minute of it. He's the sort that would."

She had felt no doubt then, nor ever since, until this moment. And now—now it came upon her and overwhelmed her. She glanced about her, almost as one seeking escape.

"I've fixed everything up. Come along to the railway hotel! You must be pretty tired." He had returned to her, and he stood looking at her with those strangely keen eyes, almost as if he had never seen her before, she thought to herself desolately.

She looked back at him with unconscious appeal in her own. "I am tired," she said, and was aware of a sudden difficulty in speaking. "Is it far?"

"No," he said; "only a step."

He gathered up her hand-baggage and led the way, making a path for her through the throng.

She scarcely noticed where she went, so completely did he fill her mind. He had changed enormously, developed in a fashion that she had never deemed possible. He walked with a free swing, and carried himself as one who counted. He had the look of one accustomed to command. She seemed to read prosperity in every line. But was he prosperous? If so, why had he not sent for her long ago?

They reached the hotel. He led the way without pause straight to a small private room where a table had been prepared for a meal.

"Sit down!" he said. "Take off your things! You must be starved."

He rang the bell and gave an order while she mutely obeyed. All her confidence was gone. She had begun to tremble. The wonder crossed

her mind if perhaps she, too, had altered, grown
beyond all his previous conception of her. Possibly she was as much a stranger to him as he to
her. Was that why he had looked at her with
that oddly critical expression? Was that why
he did not now take her in his arms?

Impulsively she took off her hat and turned
round to him.

He was looking at her still, and again that awful
sense of doubt mastered and possessed her. A
great barrier seemed to have sprung up between
them. He was formidable, actually formidable.
The Guy of old days, impetuous, hot-tempered
even, had never been that.

She stood before him, controlling her rising
agitation with a great effort. "Why do you look
at me like that?" she said. "I feel—you make
me feel—as if—you are a total stranger!"

His face changed a little, but still she could not
read his look. "Sit down!" he said. "We must
have a talk."

She put out her hand to him. The aloofness
of his speech cut her with an anguish intolerable.
"What has happened?" she said. "Quick! Tell
me! Don't you want to—marry me?"

He took her hand. She saw that in some fashion
he was moved, though still she could not under-

stand. "I'm trying to tell you," he said; "but—to be honest—you've hit me in the wind, and I don't know how. I think you have forgotten in all these years what Guy was like."

She gazed at him blankly. Again Jeffcott's words were running in her mind. And something —something hidden behind them—arose up like a menace and terrified her.

"I haven't forgotten," she whispered voice-lessly. "I couldn't forget. But go on! Don't—don't mind telling me!"

She was white to the lips. All the blood in her body seemed concentrated at her heart. It was beating in heavy, sickening throbs like the labour-ing of some clogged machinery.

He put his free hand on her shoulder with an abrupt movement that made him for the moment oddly familiar. "It's a damned shame," he said, and though his voice was low he spoke with feeling. "Look here, child! This is no fault of mine. I never thought you could make this mistake, never dreamed of such a possibility. I'm not Guy at all. I am Burke Ranger—his cousin. And let me tell you at once, we are not much alike now—whatever we have been in the past. Here, don't faint! Sit down!"

He shifted his hand from her shoulder to her

elbow, and supported her to a chair. But she remained upon her feet, her white face upraised, gazing at him—gazing at him.

"Not Guy! Not Guy!" She said it over and over as if to convince herself. Then: "But where is Guy?" She clutched at his arm desperately, for all her world was shaking. "Are you going to tell me he is—dead?"

"No." Burke Ranger spoke with steady eyes looking straight into hers. "He is not."

"Then why—then why—" She could get no further. She stopped, gasping. His face swam blurred before her quivering vision,—Guy's face, yet with an inexplicable something in it that was not Guy.

"Sit down!" he said again, and put her with quiet insistence into the chair. "Wait till you have had something to eat! Then we'll have a talk and decide what had better be done."

She was shivering from head to foot, but she faced him still. "I can't eat," she said through white lips. "I can't do anything till—till I know —all there is to know."

He stood looking down at her. The fingers of his right hand were working a little, but his face was perfectly calm, even grim.

As he did not speak immediately, she went on

with piteous effort. "You must forgive me for making that stupid mistake. I see now—you are not Guy, though there is a strong likeness. You see, I have not seen Guy for five years, and I—I was allowing for certain changes."

"He is changed," said Burke Ranger.

That nameless terror crept closer about her heart. Her eyes met his imploringly.

"Really I am quite strong," she said. "Won't you tell me what is wrong? He—cabled to me to come to him. It was in answer to my cable."

"Yes, I know," said Ranger.

He turned from her abruptly and walked to the window. The darkness had drawn close. It hung like a black curtain beyond the pane. The only light in the room was a lamp that burned on a side table. It illumined him but dimly, and again it seemed to the girl who watched him that this could be no other than the Guy of her dreams —the Guy she had loved so faithfully, for whose sake she had waited so patiently for so many weary years. Surely it was he who had made the mistake! Surely even yet he would turn and gather her to his heart, and laugh at her folly for being so easily deluded!

Ah! He had turned. He stood looking at her

across the dimly-lighted space. Her very heart
stood still to hear his voice.

He spoke. "The best thing you can do is to
go back to the place you came from—and marry
someone else."

The words went through her. They seemed
to tear and lacerate her. As in a nightmare
vision she saw the bitterness that lay behind her,
the utter emptiness before. She still stared full
at him, but she saw him not. Her terror had
taken awful shape before her, and all her courage
was gone. She cowered before it.

"I can't—I can't!" she said, and even to herself her voice sounded weak and broken, like the
cry of a lost child. "I can't go back!"

He came across the room to her, moving quickly,
as if something urged him. She did not know
that she had flung out her hands in wild despair
until she felt him gather them together in his own.

He bent over her, and she saw very clearly in
his countenance that which had made her realize
that he was not Guy. "Look here!" he said.
"Have a meal and go to bed! We will talk it out
in the morning. You are worn out now."

His voice held insistence. There was no soft-
ness in it. Had he displayed kindness in that
moment she would have burst into tears. But

he put her hands down again with a brief, repressive gesture, and the impulse passed. She yielded him obedience, scarcely knowing what she did.

He brought her food and wine, and she ate and drank mechanically while he watched her with his grey, piercing eyes, not speaking at all.

Finally she summoned strength to look up at him with a quivering smile. "You are very kind. I am sorry to have given you so much trouble."

He made an abrupt movement that she fancied denoted impatience. "Can't you eat any more?" he said.

She shook her head, still bravely smiling. "I can't—really. I think—I think perhaps you are right. I had better go to bed, and you will tell me everything in the morning."

"Finish the drink anyhow!" he said.

She hesitated momentarily, but he pushed the glass firmly towards her and she obeyed.

She stood up then and faced him. "Will you please tell me one thing—to—to set my mind at rest? Guy—Guy isn't ill?"

He looked her straight in the face. "No."

"You are sure?" she said.

"Yes." He spoke with curt decision, yet oddly she wondered for a fleeting second if he had told her the truth.

His look seemed to challenge the doubt, to beat it down. Half shyly, she held out her hand.

"Good night," she said.

His fingers grasped and released it. He turned with her to the door. "I will show **you** your room," he said.

CHAPTER VII

THE WRONG TURNING

SYLVIA slept that night the heavy, unstirring sleep of utter weariness though when she lay down she scarcely expected to sleep at all. The shock, the bewilderment, the crushing dread, that had attended her arrival after the long, long journey had completely exhausted her mentally and physically. She slept as a child sleeps at the end of a strenuous day.

When she awoke, the night was gone and all the world was awake and moving. The clouds had all passed, and a brilliant morning sun shone down upon the wide street below her window. She felt refreshed though the heat was still great. The burden that had overwhelmed her the night before did not seem so intolerable by morning light. Her courage had come back to her.

She dressed with a firm determination to carry a brave face whatever lay before her. Things could not be quite so bad as they had seemed the previous night. Guy could not really have changed so fundamentally. Perhaps he only feared that she could not endure poverty with him. If that were all, she would soon teach him otherwise. All she wanted in life now was his love.

She had almost convinced herself that this was practically all she had to contend with, and the ogre of her fears was well in the background, when she finally left her room and went with some uncertainty through the unfamiliar passages.

She found the entrance, but a crowd of curious Boers collected about the door daunted her somewhat, and she was turning back from their staring eyes when Burke Ranger suddenly strode through the group and joined her.

She gave him a quick, half-startled glance as they met, and the first thing that struck her about him was the obvious fact that he had shaved. His eyes intercepted hers, and she saw the flicker of a smile pass across them and knew he had read her thought.

She flushed as she held out her hand to him. "Good morning," she said with a touch of shyness. "I hope you haven't been wasting your time waiting for me."

He took her hand and turned her towards the small room in which they had talked together the previous night. "No, I haven't wasted my time," he said. "I hope you have had a good rest?"

"Oh, quite, thank you," she answered. "I slept like the dead. I feel—fit for anything."

"That's right," he said briefly. "We will have some breakfast before we start business."

"Oh, you have been waiting!" she exclaimed with compunction. "I'm so sorry. I'm not generally so lazy."

"Don't apologize!" he said. "You've done exactly what I hoped you'd do. Sit down, won't you? Take the end of the table!"

His manner was friendly though curt. Her embarrassment fell from her as she complied. They sat, facing one another, and, the light being upon him, she gave him a steady look. He was not nearly so much like Guy as she had thought the previous night, though undoubtedly there was a strong resemblance. On a closer inspection she did not think him handsome, but the keen alertness of him attracted her. He looked as if physical endurance were a quality he had brought very near to perfection. He had the stamp of the gladiator upon him. He had wrestled against odds.

After a moment or two he turned his eyes unexpectedly to hers. It was a somewhat disconcerting habit of his.

"A satisfactory result, I hope?" he said.

She did not look away. "I don't consider myself a good character reader," she said. "But you are certainly not so much like Guy as I thought at first sight."

"Thank you," he said. "I must confess I prefer to be like myself."

She laughed a little. "It was absurd of me to make such a mistake. But yours was the only face that looked in the least familiar in all that crowd. I was so glad to see it."

"You have never been in this country before?" he asked.

She shook her head. "Never. I feel a dreadful outsider at present. But I shall soon learn.'

"Do you ride?" he said.

Her eyes kindled. "Yes. I was keen on hunting in England. That will be a help, won't it?"

"It would be," he said, "if you stayed."

"I have come to stay," she said with assurance.

"Wait a bit!" said Burke Ranger.

His manner rather than his words checked her. She felt again that cold dread pressing against her heart. She turned from the subject as one seeking escape.

She ate a good breakfast almost in spite of herself. Ranger insisted upon it, and since he was evidently hungry himself it seemed churlish not to keep him company. He told her a little about the country, while they ate, but he strenuously avoided all things personal, and she felt compelled to follow his lead. He imposed a certain restraint upon her, and even when he rose from the table at length with the air of a man about to face the inevitable, she did not feel it to be wholly removed.

She got up also and watched him fill his pipe with something of her former embarrassment. She expected him to light it when he had finished, but he did not. He put it in his pocket, and somewhat abruptly turned to her.

"Now!" he said.

She met his look with a brave face. She even smiled—a gallant, little smile to which he made no response. "Well, now," she said, "I want you to tell me the quickest way to get to Guy."

He faced her squarely. "I've got to tell you something about him first," he said.

"Yes?" Her heart was beating very quickly, but she had herself well in hand. "What is it?"

But he stood mutely considering her. It was as if the power of speech had suddenly gone from him.

"What is it?" she said again. "Won't you tell me?"

He made a curious gesture. It was almost a movement of flinching. "You're so young," he said.

"Oh, but I'm not—I'm not!" she assured him. "It's only my face. I'm quite old really. I've been through a lot."

"You've never seen life yet," he said.

"I have!" she declared with an odd vehemence. "I've learnt lots of things. Why—do you look like that? I'm not a child."

Her voice quivered a little in spite of her. Why did he look like that? The compassion in his eyes smote her with a strange pain. Why—why was he sorry for her?

He saw her rising agitation, and spoke, slowly, choosing his words. "The fact is, Guy isn't what you take him for—isn't the right man for you. Nothing on this earth can make him so now, whatever he may have been once. He's taken the wrong turning, and there's no getting back."

She gazed at him with wide eyes. Her lips felt stiff and cold. "What—what—do you mean, please?" she said.

She saw his hands clench. "I don't want to tell you what I mean," he said. "Haven't I said enough?"

She shook her head slowly, with drawn brows.

"No—no! I've got to understand. Do you
mean Guy doesn't want me after all? Didn't he
really mean me to come? He—sent a message."

"I know. That's the infernal part of it."
Burke Ranger spoke with suppressed force. "He
was blind drunk when he sent it."

"Oh!" She put up her hands to her face for a
moment as if to shield herself from a blow. "He—
drinks, does he?"

"He does everything he ought not to do, except
steal," said Ranger bluntly. "I've tried to keep
him straight—tried every way. I can't. It isn't
to be done."

Sylvia's hands fell again. "Perhaps," she said
slowly, " perhaps I could."

The man started as if he had been shot. "You!"
he said.

She met his look with her wide eyes. "But
why not?" she said. "We love each other."

He turned from her, grinding the floor with his
heel. "God help me to make myself intelligible!"
he said.

It was the most forcible prayer she had ever
heard. It struck through to her very soul. She
stood motionless, but she felt crushed and numb.

Ranger walked to the end of the room and then
came straight back to her.

"Look here!" he said. "This is the most damnable thing I've ever had to do. Let's get it over! He's a rotter and a blackguard. Can you grasp that? He hasn't lived a clean life all these years he's been away from you. He went wrong almost at the outset. He's the sort that always does go wrong. I've done my best for him. Anyhow, I've kept him going. But I can't make a decent man of him. No one can. He has lucid intervals, but they get shorter and shorter. Just at present—" he paused momentarily, then plunged on—"I told you last night he wasn't ill. That was a lie. He is down with delirium tremens, and it isn't the first time."

"Ah!" Sylvia said. He had made her understand at last. She stood for a space staring at him, then with a groping movement she found and grasped the back of a chair. "Why—why did you lie to me?" she said.

"I did it for your sake," he answered briefly. "You couldn't have faced it then."

"I see," she said, and paused to collect herself. "And does he—does he realize that I am here?" she asked painfully. "Doesn't he—want to see me?"

"Just now," said Ranger grimly, "he is too busy thinking about his own troubles to worry

about anyone else's. He does know you are coming. He was raving about it two nights ago. Then
came your wire from Cape Town. That was
what brought me here to meet you."

"I see," she said again. "You—you have been
very good. It would have been dreadful if—if I
had been stranded here alone."

"I'd have stopped you at Cape Town if I could,"
he said.

"No, you wouldn't have stopped me," she
answered, with a drear little smile. "I should
have had to come on and see Guy in any case. I
shall have to see him now. Where is he?"

Ranger stood close to her. He bent slightly,
looking into her eyes. "You have understood
me?" he questioned.

She looked straight back at him; it was no moment for shrinking avoidance. "Yes," she said.

"And you believe me?" he proceeded.

Her red-brown eyes widened a little. "But of
course I believe you."

"And, still you want to see him?" said Burke
Ranger.

"I must see him," she answered quietly. "You
must realize that. You would do the same in my
place."

"If I did," said Ranger, dropping his voice,

"it would be to tell him to go to hell!" Then, as involuntarily she drew back: "No, I shouldn't put it like that to you, I know. But what's the point of your seeing him? It will only make things worse for you."

"I must see him," she said firmly. "Please tell me where he is!"

He looked at her for a moment or two in silence. "He is in his own shanty on my farm," he said then. "Blue Hill Farm it is called. You can't go to him there. It's a twenty-mile ride from here."

"Can't I get a horse to take me?" she asked.

"I could take you in my cart," said Burke slowly.

"And will you?" Sylvia said.

"I suppose you will go in any case," he said.

"I must go," she answered steadily.

"I don't see why," he said. "It's a degrading business. It won't do any good."

Her face quivered. She controlled it swiftly. "Will you take me?" she said.

He frowned. "What is going to happen afterwards? Have you thought of that?"

She shook her head. "No. I can't see the future at all. I only know that I must see Guy, and I can't go back to England."

"Why not?" he said.

She pressed a hand to her throat as if she found speaking a difficulty. "I have no place there. My father has married again. I must earn my living here somehow."

He moved abruptly. "You!" he said again.

She tried to smile. "You seem to think I am very helpless. I assure you I am not. I have managed my father's house for five years. I am quite willing to learn anything, and I am very strong."

"You are very brave," he said, almost as if he spoke in spite of himself. But—you've got to be sensible too. You won't marry him?"

She hesitated. "I must see him. I must judge for myself."

He nodded, still frowning. "Very well,—if you must. But you won't marry him as a way out of your difficulties? You've got to promise me that."

"Why?" she said.

He answered her with that sudden force which before had startled her. "Because I can't stand by and see purity joined to corruption. Some women will sacrifice anything for sentiment. You wouldn't do anything so damn' foolish as that."

"No," said Sylvia.

"Then it's a promise?" he said.

She held out her hand to him with her brave little smile. "I promise you I won't do anything damn' foolish for the sake of—sentiment. Will that do?"

He gripped her hand for a moment. "Yes. I think it will," he said.

"And thank you for being so good to me," she added.

He dropped her hand, and turned away. "As to that—I please myself," he said briefly. "Be ready to start in an hour from now!"

6

CHAPTER VIII

THE COMRADE

THAT twenty-mile ride in Burke Ranger's high cart, with a pair of skittish young horses pulling at the reins, was an experience never to be eradicated from Sylvia's memory. They followed a course across the *veldt* that began as a road and after a mile or two deteriorated into a mere rough track. Up and down many slopes they travelled, but the far hills never seemed to draw any nearer. Here and there they passed *kopjes* stacked against the blazing blue of the sky. They held a weird attraction for her. They were like the stark bones of the earth pushing up through the coarse desert grasses. Their rugged strength and their isolation made her marvel. The *veldt* was swept by a burning wind. The clouds of the night before had left no rain behind.

Sylvia would have liked to ask many things of her companion but his attention was completely absorbed by the animals he drove. Also talking was wellnigh impossible during that wild progress, for though the horses presently sobered down somewhat, the roughness of the way was such that most of the time her thoughts were concentrated upon maintaining her seat. She clung to her perch with both hands, and mutely admired Burke Ranger's firm control and deftness. He seemed to know by instinct when to expect any sudden strain.

The heat of the sun was intense, notwithstanding the shelter afforded by the hood of the cart. The air seemed to quiver above the burning earth. She felt after a time as if her eyes could endure the glare no longer. The rapid, bumping progress faded into a sort of fitful unpleasant dream through which the only actual vivid consciousness that remained to her centred in the man beside her. She never lost sight of his presence. It dominated all besides, though he drove almost entirely in silence and never seemed to look her way.

At the end of what appeared an interminable stretch of time during which all her sensibilities had gradually merged into one vast discomfort, Burke spoke at her side.

"We've got a bit of tough going before us. Hang on tight! We'll have a rest after it."

She opened her eyes and saw before her a steep slant between massive stones, leading down to a

wide channel of running water. On the further
side a similar steep ascent led up again.

"Ritter Spruit," said Ranger. "It's not deep
enough to be dangerous. Hold on! We shall
soon be through."

He spoke to the horses and they gathered themselves as if for a race. They thundered down the
incline and were dashing through the stony watercourse almost before Sylvia, clinging dazed to her
seat, realized what was happening. Her sensa-
tions were indescribable. The water splashed
high around them, and every bone in her body
seemed to suffer a separate knock or jar. If
Ranger had not previously impressed her with
his level-headedness she would have thought him
mad. But her confidence in him remained un-
shaken, and in a very few seconds it proved to be
justified. They were through the *spruit* and half-
way up the further side before she drew breath.
Then she found that they were slackening pace.

She turned to Ranger with kindling eyes. "Oh,
you are a sportsman!" she said. "How I should
love to be able to drive like that!"

He smiled without turning his head. "I'm
afraid this last is a man's job. So you are awake
now, are you? I was afraid you were going to
tumble out."

She laughed. "The heat makes one drowsy. I shall get used to it."

He was pulling in the horses. "There's some shade round the corner. We'll rest for an hour or two."

"I shall like that," said Sylvia.

A group of small larch-trees grew among the stones at the top of the slope, and by these he stopped. Sylvia looked around her with appreciation as she alighted.

"I am going to like South Africa," she said.

"I wonder!" said Ranger.

He began to unbuckle the traces, and she went round to the other side and did the same.

"Poor dears, they are hot!" she said.

"Don't you do that!" said Ranger.

She was tugging at the buckle. "Why not? I like doing it. I love horses, don't you? But I know you do by the way you handle them. Do you do your own horse-breaking? That's a job you might give me."

"Am I going to find you employment, then?" said Burke.

She laughed a little, bending her flushed face down. "Don't women do any work out here?"

"Yes. They work jolly hard, some of 'em."

"Are you married?" said Sylvia.

"No."

She heaved a sigh.

"Sorry?" he enquired.

She finished her task and looked up. Her frank eyes met his across the horses' backs. "No. I think I'm rather glad. I don't like feminine authority at all."

"That means you like your own way," observed Burke.

She nodded. "Yes. But I don't always get it."

"Are you a good loser?" he said.

She hesitated. "I hope I'm a sportsman. I try to be."

He moved to the horses' heads. "Come and hold this animal for me while I hobble the other!" he said.

She obeyed him readily. There was something of boyish alertness in her movements that sent a flicker of approval into the man's eyes. She drew the horse's head to her breast with a crooning sound.

"He is a bit tricky with strangers," observed Burke, as he led the other away.

"Oh, not with me!" said Sylvia. "He knows I love him."

When he returned to relieve her of her charge

she was kissing the forehead between the full soft eyes that looked at her with perfect confidence.

"See!" she said. "We are friends already."

"I shall call you The Enchantress," said Burke. "Will you see if you can find a suitable spot for a picnic now?"

"Yes, but I can't conjure up a meal," said Sylvia.

"I can," he said. "There's a basket under the seat."

"How ripping!" she said. "I think you are the magician."

He smiled. "Rather a poor specimen, I am afraid. You go and select the spot, and I will bring it along!"

Again she obeyed with cheerful alacrity. Her choice was unhesitating. A large boulder threw an inviting shade, and she sat down among the stones and took off her hat.

Her red-gold hair gleamed against the dark background. Burke Ranger's eyes dwelt upon it as he moved to join her. She looked up at him.

"I love this place. It feels so—good."

He glanced up at the brazen sky. "You wouldn't say so if you wanted rain as badly as I do," he observed. "We haven't had nearly enough this season.   But I am glad you can enjoy it."

"I like it more and more," said Sylvia.   She stretched an arm towards the wide *veldt* all about them.   "I am simply aching for a gallop over that—a gallop in the very early morning, and to see the sun rise from that knoll!"

"That's a *kopje*," said Burke.

Again half-unconsciously his eyes dwelt upon her vivid face.   She seemed to draw his look almost in spite of him.   He set down the basket by her side.

"Am I to unpack?" said Sylvia.

He dropped his eyes.   "No.   I will.   It isn't much of a feed; only enough to keep us from starvation.   Tell me some more about yourself!   Tell me about your people—your home!"

"Have you never heard of me before?" she asked.   "Did—Guy—never speak of me?"

"I knew there was someone."   Burke spoke rather unwillingly.   "I don't think he ever actually spoke of you to me.   We're not exactly—kindred spirits, he and I."

"You don't like him," said Sylvia.

"Nor he me," said Burke Ranger.

She looked at him with her candid eyes.   "I don't think you are very tolerant of weakness, are you?" she said gently.

"I don't know," he said non-committally. "Won't you tell me about yourself?"

The subject of Guy was obviously distasteful to him, yet her whole life during the past five years had been so closely linked to the thought of that absent lover of hers that it was impossible to speak of the one without the other. She told him all without reservation, feeling in a fashion that it was his right to know.

He listened gravely, without comment, until she ended, when he made one brief observation. "And so you chose the deep sea!"

"Could I have done anything else?" she said. "Would you have done anything else?"

"Probably not," he said. "But a man is better equipped to fight the undercurrents!"

"You think I was very rash?" she questioned.

He smiled. "One doesn't look for caution in a girl. I think your father deserved a horsewhipping for letting you go."

"He couldn't prevent me," said Sylvia quickly.

"Pshaw!" said Burke Ranger.

"You're very rude," she protested.

His smile became a laugh. "I could have prevented you," he said.

She flushed. "Indeed you couldn't! I am not a namby-pamby miss. I go my own way. I——"

She broke off suddenly. Burke's eyes, grey as steel in his sun-tanned face, were upon her. He looked amused at her vehemence.

"Well?" he said encouragingly. "Finish!"

She laughed in spite of herself. "No, I shan't say any more. I never argue with the superior male. I just—go my own way, that's all."

"From which I gather that you are not particularly partial to the superior male," said Burke.

"I hate the species," said Sylvia with simplicity.

"Except when it kneels at your feet," he suggested, looking ironical.

"No, I want to kick it then," she said.

"You seem difficult to please," he observed.

Sylvia looked out across the *veldt*. "I like a man to be just a jolly comrade," she said. "If he can't be that, I've no use for him."

"I see," said Burke slowly. "That's to be my *rôle*, is it?"

She turned to him impulsively with extended hand. "I think you can fill it if you try."

He took the hand, grasping it strongly. "All right. I'll try," he said.

"You don't mind?" she said half-wistfully. "You see, it makes such a difference to feel there's someone like that to turn to in trouble—someone who won't let you down."

"I shan't let you down," said Burke.

Her fingers closed hard on his. "You're a brick," she said. "Now let's have some lunch, and then, if you don't mind, I'm going to sleep!"

"Best thing you can do," said Burke.

They rested for the greater part of the afternoon in the shadow of their boulder. Sylvia lay with her head on a light rug that he spread for her, and he sat with his back to the rock and smoked with eyes fixed straight before him.

Sleep came to the girl very quickly for she was tired, and her healthy young body was swift to find repose. But the man, watching beside her, did not even doze. He scarcely varied his position throughout his vigil, scarcely glanced at the figure nestled in the long grass so close to him. But his attitude had the alertness of the man on guard, and his brown face was set in grimly resolute lines. It gave no indication whatever of that which was passing in his mind.

CHAPTER IX

THE ARRIVAL

It was drawing towards evening when Sylvia at length stirred, stretched, and opened her eyes. A momentary bewilderment showed in them, then with a smile she saw and recognized her companion.

She sat up quickly. "I must have been asleep for ages. Why didn't you wake me?"

"I didn't want to," he said.

She looked at him. "What have you been doing? Have you been asleep?"

He raised his shoulders to the first question. To the second he replied merely, "No."

"Why didn't you smoke?" she asked next.

For an instant he looked half-ashamed, then very briefly, "I don't live on tobacco," he said.

"How very silly of you!" said Sylvia. "It wouldn't have disturbed me in the least. I smoke cigarettes myself."

Burke said nothing. After a moment he got to his feet.

"Time to go?" she said.

"Yes. I think we ought to be moving. We have some miles to go yet. You sit still while I get the horses in!"

But Sylvia was on her feet. "No. I'm coming to help. I like to do things. Isn't it hot? Do you think there will be a storm?"

He looked up at the sky. "No, not yet. It'll take some time to break. Are you afraid of storms?"

"Of course not!" said Sylvia.

He smiled at her prompt rejoinder. "Not afraid of anything?" he suggested.

She smiled back. "Not often anyway. And I hope I don't behave like a muff even when I am."

"I shouldn't think that very likely," he observed.

They put in the horses, and started again across the *veldt*. The burning air that blew over the hot earth was like a blast from a furnace. Over the far hills the clouds hung low and menacing. A mighty storm seemed to be brewing somewhere on the further side of those distant heights.

"It is as if someone had lighted a great fire just out of sight," said Sylvia. "Is it often like this?"

"Very often," said Burke.

"How wonderful!" she said.

They drove on rapidly, and as they went, the brooding cloud-curtain seemed to advance to meet them, spreading ominously across the sky as if it were indeed the smoke from some immense conflagration.

Sylvia became silent, awed by the spectacle. All about them the *veldt* took on a leaden hue. The sun still shone; but vaguely, as if through smoked glass. The heat seemed to increase.

Sylvia sat rapt. She did not for some time wake to the fact that Burke was urging the horses, and only when they stretched themselves out to gallop in response to his curt command did she rouse from her contemplation to throw him a startled glance. He was leaning slightly forward, and the look on his face sent a curious thrill through her. It was the look of a man braced to utmost effort. His eyes were fixed steadily straight ahead, marking the road they travelled. His driving was a marvel of skill and confidence. The girl by his side forgot to watch the storm in front of them in her admiration of his ability. It was to her the most amazing exhibition of strength and adroitness combined that she had ever witnessed. The wild enjoyment of that drive was fixed in her memory for all time.

At the end of half-an-hour's rapid travelling a great darkness had begun to envelope them, and obscurity so pall-like that even near objects were seen as it were through a dark veil.

Burke broke his long silence. "Only two miles more!"

She answered him exultantly. "I could go on for ever!"

They seemed to fly on the wings of the wind those last two miles. She fancied that they had turned off the track and were racing over the grass, but the darkness was such that she could discern nothing with any certainty. At last there came a heavy jolting that flung her against Burke's shoulder, and on the top of it a frightful flash and explosion that made her think the earth had rent asunder under their feet.

Half-stunned and wholly blinded, she covered her face, crouching down almost against the footboard of the cart, while the dreadful echoes rolled away.

Then again came Burke's voice, brief yet amazingly reassuring. "Get down and run in! It's all right."

She realized that they had come to a standstill, and mechanically she raised herself to obey him.

As she groped for the step, he grasped her arm.

"Get on to the *stoep!* There's going to be rain.
I'll be with you in a second."

She thanked him, and found herself on the
ground. A man in front of her was calling out
unintelligibly, and somewhere under cover a
woman's voice was uplifted in shrill tones of dismay. This latter sound made her think of the
chattering of an indignant monkey, so shrill was
it and so incessant.

A dark pile of building stood before her, and she
blundered towards it, not seeing in the least where
she was going. The next moment she kicked
against some steps, and sprawled headlong.

Someone—Burke—uttered an oath behind her,
and she heard him leap to the ground. She made
a sharp effort to rise, and cried out with a sudden
pain in her right knee that rendered her for an
instant powerless. Then she felt his hands upon
her, beneath her. He lifted her bodily and bore
her upwards.

She was still half-dazed when he set her down
in a chair. She held fast to his arm. "Please
stay with me just a moment—just a moment!"
she besought him incoherently.

He stayed, very steady and quiet beside her.
"Are you hurt?" he asked her.

She fought with herself, but could not answer

him. A ridiculous desire to dissolve into tears possessed her. She gripped his arm with both hands, saying no word.

"Stick to it!" he said.

"I—I'm an awful idiot!" she managed to articulate.

"No, you're not. You're a brave girl," he said. "I was a fool not to warn you. I forgot you didn't know your way. Did you hurt yourself when you fell?"

"My knee—a little," she said. "It'll be all right directly." She released his arm. "Thank you. I'm better now. Oh, what is that? Rain?"

"Yes, rain," he said.

It began like the rushing of a thousand wings, sweeping irresistibly down from the hills. It swelled into a pandemonium of sound that was unlike anything she had ever heard. It was as if they had suddenly been caught by a seething torrent. Again the lightning flared, dancing a quivering, zigzag measure across the verandah in which she sat, and the thunder burst overhead, numbing the senses.

By that awful leaping glare Sylvia saw her companion. He was stooping over her. He spoke; but she could not hear a word he uttered.

Then again his arms were about her and he

lifted her. She yielded herself to him with the
confidence of a child, and he carried her into his
home while the glancing lightning showed the
way.

The noise within the house was less overwhelming. He put her down on a long chair in almost
total darkness, but a few moments later the lightning glimmered again and showed her vividly the
room in which she lay. It was a man's room,
half-office, half-lounge, extremely bare, and devoid
of all ornament with the exception of a few native
weapons on the walls.

The kindling of a lamp confirmed this first impression, but the presence of the man himself
diverted her attention from her surroundings.
He turned from lighting the lamp to survey her.
She thought he looked somewhat stern.

"What about this knee of yours?" he said. "Is
it badly damaged?"

"Oh, not badly," she answered. "I'm sure not
badly. What a lot of trouble I am giving you!
I am so sorry."

"You needn't be sorry on that account," he
said. "I blame myself alone. Do you mind letting me see it? I am used to giving first-aid."

"Oh, I don't think that is necessary," said
Sylvia. "I—can quite easily doctor myself."

"I thought we were to be comrades," he observed bluntly.

She coloured and faintly laughed. "You can see it if you particularly want to."

"I do," said Burke.

She sat up without further protest, and uncovered the injured knee for his inspection. "I really don't think anything of a tumble like that," she said, as he bent to examine it. But the next moment at his touch she flinched and caught her breath.

"That hurts, does it?" he said. "It's swelling up. I'm going to get some hot water to bathe it."

He stood up with the words and turned away. Sylvia leaned back again, feeling rather sick. Certainly the pain was intense.

The rain was still battering on the roof with a sound like the violent jingling together of tin cans. She listened to it with a dull wonder. The violence of it would have made a deeper impression upon her had she been suffering less. But she felt as one immersed in an evil dream which clogged all her senses save that of pain.

When Burke returned she was lying with closed eyes, striving hard to keep herself under control. The clatter of the rain had abated somewhat, and she heard him speak over his shoulder to someone behind him. She looked up and saw an old Kaffir woman carrying a basin.

"This is Mary Ann," said Burke, intercepting her glance of surprise. "A useful old dog except when there is any dope about! Hope you don't mind niggers."

"I shall get used to them," said Sylvia rather faintly.

"There's nothing formidable about this one," he said. "She can't help being hideous. She is quite tame."

Sylvia tried to smile. Certainly Mary Ann was hideous, but her tameness was equally obvious. She evidently stood in considerable awe of her master, obeying his slighest behest with clumsy solicitude and eyes that rolled unceasingly in his direction.

Burke kept her in the room while he bathed the injury. He was very gentle, and Sylvia was soon conscious of relief. When at length he applied a pad soaked in ointment and proceeded to bandage with a dexterity that left nothing to be desired, she told him with a smile that he was as good as a professional.

"One has to learn a little of this sort of thing," he said. "How does it feel now?"

"Much better," she answered. "I shall have forgotten all about it by to-morrow."

"No, you won't," said Burke. "You will rest it for three days at least. You don't want to get water on the joint."

"Three days!" she echoed in dismay. "I can't—possibly—lie up here."

He raised his eyes from his bandaging for a moment, and a curious thrill went through her; it was as if his look pierced her. "The impossible often happens here," he said briefly.

She expressed a sharp tremor that caught her unawares. "What does that mean?" she asked, striving to speak lightly.

He replied with his eyes lowered again to his task. "It means among other things that you can't get back to Ritzen until the floods go down. Ritter Spruit is a foaming torrent by this time."

"Good heavens!" she exclaimed. "But isn't there—isn't there a bridge anywhere?"

"Forty miles away," said Burke Ranger laconically.

"Good—heavens!" she gasped again.

He finished his bandaging and stood up. "Now I am going to carry you to bed," he said, "and Mary Ann shall wait on you. You won't be frightened?"

She smiled in answer. "You've taken my breath away, but I shall get it again directly. I don't think I want to go to bed yet. Mayn't I stay here for a little?"

He looked down at her. "You've got some pluck, haven't you?" he said.

She flushed. "I hope so—a little."

He touched her shoulder unexpectedly, with a hint of awkwardness. "I'm afraid I can only offer you—rough hospitality. It's the best I can do. My guests have all been of the male species till now. But you will put up with it? You won't be scared anyhow?"

She reached up an impulsive hand and put it into his. "No, I shan't be scared at all. You make me feel quite safe. I'm only—more grateful than I can say."

His fingers closed upon hers. "You've nothing to be grateful for. Let me take you to the guest-room and Mary Ann shall bring you supper. You'll be more comfortable there. Your baggage is there already."

She clung to his hand for an instant, caught by an odd feeling of forlornness. "I will do whatever you wish. But—but—you will let me see Guy in the morning?"

He stooped to lift her. For a moment his eyes

looked straight into hers. Then: "Wait till the morning comes!" he said quietly.

There was finality in his tone, and she knew that it was no moment for discussion. With a short sigh she yielded to the inevitable, and suffered him to carry her away.

CHAPTER X

THE DREAM

SHE had no further communication with Burke
that night. The old Kaffir woman helped her,
brought her a meal on a tray, and waited upon her
until dismissed.

Sylvia had no desire to detain her. She longed
for solitude. The thought of Guy tormented her
perpetually. She ached and yearned—even while
she dreaded—to see him. But Burke had decreed
that she must wait till the morning, and she had
found already that what Burke decreed usually
came to pass. Besides, she knew that she was
worn out and wholly unfit for any further strain.

Very thankfully she sank down at last upon the
bed in the bare guest-room. Her weariness was
such that she thought that she must sleep, yet for
hours she lay wide awake, listening to the rain
streaming down and pondering—pondering the
future. Her romance was ended. She saw that
very clearly. Whatever came of her meeting
with Guy, it would not be—it could not be—the

consummation to which she had looked forward so
confidently during the past five years. Guy had
failed her. She faced the fact with all her courage.
The Guy she had loved and trusted did not exist
any longer, if he ever had existed. Life had
changed for her. The path she had followed had
ended suddenly. She must needs turn back and
seek another. But whither to turn she knew not.
It seemed that there was no place left for her anywhere.

Slowly the long hours dragged away. She
thought the night would never pass. Her knee
gave her a good deal of pain, and she relinquished
all hope of sleep. Her thoughts began to circle
about Burke Ranger in a worried, confused
fashion. She felt she would know him better
when she had seen Guy. At present the likeness
between them alternately bewildered her or hurt
her poignantly. She could not close her mind to
the memory of having taken him for Guy. He
was the sort of man—only less polished—that
she had believed Guy would become. She tried to
picture him as he must have been when younger,
but she could see only Guy. And again the bitter
longing, the aching disappointment, tore her soul.

Towards morning she dozed, but physical discomfort and torturing anxiety went with her un-

ceasingly, depriving her of any real repose. She
was vaguely aware of movements in the house
long before a low knock at the door called her back
to full consciousness.

She started up on her elbows. "Come in! I
am awake."

Burke Ranger presented himself. "I was afraid
Mary Ann might give you a shock if she woke you
suddenly," he said. "Can I come in?"

"Please do!" she said.

The sight of his tanned face and keen eyes came
as a great relief to her strained and weary senses.
She held out a welcoming hand, dismissing con-
vention as superfluous.

He came to her side and took her hand, but in
a moment his fingers were feeling for her pulse.
He looked straight down at her. "You've had a
bad night," he said.

She admitted it, mustering a smile as she did so.
"It rained so hard, I couldn't forget it. Has it
left off yet?"

He paid no attention whatever to the question.
"What's the trouble?" he said. "Knee bad?"

"Not very comfortable," she confessed. "It
will be better presently, no doubt."

"I'll dress it again," said Burke, "when you've
had some tea. You had better stay in bed to-day."

"Oh, must I?" she said in dismay.

"Don't you want to?" said Burke.

"No. I hate staying in bed. It makes me so miserable." She spoke with vehemence. Besides—besides——"

"Yes?" he said.

"I want—to see Guy," she ended, colouring very deeply.

"That's out of the question," said Burke, with quiet decision. "You certainly won't see him to-day."

"Oh, but I must! I really must!" she pleaded desperately. "My knee isn't very bad. Have you—have you told him I am here yet?"

"No," said Burke.

"Then won't you? Please won't you?" She was urging him almost feverishly now. "I can't rest till I have seen him—indeed. I can't see my way clearly. I can't do anything until—until I have seen him."

Burke was frowning. He looked almost savage. But she was not afraid of him. She could think only of Guy at that moment and of her urgent need to see him. It was all that mattered. With nerves stretched and quivering, she waited for his answer.

It did not come immediately. He was still

holding her hand in one of his and feeling her pulse with the other.

"Listen!" he said at length. "There is no need for all this wearing anxiety. You must make up your mind to rest to-day, or you will be ill. It won't hurt you—or him either—to wait a few hours longer."

"I shan't be ill!" she assured him earnestly. "I am never ill. And I want to see him—oh, so much. I must see him. He isn't—he isn't worse?"

"No," said Burke.

"Then why mustn't I see him?" she urged. "Why do you look like that? Are you keeping back something? Has—has something happened that you don't want me to know? Ah, that is it! I thought so! Please tell me what it is! It is far better to tell me."

She drew her hand from his and sat up, steadily facing him. She was breathing quickly, but she had subdued her agitation. Her eyes met his unflinchingly.

He made an abrupt gesture—as if compelled against his will. "Well—if you must have it! He has gone."

"Gone!" she repeated. "What—do you mean by that?"

He looked down into her whitening face, and his own grew sterner. "Just what I say. He cleared out yesterday morning early. No one knows where he is."

Sylvia's hand unconsciously pressed her heart. It was beating very violently. She spoke with a great effort. "Perhaps he has gone to Ritzen—to look for me."

"I think not," said Burke drily.

His tone said more than his words. She made a slight involuntary movement of shrinking. But in a moment she spoke again with a pathetic little smile.

"You are very good to me. But I mustn't waste any more of your time. Please don't worry about me any more! I can quite well bandage my knee myself."

The grimness passed from his face. "I shall have to see it to satisfy myself it is going on all right," he said. "But I needn't bother you now. I'll send Mary Ann in with some tea."

"Thank you," said Sylvia. She was gathering her scattered forces again after the blow; she spoke with measured firmness. "Now please don't think about me any more! I am not ill—or going to be. You may look at my knee this evening—if you are very anxious. But not before."

"Then you will stay in bed?" said Burke.

"Very well; if I must," she conceded.

He turned to go; then abruptly turned back. "And you won't lie and worry? You've too much pluck for that."

She smiled again—a quivering, difficult smile. "I am not at all plucky, really. I am only pretending."

He smiled back at her suddenly. "You're a brick! I've never seen any woman stand up to hard knocks as you do. They generally want to be carried over the rough places. But you—you stand on your feet."

The genuine approbation of his voice brought the colour back to her face. His smile too, though it reminded her piercingly of Guy, sent a glow of comfort to her chilled and trembling heart.

"I want to if I can," she said. "But I've had rather a—knock-out this time. I shall be all right presently, when I've had time to pull myself together."

He bent abruptly and laid his hand upon hers. "Look here!" he said. "Don't worry!"

She lifted clear eyes to his. "No—I won't! There is always a way out of every difficulty, isn't there?"

"There certainly is out of this one," he said.

"I'll show it you presently—if you'll promise not to be offended."

"Offended!" said Sylvia. "That isn't very likely, is it?"

"I don't know," said Burke. "I hope not. Good-bye!" He straightened himself, stood a moment looking down at her, then turned finally and left her.

There was something in the manner of his going that made her wonder.

The entrance of the old Kaffir woman a few minutes later diverted her thoughts. She found Mary Ann an interesting study, being the first of her kind that she had viewed at close quarters. She was very stout and ungainly. She moved with elephantine clumsiness, but her desire to please was so evident that Sylvia could not regard her as wholly without charm. Her dog-like amiability outweighed her hideousness. She found it somewhat difficult to understand Mary Ann's speech, for it was more like the chattering of a monkey than human articulation, and being very weary she did not encourage her to talk.

There was so much to think about, and for a while her tired brain revolved around Guy and all that his departure meant to her. She tried to take a practical view of the situation, to grapple

with the difficulties that confronted her. Was
there the smallest chance of his return? And
even if he returned, what could it mean to her?
Would it help her in any way? It was impossible
to evade the answer to that question. He had
failed her finally. She was stranded in a strange
land and only her own efforts could avail her now.

She wondered if Burke would urge her to return
to her father's house. If so, he would not succeed. She would face any hardship sooner than
that. She was not afraid of work. She would
make a living for herself somehow if she worked in
the fields with Kaffir women. She would be
independent or die in the attempt. After all, she
reflected forlornly, it would not matter very much
to anyone if she did die. She stood or fell alone.

Thought became vague at last and finally obscured in the mists of sleep. She lay still on the
narrow bed and slept long and deeply.

It must have been after several hours that her
dream came to her. It arose out of a sea of oblivion—a vision unsummoned, wholly unexpected.
She saw Burke Ranger galloping along the side
of a dry and stony ravine where doubtless water
flowed in torrents when the rain came. He was
bending low in the saddle, his dark face set forward scanning the path ahead. With a breath-

less interest she watched him, and the thunder of
his horse's hoofs drummed in her brain. Suddenly, turning her eyes further along the course
he followed, she saw with horror round a bend
that which he could not see. She beheld another
horseman galloping down from the opposite direction. The face of this horseman was turned from
her, but she did not need to see it. She knew, as
it is given in dreams to know beyond all doubting, that it was Guy. She recognized his easy
seat in the saddle, the careless grace of his carriage. He was plunging straight ahead with never
a thought of danger, and though he must have
seen the turn as he approached it, he did not
attempt to check the animal under him. Rather
he seemed to be urging it forward. And ever
the thunder of the galloping hoofs filled her
brain.

Tensely she watched, in a suspense that racked
her whole body. Guy reached the bend first.
There was room for only one upon that narrow
ledge. He went round the curve with the confidence of one who fully expected a clear path
ahead. And then—on the very edge of the preci-
pice—he caught sight of the horseman galloping
towards him. He reined back. He threw up
one hand as his animal staggered under him, and

8

called a warning. But the thudding of the hoofs drowned all other sound.

Sylvia's heart stood still as if it could never beat again. Her look flashed to Burke Ranger. He was galloping still—galloping hard. One glimpse she had of his face as he drew near, and she knew that he saw the man ahead of him, for it was set and terrible—the face of a devil.

The next instant she heard the awful crash of collision. There was a confusion indescribable, there on the very brink of the ravine. Then one horse and its rider went hurling headlong down that wall of stones. The other horseman struck spurs into his animal and galloped up the narrow path to the head of the ravine without a backward glance.

She was left transfixed by horror in a growing darkness that seemed to penetrate to her very soul. Which of the two had galloped free? Which lay shattered there, very far below her in an abyss that had already become obscure? She agonized to know, but the darkness hid all things. At last she tore it aside as if it had been a veil. She went down, down into that deep place. She stumbled through a valley of awful desolation till she came to that which she sought;—a fallen horse, a rider with glassy eyes upturned.

But the hand of Death had wiped out every distinguishing mark. Was it Guy? Was it Burke? She knew not. She turned from the sight with dread unspeakable. She went from the accursed spot with the anguish of utter bewilderment in her soul. She was bereft of all. She walked alone in a land of strangers.

CHAPTER XI

THE CROSS-ROADS

WHEN Sylvia started awake from that terrible dream it was to hear the tread of horses' feet outside the house and the sound of men's voices talking to each other. As she listened, these drew nearer, and soon she heard footsteps on the *stoep* outside. It was drawing towards sunset, and she realized that she had slept for a long time.

She felt refreshed in spite of her dream and very thankful to regain possession of her waking senses. Her knee too was decidedly better. She found with relief that with care she could use it.

The smell of tobacco wafted in, and she realized that the two men were sitting smoking together on the *stoep*. One of them, she felt sure, was Burke Ranger, though it very soon dawned upon her that they were conversing in Dutch. She lay for awhile watching the orange light of evening gleaming through the creeper that entwined the corner of the *stoep* outside her window. Then, growing weary of inaction, she slipped from her bed and began to dress.

Her cabin-trunk had been placed in a corner of the bare room. She found her key and opened it. Guy's photograph—the photograph she had cherished for five years—lay on the top. She saw it with a sudden, sharp pang, remembering how she had put it in at the last moment and smiled to think how soon she would behold him in the flesh. The handsome, boyish face looked straight into hers. Ah, how she had loved him. A swift tremor went through her. She closed her eyes upon the smiling face. And suddenly great tears welled up from her heart. She laid her face down upon the portrait and wept.

The voices on the *stoep* recalled her. She remembered that she had a reputation for courage to maintain. She commanded herself with an effort and finished her dressing. She did not dare to look at the portrait again, but hid it deep in her trunk.

Mary Ann seemed to have forsaken her, and she was in some uncertainty as to how to proceed when she was at length ready to leave her room. She did not want to intrude upon Burke and his visitor, but a great longing to breathe the air of the *veldt* was upon her. She wondered if she could possibly escape unseen.

Finally, she ventured out into the passage, and followed it to an open door that seemed to lead whither she desired to go. She fancied that it was out of sight of the two men on the *stoep*, but as she reached it, she realized her mistake. For there fell a sudden step close to her, and as she paused irresolute, Burke's figure blocked the opening. He stood looking at her, pipe in hand.

"So—you are up!" he said.

His voice was quite friendly, yet she was possessed by a strong feeling that he did not want her there.

She looked back at him in some embarrassment. "I hope you don't mind, she said. "I was only coming out for a breath of air."

"Why should I mind?" said Burke. "Come and sit on the *stoep*! My neighbour, Piet Vreiboom, is there, but he is just going."

He spoke the last words with great distinctness, and it occurred to her that he meant them to be overheard.

She hung back. "Oh, I don't think I will. I can't talk Dutch. Really I would rather——"

"He understands a little English," said Burke. "But don't be surprised at anything he says! He isn't very perfect."

He stood against the wall for her to pass him,

and she did so with a feeling that she had no choice. Very reluctantly she moved out on to the wooden *stoep*, and turned towards the visitor. The orange of the sunset was behind her, turning her hair to living gold. It fell full upon the face of the man before her, and she was conscious of a powerful sense of repugnance. Low-browed, wide-nosed, and prominent of jaw, with close-set eyes of monkeyish craft, such was the countenance of Piet Vreiboom. He sat and stared at her, his hat on his head, his pipe in his mouth.

"How do you do, Mrs. Ranger?" he said.

Sylvia checked her advance, but in a moment Burke Ranger's hand closed upon her elbow, quietly impelling her forward.

"Mr. Vreiboom saw you with me at Ritzen yesterday," he said, and she suddenly remembered the knot of Boer farmers at the hotel-door and the staring eyes that had abashed her.

She glanced up at Burke, but his face was quite emotionless. Only something about him—an indefinable something—held her back from correcting the mistake that Vreiboom had made.

She looked at the seated Boer with a dignity wholly unconscious. "How do you do?" she said coolly.

He stretched out a hand to her. His smile was

familiar. "I hope you like the farm, Mrs. Ranger," he said.

"She has hardly seen it yet," said Burke.

There was a slight pause before Sylvia gave her hand. This man filled her with distaste. She resented his manner. She resented the look in his eyes.

"I have no doubt I shall like it very much," she said, removing her hand as speedily as possible.

"You like to be—a farmer's wife?" questioned Piet, still freely staring.

She resented this question also, but she had to respond to it. "It is what I came out for," she said.

"You do not look like a farmer's wife," said Piet.

Sylvia stiffened.

"Give him a little rope!" said Burke. "He doesn't know much. Sit down! I'll get him on the move directly."

She sat down not very willingly, and he resumed his talk with Vreiboom in Dutch, lounging against the wall. Sylvia sat quite silent, her eyes upon the glowing sky and the far-away hills. In the foreground was a *kopje* shaped like a sugar-loaf. She wished herself upon its summit which was bathed in the sunset light.

Once or twice she was moved to glance up at the brown face of the man who leaned between herself and the objectionable visitor. His attitude was one of complete ease, and yet something told her that he desired Piet's departure quite as sincerely as she did.

He must have given a fairly broad hint at last, she decided; for Piet moved somewhat abruptly and knocked out the ashes of his pipe on the floor with a noisy energy that made her start. Then he got up and addressed her in his own language.

She did not understand in the least what he said, but she gave him a distant smile realizing that he was taking leave of her. She was somewhat surprised to see Burke take him unceremoniously by the shoulder as he stood before her and march him off the *stoep*. Piet himself laughed as if he had said something witty, and there was that in the laugh that sent the colour flaming to her cheeks.

She quivered with impotent indignation as she sat. She wished with all her heart that Burke would kick him down the steps.

The sunset-light faded, and a soft dusk stole up over the wide spaces. A light breeze cooled her hot face, and after the lapse of a few minutes she began to chide herself for her foolishness. Probably the man had not meant to be offensive. She was certain Burke would never permit her to be insulted in his presence. She heard the sound of hoof-beats retreating away into the distance, and, with it, the memory of her dream came back upon her. She felt forlorn and rather frightened. It was only a dream of course; it was only a dream! But she wished that Burke would come back to her. His substantial presence would banish phantoms.

He did not come for some time, but she heard his step at last. And then a strange agitation took her so that she wanted to spring up and avoid him. She did not do so; she forced herself to appear normal. But every nerve tingled as he approached, and she could not keep the quick blood from her face.

He was carrying a tray which he set down on a rough wooden table near her.

"You must be famished," he said.

She had not thought of food, but certainly the sight of it cheered her failing spirits. She smiled at him.

"Are we going to have another picnic?"

He smiled in answer, and she felt oddly relieved. All sense of strain and embarrassment left her. She sat up and helped him spread the feast.

The fare was very simple, but she found it amply

satisfying. She partook of Mary Ann's butter with appreciation.

"I can make butter," she told him presently.

"And bake bread?" said Burke.

She nodded, laughing. "Yes, and cook joints and mend clothes, too. Who does your mending? Mary Ann?"

"I do my own," said Burke. "I cook, too, when Mary Ann takes leave of absence. But I have a Kaffir house boy, Joe, for the odd jobs. And there's a girl, too, uglier than Mary Ann, a relation of hers —called Rose, short for Fair Rosamond. Haven't you seen Rose yet?"

Sylvia's laugh brought a smile to his face. It was a very infectious laugh. Though she sobered almost instantly, it left a ripple of mirth behind on the surface of their conversation. He carried the tray away again when the meal was over, firmly refusing her offer to wash up.

"Mary Ann can do it in the morning," he said.

"Where is she now?" asked Sylvia.

He sat down beside her, and took out his pipe. "They are over in their own huts. They don't sleep in the house."

"Does no one sleep in the house?" she asked quickly.

"I do," said Burke.

A sudden silence fell. The dusk had deepened into a starlit darkness, but there was a white glow behind the hills that seemed to wax with every instant that passed. Very soon the whole *veldt* would be flooded with moonlight.

In a very small voice Sylvia spoke at length. "Mr. Ranger!"

It was the first time she had addressed him by name. He turned directly towards her. "Call me Burke!" he said.

It was almost a command. She faced him as directly as he faced her. "Burke—if you wish it!" she said. "I want to talk things over with you, to thank you for your very great goodness to me, and—and to make plans for the future."

"One moment!" he said. "You have given up all thought of marrying Guy?"

She hesitated. "I suppose so," she said slowly.

"Don't you know your own mind?" he said.

Still she hesitated. "If—if he should come back——"

"He will come back," said Burke.

She started. "He will?"

"Yes, he will." His voice held grim confidence, and somehow it sounded merciless also to her ears. "He'll turn up again some day. He always does. I'm about the only man in South Africa who wouldn't kick him out within six months. He knows that. That's why he'll come back."

"You are—good to him," said Sylvia, her voice very low.

"No, I'm not; not specially. He knows what I think of him anyhow." Burke spoke slowly. "I've done what I could for him, but he's one of my failures. You've got to grasp the fact that he's a rotter. Have you grasped that yet?"

"I'm beginning to," Sylvia said, under her breath.

"Then you can't—possibly—marry him," said Burke.

She lowered her eyes before the keenness of his look. She wished the light in the east were not growing so rapidly.

"The question is, What am I going to do?" she said.

Burke was silent for a moment. Then with a slight gesture that might have denoted embarrassment he said, "You don't want to stay here, I suppose?"

She looked up again quickly. "Here—on this farm, do you mean?"

"Yes." He spoke brusquely, but there was a certain eagerness in his attitude as he leaned towards her.

A throb of gratitude went through her.   She put out her hand to him very winningly.   "What a pity I'm not a boy!" she said, genuine regret in her voice.

He took her hand and kept it.   "Is that going to make any difference?" he said.

She looked at him questioningly.   It was difficult to read his face in the gloom.   "All the difference, I am afraid," she said.   "You are very generous—a real good comrade.   If I were a boy, there's nothing I'd love better.   But, being a woman, I can't live here alone with you, can I? Not even in South Africa!"

"Why not?" he said.

His hand grasped hers firmly; she grasped his in return.   "You heard what your Boer friend called me," she said.   "He wouldn't understand anything else."

"I told him to call you that," said Burke.

"You—told him!"   She gave a great start.   His words amazed her.

"Yes."   There was a dogged quality in his answer.   "I had to protect you somehow.   He had seen us together at Ritzen.   I said you were my wife."

Sylvia gasped in speechless astonishment.

He went on ruthlessly.   "It was the only thing to do.   They're not a particularly moral crowd here, and, as you say, they wouldn't understand anything else—decent. Do you object to the idea? Do you object very strongly?"

There was something masterful in the persistence with which he pressed the question. Sylvia had a feeling as of being held down and compelled to drink some strangely paralyzing draught.

She made a slight, half-scared movement and in a moment his hand released hers.

"You do object!" he said.

She clasped her hands tightly together. "Please don't say—or think—that! It is such a sudden idea, and—it's rather a wild one, isn't it?" Her breath came quickly. "If—if I agreed—and let the pretence go on—people would be sure to find out sooner or later. Wouldn't they?"

"I am not suggesting any pretence," he said.

"What do you mean then?" Sylvia said, compelling herself to speak steadily.

"I am asking you to marry me," he said, with equal steadiness.

"Really, do you mean? You are actually in earnest?" Her voice had a sharp quiver in it. She was trembling suddenly. "Please be quite plain with me!" she said. "Remember, I don't know you very well. I have got to get used to the ways out here."

"I am quite in earnest," said Burke. "You know me better than you knew the man you came out here to marry. And you will get used to things more quickly married to me than any other way. At least, you will have an assured position That ought to count with you."

"Of course it would! It does!" she said rather incoherently. "But—you see—I've no one to help me—no one to advise me. I'm on a road I don't know. And I'm so afraid of taking a wrong turning."

"Afraid!" he said. "You!"

She tried to laugh. "You think me a very bold person, don't you? Or you wouldn't have suggested such a thing."

"I think you've got plenty of grit," he said, "but that wasn't what made me suggest it." He paused a moment. "Perhaps it's hardly worth while going on," he said then. "I seem to have gone too far already. Please believe I meant well, that's all!"

"Oh, I know that!" she said.

And then, moved by a curious impulse, she did an extraordinary thing. She leaned forward and laid her clasped hands on his knee.

"I'm going to be—awfully frank with you," she said rather tremulously. "You—won't mind?"

He sat motionless for a second. Then very quietly he dropped his pipe back into his pocket and grasped her slender wrists. "Go on!" he said.

Her face was lifted, very earnest and appealing, to his. "You know," she said, "we are not strangers. We haven't been from the very beginning. We started comrades, didn't we?"

"We should have been married by this time, if I hadn't put the brake on," said Burke.

"Yes," Sylvia said. "I know. That is what makes me feel so—intimate with you. But it is different for you. I am a total stranger to you. You have never met me—or anyone like me—before. Have you?"

"And I have never asked anyone to marry me before," said Burke.

The wrists he held grew suddenly rigid. "You have asked me out of—out of pity—and the goodness of your heart?" she whispered.

"Quite wrong," said Burke. "I want a capable woman to take care of me—when Mary Ann goes on the bust."

"Please don't make me laugh!" begged Sylvia rather shakily. "I haven't done yet. I'm going to ask you an awful thing next. You'll tell me the truth, won't you?"

"I'll tell you before you ask," he said. "I can

9

be several kinds of beast, but not the kind you are afraid of. I am not a faddist, but I am moral. I like it best."

The curt, distinct words were too absolute to admit of any doubt. Sylvia breathed a short, hard sigh.

"I wonder," she said, "if it would be very wrong to marry a person you only like."

"Marriage is a risk—in any case," said Burke. "But if you're not blindly in love, you can at least see where you are going."

"I can't," she said rather piteously.

"You're afraid of me," he said.

"No, not really—not really. It's almost as big a risk for you as for me. You haven't bothered about—my morals, have you?" Her faint laugh had in it a sound of tears.

The hands that held her wrists closed with a steady pressure. "I haven't," said Burke with simplicity.

"Thank you," she said. "You've been very kind to me. Really I am not afraid of you."

"Sure?" said Burke.

"Only I still wish I were a boy," she said. "You and I could be just pals then."

"And why not now?" he said.

"Is it possible?" she asked.

"I should say so. Why not?"

She freed her hands suddenly and laid them upon his arms. "If I marry you, will you treat me just as a pal?"

"I will," said Burke.

She was still trembling a little. "You won't interfere with my—liberty?"

"Not unless you abuse it," he said.

She laughed again faintly. "I won't do that. I'll be a model of discretion. You may not think it, but I am—very discreet."

"I am sure of it," said Burke.

"No, you're not. You're not in the least sure of anything where I am concerned. You've only known me—two days."

He laughed a little. "It doesn't matter how long it has taken. I know you."

She laughed with him, and sat up. "What must you have thought of me when I told you you hadn't shaved?"

He took out his pipe again. "If you'd been a boy, I should probably have boxed your ears," he said. "By the way, why did you get up when I told you to stay in bed?"

"Because I knew best what was good for me," said Sylvia. "Have you got such a thing as a cigarette?"

He got up. "Yes, in my room. Wait while I fetch them!"

"Oh, don't go on purpose!" she said. "I daresay I shouldn't like your kind, thanks all the same."

He went nevertheless, and she leaned back with her face to the hills and waited. The moon was just topping the great summits. She watched it with a curious feeling of weakness. It had not been a particularly agitating interview, but she knew that she had just passed a cross-roads, in her life.

She had taken a road utterly unknown to her, and though she had taken it of her own accord, she did not feel that the choice had really been hers. Somehow her faculties were numbed, were paralyzed. She could not feel the immense importance of what she had done, or realize that she had finally, of her own action, severed her life from Guy's. He had become such a part of herself that she could not all at once divest herself of that waiting feeling, that confident looking forward to a future with him. And yet, strangely, her memory of him had receded into distance, become dim and remote. In Burke's presence she could not recall him at all. The two personalities, dissimilar though she knew them to be, seemed in some curious fashion to have become merged into one. She could not understand her own feelings, but she was conscious of relief that the die was cast. Whatever lay before her, she was sure of one thing. Burke Ranger would be her safeguard against any evil that might arise and menace her. His protection was of the solid quality that would never fail her. She felt firm ground beneath her feet at last.

At the sound of his returning step, she turned with the moonlight on her face and smiled up at him with complete confidence.

CHAPTER XII

THE STAKE

WHENEVER in after days Sylvia looked back upon her marriage, it seemed to be wrapped in a species of hazy dream like the early mists on that far-off range of hills.

They did not go again to Ritzen, but to a town of greater importance further down the line, a ride of nearly forty miles across the *veldt*. It was a busy town in the neighbourhood of some mines, and its teeming life brought back again to her that sense of aloneness in a land of strangers that had so oppressed her in the beginning. It drove her to seek Burke's society whenever possible. He was the shield between her and desolation, and in his presence her misgivings always faded into the background. He knew some of the English people at Brennerstadt, but she dreaded meeting them, and entreated him not to introduce anyone to her until they were married.

"People are all so curious. I can't face it," she said. "Mine is rather a curious story, too.

It will only set them talking, and I do so hate gossip."

He smiled a little and conceded the point. And so she was still a stranger to everyone on the day she laid her hand in Burke's and swore to be faithful to him. The marriage was a civil one. That also robbed it of all sense of reality for her. The ceremony left her cold. It did not touch so much as the outer tissues of her most vital sensibilities. She even felt somewhat impatient of the formalities observed, and very decidedly glad when they were over.

"Now let's go for a ride and forget it all!" she said. "We'll have a picnic on the *veldt*."

They had their picnic, but the heat was so great as to rob it of much enjoyment. Sylvia was charmed by a distant view of a herd of springbok, and her eyes shone momentarily when Burke said that they would have to do some shooting together. But almost immediately she shook her head.

"No, they are too pretty to kill. I love the hunt, but I hate the kill. Besides, I shall be too busy. If I am going to be your partner, one of us will have to do some work."

He laughed at that. "When do you want to begin?"

"Very soon," she said energetically. "To-morrow if you like. I don't think much of Brennerstadt, do you? It's such a barren sort of place."

He looked at her. "I believe you'll hate the winter on the farm."

"No, I shan't. I shan't hate anything. I'm not so silly as to expect paradise all the time."

"Is this paradise?" said Burke.

She glanced at him quickly. "No, I didn't say that. But I am enjoying it. And," she flushed slightly, "I am very grateful to you for making that possible."

"You've nothing to be grateful to me for," he said.

"Only I can't help it," said Sylvia.

Burke's eyes were scanning the far stretch of *veldt* towards the sinking sun, with a piercing intentness. She wondered what he was looking for.

There fell a silence between them, and a vague feeling of uneasiness began to grow up within her. His brown face was granite-like in its immobility, but it was exceedingly grim.

Something stirred within her at last, impelling her to action. She got up.

"Do you see that blasted tree right away over there with horrid twisted arms that look as if they are trying to clutch at something?"

His eyes came up to hers on the instant. "What of it?" he said.

She laughed down at him. "Let's mount! I'll race you to it."

He leapt to his feet like a boy. "What's the betting?"

"Anything you like!" she threw back gaily. "Whoever gets there first can fix the stakes."

He laughed aloud, and the sound of his laugh made her catch her breath with a sharp, involuntary start. She ran to her mount feeling as if Guy were behind her, and with an odd perversity she would not look round to disillusion herself.

During the fevered minutes that followed, the illusion possessed her strongly, so strongly that she almost forgot the vital importance of being first. It was the thudding hoofs of his companion that made her animal gallop rather than any urging of hers. But once started, with the air swirling past her and the excitement of rapid motion setting her veins on fire, the spirit of the race caught her again, and she went like the wind.

The blasted tree stood on a slope nearly a mile away. The ground was hard, and the grass seemed to crackle under the galloping hoofs. The horse she rode carried her with superb ease. He was the finest animal she had ever ridden, and from the first she believed the race was hers.

On she went through the orange glow of even-

ing. It was like a swift entrancing dream. And
the years fell away from her as if they had never
been, and she and Guy were racing over the slopes
of her father's park, as they had raced in the old
sweet days of youth and early love. She heard
him urging his horse behind her, and remembered
how splendid he always looked in the saddle.

The distance dwindled. The stark arms of the
naked tree seemed to be stretching out to receive
her. But he was drawing nearer also. She
could hear the thunder of his animal's hoofs close
behind. She bent low in the saddle, gasping
encouragement to her own.

There came a shout beside her—a yell of triumph such as Guy had often uttered. He passed
her and drew ahead. That fired her. She saw
victory being wrested from her.

She cried back at him "You—bounder!" and
urged her horse to fresh effort.

The ground sped away beneath her. The
heat-haze seemed to spin around. Her eyes were
fixed upon their goal, her whole being was concentrated upon reaching it. In the end it was as
if the ruined tree shot towards her. The race
was over. A great giddiness came upon her. She
reeled in the saddle.

And then a hand caught her; or was it one of

those outstretched skeleton arms? For a moment she hung powerless; then she was drawn close—close—to a man's breast, and felt the leap and throb of a man's heart against her own.

Breathless and palpitating, she lifted her face. His eyes looked deeply into hers, eyes that glowed like molten steel, and in an instant her illusion was swept away. It seemed to her that for the first time she looked upon Burke Ranger as he was, and her whole being recoiled in sudden wild dismay from what she saw.

"Ah! Let me go!" she said.

He held her still, but his hold slackened. "I won the race," he said.

"Yes, but—but it was only a game," she gasped back incoherently. "You — you can't — you won't——"

"Kiss you?" he said. "Not if you forbid it."

That calmed her very strangely. His tone was so quiet; it revived her courage. She uttered a faint laugh. "Is that the stake? I can't refuse to pay—a debt of honour."

"Thank you," he said, and she saw a curious smile gleam for a moment on his face. "That means you are prepared to take me like a nasty pill, doesn't it? I like your pluck. It's the best thing about you. But I won't put it to the test this time."

He made as if he would release her, but with an odd impulse she checked him. Somehow it was unbearable to be humoured like that. She looked him straight in the eyes.

"We are pals, aren't we?" she said.

The smile still lingered on Burke's face; it had an enigmatical quality that disquieted her, she could not have said wherefore. "It's rather an ambiguous term, isn't it?" he said.

"No, it isn't," she assured him, promptly and very earnestly. "It means that we are friends, but we are not in love and we are not going to pretend we are. At least," she flushed suddenly under his look, "that is what it means to me."

"I see," said Burke. "And what would happen if we fell in love with each other?"

Her eyes sank in spite of her. "I don't think we need consider that," she said.

"Why not?" said Burke.

"I could never be in love with anyone again," she said, her voice very low.

"Quite sure?" said Burke.

Something in his tone made her look up sharply. His eyes were intently and critically upon her,

but the glow had gone out of them. They told
her nothing.

"Do you think we need discuss this subject?"
she asked him uneasily.

"Not if you prefer to shirk it," he said.

She flushed a little. "But I don't shirk. I'm
not that sort."

"No," he said. "I don't think you are. You
may be frightened, but you won't run away."

"But I'm not frightened," she asserted boldly,
looking him squarely in the face. "We are
friends, you and I. And—we are going to trust
each other. Being married isn't going to make
any difference to us. It was just a matter of
convenience and—we are going to forget it."

She paused. Burke's face had not altered. He
was looking back at her with perfectly steady
eyes.

"Very simple in theory," he said. "Won't
you finish?"

"That's all," she said lightly. "Except—if you
really want to kiss me now and then—you can do
so. Only don't be silly about it!"

Burke's quick movement of surprise told her
that this was unexpected. The two horses had
recovered their wind and begun to nibble at one
another. He checked them with a growling

rebuke. Then very quietly he placed Sylvia's bridle in her hand, and put her from him.

"Thank you," he said again. "But you mustn't be too generous at the outset. I might begin to expect too much. And that would be—silly of me, wouldn't it?"

There was no bitterness in voice or action, but there was unmistakable irony. A curious sense of coldness came upon her, as if out of the heart of a distant storm-cloud an icy breath had reached her.

She looked at him rather piteously. "You are not angry?" she said.

He leaned back in the saddle to knock a blood-sucking fly off his horse's flank. Then he straightened himself and laughed.

"No, not in the least," he said.

She knew that he spoke the truth, yet her heart misgave her. There was something baffling, something almost sinister to her, in the very carelessness of his attitude. She turned her horse's head and walked soberly away.

He did not immediately follow her, and after a few moments she glanced back for him. He had dismounted and was scratching something on the trunk of the blasted tree with a knife. The withered arms stretched out above his head. They looked weirdly human in the sunset glow. She wished he would not linger in that eerie place.

She waited for him, and he came at length, riding with his head up and a strange gleam of triumph in his eyes.

"What were you doing?" she asked him, as he joined her.

He met her look with a directness oddly disconcerting. "I was commemorating the occasion," he said.

"What do you mean?" she said.

"Never mind now!" said Burke, and took out his pipe.

The light still lingered in his eyes, firing her to something deeper than curiosity. She turned her horse abruptly.

"I am going back to see for myself."

But in the same moment his hand came out, grasping her bridle. "I shouldn't do that," he said. "It isn't worth it. Wait till we come again!"

"The tree may be gone by then," she objected.

"In that case you won't have missed much," he rejoined. "Don't go now!"

He had his way though she yielded against her will. They turned their animals towards Brennerstadt, and rode back together over the sunscorched *veldt*.

PART II

CHAPTER I

COMRADES

SOME degree of normality seemed to come back into Sylvia's life with her return to Blue Hill Farm. She found plenty to do there, and she rapidly became accustomed to her surroundings.

It would have been a monotonous and even dreary existence but for the fact that she rode with Burke almost every evening, and sometimes in the early morning also, and thus saw a good deal of the working of the farm. Her keen interest in horses made a strong bond of sympathy between them. She loved them all. The mares and their foals were a perpetual joy to her, and she begged hard to be allowed to try her powers at breaking in some of the young animals. Burke, however, would not hear of this. He was very kind to her, unfailingly considerate in his treatment of her, but by some means he made her aware that his orders were to be respected. The Kaffir

servants were swift to do his bidding, though she
did not find them so eager to fulfil their duties
when he was not at hand.

She laughingly commented upon this one day
to Burke, and he amazed her by pointing to the
riding-whip she chanced to be holding at the time.

"You'll find that's the only medicine for that
kind of thing," he said. "Give 'em a taste of
that and they'll respect you!".

She decided he must be joking, but only a few
days later he quite undeceived her on that point
by dragging Joe, the house boy, into the yard and
chastising him with a *sjambok* for some neglected
duty.

Joe howled lustily, and Sylvia yearned to fly
to the rescue, but there was something so judicial
about Burke's administration of punishment that
she did not venture to intervene.

When he came in a little later, she was sitting
in their living-room nervously stitching at the
sleeve of a shirt that he had managed to tear on
some barbed wire. He had his pipe in his hand,
and there was an air of grim satisfaction about him
that seemed to denote a consciousness of something well done.

Sylvia set her mouth hard and stitched rapidly,
trying to forget Joe's piercing yells of a few minutes

before. Burke went to the window and stood there, pensively filling his pipe.

Suddenly, as if something in her silence struck him, he turned and looked at her. She felt his eyes upon her though she did not raise her own.

After a moment or two he came to her. "What are you doing there?" he said.

It was the first piece of work she had done for him. She glanced up. "Mending your shirt," she told him briefly.

He laid his hand abruptly upon it. "What are you doing that for? I don't want you to mend my things."

"Oh, don't be silly, Burke!" she said. "You can't go in tatters. Please don't hinder me! I want to get it done."

She spoke with a touch of sharpness, not feeling very kindly disposed towards him at the moment. She was still somewhat agitated, and she wished with all her heart that he would go and leave her alone.

She almost said as much in the next, breath as he did not remove his hand. "Why don't you go and shoot something? There's plenty of time before supper."

"What's the matter?" said Burke.

"Nothing," she returned, trying to remove her work from his grasp.

"Nothing!" he echoed. "Then why am I told not to be silly, not to hinder you, and to go and shoot something?"

Sylvia sat up in her chair, and faced him. "If you must have it—I think you've been—rather brutal," she said, lifting her clear eyes to his. "No doubt you had plenty of excuse, but that doesn't really justify you. At least—I don't think so."

He met her look in his usual direct fashion. Those eagle eyes of his sent a little tremor through her. There was a caged fierceness about them that strangely stirred her.

He spoke after the briefest pause with absolute gentleness. "All right, little pal! It's decent of you to put it like that. You're quite wrong, but that's a detail. You'll change your views when you've been in the country a little longer. Now forget it, and come for a ride!"

It was disarmingly kind, and Sylvia softened in spite of herself. She put her hand on his arm. "Burke, you won't do it again?" she said.

He smiled a little. "It won't be necessary for some time to come. If you did the same to Fair Rosamond now and then you would marvellously improve her. Idle little cuss!"

"I never shall," said Sylvia with emphasis.

He heaved a sigh. "Then I shall have to kick

her out I suppose.   I can see she is wearing your temper to a fine edge."

She bit her lip for a second, and then laughed. "Oh, go away, do! You're very horrid. Rose may be trying sometimes, but I can put up with her."

"You can't manage her," said Burke.

"Anyway, you are not to interfere," she returned with spirit.   "That's my department."

He abandoned the discussion.   "Well, I leave it to you, partner.   You're not to sit here mending shirts anyhow.   I draw the line at that."

Sylvia's delicate chin became suddenly firm. "I never leave a thing unfinished," she said. "You will have to ride alone this evening."

"I refuse," said Burke.

She opened her eyes wide. "Really"—she began.

"Yes, really," he said. "Put the thing away! It's a sheer fad to mend it at all. I don't care what I wear, and I'm sure you don't."

"But I do," she protested. "You must be respectable."

"But I am respectable—whatever I wear," argued Burke.   "It's my main characteristic."

His brown hand began to draw the garment in dispute away from her, but Sylvia held it tight.

"Burke, don't—please—be tiresome! Every woman mends her husband's clothes if there is no one else to do it. I want to do it. There!"

"You don't like doing it!" he challenged.

"It's my duty," she maintained.

He gave her an odd look. "And do you always do—your duty?"

"I try to," she said.

"Always?" he insisted.

Something in his eyes gave her pause. She wanted to turn her own aside, but could not. "To —to the best of my ability," she stammered.

He looked ironical for an instant, and then abruptly he laughed and released her work. "Bless your funny little heart!" he said. "Peg away, if you want to! It looks rather as if you're starting at the wrong end, but, being a woman, no doubt you will get there eventually."

That pierced her. It was Guy—Guy in the flesh—tenderly taunting her with some feminine weakness. So swift and so sharp was the pain that she could not hide it. She bent her face over her work with a quick intake of the breath.

"Why—Sylvia!" he said, bending over her.

She drew away from him. "Don't—please! I—I am foolish. Don't—take any notice!"

He stood up again, but his hand found her

shoulder and rubbed it comfortingly. "What is it, partner? Tell a fellow!" he urged, his tone an odd mixture of familiarity and constraint.

She fought with herself, and at last told him. "You—you—you were so like—Guy—just then."

"Oh, damn Guy!" he said lightly. "I am much more like myself at all times. Cheer up, partner! Don't cry for the moon!"

She commanded herself and looked up at him with a quivering smile. "It is rather idiotic, isn't it? And ungrateful too. You are very good not to lose patience."

"Oh, I am very patient," said Burke with a certain grimness. "But look here! Must you mend that shirt? I've got another somewhere."

Her smile turned to a laugh. She sprang up with a lithe, impulsive movement, "Come along then! Let's go! I don't know why you want to be bothered with me, I'm sure. But I'll come."

She took him by the arm and went with him from the room.

They rode out across Burkes land. The day had been one of burning heat. Sylvia turned instinctively towards the *kopje* that always attracted her. It had an air of aloofness that drew her fancy. "I must climb that very early some morning," she said, "in time for the sunrise."

"It will mean literal climbing," said Burke. "It's too steep for a horse."

"Oh, I don't mind that," she said. "I have a steady head. But I want to get round it to-night. I've never been round it yet. What is there on the other side?"

"*Veldt*," he said.

She made a face. "And then *veldt*—and then *veldt*. Plenty of nice, sandy *karoo* where all the sand-storms come from! But there are always the hills beyond. I am going to explore them some day."

"May I come too?" he said.

She smiled at him. "Of course, partner. We will have a castle right at the top of the world, shall we? There will be mountain gorges and great torrents, and ferns and rhododendrons everywhere. And a little further still, a great lake like an inland sea, with sandy shores and very calm water with the blue sky or the stars always in it."

"And what will the castle be like?" he said.

Sylvia's eyes were on the far hills as they rode. "The castle?" she said. "Oh, the castle will be of grey granite—the sparkling sort, very cool inside, with fountains playing everywhere; spacious rooms of course, and very lofty—always lots of air and no dust."

"Shall I be allowed to smoke a pipe in them?" asked Burke.

"You will do exactly what you like all day long," she told him generously.

"So long as I don't get in your way," he suggested.

She laughed a little. "Oh, we shall be too happy for that. Besides, you can have a farm or two to look after. There won't be any dry watercourses there like that," pointing with her whip. "That is what you call a '*spruit*,' isn't it?"

"You are getting quite learned," he said. "Yes, that is a *spruit* and that is a *kopje*."

"And that?" She pointed farther on suddenly. "What is that just above the watercourse? Is it a Kaffir hut?"

"No," said Burke.

He spoke somewhat shortly. The object she indicated was undoubtedly a hut; to Sylvia's unaccustomed eyes it might have been a cattle-shed. It was close to the dry watercourse, a little lonely hovel standing among stones and a straggling growth of coarse grass.

Something impelled Sylvia to check her horse. She glanced at her companion as if half-afraid. "What is it?" she said. "It—looks like a hermit's cell. Who lives there?"

"No one at the present moment," said Burke. His eyes were fixed straight ahead. He spoke curtly, as if against his will.

"But who generally—" began Sylvia, and then she stopped and turned suddenly white to the lips.

"I—see," she said, in an odd, breathless whisper.

Burke spoke without looking at her. "It's just a cabin. He built it himself the second year he was out here. He had been living at the farm, but he wanted to get away from me, wanted to go his own way without interference. Perhaps I went too far in that line. After all, it was no business of mine. But I can't stand tamely by and see a white man deliberately degrading himself to the Kaffir level. It was as well he went. I should have skinned him sooner or later if he hadn't. He realized that. So did I. So we agreed to part."

So briefly and baldly Burke stated the case, and every sentence he uttered was a separate thrust in the heart of the white-faced girl who sat her horse beside him, quite motionless, with burning eyes fixed upon the miserable little hovel that had enshrined the idol she had worshipped for so long.

She lifted her bridle at last without speaking a word and walked her animal forward through the sparse grass and the stones. Burke moved beside her, still gazing straight ahead, as if he were alone.

They went down to the cabin, and Sylvia dismounted. The only window space was filled with wire-netting instead of glass, and over this on the inside a piece of cloth had been firmly fastened so that no prying eyes could look in. The door was locked and padlocked. It was evident that the owner had taken every precaution against intrusion.

And yet—though he lived in this wretched place at which even a Kaffir might have looked askance —he had sent her that message telling her to come to him. This fact more than any other that she had yet encountered brought home to her the bitter, bitter truth of his failure. Out of the heart of the wilderness, out of desolation unspeakable, he had sent that message. And she had answered it—to find him gone.

The slow hot tears welled up and ran down her face. She was not even aware of them. Only at last she faced the desolation in its entirety, she drank the cup to its dregs. It was here that he had taken the downward road. It was here that he had buried his manhood. When she turned away at length, she felt as if she had been standing by his grave.

Burke waited for her and helped her to mount again in utter silence. Only as she lifted the bridle again he laid his hand for a moment on her knee. It was a dumb act of sympathy which she could not acknowledge lest she should break down utterly. But it sent a glow of comfort to her hurt and aching heart. He had given her a comrade's sympathy just when she needed it most.

CHAPTER II

THE VISITORS

It was after that ride to Guy's hut that Sylvia began at last to regard him as connected only with that which was past. It was as if a chapter in her life had closed when she turned away from that solitary hut in the wilderness. She said to herself that the man she had known and loved was dead, and she did not after that evening suffer her thoughts voluntarily to turn in his direction. Soberly she took up the burden of life. She gathered up the reins of government, and assumed the ordering of Burke Ranger's household. She did not again refer to Guy in his presence, though there were times when his step, his voice, above all, his whistle, stabbed her to poignant remembrance.

He also avoided the subject of Guy, treating her with a careless kindliness that set her wholly at ease with him. She learned more and more of the working of the farm, and her interest in the young creatures grew daily. She loved to accompany him on his rides of inspection in the early mornings showing herself so apt a pupil that he presently dubbed her his overseer, and even at last entrusted her occasionally with such errands as only a confidential overseer could execute.

It was when returning from one of these somewhat late one blazing morning that she first encountered their nearest British neighbours from a farm nearly twelve miles distant. It was a considerable shock to her to find them in possession of the *stoep* when she rode up, but the sight of the red-faced Englishman who strode out to meet her reassured her in a moment.

"How do you do, Mrs. Ranger? We've just come over to pay our respects," he announced in a big, hearty voice. "You'll hardly believe it, but we've only recently heard of Burke's marriage. It's been a nine days' wonder with us, but now I've seen you I cease to marvel at anything but Burke's amazing luck."

There was something so engagingly naïve in this compliment that Sylvia found it impossible to be formal. She smiled and slipped to the ground.

"You are Mr. Merston," she said. "How kind of you to come over! I am afraid I am alone at present, but Burke is sure to be in soon. I hope you have had some refreshment."

She gave her horse to a Kaffir boy, and went with her new friend up the steps of the *stoep*.

"My wife!" said Merston in his jolly voice.

Sylvia went forward with an eagerness that wilted in spite of her before she reached its object. Mrs. Merston did not rise to meet her. She sat prim and upright and waited for her greeting, and Sylvia knew in a moment before their hands touched each other that here was no kindred spirit.

"How do you do?" said Mrs. Merston formally.

She was a little woman, possibly ten years Sylvia's senior, with a face that had once been pink and white and now was the colour of pale brick all over. Her eyes were pale and seemed to carry a perpetual grievance. Her nose was straight and very thin, rather pinched at the nostrils. Her lips were thin and took a bitter downward curve. Her hair was quite colourless, almost like ashes; it had evidently once been light gold.

The hand she extended to Sylvia was so thin that she thought she could feel the bones rubbing together. Her skin was hot and very dry.

"I hope you like this horrible country," she said.

"Oh, come, Matilda!" her husband protested.

"That's not a very cheery greeting for a new-comer!"

She closed her thin lips without reply, and the downward curve became very unpleasantly apparent.

"I haven't found out all its horrors yet," said Sylvia lightly. "It's a very thirsty place, I think, anyway just now. Have you had anything?"

"We've only just got here," said Merston.

"Oh, I must see to it!" said Sylvia, and hastened within.

"Looks a jolly sort of girl," observed Merston to his wife. "Wonder how—and when—Burke managed to catch her. He hasn't been home for ten years and she can't be five-and-twenty."

"She probably did the catching," remarked his wife tersely. "But she will soon wish she hadn't."

Sylvia returned two minutes later bearing a tray of which Merston hastened to relieve her.

"We're wondering—my wife and I—how Burke had the good fortune to get married to you," he said. "You're new to this country, aren't you? And he hasn't been out of it as long as I have known him."

Sylvia looked up at him in momentary confusion. Then she laughed.

"We picked each other up at Ritzen," she said.

"Ritzen!" he echoed in amazement. "What on earth took you there?" Then hastily, "I say, I beg your pardon. You must forgive my impertinence. But you look so awfully like a duchess in your own right, I couldn't help being surprised."

"Well, have a drink!" said Sylvia lightly. "I'm not a duchess in my own right or anything else, except Burke's wife. We're running this farm together on the partner system. I'm junior partner of course. Burke tells me what to do, and I do it."

"You'll soon lose your complexion if you go out riding in this heat and dust," said Mrs. Merston.

"Oh, I hope not," Sylvia laughed again. "If I do, I daresay I shan't miss it much. It's rather fun to feel that sort of thing doesn't matter. Ah, here is Burke coming now!" She glanced up at the thudding of his horse's hoofs.

Merston went out again into the blinding sunlight to greet his host, and Sylvia turned to the thin, pinched woman beside her.

"I expect you would like to come inside and take off your hat and wash. It is hot, isn't it? Shall we go in and get respectable?"

She spoke with that winning friendliness of hers that few could resist. Mrs. Merston's lined face softened almost in spite of itself. She got up.

But she could not refrain from flinging another acid remark as she did so.

"I really think if Englishmen must live in South Africa, they ought to be content with Boer wives."

"Oh, should you like your husband to have married a Boer wife?" said Sylvia.

Mrs. Merston smiled grimly. "You are evidently still in the fool's paradise stage. Make the most of it! It won't last long. The men out here have other things to think about."

"I should hope so," said Sylvia energetically. "And the women, too, I should think. I should imagine that there is very little time for philandering out here."

Mrs. Merston uttered a bitter laugh as she followed her in. "There is very little time for anything, Mrs. Ranger. It is drudgery from morning till night."

"Oh, I haven't found that yet," said Sylvia.

She had led her visitor into the guest-room which she had occupied since her advent. It was not quite such a bare apartment as it had been on that first night. All her personal belongings were scattered about, and the severely masculine atmosphere had been completely driven forth.

"I'm afraid it isn't very tidy in here," she said.

11

"I generally see to things later. I don't care to turn the Kaffir girl loose among my things."

Mrs. Merston looked around her. "And where does your husband sleep?" she said.

"Across the passage. His room is about the same size as this. They are not very big, are they?"

"You are very lucky to have such a home," said Mrs. Merston. "Ours is nothing but a corrugated iron shed divided into two parts."

"Really?" Sylvia opened her eyes. "That doesn't sound very nice certainly. Haven't you got a verandah even—I beg its pardon, a *stoep?*"

"We have nothing at all that makes for comfort," declared Mrs. Merston, with bitter emphasis. "We live like pigs in a sty!"

"Good heavens!" said Sylvia. "I shouldn't like that."

"No, you wouldn't. It takes a little getting used to. But you'll go through the mill presently. All we farmers' wives do. You and Burke Ranger won't go on in this Garden of Eden style very long."

Sylvia laughed with a touch of uncertainty. "I suppose it's a mistake to expect too much of life anywhere," she said. "But it's difficult to be miserable when one is really busy, isn't it? Anyhow one can't be bored."

"Are you really happy here?" Mrs. Merston asked point-blank, in the tone of one presenting a challenge.

Sylvia paused for a moment, only a moment, and then she answered, "Yes."

"And you've been married how long? Six weeks?"

"About that," said Sylvia.

Mrs. Merston looked at her, and an almost cruel look came into her pale eyes. "Ah! You wait a little!" she said. "You're young now. You've got all your vitality still in your veins. Wait till this pitiless country begins to get hold of you! Wait till you begin to bear children, and all your strength is drained out of you, and you still have to keep on at the same grinding drudgery till you're ready to drop, and your husband comes in and laughs at you and tells you to buck up, when you haven't an ounce of energy left in you! See how you like the prison-house then! All your young freshness gone and nothing left—nothing left!"

She spoke with such force that Sylvia felt actually shocked. Yet still with that instinctive tact of hers, she sought to smooth the troubled waters. "Oh, have you children?" she said. "How many? Do tell me about them!"

"I have had six," said Mrs. Merston dully. "They are all dead."

She clenched her hands at Sylvia's quick exclamation of pity, but she gave no other sign of emotion.

"They all die in infancy," she said. "It's partly the climate, partly that I am overworked—worn out. He—" with infinite bitterness—"can't see it. Men don't—or won't. You'll find that presently. It's all in front of you. I don't envy you in the least, Mrs. Ranger. I daresay you think there is no one in the world like your husband. Young brides always do. But you'll find out presently. Men are all selfish where their own pleasures are concerned. And Burke Ranger is no exception to the rule. He has a villainous temper, too. Everyone knows that."

"Oh, don't tell me that!" said Sylvia gently. "He and I are partners, you know. Let me put a little *eau-de-cologne* in that water! It's so refreshing."

Mrs. Merston scarcely noticed the small service. She was too intent upon her work of destruction. "You don't know him—yet," she said. "But anyone you meet can tell you the same. Why, he had a young cousin here—such a nice boy—and he sent him straight to the bad with his harsh treatment,—*sjamboked* him and turned him out of the house for some slight offence. Yes, no wonder you look scandalized; but I assure you it's true. Guy Ranger was none too steady, I know. But that was absolutely the finishing touch. He was never the same again."

She paused. Sylvia was very white, but her eyes were quite resolute, unfailingly steadfast.

"Please don't tell me any more!" she said. "Whatever Burke did was—was from a good motive. I know that. I know him. And—I don't want to have any unkind feelings towards him."

"You prefer to remain blind?" said Mrs. Merston with her bitter smile.

"Yes—yes," Sylvia said.

"Then you are building your house on the sand," said Mrs. Merston, and turned from her with a shrug. "And great will be the fall thereof."

CHAPTER III

THE BARGAIN

THE visitors did not leave until the sun was well down in the west. To Sylvia it had been an inexplicably tiring day, and when they departed at length she breathed a wholly unconscious sigh of relief.

"Come for a ride!" said Burke.

She shook her head. "No, thank you. I think I will have a rest."

"All right. I'll smoke a pipe on the *stoep*," he said.

He had been riding round his land with Merston during the greater part of the afternoon, and it did not surprise her that he seemed to think that he also had earned a quiet evening. But curiously his decision provoked in her an urgent desire to ride alone. A pressing need for solitude was upon her. She yearned to get right away by herself.

She went to her room, however, and lay down for a while, trying to take the rest she needed; but when presently she heard the voice of Hans

Schafen, his Dutch foreman, talking on the verandah, she arose with a feeling of thankfulness, donned her sun-hat, and slipped out of the bungalow. It was hot for walking, but it was a relief to get away from the house. She knew it was quite possible that Burke would see her go, but she believed he would be too engrossed with business for some time to follow her. It was quite possible he would not wish to do so, but she had a feeling that this was not probable. He generally sought her out in his leisure hours.

Almost instinctively she turned her steps in the direction of the *kopje* which she had so often desired to climb. It rose steep from the *veldt* like some lonely tower in the wilderness. Curious-shaped rocks cropped out unexpectedly on its scarred sides and a few prickly pear bushes stood up here and there like weird guardians of the rugged stronghold. Sylvia had an odd feeling that they watched her with unfriendly attention as she approached. Though solitude girt her round, she did not feel herself to be really alone.

It took her some time to reach it, for the ground was rough and sandy under her feet, and it was farther away than it looked. She realized as she drew nearer that to climb to the round summit would be no easy task, but that fact did not daunt

her. She felt the need for strenuous exercise just
then.

The shadows were lengthening, and the full
glare of the sun no longer smote upon her. She
began to climb with some energy. But she soon
found that she had undertaken a greater task than
she had anticipated. The way was steep, and here
and there the boulders seemed to block further
progress completely. She pressed on with dimin-
ishing speed, taking a slanting upward course that
presently brought her into the sun again and in
view of the little cabin above the stony watercourse that had sheltered Guy for so long.

The sight of it seemed to take all the strength
out of her. She sat down on a rock to rest. All
day long she had been forcing the picture that
Mrs. Merston had painted for her into the background of her thoughts. All day long it had been
pressing forward in spite of her. It seemed to be
burning her brain, and now she could not ignore
it any longer. Sitting there exhausted in mind
and body, she had to face it in all its crudeness.
She had to meet and somehow to conquer the
sickening sensation of revolt that had come upon
her.

She sat there for a long time, till the sun sank
low in the sky and a wondrous purple glow spread

across the *veldt*. She knew that it was growing late, that Burke would be expecting her for the evening meal, but she could not summon the strength she needed to end her solitary vigil on the *kopje*. She had a feeling as of waiting for something. Though she was too tired to pray, yet it seemed to her that a message was on its way. She watched the glory in the west with an aching intensity that possessed her to the exclusion of aught beside. Somehow, even in the midst of her weariness and depression, she felt sure that help would come.

The glory began to wane, and a freshness blew across the *veldt*. Somewhere on the very top of the *kopje* a bird uttered a twittering note. She turned her face, listening for the answer, and found Burke seated on another boulder not six yards away.

So unexpected was the sight that she caught her breath in astonishment and a sharp instinctive sense of dismay. He was not looking at her, but gazing forth to the distant hills like an eagle from its eyrie. His eyes had the look of seeing many things that were wholly beyond her vision.

She sat in silence, a curious feeling of embarrassment upon her, as if she looked upon something which she was not meant to see and yet could not turn from. His brown face was so intent, almost terribly keen. The lines about the mouth were drawn with ruthless distinctness. It was the face of a hunter, and the iron resolution of it sent an odd quiver that was almost of foreboding through her heart.

And then suddenly he turned his head slightly, as if he felt her look upon him, and like a knife-thrust his eyes came down to hers. She felt the hot colour rush over her face as if she had been caught in some act of trespass. Her confusion consumed her, she could not have said wherefore. She looked swiftly away.

Quietly he left his rock and came to her.

She shrank at his coming. The pulse in her throat was throbbing as if it would choke her. She wanted to spring up and flee down the hill. But he was too near. She sat very still, her fingers gripping each other about her knees, saying no word.

He reached her and stood looking down at her. "I followed you," he said, "because I knew you would never get to the top alone."

She lifted her face, striving against her strange agitation. "I wasn't thinking of going any further," she said, struggling to speak indifferently. "It—is steeper than I thought."

"It always is," said Burke.

He sat down beside her, close to her. She made

a small, instinctive movement away from him,
but he did not seem to notice. He took off his
hat and laid it down.

"I'm sorry Mrs. Merston had to be inflicted on
you for so long," he said. "I'm afraid she is not
exactly cheery company."

"I didn't mind," said Sylvia.

He gave her a faintly whimsical look. "Not
utterly fed up with Africa and all her beastly
ways?" he questioned.

She shook her head. "I don't think I am so
easily swayed as all that."

"You would rather stay here with me than go
back home to England?" he said.

Her eyes went down to the lonely hut on the sand.
"Why do you ask me that?" she said, in a low voice.

"Because I want to know," said Burke.

Sylvia was silent.

He went on after a moment. "I've a sort of
notion that Mrs. Merston is not a person to spread
contentment around her under any circumstances.
If she lived in a palace at the top of the world she
wouldn't be any happier."

Sylvia smiled faintly at the allusion. "I don't
think she has very much to make her happy," she
said. "It's a little hard to judge her under present
conditions."

"She's got one of the best for a husband anyway," he maintained.

"Do you think that's everything?" said Sylvia.

"No, I don't," said Burke unexpectedly. "I think he spoils her, which is bad for any woman. It turns her head in the beginning and sours her afterwards."

Sylvia turned at that and regarded him, a faint light of mockery in her eyes. "What a lot you know about women!" she remarked.

He laughed in a way she did not understand. "If I had a wife," he said, "I'd make her happy, but not on those lines."

"I thought you had one," said Sylvia.

He met her eyes with a sudden mastery which made her flinch in spite of herself. "No," he said, "I've only a make-believe at present. Not very satisfying of course; but better than nothing. There is always the hope that she may some day turn into the real thing to comfort me."

His words went into silence. Sylvia's head was bent.

After a moment he leaned a little towards her, and spoke almost in a whisper. "I feel as if I have caught a very rare, shy bird," he said. "I'm trying to teach it to trust me, but it takes a mighty lot of time and patience. Do you think I shall ever succeed, Sylvia? Do you think it will ever come and nestle against my heart?"

Again his words went into silence. The girl's eyes were fixed upon the stretch of sandy *veldt* below her and that which it held.

Silently the man watched her, his keen eyes very steady, very determined.

She lifted her own at last, and met them with brave directness. "You know, partner," she said, "it isn't very fair of you to ask me such a thing as that. You can't have—everything."

"All right," said Burke, and felt in his pocket for his pipe. "Consider it unsaid!"

His abrupt acceptance of her remonstrance was curiously disconcerting. The mastery of his look had led her to expect something different. She watched him dumbly as he filled his pipe with quiet precision.

Finally, as he looked at her again, she spoke. "I don't want to seem over-critical—ungrateful, but—" her breath came quickly—"though you have been so awfully good to me, I can't help feeling—that you might have done more for Guy, if—if you had been kinder when he went wrong. And —" her eyes filled with sudden tears—"that thought spoils—just everything."

"I see," said Burke, and though his lips were

grim his voice was wholly free from harshness. "Mrs. Merston told you all about it, did she?"

Sylvia's colour rose again. She turned slightly from him. "She didn't say much," she said.

There was a pause. Then unexpectedly Burke's hand closed over her two clasped ones. "So I've got to be punished, have I?" he said.

She shook her head, shrinking a little though she suffered his touch. "No. Only—I can't forget it,—that's all."

"Or forgive?" said Burke.

She swallowed her tears with an effort. "No, not that. I'm not vindictive. But—oh, Burke—" she turned to him impulsively,—"I wish—I wish—we could find Guy!"

He stiffened almost as if at a blow. "Why?" he demanded sternly.

For a moment his look awed her, but only for a moment; the longing in her heart was so great as to overwhelm all misgiving. She grasped his arm tightly between her hands.

"If we could only find him—and save him—save him somehow from the horrible pit he seems to have fallen into! We could do it between us— I feel sure we could do it—if only—if only—we could find him!"

Breathlessly her words rushed out. It seemed

as if she had stumbled almost inadvertently upon the solution of the problem that had so tormented her. She marvelled now that she had ever been able to endure inaction with regard to Guy. She was amazed at herself for having been so easily content. It was almost as if in that moment she heard Guy's voice very far away, calling to her for help.

And then, swift as a lightning-flash, striking dismay to her soul, came the consciousness of Burke gazing straight at her with that in his eyes which she could not—dare not—meet.

She gripped his arm a little tighter. She was quivering from head to foot. "We could do it between us," she breathed again. "Wouldn't it be worth it? Oh, wouldn't it be worth it?"

But Burke spoke no word. He sat rigid, looking at her.

A feeling of coldness ran through her—such a feeling as she had experienced on her wedding-day under the skeleton-tree, the chill that comes from the heart of a storm. Slowly she relaxed her hold upon him. Her tears were gone, but she felt choked, unlike herself, curiously impotent.

"Shall we go back?" she said.

She made as if she would rise, but he stayed her with a gesture, and her weakness held her passive.

"So you have forgiven him!" he said.

His tone was curt. He almost flung the words.

She braced herself, instinctively aware of coming strain. But she answered him gently. "You can't be angry with a person when you are desperately sorry for him."

"I see. And you hold me in a great measure responsible for his fall? I am to make good, am I?"

He did not raise his voice, but there was something in it that made her quail. She looked up at him in swift distress.

"No, no! Of course not—of course not! Partner, please don't glare at me like that! What have I done?"

He dropped his eyes abruptly from her startled face, and there followed a silence so intense that she thought he did not even breathe.

Then, in a very low voice: "You've raised Cain," he said.

She shivered. There was something terrible in the atmosphere. Dumbly she waited, feeling that protest would but make matters worse.

He turned himself from her at length, and sat with his chin on his hands, staring out to the fading sunset.

When he spoke finally, the hard note had gone

out of his voice. "Do you think it's going to make life any easier to bring that young scoundrel back?"

"I wasn't thinking of that," she said. "It was only—" she hesitated.

"Only?" said Burke, without turning.

With difficulty she answered him. "Only that probably you and I are the only people in the world who could do anything to help him. And so—somehow it seems our job."

Burke digested this in silence. Then: "And what are you going to do with him when you've got him?" he enquired.

Again she hesitated, but only momentarily. "I shall want you to help me, partner," she said appealingly.

He made a slight movement that passed unexplained. "You may find me—rather in the way—before you've done," he said.

"Then you won't help me?" she said, swift disappointment in her voice.

He turned round to her. His face was grim, but it held no anger. "You've asked a pretty hard thing of me," he said. "But—yes, I'll help you."

"You will?" She held out her hand to him. "Oh, partner, thank you—awfully!"

He gripped her hand hard. "On one condition," he said.

12

"Oh, what?"   She started a little and her face whitened.

He squeezed her fingers with merciless force. "Just that you will play a straight game with me," he said briefly.

The colour came back to her face with a rush. "That!" she said.   "But of course—of course! I always play a straight game."

"Then it's a bargain?" he said.

Her clear eyes met his.   "Yes, a bargain.   But how shall we ever find him?"

He was silent for a moment, and she felt as if those steel-grey eyes of his were probing for her soul.   "That," he said slowly, "will not be a very difficult business."

"You know where he is?" she questioned eagerly.

"Yes.   Merston told me to-day."

"Oh, Burke!"   The eager kindling of her look made her radiant.   "Where is he?   What is he doing?"

He still looked at her keenly, but all emotion had gone from his face.   "He is tending a bar in a miners' saloon at Brennerstadt."

"Ah!"   She stood up quickly to hide the sudden pain his words had given.   "But we can soon get him out.   You—you will get him out, partner?"

He got to his feet also.   The sun had passed, and

only a violet glow remained. He seemed to be watching it as he answered her.

"I will do my best."

"You are good," she said very earnestly. "I wonder if you have the least idea how grateful I feel."

"I can guess," he said in a tone of constraint.

She was standing slightly above him. She placed her hand shyly on his shoulder. "And you won't hate it so very badly?" she urged softly. "It is in a good cause, isn't it?"

"I hope so," he said.

He seemed unaware of her hand upon him. She pressed a little. "Burke!"

"Yes?" He still stood without looking at her.

She spoke nervously. "I—I shan't forget— ever—that I am married. You—you needn't be afraid of—of anything like that."

He turned with an odd gesture. "I thought you were going to forget it—that you had for- gotten it—for good."

His voice had a strained, repressed sound. He spoke almost as if he were in pain.

She tried to smile though her heart was beating fast and hard. "Well, I haven't. And—I never shall now. So that's all right, isn't it? Say it's all right!"

There was more of pleading in her voice than she knew. A great tremor went through Burke. He clenched his hands to subdue it.

"Yes; all right, little pal, all right," he said.

His voice sounded strangled; it pierced her oddly. With a sudden impetuous gesture she slid her arm about his neck, and for one lightning moment her lips touched his cheek. The next instant she had sprung free and was leaping downwards from rock to rock like a startled gazelle.

At the foot of the *kopje* only did she stop and wait. He was close behind her, moving with lithe, elastic strides where she had bounded.

She turned round to him boyishly. "We'll climb to the top one of these days, partner; but I'm not in training yet. Besides,—we're late for supper."

"I can wait," said Burke.

She linked her little finger in his, swinging it carelessly. There was absolute confidence in her action; only her eyes avoided his.

"You're jolly decent to me," she said. "I often wonder why."

"You'll know one day," said Burke very quietly.

CHAPTER IV

THE CAPTURE

A DUST-STORM had been blowing practically all day, and the mining crowds of Brennerstadt were thirsty to a man. They congregated at every bar with the red sand thick upon them, and cursed the country and the climate with much heartiness and variety.

Burke Ranger was one of the thirstiest when he reached the town after his ride through the desert —a ride upon which he had flatly refused to allow Sylvia to accompany him. He went straight to the hotel where he had stayed for his marriage, and secured a room. Then he went down to the dining-room, where he was instantly greeted by an old friend, Kelly, the Irish manager of a diamond mine in the neighbourhood.

Kelly was the friend of everyone. He knew everyone's affairs and gossiped openly with a childlike frankness that few could resent. Everyone declared he could never keep a secret, yet nearly everyone confided in him. His goodness

of heart was known to all, and he was regarded
as a general arbitrator among the sometimes rest-
less population of Brennerstadt.

His delight at seeing Burke was obvious; he
hailed him with acclamations. "I've been meaning to ride over your way for ages," he declared,
his rubicund face shining with geniality as he
wrung his friend's hand hard. "I was up-country
when you came along last with your bride. Dark
horse that you are, Burke! I should as soon
have thought of getting married myself, as of seeing you in double harness."

Burke laughed his careless laugh. "You'll come
to it yet. No fun in growing old alone in this
country."

"And what's the lady like?" pursued Kelly,
keen for news as an Irish terrier after a rat. "As
fair as Eve and twice as charming?"

"Something that style," agreed Burke. "What
are you drinking, old chap? Any ice to be had?"

He conferred with the waiter, but Kelly's curiosity was far from being satisfied. He pounced
back upon the subject the moment Burke's attention was free.

"And is she new to this part of the world then?
She came out to be married, I take it? And what
does she think of it at all?"

"You'll have to come over and see for yourself," said Burke.

"So I will, old feller. I'll come on the first opportunity. I'd love to see the woman who can capture you. Done any shooting lately, or is wedded bliss still too sweet to leave?"

"I've had a few other things as well to think about," said Burke drily.

"And this is your first absence? What will the missis do without you?"

"She'll manage all right. She's very capable. She is helping me with the farm. The life seems to suit her all right, only I shall have to see she doesn't work too hard."

"That you will, my son. This climate's hard on women. Look at poor Bill Merston's wife! When she came out, she was as pretty and as sweet as a little wild rose. And now—well, it gives you the heartache to look at her."

"Does it?" said Burke grimly. "She doesn't affect me that way. If I were in Merston's place, —well, she wouldn't look like that for long."

"Wouldn't she though?" Kelly looked at him with interest. "You always were a goer, old man. And what would your treatment consist of?"

"Discipline," said Burke briefly. "No woman

is happy if she despises her husband. If I were in Merston's place, I would see to it that she did not despise me. That's the secret of her trouble. It's poison to a woman to look down on her husband."

"Egad!" laughed Kelly. "But you've studied the subject! Well, here's to the fair lady of your choice! May she fulfil all expectations and be a comfort to you all the days of your life!"

"Thanks!" said Burke. "Now let's hear a bit about yourself! How's the diamond industry?"

"Oh, there's nothing the matter with it just now. We've turned over some fine stones in the last few days. Plenty of rubbish, too, of course. You don't want a first-class speculation, I presume? If you've got a monkey to spare, I can put you on to something rather great."

"Thanks, I haven't," said Burke. "I never have monkeys to spare. But what's the gamble?"

"Oh, it's just a lottery of Wilbraham's. He has a notion for raffling his biggest diamond. The draw won't take place for a few weeks yet; and then only monkeys need apply. It's a valuable stone. I can testify to that. It would be worth a good deal more if it weren't for a flaw that will have to be taken out in the cutting and will reduce it a lot. But even so, it's worth some thousands, worth risking a monkey for, Burke. Think what a splendid present it would be for your wife!"

Burke laughed and shook his head. "She isn't that sort if I know her."

"Bet you you don't know her then," said Kelly, with a grin. "It's a good sporting chance anyway. I don't fancy there will be many candidates, for the stone has an evil name."

Burke looked slightly scornful. "Well, I'm not putting any monkeys into Wilbraham's pocket, so that won't trouble me. Have you seen anything of Guy Ranger lately?"

The question was casually uttered, but it sent a sharp gleam of interest into Kelly's eyes. "Oh, it's him you've come for, is it?" he said. "Well, let me tell you this for your information! He's had enough of Blue Hill Farm for the present."

Burke said nothing, but his grey eyes had a more steely look than usual as he digested the news.

Kelly looked at him curiously. "The boy's a wreck," he said. "Simply gone to pieces; nerves like fiddle-strings. He drinks like hell, but it's my belief he'd die in torment if he didn't."

Still Burke said nothing, and Kelly's curiosity grew.

"You know what he's doing, don't you?" he said. "He's doing a Kaffir's job for Kaffir's pay.

It's about the vilest hole this side of perdition, my son. And I'm thinking you won't find it specially easy to dig him out."

Burke's eyes came suddenly straight to the face of the Irishman. He regarded him for a moment or two with a faintly humorous expression; then: "That's just where you can lend me a hand, Donovan," he said. "I'm going to ask you to do that part."

"The deuce you are!" said Kelly. "You're not going to ask much then, my son. Moreover, it's well on the likely side that he'll refuse to budge. Better leave him alone till he's tired of it."

"He's dead sick of it already," said Burke with conviction. "You go to him and tell him you've a decent berth waiting for him. He'll come along fast enough then."

"I doubt it," said Kelly. "I doubt it very much. He's in just the bitter mood to prefer to wallow. He's right under, Burke, and he isn't making any fight. He'll go on now till he's dead."

"He won't!" said Burke shortly. "Where exactly is he? Tell me that!"

"He's barkeeping for that brute Hoffstein, and taking out all his wages in drink. I saw him three days ago. I assure you he's past help. I believe he'd shoot himself if you took any trouble over him. He's in a pretty desperate mood."

"Not he!" said Burke. "I'm going to have him out anyway."

Again Kelly looked at him speculatively. "Well, what's the notion?" he asked after a moment, frankly curious. "You've never worried after him before."

Burke's eyes were grim. "You may be sure of one thing, Donovan," he said, "I'm not out for pleasure this journey."

"I've noted that," observed Kelly.

"I don't want you to help me if you have anything better to do," pursued Burke. "I shall get what I've come for in any case."

"Oh, don't you worry yourself! I'm on," responded Kelly, with his winning, Irish smile. "When do you want to catch your hare? To-night?"

"Yes; to-night," said Burke soberly. "I'll come down with you to Hoffstein's, and if you can get him out, I'll do the rest."

"Hurrah!" crowed Kelly softly, lifting his glass. "Here's luck to the venture!"

But though Burke drank with him, his face did not relax.

A little later they left the hotel together. A

strong wind was still blowing, sprinkling the dust of the desert everywhere. They pushed their way against it, striding with heads down through the swirling darkness of the night.

Hoffstein's bar was in a low quarter of the town and close to the mine-workings. A place of hideous desolation at all times, the whirling sand-storm made of it almost an inferno. They scarcely spoke as they went along, grimly enduring the sand-fiend that stung and blinded but could not bar their progress.

As they came within sight of Hoffstein's tavern, they encountered groups of men coming away, but no one was disposed to loiter on that night of turmoil; no one accosted them as they approached. The place was built of corrugated iron, and they heard the sand whipping against it as they drew near. Kelly paused within a few yards of the entrance. The door was open and the lights of the bar flared forth into the darkness.

"You stop here!" bawled Kelly. "I'll go in and investigate."

There was an iron fence close to them, affording some degree of shelter from the blast. Burke stood back against it, dumbly patient. The other man went on, and in a few seconds his short square figure passed through the lighted doorway.

There followed an interval of waiting that seemed interminable—an interval during which Burke moved not at all, but stood like a statue against the wall, his hat well down over his eyes, his hands clenched at his sides. The voices of men drifted to and fro through the howling night, but none came very near him.

It must have been nearly half-an-hour later that there arose a sudden fierce uproar in the bar, and the silent watcher straightened himself up sharply. The turmoil grew to a babel of voices, and in a few moments two figures, struggling furiously, appeared at the open door. They blundered out, locked together like fighting beasts, and behind them the door crashed to, leaving them in darkness.

Burke moved forward. "Kelly, is that you?"

Kelly's voice, uplifted in lurid anathema, answered him, and in a couple of seconds Kelly himself lurched into him, nearly hurling him backwards. "And is it yourself?" cried the Irishman. "Then help me to hold the damned young scoundrel, for he's fighting like the devils in hell! Here he is! Get hold of him!"

Burke took a silent hard grip upon the figure suddenly thrust at him, and almost immediately the fighting ceased.

"Let me go!" a hoarse voice said.

"Hold him tight!" said Kelly. "I'm going to take a rest. Guy, you young devil, what do you want to murder me for? I've never done you a harm in my life."

The man in Burke's grasp said nothing whatever. He was breathing heavily, but his resistance was over. He stood absolutely passive in the other man's hold.

Kelly gave himself an indignant shake and continued his tirade. "I call all the saints in heaven to witness that as sure as my name is Donovan Kelly so sure is it that I'll be damned to the last most nether millstone before ever I'll undertake to dig a man out of Hoffstein's marble halls again. You'd better watch him, Burke. His skin is about as full as it'll hold."

"We'll get back," said Burke briefly.

He was holding his captive locked in a scientific grip, but there was no violence about him. Only, as he turned, the other turned also, as if compelled. Kelly followed, cursing himself back to amiability.

Back through the raging wind they went, as though pursued by furies. They reached and entered the hotel just as the Kaffir porter was closing for the night. He stared with bulging eyes at Burke and his companion, but Burke walked straight through, looking neither to right nor left.

Only at the foot of the stairs, he paused an instant, glancing back.

"I'll see you in the morning, Donovan," he said. "Thanks for all you've done."

To which Kelly replied, fingering a bump on his forehead with a rueful grin, "All's well that ends well, my son, and sure it's a pleasure to serve you. I flatter myself, moreover, that you wouldn't have done the trick on your own. Hoffstein will stand more from me than from any other living man."

The hint of a smile touched Burke's set lips. "Show me the man that wouldn't!" he said; and turning, marched his unresisting prisoner up the stairs.

CHAPTER V

THE GOOD CAUSE

"Why can't you leave me alone? What do you want with me?"

Half-sullenly, half-aggressively, Guy Ranger flung the questions, standing with lowering brow before his captor. His head was down and his eyes raised with a peculiar, brutish expression. He had the appearance of a wild animal momentarily cowed, but preparing for furious battle. The smouldering of his look was terrible.

Burke Ranger met it with steely self-restraint. "I'll tell you presently," he said.

"You'll tell me now!" Fiercely the younger man made rejoinder. His power of resistance was growing, swiftly swallowing all sense of expediency. "If I choose to wallow in the mire, what the devil is it to you? You didn't send that accursed fool Kelly round for your own pleasure, I'll take my oath. What is it you want me for? Tell me straight!"

His voice rose on the words. His hands were

clenched; yet still he wore that half-frightened look as of an animal that will spring when goaded, not before. His hair hung black and unkempt about his burning eyes. His face was drawn and deadly pale.

Burke stood like a rock, confronting him. He blocked the way to the door. "I'll tell you all you want to know in the morning," he said. "You have a wash now and turn in!"

The wild eyes took a fleeting glance round the room, returning instantly, as if fascinated, to Burke's face.

"Why the devil should I? I've got a—sty of my own to go to."

"Yes, I know," said Burke. Yet he stood his ground, grimly emotionless.

"Then let me go to it!" Guy Ranger straightened himself, breathing heavily. "Get out!" he said. "Or—by heaven—I'll throw you!"

"You can't," said Burke. "So don't be a fool! You know—none better—that that sort of thing doesn't answer with me."

"But what do you want?" The reiterated question had a desperate ring as if, despite its urgency, the speaker dreaded the reply. "You've never bothered to dig me out before. What's the notion? I'm nothing to you. You loathe the sight of me."

Burke made a slight gesture as of repudiation, but he expressed no denial in words. "As to that," he said, "you draw your own conclusions. I can't discuss anything with you now. The point is, you are out of that hell for the present, and I'm going to keep you out."

"You!" There was a note of bitter humour in the word. Guy Ranger threw back his head as he uttered it, and by the action the likeness between them was instantly proclaimed. "That's good!" he scoffed. "You—the man who first showed me the gates of hell—to take upon yourself to pose as deliverer! And for whose benefit, if one might ask? Your own—or mine?"

His ashen face with the light upon it was still boyish despite the stamp of torment that it bore. Through all the furnace of his degradation his youth yet clung to him like an impalpable veil that no suffering could rend or destroy.

Burke suddenly abandoned his attitude of gaoler and took him by the shoulder. "Don't be a fool!" he said again, but he said it gently. "I mean what I say. It's a way I've got. This isn't the time for explanations, but I'm out to help you. Even you will admit that you're pretty badly in need of help."

"Oh, damn that!" Recklessly Guy made an-

swer, chafing visibly under the restraining hold,
yet not actually flinging it off. "I know what I'm
doing all right. I shall pull up again presently—
before the final plunge. I'm not going to attempt
it before I'm ready. I've found it doesn't answer."

"You've got to this time," Burke said.

His eyes, grey and indomitable, looked straight
into Guy's, and they held him in spite of himself.
Guy quivered and stood still.

"You've got to," he reiterated. "Don't tell
me you're enjoying yourself barkeeping at Hoffstein's! I've known you too long to swallow it.
It just won't go down."

"It's preferable to doing the white nigger on
your blasted farm!" flashed back Guy. "Starvation's better than that!"

"Thank you," said Burke. He did not flinch
at the straight hit, but his mouth hardened. "I
see your point of view of course. Perhaps it's beside the mark to remind you that you might have
been a partner if you'd only played a decent game.
I wanted a partner badly enough."

An odd spasm crossed Guy's face. "Yes. You
didn't let me into that secret, did you, till I'd been
weighed in the balances and found wanting? You
were too damned cautious to commit yourself.
And you've congratulated yourself on your mar-

vellous discretion ever since, I'll lay a wager. You hide-bound, self-righteous prigs always do. Nothing would ever make you see that it's just your beastly discretion that does the mischief,—your infernal, complacent virtue that breeds the vice you so deplore!" He broke into a harsh laugh that ended in a sharp catch of the breath that bent him suddenly double.

Burke's hand went swiftly from his shoulder to his elbow. He led him to a chair. "Sit down!" he said. "You've got beyond yourself. I'm going to get you a drink, and then you'll go to bed."

Guy sat crumpled down in the chair like an empty sack. His head was on his clenched hands. He swayed as if in pain.

Burke stood looking down at him for a moment or two. Then he turned and went away, leaving the door ajar behind him.

When he came back, Guy was on his feet again, prowling uneasily up and down, but he had not crossed the threshold. He gave him that furtive, hunted look again as he entered.

"What dope is that? Not the genuine article I'll wager my soul!"

"It is the genuine article," Burke said. "Drink it, and go to bed!"

But Guy stood before him with his hands at his sides. The smouldering fire in his eyes was leaping higher and higher. "What's the game?" he said. "Is it a damned ruse to get me into your power?"

Burke set down the glass he carrried, and turned full upon him. There was that about him that compelled the younger man to meet his look. They stood face to face.

"You are in my power," he said with stern insistence. "I've borne with you because I didn't want to use force. But—I can use force. Don't forget that!"

Guy made a sharp movement—the movement of the trapped creature. Beneath Burke's unsparing regard his eyes fell. In a moment he turned aside, and muttering below his breath he took up the glass on the table. For a second or two he stood staring at it, then lifted it as if to drink, but in an instant changed his purpose and with a snarling laugh swung back and flung glass and contents straight at Burke's grim face.

What followed was of so swift and so deadly a nature as to possess something of the quality of a whirlwind. Almost before the glass lay in shivered fragments on the floor, Guy was on his knees and being forced backwards till his head and shoulders

touched the boards. And above him, terrible
with awful intention, was Burke's face, gashed
open across the chin and dripping blood upon his
own.

The fight went out of Guy then like an extinguished flame. With gasping incoherence he
begged for mercy.

"You're hurting me infernally! Man, let me
up! I've been—I've been—a damn' fool! Didn't
know—didn't realize! Burke—for heaven's sake
—don't torture me!"

"Be still!" Burke said. "Or I'll murder you!"

His voice was low and furious, his hold without
mercy. Yet, after a few seconds he mastered his
own violence, realizing that all resistance in the
man under him was broken. In a silence that was
more appalling than speech he got to his feet,
releasing him.

Guy rolled over sideways and lay with his face
on his arms, gasping painfully. After a pause,
Burke turned from him and went to the washing-
stand.

The blood continued to flow from the wound
while he bathed it. The cut was deep. He
managed, however, to staunch it somewhat at
length, and then very steadily he turned back.

"Get up!" he said.

Guy made a convulsive movement in response, but he only half-raised himself, sinking back immediately with a hard-drawn groan.

Burke bent over him. "Get up!" he said again. "I'll help you."

He took him under the arms and hoisted him slowly up. Guy blundered to his feet with shuddering effort.

"Now—fire me out!" he said.

But Burke only guided him to the bed. "Sit down!" he said.

Numbly he obeyed. He seemed incapable of doing otherwise. But when, still with that unwavering steadiness of purpose, Burke stooped and began to unfasten the straps of his gaiters, he suddenly cried out as if he had been struck unawares in a vital place.

"No—no—no! I'm damned—I'm damned if you shall! Burke—stop, do you hear? Burke!"

"Be quiet!" Burke said.

But Guy flung himself forward, preventing him. They looked into one another's eyes for a tense interval, then, as the blood began to trickle down his chin again, Burke released himself.

In the same moment, Guy covered his face and burst into agonized sobbing most terrible to hear.

Burke stood up again. Somehow all the hardness had gone out of him though the resolution remained. He put a hand on Guy's shoulder, and gently shook him.

"Don't do it, boy! Don't do it! Pull yourself together for heaven's sake! Drink—do anything—but this! You'll want to shoot yourself afterwards."

But Guy was utterly broken, his self-control beyond recovery. The only response he made was to feel for and blindly grip the hand that held him.

So for a space they remained, while the anguish possessed him and slowly passed. Then, with the quiescence of complete exhaustion, he suffered Burke's ministrations in utter silence.

Half-an hour later he lay in a dead sleep, motionless as a stone image, while the man who dragged him from his hell rested upon two chairs and grimly reviewed the problem which he had created for himself. There was no denying the fact that young Guy had been a thorn in his side almost ever since his arrival in the country. The pity of it was that he possessed such qualities as should have lifted him far above the crowd. He had courage, he had resource. Upon occasion he was even brilliant. But ever the fatal handicap existed that had pulled him down. He lacked moral strength, the power to resist temptation. As long as he lived, this infirmity of character would dog his steps, would ruin his every enterprise. And Burke, whose stubborn force made him instinctively impatient of such weakness, lay and contemplated the future with bitter foreboding.

There had been a time when he had thought to rectify the evil, to save Guy from himself, to implant in him something of that moral fibre which he so grievously lacked. But he had been forced long since to recognize his own limitations in this respect. Guy was fundamentally wanting in that strength which was so essentially a part of his own character, and he had been compelled at last to admit that no outside influence could supply the want. He had come very reluctantly to realize that no faith could be reposed in him, and when that conviction had taken final hold upon him, Burke had relinquished the struggle in disgust.

Yet, curiously, behind all his disappointment, even contempt, there yet lurked in his soul an odd liking for the young man. Guy was most strangely likable, however deep he sank. Unstable, unreliable, wholly outside the pale as he was, yet there ever hung about him a nameless, indescribable fascination which redeemed him from utter degradation, a charm which very curiously kept him from being classed with the swine. There was a natural gameness about him that men found good. Even at his worst, he was never revolting.

He seemed to Burke a mass of irresponsible inconsistency. He was full of splendid possibilities that invariably withered ere they approached fruition. He had come to regard him as a born failure, and though for Sylvia's sake he had made this final effort, he had small faith in its success. Only she was so hard to resist, that frank-eyed, earnest young partner of his. She was so unutterably dear in all her ways. How could he hear the tremor of her pleading voice and refuse her?

The memory of her came over him like a warm soft wave. He felt again the quick pressure of her arm about his neck, the fleeting sweetness of her kiss. How had he kept himself from catching her to his heart in that moment, and holding her there while he drank his fill of the cup she had so shyly proffered? How had he ever suffered her to flit from him down the rough *kopje* and turn at the bottom with the old intangible shield uplifted between them?

The blood raced in his veins. He clenched his hands in impotent self-contempt. And yet at the back of his man's soul he knew that by that very forbearance his every natural impulse condemned, he had strengthened his position, he had laid the foundation-stone of a fabric that would endure against storm and tempest. The house that he would build would be an abiding-place—no swiftly raised tent upon the sand. It would take time to build it, infinite care, possibly untold sacrifice. But when built, it would be absolutely solid, proof for all time against every wind that blew. For every stone would be laid with care and made fast with the cement that is indestructible. And it would be founded upon a rock.

So, as at last he drifted into sleep, Guy lying in a deathlike immobility by his side, there came to him the conviction that what he had done had been well done, done in a good cause, and acceptable to the Master Builder at Whose Behest he was vaguely conscious that all great things are achieved.

CHAPTER VI

THE RETURN

WHEN the morning broke upon Blue Hill Farm the sand-storm had blown itself out. With brazen splendour the sun arose to burn the parched earth anew, but Sylvia was before it. With the help of Fair Rosamond and Joe, the boy, she was preparing a small wooden hut close by for the reception of a guest. He should not go back to that wretched cabin on the sand if she could prevent it. He should be treated with honour. He should be made to feel that to her—and to Burke—his welfare was a matter of importance.

She longed to know how Burke had fared upon his quest. She yearned, even while she dreaded, to see the face which once had been all the world to her. That he had ceased to fill her world was a fact that she frankly admitted to herself just as she realized that she felt no bitterness towards this man who had so miserably failed her. Her whole heart now was set upon drawing him back from the evil paths down which he had strayed. When that was done, when Guy was saved from the awful destruction that menaced him, then there might come time for other thoughts, other interests. Since Burke had acceded to her urgent request so obviously against his will, her feelings had changed towards him. A warmth of gratitude had filled her. It had been so fine of him to yield to her like that.

But somehow she could not suffer her thoughts to dwell upon Burke just then. Always something held her back, restraining her, filling her with a strange throbbing agitation that she herself must check, lest it should overwhelm her. Instinctively, almost with a sense of self-preservation, she turned her mind away from him. And she was too busy— much too busy—to sit and dream.

When the noon-day heat waxed fierce, she had to rest, though it required her utmost strength of will to keep herself quiet, lying listening with strain-ing ears to the endless whirring of countless insects in the silence of the *veldt*.

It was with unspeakable relief that she arose from this enforced inactivity and, as evening drew on, resumed her work. She was determined that Guy should be comfortable when he came. She knew that it was more than possible that he would not come that day, but she could not leave any-thing unfinished. It was so important that he

should realize his welcome from the very first
moment of arrival.

All was finished at last even to her satisfaction.
She stood alone in the rough hut that she had
turned into as dainty a guest-chamber as her
woman's ingenuity could devise, and breathed a
sigh of contentment, feeling that she had not
worked in vain. Surely he would feel at home
here! Surely, even though through his weakness
they had had to readjust both their lives, by love
and patience a place of healing might be found. It
was impossible to analyze her feelings towards
him, but she was full of hope. Again she fell to
wondering how Burke had fared.

At sunset she went out and saddled the horse
he had given her as a wedding-present, Diamond,
a powerful animal, black save for a white mark on
his head from which he derived his name. She
and Diamond were close friends, and in his company her acute restlessness began to subside. She
rode him out to the *kopje*, but she did not go
round to view the lonely cabin above the stony
watercourse. She did not want to think of past
troubles, only to cherish the hope for the future
that was springing in her heart.

She was physically tired, but Diamond seemed
to understand, and gave her no trouble. For

awhile they wandered in the sunset light, she with her face to the sky and the wonderful mauve streamers of cloud that spread towards her from the west. Then, as the light faded, she rode across the open *veldt* to the rough road by which they must come.

It wound away into the gathering dusk where no lights gleamed, and a strong sense of desolation came to her, as it were, out of the desert and gripped her soul. For the first time she looked forward with foreboding.

None came along the lonely track. She heard no sound of hoofs. She tried to whistle a tune to keep herself cheery, but very soon it failed. The silent immensity of the *veldt* enveloped her. She had a forlorn feeling of being the only living being in all that vastness, except for a small uneasy spirit out of the great solitudes that wandered to and fro and sometimes fanned her with an icy breath that made her start and shiver.

She turned her horse's head at last. "Come, Diamond, we'll go home."

The word slipped from her unawares, but the moment she had uttered it she remembered, and a warm flush mounted in her cheeks. Was it really home to her—that abode in the wilderness to which Burke Ranger had brought her? Had she come already to regard it as she had once regarded that dear home of her childhood from which she had been so cruelly ousted?

The thought of the old home went through her with a momentary pang. Did her father ever think of her now, she wondered? Was he happy himself? She had written to him after her marriage to Burke, telling him all the circumstances thereof. It had been a difficult letter to write. She had not dwelt overmuch upon Guy's part because she could not bring herself to do so. But she had tried to make the position intelligible to him, and she hoped she had succeeded.

But no answer had come to her. Since leaving England, she had received letters from one or two friends, but not one from her old home. It was as if she had entered another world. Already she had grown so accustomed to it that she felt as if she had known it for years. And she had no desire to return. The thought of the summer gaieties she was foregoing inspired her with no regret. Isolated though she was, she was not unhappy. She had only just begun to realize it, and not yet could she ask herself wherefore.

A distinct chill began to creep round her with the approach of night. She lifted the bridle, and Diamond broke into a trot. Back to Blue Hill

Farm they went, leaving the silence and the loneliness behind them as they drew near. Mary Ann was scolding the girl from the open door of the kitchen. Her shrill vituperations banished all retrospection from Sylvia's mind. She found herself laughing as she slipped to the ground and handed the horse over to Joe.

Then she went within, calling to the girl to light the lamps. There was still mending to be done in Burke's wardrobe. She possessed herself of some socks, and went to their sitting-room. Her former restlessness was returning, but she resolutely put it from her, and for more than an hour she worked steadily at her task. Then, the socks finished, she took up a book on cattle-raising and tried to absorb herself in its pages.

She soon realized, however, that this was quite hopeless, and, at last, in desperation she flung on a cloak and went outside. The night was still, the sky a wonderland of stars. She paced to and fro with her face uplifted to the splendour for a long, long time. And still there came no sound of hoofs along the lonely track.

Gradually she awoke to the fact that she was getting very tired. She began to tell herself that she had been too hopeful. They would not come that night.

Her knees were getting shaky, and she went indoors. A cold supper had been spread. She sat down and partook of food, scarcely realizing what she ate. Then, reviving, she rallied herself on her foolishness. Of course they would not come that night. She had expected too much, had worn herself out to no purpose. She summoned her common sense to combat her disappointment, and commanded herself sternly to go to bed before exhaustion overtook her. She had behaved like a positive idiot. It was high time she pulled herself together.

It was certainly growing late. Mary Ann and her satellites had already retired to their own quarters some little distance from the bungalow. She was quite alone in the eerie silence. Obviously, bed was the only place if she did not mean to sit and shiver with sheer nervousness. Stoutly she collected her mental forces and retreated to her room. She was so tired that she knew she would sleep if she could control her imagination.

This she steadfastly set herself to do, with the result that sleep came to her at last, and in her weariness she sank into a deep slumber that, undisturbed by any outside influence, would have lasted throughout the night. She had left a lamp burning in the sitting-room that adjoined her bedroom, and the door between ajar, so that she was not lying in complete darkness. She had done the same the previous night, and had felt no serious qualms. The light scarcely reached her, but it was a comfort to see it at hand when she opened her eyes. It gave her a sense of security, and she slept the more easily because of it.

So for an hour or more she lay in unbroken slumber; then, like a cloud arising out of her sea of oblivion, there came to her again that dream of two horsemen galloping. It was a terrible dream, all the more terrible because she knew so well what was coming. Only this time, instead of the ledge along the ravine, she saw them clearly outlined against the sky, racing from opposite directions along a knife-edge path that stood up, sharp and jagged, between two precipices.

With caught breath she stood apart and watched in anguished expectation, watched as if held by some unseen force, till there came the inevitable crash, the terrible confusion of figures locked in deadly combat, and then the hurtling fall of a single horseman down that frightful wall of rock. His face gleamed white for an instant, and then was gone. Was it Guy? Was it Burke? She knew not. . . .

It was then that strength returned to her, and

she sprang up, crying wildly, every pulse alert and pricking her to action. She fled across the room, instinctively seeking the light, stumbled on the threshold, and fell headlong into the arms of a man who stood just beyond. They closed upon her instantly, supporting her. She lay, gasping hysterically, against his breast.

"Easy! Easy!" he said. "Did I startle you?"

It was Burke's voice, very deep and low. She felt the steady beat of his heart as he held her.

Her senses returned to her and with them an overwhelming embarrassment that made her swiftly withdraw herself from him. He let her go, and she retreated into the darkness behind her.

"What is it, partner?" he said gently. "You've nothing to be afraid of."

There was no reproach in his voice, yet something within reproached her instantly. She put on slippers and dressing-gown and went back to him.

"I've had a stupid dream," she said. "I expect I heard your horse outside. So—you have come back alone!"

"He has gone back to his own cabin," Burke said.

"Burke!" She looked at him with startled, reproachful eyes. Her hair lay in a fiery cloud about her shoulders, and fire burned in her gaze as she faced him.

He made a curious gesture as if he restrained some urging impulse, not speaking for a moment. When his voice came again it sounded cold, with an odd note of defiance. "I've done my best."

She still looked at him searchingly. "Why wouldn't he come here?" she said.

He turned from her with a movement that almost seemed to indicate impatience. "He preferred not to. There isn't much accommodation here. Besides, he can very well fend for himself. He's used to it."

"I have been preparing for him all day," Sylvia said. She looked at him anxiously, struck by something unusual in his pose, and noted for the first time a wide strip of plaster on one side of his chin. "Is all well?" she questioned. "How have you hurt your face?"

He did not look at her. "Yes, all's well," he said. "I cut myself—shaving. You go back to bed! I'm going to refresh before I turn in."

Sylvia turned to a cupboard in the room where she had placed some eatables before retiring. She felt chill with foreboding. What was it that Burke was hiding behind that curt manner? She was sure there was something.

"What will Guy do for refreshment?" she said, as she set dishes and plates upon the table.

"He'll have some tinned stuff in that shanty of his," said Burke.

She turned from the table with abrupt resolu tion. "Have something to eat, partner," she said, "and then tell me all about it!"

She looked for the sudden gleam of his smile, but she looked in vain. He regarded her, indeed, but it was with sombre eyes.

"You go back to bed!" he reiterated. "There is no necessity for you to stay up. You can see him for yourself in the morning."

He would have seated himself at the table with the words, but she laid a quick, appealing hand upon his arm, deterring him. "Burke!" she said. "What is the matter? Please tell me!"

She felt his arm grow rigid under her fingers. And then with a suddenness that electrified her he moved, caught her by the wrists and drew her to him, locking her close.

"You witch!" he said. "You—enchantress! How shall I resist you?"

She uttered a startled gasp; there was no time for more ere his lips met hers in a kiss so burning, so compelling, that it reft from her all power of resistance. One glimpse she had of his eyes, and it was as if she looked into the deep, deep heart of the fire unquenchable.

She wanted to cry out, so terrible was the sight, but his lips sealed her own. She lay helpless in his hold.

Afterwards she realized that she must have been near to fainting, for when at the end of those wild moments of passion he let her go, her knees gave way beneath her and she could not stand. Yet instinctively she gripped her courage with both hands. He had startled her, appalled her even, but there was a fighting strain in Sylvia, and she flung dismay away. She held his arm in a quivering grasp. She smiled a quivering smile. And these were the bravest acts she had ever forced herself to perform.

"You've done it now, partner!" she said shakily. "I'm nearly—squeezed—to death!"

"Sylvia!" he said.

Amazement, contrition, and even a curious dash of awe, were in his voice. He put his arm about her, supporting her.

She leaned against him, panting, her face downcast. "It's—all right," she told him. "I told you you might sometimes, didn't I? Only—you —were a little sudden, and I wasn't prepared. I believe you've been having a rotten time. Sit down now, and have something to eat!"

But he did not move though there was no longer violence in his hold. He spoke deeply, above her bent head. "I can't stand this farce much longer. I'm only human after all, and there is a limit to everything. I can't keep at arm's length for ever. Flesh and blood won't bear it."

She did not lift her head, but stood silent within the circle of his arm. It was as if she waited for something. Then, after a moment or two, she began to rub his sleeve lightly up and down, her hand not very steady.

"You're played out, partner," she said. "Don't let's discuss things to-night! They are sure to look different in the morning."

"And if they don't?" said Burke.

She glanced up at him with again that little quivering smile. "Well, then, we'll talk," she said, "till we come to an understanding."

He put his hand on her shoulder. "Sylvia, don't—play with me!" he said.

His tone was quiet, but it held a warning that brought her eyes to his in a flash. She stood so for a few seconds, facing him, and her breast heaved once or twice as if breathing had become difficult.

At last, "There was no need to say that to me, partner," she said, in a choked voice. "You don't

know me—even as well as—as you might—if you
—if you took the trouble." She paused a moment
and put her hand to her throat. Her eyes were
full of tears. "And now—good night!" she said
abruptly.

Her tone was a command. He let her go, and
in an instant the door had closed between them.

He stood motionless, waiting tensely for the
shooting of the bolt; but it did not come. He only
heard instead a faint sound of smothered sobbing.

For a space he stood listening, his face drawn
into deep lines, his hands hard clenched. Then
at length with a bitter gesture he flung himself
down at the table.

He was still sitting motionless a quarter of an
hour later, the food untouched before him, when
the intervening door opened suddenly and silently,
and like a swooping bird Sylvia came swiftly behind him and laid her two hands on his shoulders.

"Partner dear, I've been a big idiot. Will you
forgive me?" she said.

Her voice was tremulous. It still held a sound
of tears. She tried to keep out of his sight as he
turned in his chair.

"Don't—don't stare at me!" she said, and
slipped coaxing arms that trembled round his
neck, locking her hands tightly in front of him.

"You hurt me a bit—though I don't think you meant to. And now I've hurt you—quite a lot. I didn't mean it either, partner. So let's cry quits! I've forgiven you. Will you try to forgive me?"

He sat quite still for a few seconds, and in the silence shyly she laid her cheek down against the back of his head. He moved then, and very gently clasped the trembling hands that bound him. But still he did not speak.

"Say it's all right!" she urged softly. "Say you're not cross or—or anything!"

"I'm not," said Burke very firmly.

"And don't—don't ever think I want to play with you!" she pursued, a catch in her voice. "That's not me, partner. I'm sorry I'm so very unsatisfactory. But—anyhow that's not the reason."

"I know the reason," said Burke quietly.

"You don't," she rejoined instantly. "But never mind that now! You don't know anything whatever about me, partner. I can't say I even know myself very intimately just now. I feel as if—as if I've been blindfolded, and I can't see anything at all just yet. So will you try to be patient with me? Will you—will you—go on being a pal to me till the bandage comes off again? I—want a pal—rather badly, partner."

Her pleading voice came muffled against him. She was clinging to him very tightly. He could feel her fingers straining upon each other. He stroked them gently.

"All right, little girl. All right," he said.

His tone must have reassured her, for she slipped round and knelt beside him. "I'd like you to kiss me," she said, and lifted a pale face and tear-bright eyes to his.

He took her head between his hands, and she saw that he was moved. He bent in silence, and would have kissed her brow, but she raised her lips instead. And shyly she returned his kiss.

"You're so—good to me," she said, in a whisper. "Thank you—so much."

He said no word in answer. Mutely he let her go.

CHAPTER VII

THE GUEST

WHEN Sylvia met her husband again, it was as if they had never been parted or any cloud arisen to disturb the old frank comradeship.

They breakfasted at daybreak before riding out over the lands, and their greeting was of the most commonplace description. Later, as they rode together across the barren *veldt*, Burke told her a little of his finding of Guy at Brennerstadt. He did not dwell upon any details, but by much that he left unsaid Sylvia gathered that the task had not been easy.

"He knows about—me?" she ventured presently, with hesitation.

"Yes," Burke said.

"Was he—surprised?" she asked.

"No. He knew long ago."

She asked no more. It had been difficult enough to ask so much. And she would soon see Guy for herself. She would not admit even to her own secret soul how greatly she was dreading that meeting now that it was so near.

Perhaps Burke divined something of her feeling in the matter, however, for at the end of a prolonged silence he said, "I thought I would fetch him over to lunch,—unless you prefer to ride round that way first."

"Oh, thank you," she said. "That is good of you."

As they reached the bungalow, she turned to him with a sudden question. "Burke, you didn't —really—cut your chin so badly shaving. Did you?"

She met the swift flash of his eyes without trepidation, refusing to be intimidated by the obvious fact that the question was unwelcome.

"Did you?" she repeated with insistence. He uttered a brief laugh. "All right, I didn't. And that's all there is to it."

"Thank you, partner," she returned with spirit, and changed the subject. But her heart had given a little throb of dismay within her. Full well she knew the reason of his reticence.

They parted before the *stoep*, he leading her animal away, she going within to attend to the many duties of her household.

She filled her thoughts with these resolutely during the morning, but in spite of this it was the longest morning she had ever known.

She was at length restlessly superintending the laying of lunch when Joe hurried in with the news that a *baas* was waiting on the *stoep* round the corner to see her. The news startled her. She had heard no sounds of arrival, nor had Burke returned. For a few moments she was conscious of a longing to escape that was almost beyond her control, then with a sharp effort she commanded herself and went out.

Turning the corner of the bungalow, she came upon him very suddenly, standing upright against one of the pillar-supports, awaiting her. He was alone, and a little throb of thankfulness went through her that this was so. She knew in that moment that she could not have borne to meet him for the first time in Burke's presence.

She was trembling as she went forward, but the instant their hands met her agitation fell away from her, for she suddenly realized that he was trembling also.

No conventional words came to her lips. How could she ever be conventional with Guy? And it was Guy—Guy in the flesh—who stood before her, so little altered in appearance from the Guy she had known five years before that the thought flashed through her mind that he looked only as if he had come through a sharp illness. She had expected far worse, though she realized now what Burke had meant when he had said that whatever resemblance had once existed between them, they were now no longer alike. He had not developed as she had expected. In Burke she seemed to see the promise of Guy's youth. But Guy himself had not fulfilled that promise. He had degenerated. He had proved himself a failure. And yet he did not look coarsened or hardened by vice. He only looked, to her pitiful, inexperienced eyes, as if he had been ravaged by some sickness, as if he had suffered intensely and were doomed to suffer as long as he lived.

That was the first impression she received of him, and it was that that made her clasp his hand in both her own and hold it fast.

"Oh, Guy!" she said. "How ill you look!"

His fingers closed hard upon hers. He did not attempt to meet her earnest gaze. "So you got married to Burke!" he said, ignoring her exclamation. "It was the best thing you could do. He may not be exactly showy, but he's respectable. I wonder you want to speak to me after the way I let you down."

The words were cool, almost casual; yet his hand still held hers in a quivering grasp. There was something in that grasp that seemed to plead for understanding. He flashed her a swift look from eyes that burned with a fitful, feverish fire out of deep hollows. How well she remembered his eyes! But they had never before looked at her thus. With every moment that passed she realized that the change in him was greater than that first glance had revealed.

"Of course I want to speak to you!" she said gently. "I forgave you long ago—as, I hope, you have forgiven me."

"I!" he said. "My dear girl, be serious!"

Somehow his tone pierced her. There was an oddly husky quality in his voice that seemed to veil emotion. The tears sprang to her eyes before she was aware.

"Whatever happens then, we are friends," she said. "Remember that always, won't you? It —it will hurt me very much if you don't."

"Bless your heart!" said Guy, and smiled a twisted smile. "You were always generous, weren't you? Too generous sometimes. What did you want to rake me out of my own particular little corner of hell for? Was it a mistaken idea of kindness or merely curiosity? I wasn't anyhow doing you any harm there."

His words, accompanied by that painful smile, went straight to her heart. "Ah, don't—don't!"

she said. "Did you think I could forget you so easily, or be anything but wretched while you were there?"

He looked at her again, this time intently. "What can you be made of, Sylvia?" he said. "Do you mean to say you found it easy to forgive me?"

She dashed the tears from her eyes. "I don't remember that I was ever—angry with you," she said. "Somehow I realized—from the very first—that—that—it was just—bad luck."

"You amaze me!" he said.

She smiled at him. "Do I? I don't quite see why. Is it so amazing that one should want to pass on and make the best of things? That is how I feel now. It seems so long ago, Guy,—like another existence almost. It is too far away to count."

"Are you talking of the old days?" he broke in, in a voice that grated. "Or of the time a few weeks ago when you got here to find yourself stranded?"

She made a little gesture of protest. "It wasn't for long. I don't want to think of it. But it might have been much worse. Burke was—is still—so good to me."

"Is he?" said Guy.

He was looking at her curiously, and instinctively she turned away, avoiding his eyes.

"Come and have some lunch!" she said. "He ought to be in directly."

"He is in," said Guy. "He went round to the stable."

It was another instance of Burke's goodness that he had not been present at their meeting. She turned to lead the way within with a warm feeling at her heart. It was solely due to this consideration of his that she had not suff red the most miserable embarrassment. Someho w she felt that she could not possibly have endured that first encounter in his presence. But now that it was over, now that she had made acquaintance with this new Guy—this stranger with Guy's face, Guy's voice, but not Guy's laugh or any of the sparkling vitality that had been his—she felt she wanted him. She needed his help. For surely now he knew Guy better than she did!

It was with relief that she heard his step, entering from the back of the house. He came in, whistling carelessly, and she glanced instinctively at Guy. That sound had always made her think of him. Had he forgotten how to whistle also, she wondered?

She expected awkwardness, constraint; but

Burke surprised her by his ease of manner. Above all, she noticed that he was by no means kind to Guy. He treated him with a curt friendliness from which all trace of patronage was wholly absent. His attitude was rather that of brother than host, she reflected. And its effect upon Guy was of an oddly bracing nature. The semi-defiant air dropped from him. Though still subdued, his manner showed no embarrassment. He even, as time passed, became in a sardonic fashion almost jocose.

In company with Burke, he drank *lager*-beer, and he betrayed not the smallest desire to drink too much. Furtively she watched him throughout the meal, trying to adjust her impressions, trying to realize him as the lover to whom she had been faithful for so long, the lover who had written those always tender, though quite uncommunicative letters, the lover who had cabled her his welcome, and then had so completely and so cruelly failed her.

Her ideas of him were a whirl of conflicting notions which utterly bewildered her. Of one thing only did she become very swiftly and surely convinced, and that was that in failing her he had saved her from a catastrophe which must have eclipsed her whole life. Whatever he was, whatever her feelings for him, she recognized that this man was not the mate her girlish dreams had so fondly pictured. Probably she would have realized this in any case from the moment of their meeting, but circumstances might have compelled her to join her life to his. And then——

Her look passed from him to Burke, and instinctively she breathed a sigh of thankfulness. He had saved her from much already, and his rock-like strength stood perpetually between her and evil. For the first time she was consciously glad that she had entrusted herself to him.

At the end of luncheon she realized with surprise that there had not been an awkward moment. They went out on to the *stoep* to smoke cigarettes when it was over, and drink the coffee which she went to prepare. It was when she was coming out with this that she first heard Guy's cough—a most terrible, rending sound that filled her with dismay. Stepping out on to the *stoep* with her tray, she saw him bent over the back of a chair, convulsed with coughing, and stood still in alarm. She had never before witnessed so painful a struggle. It was as if he fought some demon whose clutch threatened to strangle him.

Burke came to her and took the tray from her

hands. "He'll be better directly," he said. "It was the cigarette."

With almost superhuman effort, Guy succeeded in forcing back the monster that seemed to be choking him, but for several minutes thereafter he hung over the chair with his face hidden, fighting for breath.

Burke motioned to Sylvia to sit down, but she would not. She stood by Guy's side, and at length as he grew calmer, laid a gentle hand upon his arm.

"Come and sit down, Guy. Would you like some water?"

He shook his head. "No—no! Give me—that damned cigarette!"

"Don't you be a fool!" said Burke, but he said it kindly. "Sit down and be quiet for a bit!"

He came up behind Guy, and took him by the shoulders. Sylvia saw with surprise the young man yield without demur, and suffer himself to be put into the chair where with an ashen face he lay for a space as if afraid to move.

Burke drew her aside. "Don't be scared!" he said. "It's nothing new. He'll come round directly."

Guy came round, sat slowly up, and reached a shaking hand towards the table on which lay his scarcely lighted cigarette.

"Oh, don't!" Sylvia said quickly. "See, I have just brought out some coffee. Won't you have some?"

Burke settled the matter by picking up the cigarette and tossing it away.

Guy gave him a queer look from eyes that seemed to burn like red coals, but he said nothing whatever. He took the coffee Sylvia held out to him and drank it as if parched with thirst.

Then he turned to her. "Sorry to have made such an exhibition of myself. It's all this infernal sand. Yes, I'll have some more, please. It does me good. Then I'll get back to my own den and have a sleep."

"You can sleep here," Burke said unexpectedly. "No one will disturb you. Sylvia never sits here in the afternoon."

Again Sylvia saw that strange look in Guy's eyes, a swift intent glance and then the instant falling of the lids.

"You're very—kind," said Guy. "But I think I'll get back to my own quarters all the same."

Impulsively Sylvia intervened. "Oh, Guy, please,—don't go back to that horrible little shanty on the sand! I got a room all ready for you yesterday—if you will only use it."

He turned to her. For a second his look was

upon her also, and it seemed to her in that moment that she and Burke had united cruelly to bait some desperate animal. It sent such a shock through her that she shrank in spite of herself.

And then for the first time she heard Guy laugh, and it was a sound more dreadful than his cough had been, a catching, painful sound that was more like a cry—the hunger-cry of a prowling beast of the desert.

He got up as he uttered it, and stretched his arms above his head. She saw that his hands were clenched.

"Oh, don't overdo it, I say!" he begged. "Hospitality is all very well, but it can be carried too far. Ask Burke if it can't! Besides, two's company and three's the deuce. So I'll be going—and many thanks!"

He was gone with the words, snatching his hat from a chair where he had thrown it, and departing into the glare of the desert with never a backward glance.

Sylvia turned swiftly to her husband, and found his eyes upon her.

With a gasping cry she caught his arm. "Oh, can't you go after him? Can't you bring him back?"

He freed the arm to put it round her, with the

gesture of one who comforts a hurt child. "My dear, it's no good," he said. "Let him go!"

"But, Burke—" she cried. "Oh, Burke——"

"I know," he made answer, still soothing her. "But it can't be done—anyhow at present. You'll drive him away if you attempt it. I know. I've done it. Leave him alone till the devil has gone out of him! He'll come back then—and be decent —for a time."

His meaning was unmistakable. The force of what he said drove in upon her irresistibly. She burst into tears, hiding her face against his shoulder in her distress.

"But how dreadful! Oh, how dreadful! He is killing himself. I think—the Guy—I knew—is dead already."

"No, he isn't," Burke said, and he held her with sudden closeness as he said it. "He isn't— and that's the hell of it. But you can't save him. No one can."

She lifted her face sharply. There was something intolerable in the words. With the tears upon her cheeks she challenged them.

"He can be saved! He must be saved! I'll do it somehow—somehow!"

"You may try," Burke said, as he suffered her to release herself. "You won't succeed."

She forced a difficult smile with quivering lips. "You don't know me. Where there's a will, there's a way. And I shall find it somehow."

He looked grim for an instant, then smiled an answering smile. "Don't perish in the attempt!" he said. "That do-or-die look of yours is rather ominous. Don't forget you're my partner! I can't spare you, you know."

She uttered a shaky laugh. "Of course you can't. Blue Hill Farm would go to pieces without me, wouldn't it? I've often thought I'm quite indispensable."

"You are to me," said Burke briefly; and ere the quick colour had sprung to her face, he also had gone his way.

CHAPTER VIII

THE INTERRUPTION

SYLVIA meant to ride round to Guy's hut in search of him that evening, but when the time came something held her back.

Burke's words, "You'll drive him away," recurred to her again and again, and with them came a dread of intruding that finally prevailed against her original intention. He must not think for a moment that she desired to spy upon him, even though that dreadful craving in his eyes haunted her perpetually, urging her to action. It seemed inevitable that for a time at least he must fight his devil alone, and with all her strength she prayed that he might overcome.

In the end she rode out with Burke, covering a considerable distance, and returning tired in body but refreshed in mind.

They had supper together as usual, but when it was over he surprised her by taking up his hat again.

"You are going out?" she said.

"I'm going to have a smoke with Guy," he said. "You have a game of Patience, and then go to bed!"

She looked at him uncertainly. "I'll come with you," she said.

He was filling his pipe preparatory to departure. "You do as I say!" he said.

She tried to laugh though she saw his face was grim. "You're getting rather despotic, partner. I shall have to nip that in the bud. I'm not going to stay at home and play Patience all by myself. There!"

He raised his eyes abruptly from his task, and suddenly her heart was beating fast and hard. "All right," he said. "We'll stay at home together."

His tone was brief, but it thrilled her. She was afraid to speak for a moment or two lest he should see her strange agitation. Then, as he still looked at her, "Oh no, partner," she said lightly. "That wouldn't be the same thing at all. I am much too fond of my own company to object to solitude. I only thought I would like to come, too. I love the *veldt* at night."

"Do you?" he said. "I wonder what has taught you to do that."

He went on with the filling of his pipe as he spoke, and she was conscious of quick relief. His words did not seem to ask for an answer, and she made none.

"When are you going to take me to Ritzen?" she asked instead.

"To Ritzen!" He glanced up again in surprise. "Do you want to go to Ritzen?"

"Or Brennerstadt," she said. "Whichever is the best shopping centre."

"Oh!" He began to smile. "You want to shop, do you? What do you want to buy?"

She looked at him severely. "Nothing for myself, I am glad to say."

"What! Something for me?" His smile gave him that look—that boyish look—which once she had loved so dearly upon Guy's face. She felt as if something were pulling at her heart. She ignored it resolutely.

"You will have to buy it for yourself," she told him sternly. "I've got nothing to buy it with. It's something you ought to have got long ago—if you had any sense of decency."

"What on earth is it?" Burke dropped his pipe into his pocket and gave her his full attention.

Sylvia, with a cigarette between her lips, got up to find the matches. She lighted it very deliberately under his watching eyes, then held out the match to him. "Light up, and I'll tell you."

He took the slender wrist, blew out the match, and held her, facing him.

"Sylvia," he said. "I ought to have gone into the money question with you before. But all I have is yours. You know that, don't you?"

She laughed at him through the smoke. "I know where you keep it anyhow, partner," she said. "But I shan't take any—so you needn't be afraid."

"Afraid!" he said, still holding her. "But you are to take it. Understand? It's my wish."

She blew the smoke at him, delicately, through pursed lips. "Good my lord, I don't want it. Couldn't spend it if I had it. So now!"

"Then what is it I am to buy?" he said.

Lightly she answered him. "Oh, you will only do the paying part. I shall do the choosing—and the bargaining, if necessary."

"Well, what is it?" Still he held her, and there was something of insistence, something of possession, in his hold.

Possibly she had never before seemed more desirable to him—or more elusive. For she was beginning to realize and to wield her power. Again she took a whiff from her cigarette, and wafted it at him through laughing lips.

"I want some wool—good wool—and a lot of it,

to knit some socks—for you. Your present things are disgraceful."

His look changed a little. His eyes shone through the veil of smoke she threw between them. "I can buy ready-made socks. I'm not going to let you make them—or mend them."

Sylvia's red lips expressed scorn. "Ready-made rubbish! No, sir. With your permission I prefer to make. Then perhaps I shall have less mending to do."

He was drawing her to him and she did not actively resist, though there was no surrender in her attitude.

"And why won't you have any money?" he said. "We are partners."

She laughed lightly. "And you give me board and lodging. I am not worth more."

He looked her in the eyes. "Are you afraid to take too much—lest I should want too much in return?"

She did not answer. She was trembling a little in his hold, but her eyes met his fearlessly.

He put up a hand and took the cigarette very gently from her lips. "Sylvia, I'm going to tell you something—if you'll listen."

He paused a moment. She was suddenly throbbing from head to foot.

"What is it?" she whispered.

He snuffed out the cigarette with his fingers and put it in his pocket. Then he bent to her, his hand upon her shoulder.

His lips were open to speak, and her silence waited for the words, when like the sudden rending of the heavens there came an awful sound close to them, so close that is shook the windows in their frames and even seemed to shake the earth under their feet.

Sylvia started back with a cry, her hands over her face. "Oh, what—what—what is that?"

Burke was at the window in a second. He wrenched it open, and as he did so there came the shock of a thudding fall. A man's figure, huddled up like an empty sack, lay across the threshold. It sank inwards with the opening of the window, and Guy's face white as death, with staring, senseless eyes, lay upturned to the lamplight.

Something jingled on the floor as his inert form collapsed, and a smoking revolver dropped at Burke's feet.

He picked it up sharply, uncocked it and laid it on the table. Then he stooped over the prostrate body. The limbs were twitching spasmodically, but the movement was wholly involuntary. The deathlike face testified to that. And through

the grey flannel shirt above the heart a dark stain
spread and spread.

"He is dead!" gasped Sylvia at Burke's
shoulder.

"No," Burke said.

He opened the shirt with the words and exposed
the wound beneath.   Sylvia shrank at the sight of
the welling blood, but Burke's voice steadied her.

"Get some handkerchiefs and towels," he said,
"and make a wad!   We must stop this somehow."

His quietness gave her strength.   Swiftly she
moved to do his bidding.

Returning, she found that he had stretched the
silent figure full length upon the floor.   The convulsive movements had wholly ceased.   Guy lay
like a dead man.

She knelt beside Burke.   "Tell me what to do
and I'll do it!   I'll do—anything!"

"All right," he said.   "Get some cold water!"

She brought it, and he soaked some handkerchiefs and covered the wound.

"I think we shall stop it," he said.   "Help me
to get this thing under his shoulders!   I shall have
to tie him up tight.   I'll lift him while you get it
underneath."

She was perfectly steady as she followed his
instructions, and even though in the process her

hands were stained with Guy's blood, she did not shrink again. It was no easy task, but Burke's skill and strength of muscle accomplished it at last. Across Guy's body he looked at her with a certain grim triumph.

"Well played, partner! That's the first move. Are you all right?"

She saw by his eyes that her face betrayed the horror at her heart. She tried to smile at him, but her lips felt stiff and cold. Her look went back to the ashen face on the floor.

"What—what must be done next?" she said.

"He will have to stay as he is till we can get a doctor," Burke answered. "The bleeding has stopped for the present, but— " He broke off.

"Child, how sick you look!" he said. "Here, come and wash! There's nothing more to be done now."

She got up, feeling her knees bend beneath her but controlling them with rigid effort. "I—am all right," she said. "You—you think he isn't dead?"

Burke's hand closed upon her elbow. "He's not dead,—no! He may die of course, but I don't fancy he will at present,—not while he lies like that."

He was drawing her out of the room, but she resisted him suddenly. "I can't go. I can't leave him—while he lives. Burke, don't, please, bother about me! Are you—are you going to fetch a doctor?"

"Yes," said Burke.

She looked at him, her eyes wide and piteous. "Then please go now—go quickly! I—will stay with him till you come back."

"I shall have to leave you for some hours," he said.

"Oh, never mind that!" she answered. "Just be as quick as you can, that's all! I will be with him. I—shan't be afraid."

She was urging him to the door, but he turned back. He went to the table, picked up the revolver he had laid there, and put it away in a cupboard which he locked.

She marked the action, and as he came to her again, laid a trembling hand upon his arm. "Burke! Could it—could it have been an accident?"

"No. It couldn't," said Burke. He paused a moment, looking at her in a way she did not understand. She wondered afterwards what had been passing in his mind. But he said no further word except a brief, "Good-bye!"

Ten minutes later, she heard the quick thud of his horse's hoofs as he rode into the night.

CHAPTER IX

THE ABYSS

"SYLVIA!"

Was it a voice that spoke in the overwhelming silence, or was it the echo in her soul of a voice that would never speak again? Sylvia could not decide. She had sat for so long, propped against a chair, watching that still figure on the floor, straining her senses to see or hear some sign of breathing, trying to cheat herself into the belief that he slept, and then with a wrung heart wondering if he were not better dead.

All memory of the bitterness and the cruel disappointment that he had brought into her life had rolled away from her during those still hours of watching. She did not think of herself at all; only of Guy, once so eager and full of sparkling hope, now so tragically fallen in the race of life. All her woman's tenderness was awake and throbbing with a passionate pity for this lover of her youth. Why, oh why had he done this thing? The horror of it oppressed her like a crushing, physical weight. Was it for this that she had persuaded Burke to rescue him from the depths to which he had sunk? Had she by her rash interference only precipitated his final doom—she who had suffered so deeply for his sake, who had yearned so ardently to bring him back?

Burke had been against it from the beginning; Burke knew to his cost the hopelessness of it all. Ah, would it have been better if she had listened to him and refrained from attempting the impossible? Would it not have been preferable to accept failure rather than court disaster? What had she done? What had she done?

"Sylvia!"

Surely the old Guy was speaking to her! Those pallid lips could make no sound; the new, strange Guy was dead.

As in a dream, she answered him through the silence, feeling as if she spoke into the shadows of the Unknown.

"Yes, Guy? Yes? I am here."

"Will you—forgive me," he said, "for making—a boss shot!"

Then she turned to the prostrate form beside her on the floor, and saw that the light of understanding had come back into those haunted eyes.

She knelt over him and laid her hand upon his

rough hair. "Oh, Guy, hush—hush!" she said. "Thank God you are still here!"

A very strange expression flitted over his up-turned face, a look that was indescribably boyish and yet so sad that she caught her breath to still the intolerable pain at her heart.

"I shan't be—long," he said. "Thank God for that—too! I've been—working myself up to it—all day."

"Guy!" she said.

He made a slight movement of one hand, and she gathered it close into her own. It seemed to her that the Shadow of Death had drawn very near to them, enveloping them both.

"It had—to be," he said, in the husky halting voice so unfamiliar to her. "It—was a mistake—to try to bring me back. I'm—beyond—re-demption. Ask Burke;—he knows!"

"You are not—you are not!" she told him vehemently. "Guy!" She was holding his hand hard pressed against her heart; her words came with a rush of pitying tenderness that swept over every barrier. "Guy! I want you! You must stay. If you go now—you—you will break my heart."

His eyes kindled a little at her words, but in a moment the emotion passed. "It's too late, my dear;—too late," he said and turned his head on

the pillow under it as if seeking rest. "You don't
—understand. Just as well for me perhaps. But
I'm better gone—for your sake, better gone."

The conviction of his words went through her
like a sword-thrust. He seemed to have passed
beyond her influence, almost, she fancied, not to
care. Yet why did the look in his eyes make her
think of a lost child—frightened, groping along an
unknown road in the dark? Why did his hand
cling to hers as though it feared to let go?

She held it very tightly as she made reply.
"But, Guy, it isn't for us to choose. It isn't for
us to discharge ourselves. Only God knows when
our work is done."

He groaned. "I've given all mine to the devil.
God couldn't use me if He tried."

"You don't know," she said. "You don't know.
We're none of us saints. I think He makes allowances—when things go wrong with us—just as
—just as we make allowances for each other."

He groaned again. "You would make allowances for the devil himself," he muttered. "It's
the way you're made. But it isn't justice. Burke
would tell you that."

An odd little tremor of impatience went through
her. "I know you better than Burke does," she said.
"Better, probably—than anyone else in the world."

He turned his head to and fro upon the pillow. "You don't know me, Sylvia. You don't know me—at all."

Yet the husky utterance seemed to plead with her as though he longed for her to understand.

She stooped lower over him. "Never mind, dear! I love you all the same," she said. "And that's why I can't bear you—to go—like this." Her voice shook unexpectedly. She paused to steady it. "Guy," she urged, almost under her breath at length, "you will live—you will try to live—for my sake?"

Again his eyes were upon her. Again, more strongly, the flame kindled. Then, very suddenly, a hard shudder went through him, and a dreadful shadow arose and quenched that vital gleam. For a few moments consciousness itself seemed to be submerged in the most awful suffering that Sylvia had ever beheld. His eyeballs rolled upwards under lids that twitched convulsively. The hand she held closed in an agonized grip upon her own. She thought that he was dying, and braced herself instinctively to witness the last terrible struggle, the rending asunder of soul and body.

Then—as one upon the edge of an abyss—he spoke, his voice no more than a croaking whisper.

"It's hell for me—either way. Living or dead —hell!"

The paroxysm spent itself and passed like an evil spirit. The struggle for which she had prepared herself did not come. Instead, the flickerering lids closed over the tortured eyes, the clutching hand relaxed, and there fell a great silence.

She sat for a long time not daring to move, scarcely breathing, wondering if this were the end. Then gradually it came to her, that he was lying in the stillness of utter exhaustion. She felt for his pulse and found it beating, weakly but unmistakably. He had sunk into a sleep which she realized might be the means of saving his life.

Thereafter she sat passive, leaning against a chair, waiting, watching, as she had waited and watched for so long. Once she leaned her head upon her hand and prayed "O dear God, let him live!" But something—some inner voice—seemed to check that prayer, and though her whole soul yearned for its fulfilment she did not repeat it. Only, after a little, she stooped very low, and touched Guy's forehead with her lips.

"God bless you!" she said softly. "God bless you!"

And in the silence that followed, she thought there was a benediction.

CHAPTER X

THE DESIRE TO LIVE

IN the last still hour before the dawn there came the tread of horses' feet outside the bungalow and the sound of men's voices.

Sylvia looked up as one emerging from a long, long dream, though she had not closed her eyes all night. The lamp was burning low, and Guy's face was in deep shadow; but she knew by the hand that she still held close between her own that he yet lived. She even fancied that the throb of his pulse was a little stronger.

She looked at Burke with questioning, uncertain eyes as he entered. In the dim light he seemed to her bigger, more imposing, more dominant, than he had ever seemed before. He rolled a little as he walked as if stiff from long hours in the saddle.

Behind him came another man — a small thin man with sleek black hair and a swarthy Jewish face, who moved with a catlike deftness, making no sound at all.

"Well, Sylvia?" Burke said. "Is he alive?"

He took the lamp from the table, and cast its waning light full upon her. She shrank a little involuntarily from the sudden glare. Almost without knowing it, she pressed Guy's inert hand to her breast. The dream was still upon her. It was hardly of her own volition that she answered him.

"Yes, he is alive. He has been speaking. I think he is asleep."

"Permit me!" the stranger said.

He knelt beside the still form while Burke held the lamp. He opened the shirt and exposed the blood-soaked bandage.

Then suddenly he looked at Sylvia with black eyes of a most amazing brightness. "Madam, you cannot help here. You had better go."

Somehow he made her think of a raven, unscrupulous, probably wholly without pity, possibly wicked, and overwhelmingly intelligent. She avoided his eyes instinctively. They seemed to know too much.

"Will he—do you think he will—live?" she whispered.

He made a gesture of the hands that seemed to indicate infinite possibilities. "I do not think at present. But I must be undisturbed. Go to your room, madam, and rest! Your husband will come to you later and tell you what I have done—or failed to do."

He spoke with absolute fluency but with a foreign accent. His hands were busy with the bandages, dexterous, clawlike hands that looked as if they were delving for treasure.

She watched him, speechless and fascinated, for a few seconds. Then Burke set the lamp upon the chair against which she had leaned all the night, and bent down to her.

"Let me help you!" he said.

A shuddering horror of the sight before her came upon her. She yielded herself to him in silence. She was shivering violently from head to foot. Her limbs were so numb she could not stand. He raised her and drew her away.

The next thing she knew was that she was sitting on the bed in her own room, and he was making her drink brandy and water in so burning a mixture that it stung her throat.

She tried to protest, but he would take no refusal till she had swallowed what he had poured out. Then he put down the glass, tucked her feet up on the bed with an air of mastery, and spread a rug over her.

He would have left her then with a brief injunction to remain where she was, but she caught and held his arm so that he was obliged to pause.

"Burke, is that dreadful man a doctor?"

"The only one I could get hold of," said Burke. "Yes, he's a doctor all right. Saul Kieff his name is. I admit he's a scoundrel, but anyway he's keen on his job."

"You think he'll save Guy?" she said tremulously. "Oh, Burke, he must be saved! He must be saved!"

An odd look came into Burke's eyes. She remembered it later, though it was gone in an instant like the sudden flare of lightning across a dark sky.

"We shall do our best," he said. "You stay here till I come back!"

She let him go. Somehow that look had given her a curious shock though she did not understand it. She heard the door shut firmly behind him, and she huddled herself down upon the pillow and lay still.

She wished he had not made her drink that fiery draught. All her senses were in a tumult, and yet her body felt as if weighted with lead. She lay listening tensely for every sound, but the silence was like a blanket wrapped around her—a blanket which nothing seemed to penetrate.

It seemed to overwhelm her at last, that silence, to blot out the clamour of her straining nerves, to deprive her of the power to think. Though she did not know it, the stress of that night's horror and vigil had worn her out. She sank at length into a deep sleep from which it seemed that nought could wake her. And when more than an hour later, Burke came, treading softly, and looked upon her, he did not need to keep that burning hunger-light out of his eyes. For she was wholly unconscious of him as though her spirit were in another world.

He looked and looked with a gaze that seemed as if it would consume her. And at last he leaned over her, with arms outspread, and touched her sunny, disordered hair with his lips. It was the lightest touch, far too light to awaken her. But, as if some happy thought had filtered down through the deeps of her repose, she stirred in her sleep. She turned her face up to him with the faint smile of a slumbering child.

"Good night!" she murmured drowsily.

Her eyes half-opened upon him. She gave him her lips.

And as he stooped, with a great tremor, to kiss them, "Good night, dear—Guy!" Her voice was fainter, more indistinct. She sank back again into that deep slumber from which she had barely been roused.

And Burke went from her with the flower-like memory of her kiss upon his lips, and the dryness of ashes in his mouth.

It was several hours later that Sylvia awoke to full consciousness and a piercing realization of a strange presence that watched by her side.

She opened her eyes wide with a curious conviction that there was a cat in the room, and then all in a moment she met the cool, repellent stare of the black-browed doctor whom Burke had brought from Ritzen.

A little quiver of repugnance went through her at the sight, swiftly followed by a sharp thrill of indignation. What was he doing seated there by her side—this swarthy-faced stranger whom she had disliked instinctively at first sight?

And then—suddenly it rushed through her mind that he was the bearer of evil tidings, that he had come to tell her that Guy was dead. She raised herself sharply.

"Oh, what is it? What is it?" she gasped. "Tell me quickly! It's better for me to know. It's better for me to know."

He put out a narrow, claw-like hand and laid it

upon her arm. His eyes were like onyxes, Oriental, quite emotionless.

"Do not agitate yourself, madam!" he said. "My patient is better. I think, that with care— he may live. That is, if he finds it worth while."

"What do you mean?" she said in a whisper.

That there was a veiled meaning to his words she was assured at the outset. His whole bearing conveyed something mysterious, something sinister, to her startled imagination. She wanted to shake off the hand upon her arm, but she had to suffer it though the man's bare touch revolted her.

He was leaning slightly towards her, but yet his face was utterly inanimate. It was obvious that though he had imposed his personality upon her with a definite end in view, he was personally totally indifferent as to whether he achieved that end or not.

"I mean," he said, after a quiet pause, "that the desire to live is sometimes the only medicine that is of any avail. I know Guy Ranger. He is a fool in many ways, but not in all. He is not for instance fool enough to hang on to life if it holds nothing worth having. He was born with an immense love of life. He would not have done this thing if he had not somehow lost this gift—

for it is a gift.   If he does not get it back—some-how—then," the black, stony eyes looked into hers without emotion—"he will die."

She shrank at the cold deliberation of his words. "Oh no—no! Not like this! Not—by his own hand!"

"Ah!" He leaned towards her, bringing his sallow, impassive countenance close to hers, re-pulsively close, to her over-acute sensibilities. "And how is that to be prevented? Who is to give him that priceless remedy—the only medi-cine that can save him? Can I?" He lifted his shoulders expressively, indicating his own help-lessness. And then in a voice dropped to a whisper, "Can you?"

She did not answer him.   There was something horrible to her in that low-spoken question, something that yet possessed for her a species of evil fascination that restrained her from open revolt.

He waited for a while, his eyes so immovably fixed upon hers that she had a mild wonder if they were lidless—as the eyes of a serpent.

Then at last, through grim pale lips that did not seem to move, he spoke again. "Madam, it lies with you whether Guy Ranger lives or dies. You can open to him the earthly paradise or you can hurl him back to hell. I have only brought him a little way. I cannot keep him. Even now, he is slipping—he is slipping from my hold. It is you, and you alone, who can save him. How do I know this thing? How do I know that the sun rises in the east? I—have—seen. It is you who have taken from him the desire to live—perhaps unintentionally; that I do not know. It is you—and you alone—who can restore it. Need I say more than this to open your eyes? Perhaps they are already open. Perhaps already your heart has been in communion with his. If so, then you know that I have told you the truth. If you really desire to save him—and I think you do—then everything else in life must go to that end. Women were made for sacrifice, they say." A sardonic flicker that was scarcely a smile touched his face. "Well, that is the only way of saving him. If you fail him, he will go under."

He got up with the words. He had evidently said his say. As his hand left hers, Sylvia drew a deep hard breath, as of one emerging from a suffocating atmosphere. She had never felt so oppressed, so fettered, with evil in the whole of her life. And yet he had not urged her to any line of action. He had merely somewhat baldly, wholly dispassionately, told her the truth, and the very

17

absence of emotion with which he had spoken **had** driven conviction to her soul.   She saw him go with relief, but his words remained like a stone at the bottom of her heart.

CHAPTER XI

THE REMEDY

WHEN Sylvia went to Guy a little later, she found him installed in Burke's room. Burke himself was out on the farm, but it was past the usual hour for luncheon, and she knew he would be returning soon.

Keiff rose up noiselessly from the bedside at her entrance, and she saw that Guy was asleep. She was conscious of a surging, passionate longing to be alone with him as she crept forward. The silent presence of this stranger had a curious, nauseating effect upon her. She suppressed a shudder as she passed him.

He stood behind her in utter immobility as she bent over the bed. Guy was lying very still, but though he was pale, the deathly look had gone from his face. He looked unutterably tired, but very peaceful.

Lying so, with all the painful lines of his face relaxed, she saw the likeness of his boyhood very clearly on his quiet features, and her heart gave a quick hard throb within her that sent the hot tears to her eyes. The sight of him grew blurred and dim. She just touched his black hair with trembling fingers as she fought back a sob.

And then quite suddenly his eyes were open, looking at her. The pupils were enormously enlarged, giving him an unfamiliar look. But at sight of her, a quick smile flashed across his face— his old glad smile of welcome, and she knew him again. "Hullo—darling!" he said.

She could not speak in answer. She could only lay her hand over his and hold it fast.

He went on, his speech rapid, slighty incoherent. Guy had been like that, she remembered, in moments of any excitement or stress.

"I've had a beastly bad dream, sweetheart. Thought I'd lost you—somehow I was messing about in a filthy fog, and there were beastly precipices about. And you—you were calling somewhere—telling me not to forget something. What was it? I'm dashed if I can remember now."

"It—doesn't matter," she managed to say, though her voice was barely audible.

He opened his eyes a little wider. "Are you crying, I say? What's the matter? What, darling? You're not crying for me? Eh? I shall get over it. I always come up again. Ask Kelly! Ask Keiff!"

"Yes, you always come up again," Kieff said, in his brief, mechanical voice.

Guy threw him a look that was a curious blend of respect and disgust. "Hullo, Lucifer!" he said. "What are you doing here? Come to show us the quickest way to hell? He's an authority on that, Sylvia. He knows all the shortest cuts."

He broke off with a sudden hard breath, and Sylvia saw again that awful shadow gather in his eyes. She made way for Kieff, though not consciously at his behest, and there followed a dreadful struggling upon which she could not look. Kieff spoke once or twice briefly, authoritatively, and was answered by a sound more anguished than any words. Then at the end of several unspeakable seconds she heard Burke's footstep outside the door. She turned to him as he entered, with a thankfulness beyond all expression.

"Oh, Burke, he is suffering—so terribly. Do see if you can help!"

He passed her swiftly and went to the other side of the bed. Somehow his presence braced her. She looked again upon Guy in his extremity.

He was propped against Kieff's shoulder, his face quite livid, his eyes roaming wildly round the room, till suddenly they found and rested upon her own. All her life Sylvia was to remember the appeal those eyes held for her. It was as if his soul were crying aloud to her for freedom.

She came to the foot of the bed. The anguish had entered into her also, and it was more than she could bear.

She turned from Burke to Kieff. "Oh, do anything—anything—to help him!" she implored him. "Don't let him suffer—like this!"

Kieff's hand went to his pocket. "There is only one thing," he said.

Burke, his arm behind Guy's convulsed body, made an abrupt gesture with his free hand. "Wait! He'll come through it. He did before."

And still those tortured eyes besought Sylvia, urged her, entreated her.

She left the foot of the bed, and went to Kieff. Her lips felt stiff and numb, but she forced them to speak.

"If you have anything that will help him, give it to him now! Don't wait! Don't wait!"

Kieff the impassive, nodded briefly, and took his hand from his pocket.

"Wait! He is better," Burke said.

But, "Don't wait! Don't wait!" whispered Sylvia. "Don't let him die—like this!"

Kieff held out to her a small leather case. "Open it!" he said.

She obeyed him though her hands were trembling. She took out the needle and syringe it contained.

Burke said no more. Perhaps he realized that the cause was already lost. And so he looked on in utter silence while Sylvia and Kieff between them administered the only thing that could ease the awful suffering that seemed greater than flesh and blood could bear.

It took effect with marvellous quickness—that remedy of Kieff's. It was, to Sylvia's imagination, like the casting forth of a demon. Guy's burning eyes ceased to implore her. He strained no longer in the cruel grip. His whole frame relaxed, and he even smiled at her as they laid him back against the pillows.

"That's better," he said.

"Thank God!" Sylvia whispered.

His eyes were drooping heavily. He tried to keep them open. "Hold my hand!" he murmured to her.

She sat on the edge of the bed, and took it between her own.

His finger pressed hers. "That's good, darling. Now I'm happy. Wish we—could go on like this—always. Don't you?"

"No," she whispered back. "I want you well again."

"Ah!" His eyes were closing; he opened them again. "You mean that, sweetheart? You really want me?"

"Of course I do," she said.

Guy was still smiling but there was pathos in his smile. "Ah, that makes a difference," he said, "—all the difference. That means you've quite forgiven me. Quite, Sylvia?"

"Quite," she answered, and she spoke straight from her heart. She had forgotten Burke, forgotten Kieff, forgotten everyone in that moment save Guy, the dear lover of her youth.

And he too was looking at her with eyes that saw her alone. "Kiss me, little sweetheart!" he said softly. "And then I'll know—for sure."

It was boyishly spoken, and she could not refuse. She had no thought of refusing.

As in the old days when they had been young together, her heart responded to the call of his. She leaned down to him instantly and very lovingly, and kissed him.

"Sure you want me?" whispered Guy.

"God knows I do," she answered him very earnestly.

He smiled at her and closed his eyes. "Good night!" he murmured.

"Good night, dear!" she whispered back.

And then in the silence that followed she knew that he fell asleep.

Someone touched her shoulder, and she looked up. Burke was standing by her side.

"You can leave him now," he said. "He won't wake."

He spoke very quietly, but she thought his face was stern. A faint throb of misgiving went through her. She slipped her hand free and rose.

She saw that Kieff had already gone, and for a moment she hesitated. But Burke took her steadily by the arm, and led her from the room.

"He won't wake," he reiterated. "You must have something to eat."

They entered the sitting-room, and she saw with relief that Kieff was not there either. The table was spread for luncheon, and Burke led her to it.

"Sit down!" he said. "Never mind about Kieff! He can look after himself."

She sat down in silence. Somehow she felt out of touch with Burke at that moment. Her long vigil beside Guy seemed in some inexplicable fashion to have cut her off from him. Or was it those strange words that Kieff had uttered and which even yet were running in her brain? Whatever it was, it prevented all intimacy between them. They might have been chance-met strangers sitting at the same board. He waited upon her as if he were thinking of other things.

Her own thoughts were with Guy alone. She ate mechanically, half unconsciously watching the door, her ears strained to catch any sound.

"He will probably sleep for hours," Burke said, breaking the silence.

She looked at him with a start. She had almost forgotten his presence. She met his eyes and felt for a few seconds oddly disconcerted. It was with an effort she spoke in answer.

"I hope he will. That suffering is so terrible."

"It's bad enough," said Burke. "But the morphia habit is worse. That's damnable."

She drew a sharp breath. She felt almost as if he had struck her over the heart. "Oh, but surely—" she said— "surely—having it just once —like that——"

"Do you think he is the sort of man to be satisfied with just once of anything?" said Burke.

The question did not demand an answer, she made none. With an effort she controlled her distress and changed the subject.

"How long will Dr. Kieff stay?"

Burke's eyes were upon her again. She wished he would not look at her so intently. "He will probably see him through," he said. "How long that will take it is impossible to say. Not long, I hope."

"You don't like him?" she ventured.

"Personally," said Burke, "I detest him. He is not out here in his professional capacity. In fact I have a notion that he was kicked out of that some years ago. But that doesn't prevent him being a very clever surgeon. He likes a job of this kind."

Sylvia caught at the words. "Then he ought to succeed," she said. "Surely he will succeed!"

"I think you may trust him to do his best," Burke said.

They spoke but little during the rest of the meal. There seemed to be nothing to say. In some curious fashion Sylvia felt paralyzed. She could not turn her thought in any but the one direction, and she knew subtly but quite unmistakably that in this they were not in sympathy. It was a relief to her when Burke rose from the table. She was longing to get back to Guy. She had an almost overwhelming desire to be alone with him, even though he lay unconscious of her. They had known each other so long ago, before she had come to this land of strangers. Was it altogether unnatural that meeting thus again the old link should have been forged anew? And his need of

her was so great—infinitely greater now than it
had ever been before.

She lingered a few moments to set the table in
order for Kieff; then turned to go to him, and was
surprised to find Burke still standing by the door.

She looked at him questioningly, and as if in
answer he laid his hand upon her shoulder, detaining her. He did not speak immediately, and
she had a curious idea that he was embarrassed.

"What is it, partner?" she said, withdrawing
her thoughts from Guy with a conscious effort.

He bent slightly towards her. His hold upon
her was not wholly steady. It was as if some
hidden force vibrated strongly within him, making
itself felt to his very finger-tips. Yet his face
was perfectly composed, even grim, as he said,
"There is one thing I want to say to you before
you go. Sylvia, I haven't asserted any right over
you so far. But don't forget—don't let anyone
induce you to forget—that the right is mine! I
may claim it—some day."

That aroused her from preoccupation very effectually. The colour flamed in her face. "Burke!
I don't understand you!" she said, speaking
quickly and rather breathlessly, for her heart was
beating fast and hard. "Have you gone mad?"

"No, I am not mad," he said, and faintly smiled.

"I am just looking after our joint interests, that's all."

She opened her eyes wide. "Still I don't understand you," she said. "I thought you promised—I thought we agreed—that you were never to interfere with my liberty."

"Unless you abused it," said Burke.

She flinched a little in spite of herself, so uncompromising were both his tone and attitude. But in a moment she drew herself erect, facing him fearlessly.

"I don't think you know—quite—what you are saying to me," she said. "You are tired, and you are looking at things—all crooked. Will you please take a rest this afternoon? I am sure you need it. And to-night—" She paused a moment, for, her courage notwithstanding, she had begun to tremble—"to-night,"—she said again, and still paused, feeling his hand tighten upon her, feeling her heart quicken almost intolerably under its weight.

"Yes?" he said, his voice low, intensely quiet. "Please finish! What am I to do to-night?"

She faced him bravely, with all her strength. "I hope," she said, "you will come and tell me you are sorry."

He threw up his head with a sharp gesture. She

saw his eyes kindle and burn with a flame she dared not meet.

A swift misgiving assailed her. She tried to release herself, but he took her by the other shoulder also, holding her before him.

"And if I do all that," he said, a deep quiver in his voice that thrilled her through and through, "what shall I get in return? How shall I be rewarded?"

She gripped her self-control with a great effort, summoning that high courage of hers which had never before failed her.

She smiled straight up at him, a splendid, resolute smile. "You shall have—the kiss of peace," she said.

His expression changed. For a moment his hold became a grip that hurt her—bruised her. She closed her eyes with an involuntary catch of the breath, waiting, expecting she knew not what. Then, very suddenly, the strain was over. He set her free and turned from her.

"Thank you," he said, in a voice that sounded oddly strangled. "But I don't find that—especially satisfying—just now."

His hands were clenched as he left her. She did not dare to follow him or call him back.

PART III

CHAPTER I

THE NEW ERA

LOOKING back later, it almost seemed to Sylvia that the days that followed were as an interval between two acts in the play of life. It was a time of transition, though what was happening within her she scarcely realized.

One thing only did she fully recognize, and that was that the old frank comradeship between herself and Burke had come to an end. During all the anxiety of those days and the many fluctuations through which Guy passed, Burke came and went as an outsider, scarcely seeming to be interested in what passed, never interfering. He never spoke to Kieff unless circumstances compelled him, and with Sylvia herself he was so reticent as to be almost forbidding. Her mind was too full of Guy, too completely occupied with the great struggle for his life, to allow her thoughts to dwell very much upon any other subject. She saw that

Burke's physical wants were attended to, and
that was all that she had time for just then.   He
was sleeping in the spare hut which she had prepared for Guy with such tender care, and she was
quite satisfied as to his comfort there.   It came
to be something of a relief when every evening he
betook himself thither.   Though she never actually admitted it to herself, she was always more at
ease when he was out of the bungalow.

She and Kieff were fighting inch by inch to save
Guy, and she could not endure any distractions
while the struggle lasted.   For it was a desperate
fight, and there was little rest for either of them.
Her first sensation of repugnance for this man had
turned into a species of unwilling admiration.
His adroitness, his resource, the almost uncanny
power of his personality, compelled her to a curious allegiance.   She gave him implicit obedience,
well knowing that, though in all else they were
poles asunder, in this thing they were as one.
They were allied in the one great effort to defeat
the Destroyer.   They fought day and night,
shoulder to shoulder, never yielding, never
despairing, never slacking.

And very gradually at last the tide that had
ebbed so low began to turn.   Through bitter suffering, often against his will, Guy Ranger was

drawn slowly back again to the world he had so
nearly left. Kieff never let him suffer for long.
He gave him oblivion whenever the weakened endurance threatened to fail. And Sylvia, seeing
that the flickering strength was always greater
under the influence of Kieff's remedy, raised no
protest. They fought death with the weapon of
death. It would be time enough when the battle
was won to cast that weapon aside.

During those days of watching and conflict,
she held little converse with Guy. He was like a
child, content in his waking hours to have her
near him, and fretful if she were ever absent.
Under Kieff's guidance, she nursed him with unfailing care, developing a skill with which she had
never credited herself. As gradually his strength
returned, he would have her do everything for him,
resenting even Kieff's interference though never
actively resisting his authority. He seemed to
stand in awe of Kieff, Sylvia noticed, a feeling
from which she herself was not wholly free.
For there was a subtle mastery about him which
influenced her in spite of herself. But she
had put aside her instinctive dislike of the man
because of the debt she owed him. He had
brought Guy back, had wrenched him from
the very jaws of Death, and she would never

forget it.   He had saved her from a life-long sorrow.

And so, as slowly Guy returned, she schooled herself to subdue a certain distrust of him which was never wholly absent from her consciousness. She forced herself to treat him as a friend. She silenced the warning voice within her that had bade her so constantly beware. Perhaps her own physical endurance had begun to waver a little after the long strain. Undoubtedly his influence over her was such as it could scarcely have become under any other circumstances. Her long obedience to his will in the matter of Guy had brought her to a state of submission at which once she would have scoffed. And when at last, the worst of the battle over, she was overtaken by an over-powering weariness of mind and body, all things combined to place her at a hopeless disadvantage.

One day, after three weeks of strenuous nursing, she quitted Guy's room very suddenly to battle with a ghastly feeling of faintness which threatened to overwhelm her. Kieff, who had been present with Guy, followed her almost immediately to her own room, and found her with a deathly face groping against the wall as one stricken blind.

He took her firmly by the shoulders and forced

her down over the back of a chair, holding her so with somewhat callous strength of purpose, till with a half-hysterical gasp she begged him to set her free. The colour had returned to her face when she stood up, but those few moments of weakness had bereft her of her self-control. She could not restrain her tears.

Kieff showed no emotion of any sort. With professional calm, he put her down upon the bed, and stood over her, feeling her pulse.

"You want sleep," he said.

She turned her face away from him, ashamed of the weakness she could not hide. "Yes, I know. But I can't sleep. I'm always listening. I can't help it. My brain feels wound up. Sometimes— sometimes it feels as if it hurts me to shut my eyes."

"There's a remedy for that," said Kieff, and his hand went to his pocket.

She looked at him startled. "Oh, not that! Not that! I couldn't. It would be wrong."

"Not if I advise it," said Kieff, with a self-assurance that seemed to knock aside her resistance as of no account.

She knew she ought to have resisted further, but somehow she could not. His very impassivity served to make opposition impossible. It came to her that the inevitable was upon her, and whatever she said would make no difference. Moreover, she was too tired greatly to care.

She uttered a little cry when a few seconds later she felt the needle pierce her flesh, but she submitted without a struggle. After all, what did it matter for once? And she needed rest so much.

With a sigh she surrendered herself, and was amazed at the swift relief that came to her. It was like the rolling away of an immense weight, and immediately she seemed to float upwards, upwards, like a soaring bird.

Kieff remained by her side, but his presence did not trouble her. She was possessed by an ecstasy so marvellous that she had no room for any other emotion. She was as one borne on wings, ascending, ever ascending, through an atmosphere of transcendent gold.

Once he touched her forehead, and bringing his hand slowly downwards compelled her to close her eyes. A brief darkness came upon her, and she uttered a muffled protest. But when he lifted his hand again, her eyes did not open. The physical had fallen from her, material things had ceased to matter. She was free—free as the ether through which she floated. She was mounting upwards, upwards, upwards, through celestial

morning to her castle at the top of the world.
And the magic—the magic that beat in her veins—
was the very elixir of life within her, inspiring her,
uplifting her. For a space she hovered thus, still
mounting, but imperceptibly, caught as it were
between earth and heaven. Then the golden
glamour about her turned to a mystic haze.
Strange visions, but half comprehended, took
shape and dissolved before her. She believed that
she was floating among the mountain-crests with
the Infinite all about her. The wonder of it and
the rapture were beyond all utterance, beyond the
grasp of human knowledge; the joy exceeded all
that she had ever known. And so by exquisite
phases, she entered at last a great vastness—a
slumber-space where all things were forgotten,
lost in the radiance of an unbroken peace.

She folded the wings of her enchantment with
absolute contentment and slept. She had come to
a new era in her existence. She had reached the
top of the world. . . .

It was long, long after that she awoke, returning
to earth with the feeling of one revisiting old
haunts after half a lifetime. She was very tired,
and her head throbbed painfully, but at the back
of her brain was an urgent sense of something
needed, something that must be done. She

raised herself with immense effort,—and met the eyes of Burke seated by her side.

He was watching her with a grave, unstirring attention that did not waver for an instant as she moved. It struck her that there was a strange remoteness about him, almost as if he belonged to another world. Or was it she—she who had for a space overstepped the boundary and wandered awhile through the Unknown?

He spoke, and in his voice was a depth that awed her.

"Do you know me?" he said.

She gazed at him, bewildered, wondering. "But of course I know you! Why do you ask? Are you—changed in any way?"

He made an odd movement, as if the question in her wide eyes pierced him. He did not answer her in words; only after a moment he took her hand and pushed up the sleeve as though looking for something.

She lay passive for a few seconds, watching him. Then suddenly, blindly, she realized what was the object of his search. She made a quick, instinctive movement to frustrate him.

His hand tightened instantly upon hers; he pointed to a tiny mark upon the inside of her arm. "How did you get that?" he said.

His eyes looked straight into hers. There was something pitiless, something almost brutal, in their regard. In spite of herself she flinched, and lowered her own.

"Answer me!" he said.

She felt the hot colour rush in a guilty flood over her face. "It was only—for once," she faltered. "I wanted sleep, and I couldn't get it."

"Kieff gave it you," he said, his tone grimly insistent.

She nodded. "Yes. He meant well. He saw I was fagged out."

Burke was silent for a space, still grasping her hand. Her head was throbbing dizzily, but she would not lower it to the pillow again in his presence. She felt almost like a prisoner awaiting sentence.

"Did he give it you against your will?" he asked at length.

"Not altogether." Her voice was almost a whisper. Her heart was beating with hard, uneven strokes. She felt sick and faint.

Burke moved suddenly, releasing her hand. He rose with that decision characteristic of him and walked across the room. She heard the splash of water in a basin, and then he came back to her. As if she had been a child, he raised her to lean against him, and proceeded very quietly to bathe her face and head with ice-cold water.

She shrank at the chill of it, but he persisted in his task, and very soon she began to feel refreshed.

"Thank you," she murmured at last. "I am better now. I will get up."

"You had better lie still for the present," he said. "I will send you in some supper later."

His tone was repressive. She could not look him in the face. But, as he made as if he would rise, something impelled her to lay a detaining hand upon his arm.

"Please wait a minute!" she said.

He waited, and in a moment, with difficulty, she went on.

"Burke, I have done wrong, I know. I am sorry. Please don't be angry with me! I—can't bear it."

There was a catch in her voice that she could not restrain. She had a great longing to hide her face on his shoulder and burst into tears. But something—some inner, urgent warning—held her back.

Burke sat quite still. There was a touch of rigidity in his attitude. "All right," he said at last. "I am not angry—with you."

Her fingers closed upon his arm. "Please don't

quarrel with Dr. Kieff about it!" she said nervously. "It won't happen again."

She felt him stiffen still further at her words. "It certainly won't," he said briefly. "Tell me, have you got any of the infernal stuff by you?"

She glanced up at him, startled by the question. "Of course I haven't!" she said.

His eyes held a glitter that was almost bestial. She dropped her hand from his arm as if she had received an electric shock. He got up instantly.

"Very well. I will leave you now. You had better go to bed."

"I must see Guy first," she objected.

"I am attending to Guy," he said.

That opened her eyes. She started up, facing him, a sudden sharp misgiving at her heart. "Burke! You! Where—is Dr. Kieff?"

He uttered a grim, exultant sound that made her quiver. "He is on his way back to Ritzen— or Brennerstadt. He didn't mention which."

"Ah!" Her hands were tightly clasped upon her breast. "What—what have you done to him?" she panted.

Burke had risen to his feet. "I have—helped him on his way, that's all," he said.

She tried to stand up also, but the moment she touched the ground, she reeled. He caught her, and held her, facing him. His eyes shone with a glow as of molten metal.

"Do you think," he said, breathing deeply, "that I would suffer that accursed fiend to drag my wife—my wife—down into that infernal slough?"

She was trembling from head to foot; her knees doubled under her, but he held her up. The barely repressed violence of his speech was perceptible in his hold also. She had no strength to meet it.

"But what of Guy?" she whispered voicelessly. "He will die!"

"Guy!" he said, and in the word there was a bitterness indescribable. "Is he to be weighed in the balance against you?"

She was powerless to reason with him, and perhaps it was as well for her that this was so, for he was in no mood to endure opposition. His wrath seemed to beat about her like a storm-blast. But yet he held her up, and after a moment, seeing her weakness, he softened somewhat.

"There! Lie down again!" he said, and lowered her to the bed. "I'll see to Guy. Only remember," he stooped over her, and to her strained senses he loomed gigantic, "if you ever touch that stuff again, my faith in you will be gone.

And where there is no trust, you can't expect—honour."

The words seemed to pierce her, but he straightened himself the moment after and turned to go.

She covered her face with her hands as the door closed upon him. She felt as if she had entered upon a new era, indeed, and she feared with a dread unspeakable to look upon the path which lay before her.

CHAPTER II

INTO BATTLE

WHEN Sylvia saw Guy again, he greeted her with an odd expression in his dark eyes, half-humorous, half-speculative. He was lying propped on pillows by the open window, a cigarette and a box of matches by his side.

"Hullo, Sylvia!" he said. "You can come in. The big *baas* has set his house in order and gone out."

The early morning sunshine was streaming across his bed. She thought he looked wonderfully better, and marvelled at the change.

He smiled at her as she drew near. "Yes, I've been washed and fed and generally made respectable. Thank goodness that brute Kieff has gone anyway! I couldn't have endured him much longer. What was the grand offence? Did he make love to you or what?"

"Make love to me! Of course not!" Sylvia flushed indignantly at the suggestion.

Guy laughed; he seemed in excellent spirits.

284

"He'd better not, what? But the big *baas* was very angry with him, I can tell you. And I can't think it was on my account. I'm inoffensive enough, heavens knows."

He reached up a hand as she stood beside him, and took and held hers.

"You're a dear girl, Sylvia," he said. "Just the very sight of you does me good. You're not sorry Kieff has gone?"

"Sorry! No!" She looked down at him with doubt in her eyes. "Only—we owe him a good deal, remember. He saved your life."

"Oh, that!" said Guy lightly. "You may set your mind quite at rest on that score, my dear. He wouldn't have done it if he hadn't felt like it. He pleases himself in all he does. But I should like to have witnessed his exit last night. That, I imagine, was more satisfactory from Burke's point of view than from his. He—Burke—came back with that smile-on-the-face-of-the-tiger expression of his. You've seen it, I daresay. It was very much in evidence last night."

Sylvia repressed a sudden shiver. "Oh, Guy! What do you think happened?"

He gave her hand a sudden squeeze. "Nothing to worry about, I do assure you. He's a devil of a fellow when he's roused, isn't he? But—so far as my knowledge goes—he's never killed anyone yet. Sit down, old girl, and let's have a smoke together! I'm allowed just one to-day—as a reward for good behaviour."

"Are you being good?" said Sylvia.

Guy closed one eye. "Oh, I'm a positive saint to-day. I've promised—almost—never to be naughty again. Do you know Burke slept on the floor in here last night? Decent of him, wasn't it?"

Sylvia glanced swiftly round. "Did he? How uncomfortable for him! He mustn't do that again."

"He didn't notice," Guy assured her. "He was much too pleased with himself. I rather like him for that, you know. He has a wonderful faculty for—what shall we call it?—mental detachment? Or, is it physical? Anyway, he knows how to enjoy his emotions, whatever they are, and he doesn't let any little personal discomfort stand in his way."

He ended with a careless laugh from which all bitterness was absent, and after a little pause Sylvia sat down by his side. His whole attitude amazed her this morning. Some magic had been at work. The fretful misery of the past few weeks had passed like a cloud. This was her own Guy come back to her, clean, sane, with the boyish humour that she had always loved in him, and the old quick light of understanding and sympathy in his eyes.

He watched her with a smile. "Aren't you going to light up, too? Come, you'd better. It'll tone you up."

She looked back at him. "Had you better smoke?" she said. "Won't it start your cough?"

He lifted an imperious hand. "It won't kill me if it does. Why are you looking at me like that?"

"Like what?" she said.

"As if I'd come back from the dead." He frowned at her abruptly though his eyes still smiled. "Don't!" he said.

She smiled in answer, and picked up the matchbox. It was of silver and bore his initials.

"Yes," Guy said. "I've taken great care of it, haven't I? It's been my mascot all these years."

She took out a match and struck it without speaking. There was something poignant in her silence. She was standing again in the wintry dark of her father's park, pressed close to Guy's heart, and begging him brokenly to use that little parting gift of hers with thoughts of her when more than half the word lay between them. Guy's cigarette was in his mouth. She stooped forward to light it. Her hand was trembling. In a moment he reached up, patted it lightly, and took the match from her fingers. The action said more than words. It was as if he had gently turned a page in the book of life, and bade her not to look back.

"Now don't you bother about me!" he said. "I'm being good—as you see. So go and cook the dinner or do anything else that appeals to your housekeeper's soul! That is, if you feel it's immoral to smoke a cigarette at this early hour. Needless to say, I shall be charmed if you will join me."

But he did not mean to talk upon intimate subjects, and his tone conveyed as much. She lingered for a while, and they spoke of the farm, the cattle, Burke's prospects, everything under the sun save personal matters. Yet there was no barrier in their reserve. They avoided these by tacit consent.

In the end she left him, feeling strangely comforted. Burke had been right. The devil had gone out of Guy, and he had come back.

She pondered the matter as she went about her various tasks, but she found no solution thereof. Something must have happened to cause the change in him; she could not believe that Kieff's departure had effected it. Her thoughts went involuntarily to Burke—Burke whose wrath had been so terrible the previous night. Was it due to him? Had he accomplished what neither Kieff's skill nor her devotion had been able to achieve? Yet he had spoken of Guy as one of his failures. He had impressed upon her the fact that Guy's case was hopeless. She had even been convinced of it herself until to-day. But to-day all things were changed. Guy had come back.

The thought of her next meeting with Burke tormented her continually, checking all gladness. She dreaded it unspeakably, listening for him with nerves on edge during the busy hours that followed.

She made the Kaffir boy bring the camp-bed out of the guest-hut which Burke had occupied of late and set it up in a corner of Guy's room. Kieff had slept on a long-chair in the sitting-room, taking his rest at odd times and never for any prolonged spell. She had even wondered sometimes if he ever really slept at all, so alert had he been at the slightest sound. But she knew that Burke hated the long-chair because it creaked at every movement, and she was determined that he should not spend another night on the floor. So, while with trepidation she awaited him, she made such preparations as she could for his comfort.

Joe, the house-boy, was very clumsy in all his ways, and Guy, looking on, seemed to derive considerable amusement from his performance. "I always did like Joe," he remarked. "There's something about his mechanism that is irresistibly comic. Oh, do leave him alone, Sylvia! Let him arrange the thing upside down if he wants to!"

Joe's futility certainly had something of the comic order about it. He had a dramatic fashion of rolling his eyes when expectant of rebuke, which was by no means seldom. And the vastness of his smile was almost bewildering. Sylvia had never been able quite to accustom herself to his smile.

"He's exactly like a golliwog, isn't he?" said Guy. "His head will split in two if you encourage him."

But Sylvia, hot and anxious, found it impossible to view Joe's exhibition with enjoyment. He was more stupid in the execution of her behests than she had ever found him before, and at length, losing patience, she dismissed him and proceeded to erect the bed herself.

She was in the midst of this when there came the sound of a step in the room, and Guy's quick,

"Hullo!" told her of the entrance of a third person. She stood up sharply, and met Burke face to face.

She was panting a little from her exertions, and her hand went to her side. For the moment a horrible feeling of discomfiture overwhelmed her. His look was so direct; it seemed to go straight through her.

"What is this for?" he said.

She mastered her embarrassment with a swift effort. "Guy said you slept on the floor last night. I am sure it wasn't very comfortable, so I have brought this in instead. You don't mind?" with a glance at him that held something of appeal.

"I mind you putting it up yourself," he said briefly. "Sit down! Where's that lazy hound, Joe?"

"Oh, don't call Joe!" Guy begged. "He has already reduced her to exasperation. She won't listen to me either when I tell her that I can look after myself at night. You tell her, Burke! She'll listen to you perhaps."

But Burke ended the matter without further discussion by putting her on one side and finishing the job himself. Then he stood up.

"Let Mary Ann do the rest! You have been

working too hard. Come and have some lunch!
You'll be all right, Guy?"

"Oh, quite," Guy assured him. "Mary Ann
can take care of me. She'll enjoy it."

Sylvia looked back at him over her shoulder as
she went out, but she did not linger. There was
something imperious about Burke just then.

They entered the sitting-room together. "Look
here!" he said. "You're not to tire yourself out.
Guy is convalescent now. Let him look after
himself for a bit!"

"I haven't been doing anything for Guy," she
objected. "Only I can't have you sleeping on the
floor."

"What's it matter," he said gruffly, "where or
how I sleep?" And then suddenly he took her by
the shoulders and held her before him. "Just
look at me a moment!" he said.

It was a definite command. She lifted her eyes,
but the instant they met his that overwhelming
confusion came upon her again. His gaze was so
intent, so searching. All her defences seemed to
go down before it.

Her lip suddenly quivered, and she turned her
face aside. "Be—kind to me, Burke!" she said,
under her breath.

He let her go; but he stood motionless for some

seconds after as if debating some point with himself. She went to the window and nervously straightened the curtain. After a considerable pause his voice came to her there.

"I want you to rest this afternoon, and ride over with me to the Merstons after tea. Will you do that?"

She turned sharply. "And leave Guy? Oh, no!"

Across the room she met his look, and she saw that he meant to have his way. "I wish it," he said.

She came slowly back to him. "Burke,—please! I can't do that. It wouldn't be right. We can't leave Guy to the Kaffirs."

"Guy can look after himself," he reiterated. "You have done enough—too much—in that line already. He doesn't need you with him all day long."

She shook her head. "I thinks he needs—someone. It wouldn't be right—I know it wouldn't be right to leave him quite alone. Besides, the Merstons won't want me. Why should I go?"

"Because I wish it," he said again. And, after a moment, as she stood silent, "Doesn't that count with you?"

She looked up at him quickly, caught by something in his tone, "Of course your wishes count with me!" she said. "You know they do. But all the same—" She paused, searching for words.

"Guy comes first," he suggested, in the casual voice of one stating an acknowledged fact.

She felt the hot colour rise to her temples. "Oh, it isn't fair of you to say that!" she said.

"Isn't it true?" said Burke.

She collected herself to answer him. "It is only because his need has been so great. If we had not put him first—before everything else—we should never have saved him."

"And now that he is saved," Burke said, a faint ring of irony in his voice, "isn't it almost time to begin to consider—other needs? Do you know you are looking very ill?"

He asked the question abruptly, so abruptly that she started. Her nerves were on edge that day.

"Am I? No, I didn't know. It isn't serious anyway. Please don't bother about that!"

He smiled faintly. "I've got to bother. If you don't improve very quickly, I shall take you to Brennerstadt to see a decent doctor there."

"Oh, don't be absurd!" she said, with quick annoyance. "I'm not going to do anything so silly."

He put his hand on her arm. "Sylvia, I've got something to say to you," he said.

She made a slight movement as if his touch were unwelcome. "Well? What is it?" she said.

"Only this." He spoke very steadily, but while he spoke his hand closed upon her. "You've gone your own way so far, and it hasn't been specially good for you. That's why I'm going to pull you up now, and make you go mine."

"Make me!" Her eyes flashed sudden fire upon him. She was overwrought and weary, and he had taken her by surprise, or she would have dealt with the situation—and with him—far otherwise. "Make me!" she repeated, and in second, almost before she knew it, she was up in arms, facing him with open rebellion. "I'll defy you to do that!" she said.

The moment she had said it, the word still scarcely uttered, she repented. She had not meant to defy him. The whole thing had come about so swiftly, so unexpectedly, hardly, she felt, of her own volition. And now, more than half against her will, she stood committed to carry through an undertaking for which even at the outset, she had no heart. For there was no turning back. The challenge, once uttered, could not be withdrawn. She was no coward. The idea came to her that if she blenched then she would for all time forfeit his respect as well as her own.

So she stood her ground, slim and upright, braced to defiance, though at the back of all her bravery there lurked a sickening fear.

Burke did not speak at once. His look scarcely altered, his hold upon her remained perfectly steady and temperate. Yet in the pause the beating of her heart rose between them—a hard, insistent throbbing like the fleeing feet of a hunted thing.

"You really mean that?" he asked at length.

"Yes." Straight and unhesitating came her answer. It was now or never, she told herself. But she was trembling, despite her utmost effort.

He bent a little, looking into her eyes. "You really wish me to show you who is master?" he said.

She met his look, but her heart was beating wildly, spasmodically. There was that about him, a ruthlessness, a deadly intention, that appalled her. The ground seemed to be rocking under her feet, and a dreadful consciousness of sheer, physical weakness rushed upon her. She went back against the table, seeking for support.

But through it all, desperately she made her gallant struggle for freedom. "You will never

master me against my will," she said. "I—I—
I'll die first!"

And then, as the last shred of her strength went
from her she covered her face with her hands,
shutting him out.

"Ah!" he said. "But who goes into battle
without first counting the cost?"

He spoke sombrely, without anger; yet in the
very utterance of the words there was that which
made her realize that she was beaten. Whether
he chose to avail himself of the advantage or not,
the victory was his.

At the end of a long silence, she lifted her head.
"I give you best, partner," she said, and held out
her hand to him with a difficult smile. "I'd no
right—to kick over the traces—like that. I'm
going to be good now—really."

It was a frank acceptance of defeat; so frank
as to be utterly disarming. He took the proffered
hand and held it closely, without speaking.

She was still trembling a little, but she had re-
gained her self-command. "I'm sorry I was such
a little beast," she said. "But you've got me
beat. I'll try and make good somehow."

He found his voice at that. It came with an odd
harshness. "Don't!" he said. "Don't!—You're
not—beat. The battle isn't always to the strong."

She laughed faintly with more assurance, though still somewhat shakily. "Not when the strong are too generous to take advantage, perhaps. Thank you for that, partner. Now—do you mind if I take Guy his nourishment?"

She put the matter behind her with that inimitable lightness of hers which of late she had seemed to have lost. She went from him to wait upon Guy with the tremulous laugh upon her lips, and when she returned she had fully recovered her self-control, and talked with him upon many matters connected with the farm which he had not heard her mention during all the period of her nursing. She displayed all her old zest. She spoke as one keenly interested. But behind it all was a feverish unrest, a nameless, intangible quality that had never characterized her in former days. She was elusive. Her old delicate confidence in him was absent. She walked warily where once she had trodden without the faintest hesitation.

When the meal was over, she checked him as he was on the point of going to Guy. "How soon ought we to start for the Merstons?" she asked.

He paused a moment. Then, "I will let you off to-day," he said. "We will ride out to the *kopje* instead."

He thought she would hail this concession with

relief, but she shook her head instantly, her face deeply flushed.

"No, I think not! We will go to the Merstons —if Guy is well enough. We really ought to go."

She baffled him completely. He turned away. "As you will," he said. "We ought to start in two hours."

"I shall be ready," said Sylvia.

CHAPTER III

THE SEED

"WELL!" said Mrs. Merston, with her thin smile. "Are you still enjoying the Garden of Eden, Mrs. Ranger?"

Sylvia, white and tired after her ride, tried to smile in answer and failed. "I shall be glad when the winter is over," she said.

Mrs. Merston's colourless eyes narrowed a little, taking her in. "You don't look so blooming as you did," she remarked. "I hear you have had Guy Ranger on your hands."

"Yes," Sylvia said, and coloured a little in spite of herself.

"What has been the matter with him?" demanded Mrs. Merston.

Sylvia hesitated, and in a moment the older woman broke into a grating laugh.

"Oh, you needn't trouble to dress it up in polite language. I know the malady he suffers from. But I wonder Burke would allow you to have anything to do with it. He has a reputation for being rather particular."

"He is particular," Sylvia said.

Somehow she could not bring herself to tell Mrs. Merston the actual cause of Guy's illness. She did not want to talk of it. But Mrs. Merston was difficult to silence.

"Is it true that that scroundrel Kieff has been staying at Blue Hill Farm?" she asked next, still closely observant of her visitor's face.

Sylvia looked at her with a touch of animation. "I wonder why everyone calls him that," she said. "Yes, he has been with us. He is a doctor, a very clever one. I never liked him very much, but I often wondered what he had done to be called that."

"Oh, I only know what they say," said Mrs. Merston. "I imagine he was in a large measure responsible for young Ranger's fall from virtue in the first place—and that of a good many besides. He's something of a vampire, so they say. There are plenty of them about in this charming country."

"How horrible!" murmured Sylvia, with a slight shudder as a vision of the motionless, onyx eyes which had so often watched her rose in her mind.

"You're looking quite worn out," remarked Mrs. Merston. "Why did you let your husband drag you over here? You had better stay the night and have a rest."

But Sylvia hastened to decline this invitation with much decision. "I couldn't possibly do that, thank you. There is so much to be seen to at home. It is very kind of you, but please don't suggest it to Burke!"

Mrs. Merston gave her an odd look. "Do you always do as your husband tells you!" she said. "What a mistake!"

Sylvia blushed very deeply. "I think—one ought," she said in a low voice.

"How old-fashioned of you!" said Mrs. Merston. "I don't indulge mine to that extent. Are you going to Brennerstadt for the races next month? Or has the oracle decreed that you are to stay behind?"

"I don't know. I didn't know there were any." Sylvia looked out through the mauve-coloured twilight to where Burke stood talking with Merston by one of the hideous corrugated iron cattle-sheds. The Merstons' farm certainly did not compare favourably with Burke's. She could not actively condemn Mrs. Merston's obvious distaste for all that life held for her. So far as

she could see, there was not a tree on the place,
only the horrible prickly pear bushes thrusting
out their distorted arms as if exulting in their own
nakedness.

They had had their tea in front of the bungalow,
if it could be dignified by such a name. It was
certainly scarcely more than an iron shed, and the
heat within during the day was, she could well
imagine, almost unbearable. It was time to be
starting back, and she wished Burke would come.
Her hostess's scoffing reference to him made her
long to get away. Politeness, however, forbade
her summarily to drop the subject just started.

"Do you go to Brennerstadt for the races?"
she asked.

"I?" said Mrs. Merston, and laughed again her
caustic, mirthless laugh. "No! My acquaintance
with Brennerstadt is of a less amusing nature.
When I go there, I merely go to be ill, and as soon
as I am partially recovered, I come back—to
this." There was inexpressible bitterness in her
voice. "Some day," she said, "I shall go there
to die. That is all I have to look forward to
now."

"Oh, don't!" Sylvia said, with quick feeling.
"Don't, please! You shouldn't feel like that."

Mrs. Merston's face was twisted in a painful

smile. She looked into the girl's face with a kind
of cynical pity. "You will come to it," she said.
"Life isn't what it was to you even now. You're
beginning to feel the thorns under the rose-leaves.
Of course you may be lucky. You may bear
children, and that will be your salvation. But
if you don't—if you don't——"

"Please!" whispered Sylvia. "Please don't
say that to me!"

The words were almost inarticulate. She got
up as she uttered them and moved away. Mrs.
Merston looked after her, and very strangely her
face altered. Something of that mother-love in
her which had so long been cheated showed in her
lustreless eyes.

"Oh, poor child!" she said. "I am sorry."

It was briefly spoken. She was ever brief in her
rare moments of emotion. But there was a throb
of feeling in the words that reached Sylvia. She
turned impulsively back again.

"Thank you," she said, and there were tears in
her eyes as she spoke. "I think perhaps—" her
utterance came with an effort "—my life is—in
its way—almost as difficult as yours. That ought
to make us comrades, oughtn't it? If ever there
is anything I can do to help you, please tell
me!"

"Let it be a mutual understanding!" said Mrs. Merston, and to Sylvia's surprise she took and pressed her hand for a moment.

There was more comfort in that simple pressure than Sylvia could have believed possible. She returned it with that quick warmth of hers which never failed to respond to kindness, and in that second the seed of friendship was sown upon fruitful ground.

The moment passed, sped by Mrs. Merston who seemed half-afraid of her own action.

"You must get your husband to take you to Brennerstadt for the races," she said. "It would make a change for you. It's a shame for a girl of your age to be buried in the wilderness."

"I really haven't begun to be dull yet," Sylvia said.

"No, perhaps not. But you'll get nervy and unhappy. You've been used to society, and it isn't good for you to go without it entirely. Look at me!" said Mrs. Merston, with her short laugh. "And take warning!"

The two men were sauntering towards them, and they moved to meet them. Far down in the east an almost unbelievably huge moon hung like a brazen shield. The mauve of the sunset had faded to pearl.

"It is rather a beautiful world, isn't it?" Sylvia said a little wistfully.

"To the favoured few—yes," said Mrs. Merston.

Sylvia gave her a quick glance. "I read somewhere—I don't know if it's true—that we are all given the ingredients of happiness, but the mixing is left to ourselves. Perhaps you and I haven't found the right mixture yet."

"Ah!" said Mrs. Merston. "Perhaps not."

"I'm going to have another try," said Sylvia, with sudden energy.

"I wish you luck," said Mrs. Merston somewhat grimly.

CHAPTER IV

MIRAGE

FROM the day of her visit to the Merstons
Sylvia took up her old life again, and pursued all
her old vocations with a vigour that seemed even
more enthusiastic than of yore. Her ministrations
to Guy had ceased to be of an arduous character,
or indeed to occupy much of her time. It was
mainly Burke who filled Kieff's place and looked
after Guy generally with a quiet efficiency that
never encouraged any indulgence. They seemed
to be good friends, yet Sylvia often wondered with
a dull ache at the heart if this were any more than
seeming. There was so slight a show of intimacy
between them, so little of that *camaraderie* generally so noticeable between dwellers in the wilderness. Sometimes she fancied she caught a mocking
light in Guy's eyes when they looked at Burke.
He was always perfectly docile under his management, but was he always genuine? She could not
tell. His recovery amazed her. He seemed to
possess an almost boundless store of vitality. He

cast his weakness from him with careless jesting,
laughing down all her fears.   She knew well that
he was not so strong as he would have had her
believe, that he fought down his demon of suffering in solitude, that often he paid heavily for deeds
of recklessness.   But the fact remained that he
had come back from the gates of death, and each
day she marvelled anew.

She and Burke seldom spoke of him when together.   That intangible reserve that had grown
up between them seemed to make it impossible.
She had no longer the faintest idea as to Burke's
opinion of the returned prodigal, whether he still
entertained his previous conviction that Guy was
beyond help, or whether he had begun at length
to have any confidence for the future.   In a vague
fashion his reticence hurt her, but she could not
bring herself to attempt to break through it.   He
was a man perpetually watching for something,
and it made her uneasy and doubtful, though for
what he watched she had no notion.   For it was
upon herself rather than upon Guy that his attention seemed to be concentrated.   His attitude
puzzled her.   She felt curiously like a prisoner,
though to neither word, nor look, nor deed could
she ascribe the feeling.   She was even at times
disposed to put it down to the effect of the weather

upon her physically. It did undoubtedly try her
very severely. Though the exercise that she
compelled herself to take had restored to her the
power to sleep, she always felt as weary when she
arose as when she lay down. The heat and the
drought combined to wear her out. Valiantly
though she struggled to rally her flagging energies,
the effort became increasingly difficult. She
lived in the depths of a great depression, against
which, strive as she might, she ever strove in vain.
She was furious with herself for her failure, but it
pursued her relentlessly. She found the Kaffir
servants more than usually idle and difficult to deal
with, and this added yet further to the burden
that weighed her down.

One day, returning from a ride to find Fair
Rosamond swabbing the floor of the *stoep* with her
bath-sponge, she lost her temper completely and
wholly unexpectedly, and cut the girl across her
naked shoulders with her riding-switch. It was
done in a moment—a single, desperate moment of
unbearable exasperation. Rosamond screamed
and fled, upsetting her pail inadvertently over
her mistress's feet as she went. And Sylvia, with
a burning sense of shame for her violence, retreated
as precipitately to her own room.

She entered by the window, and, not even notic-

ing that the door into the sitting-room stood ajar,
flung herself down by the table in a convulsion of
tears. She hated herself for her action, she hated
Rosamond for having been the cause of it. She
hated the blazing sky and the parched earth, the
barren *veldt*, the imprisoning *kopjes*, the hopeless
sense of oppression, of being always somehow in
the wrong. A wild longing to escape was upon
her, to go anywhere—anywhere, so long as she
could get right away from that intolerable weight
of misgiving, doubt, dissatisfaction, foreboding,
that hung like a galling chain upon her.

She was getting like Mrs. Merston, she told herself passionately. Already her youth had gone,
and all that made life worth living was going with
it. She had made her desperate bid for happiness, and she had lost. And Burke—Burke was
only watching for her hour of weakness to make
himself even more completely her master than he
was already. Had he not only that morning—
only that morning—gruffly ordered her back from
a distant cattle-run that she had desired to in-
spect? Was he not always asserting his authority
in some fashion over her, crumbling away her
resistance piece by piece till at last he could stride
in all-conquering and take possession? He was
always so strong, so horribly strong, so sure of

himself. And though it had pleased him to be
generous in his dealings with her, she had seen far
less of that generosity since Guy's recovery. They
were partners no longer, she told herself bitterly.
That farce was ended. Perhaps it was her own
fault. Everything seemed to be her fault nowa-
days. She had not played her cards well during
Guy's illness. Somehow she had not felt a free
agent. It was Kieff who had played the cards,
had involved her in such difficulties as she had
never before encountered, and then had left her
perforce to extricate herself alone; to extricate herself—or to pay the price. She seemed to have
been struggling against overwhelming odds ever
since. She had fought with all her strength to
win back to the old freedom, but she had failed.
And in that dark hour she told herself that freedom was not for her. She was destined to be a
slave for the rest of her life.

The wild paroxysm of crying could not last.
Already she was beginning to be ashamed of her
weakness. And ere long she would have to face
Burke. The thought of that steady, probing
look made her shrink in every fibre. Was there
anything that those shrewd eyes did not see?

What was that? She started at a sound.
Surely he had not returned so soon!

For a second there was something very like panic at her heart. Then, bracing herself, she lifted her head, and saw Guy.

He had entered by the sitting-room door and in his slippers she had not heard him till he was close to her. He was already bending over her when she realized his presence.

She put up a quick hand. "Oh, Guy!" she said with a gasp.

He caught and held it in swift response. "My own girl!" he said. "I heard you crying. I was in my room dressing. What's it all about?"

She could not tell him, the anguish was still too near. She bowed her head and sat in throbbing silence.

"Look here!" said Guy. "Don't!" He stooped lower over her, his dark face twitching. "Don't!" he said again. "Life isn't worth it. Life's too short. Be happy, dear! Be happy!"

He spoke a few words softly against her hair. There was entreaty in their utterance. It was as if he pleaded for his own self.

She made a little movement as if something had pierced her, and in a moment she found her voice.

"Life is so—difficult," she said, with a sob.

"You take it too hard," he answered rapidly. "You think too much of—little things. It isn't

the way to be happy. What you ought to do is to
grab the big things while you can, and chuck the
little ones into the gutter. Life's nothing but a
farce. It isn't meant to be taken—really seriously. It isn't long enough for sacrifice. I tell
you, it isn't long enough!"

There was something passionate in the reiterated
declaration. The clasp of his hand was feverish.
That strange vitality of his that had made him
defy the death he had courted seemed to vibrate within him like a stretched wire. His attitude was tense
with it. And a curious thrill went through her, as
though there were electricity in his touch.

She could not argue the matter with him though
every instinct told her he was wrong. She was
too overwrought to see things with an impartial
eye. She felt too tired greatly to care.

"I feel," she told him drearily, "as if I want to
get away from everything and everybody."

"Oh no, you don't!" he said. "All you want
is to get away from Burke. That's your trouble—
and always will be under present conditions. Do
you think I haven't looked on long enough? Why
don't you go away?"

"Go away!" She looked up at him again,
startled.

Guy's sunken eyes were shining with a fierce

intensity.   They urged her more poignantly than words. "Don't you see what's going to happen —if you don't?" he said.

That moved her.   She sprang up with a sound that was almost a cry, and stood facing him, her hand hard pressed against her heart.

"Of course I know he's a wonderful chap and all that," Guy went on. "But you haven't cheated yourself yet into believing that you care for him, have you?   He isn't the sort to attract any woman at first sight, and I'll wager he has never made love to you.   He's far too busy with his cattle and his crops.   What on earth did you marry him for?   Can't you see that he makes a slave of everyone who comes near him?"

But she lifted her head proudly at that.   "He has never made a slave of me," she said.

"He will," Guy rejoined relentlessly.   "He'll have you under his heel before many weeks.   You know it in your heart.   Why did you marry him, Sylvia?   Tell me why you married him!"

The insistence of the question compelled an answer.   Yet she paused, for it was a question she had never asked herself.   Why had she married Burke indeed?   Had it been out of sheer expediency?   Or had there been some deeper and more subtle reason?   She knew full well that there was probably not another man in Africa to whom she would have thus entrusted herself, however urgent the circumstances. How was it then that she had accepted Burke?

And then, looking into Guy's tense face, the answer came to her, and she had uttered it almost before she knew. "I married him because he was so like you."

The moment she had uttered the words she would have recalled them, for Guy made an abrupt movement and turned so white that she thought he would faint. His eyes went beyond her with a strained, glassy look, and for seconds he stood so, as one gone suddenly blind.

Then with a jerk he pulled himself together, and gave her an odd smile that somehow cut her to the heart.

"That was a straight hit anyway," he said. "And are you going to stick to him for the same reason?"

She turned her face away with the feeling of one who dreads to look upon some grievous hurt. "No," she said, in a low voice. "Only because— I am his wife."

Guy made a short, contemptuous sound. "And for that you're going to let him ride rough-shod over you—give him the right to control your every movement? Oh, forgive me, but you good people hold such ghastly ideas of right and wrong. And what on earth do you gain by it all? You sacrifice everything to the future, and the future is all mirage—all mirage. You'll never get there, never as long as you live."

Again that quick note of passion was in his voice, and she tingled at the sound, for though she knew so well that he was wrong something that was quick and passionate within her made instinctive response. She understood him. Had she not always understood him?

She did not answer him. She had given him her answer. And he, realizing this, turned aside to open the window. Yet, for a moment he stood looking back at her, and all her life she was to remember the love and the longing of his eyes. It was as if for that second a veil had been rent aside, and he had shown her his naked soul.

She wondered afterwards if he had really meant her to see. For immediately, as he went out, he broke into a careless whistle, and then, an instant later, she heard him fling a greeting to someone out in the blinding sunshine.

An answer came back from much nearer than she had anticipated. It was in the guttural tones of Hans Schafen the overseer, and with a jerk she remembered that the man always sat on the corner of the *stoep* to await Burke if he arrived before their return from the lands. It was his custom to wear rubber soles to his boots, and no one ever heard him come or go. For some reason this fact had always prejudiced her against Hans Schafen.

CHAPTER V

EVERYBODY'S FRIEND

WHEN Burke came in to lunch half an hour later, he found Sylvia alone in the sitting-room, laying the cloth.

She glanced up somewhat nervously at his entrance. "I've frightened Rosamond away," she said.

"Little cuss! Good thing too!" he said.

She proceeded rapidly with her occupation. "I believe there's a sand-storm coming," she said, after a moment.

"Yes, confound it!" said Burke.

He went to the window and stood gazing out with drawn rows.

With an effort she broke the silence. "What has Schafen to report? Is all well?"

He wheeled round abruptly and stood looking at her. For a few seconds he said nothing whatever, then as with a startled sense of uncertainty she turned towards him he spoke. "Schafen? Yes, he reported—several things. The dam over by Ritter Spruit is dried up for one thing. The animals will all have to be driven down here. Then there have been several bad *veldt*-fires over to the north. It isn't only sand that's coming along. It's cinders too. We've got to take steps to protect the fodder, or we're done. It's just the way of this country. A single night may bring ruin."

He spoke with such unwonted bitterness that Sylvia was aroused out of her own depression. She had never known him take so pessimistic a view before. With an impulsiveness that was warm and very womanly, she left her task and went to him.

"Oh, Burke!" she said. "But the worst doesn't happen, does it? Anyway not often!"

He made an odd sound that was like a laugh choked at birth. "Not often," he agreed. And then abruptly, straightening himself, "Suppose it did,—what then?"

"What then?" She looked at him for a moment, still feeling curiously unsure of her ground. "Well, we'd weather it somehow, partner," she said, and held out her hand to him with a little quivering smile.

He made no movement to take her hand. Perhaps he had already heard what a few seconds later reached her own ears,—the sound of Guy's feet upon the *stoep* outside the window.   But during those seconds his eyes dwelt upon her, holding her own with a fixed intentness that somehow made her feel cold.   It was an unspeakable relief to her when he turned them from her, as it were setting her free.

Guy came in with something of his old free swing, and closed the window behind him.   "Better to stew than to eat sand," he remarked.   "I've just heard from one of the Kaffirs that Piet Vreiboom's land is on fire."

"What?" said Burke sharply.

"It's all right at present," said Guy.   "We can bear it with equanimity.   The wind is the other way."

"The wind may change," said Burke.

"That wouldn't be like your luck," remarked Guy, as he seated himself.

They partook of the meal almost in silence.   To Sylvia the very air was laden with foreboding. Everything they ate was finely powered with sand, but she alone was apparently aware of the fact. The heat inside the bungalow was intense.   Outside a fierce wind had begun to blow, and the sky was dark.

At the end of a very few minutes Burke arose. Guy sprang instantly to his feet.

"Are you off? I'm coming!"

"No—no," Burke said shortly. "Stay where you are!"

"I tell you I'm coming," said Guy, pushing aside his chair.

Burke, already at the door, paused and looked at him. "Better not," he said. "You're not up to it—and this infernal sand——"

"Damn the sand!" said Guy, with vehemence. "I'm coming!"

He reached Burke with the words. His hand sought the door. Burke swallowed the rest of his remonstrance.

"Please yourself!" he said, with a shadowy smile; and then for a moment his eyes went to Sylvia. "You will stay in this afternoon," he said.

It was a definite command, and she had no thought of defying it. But the tone in which it was uttered hurt her.

"I suppose I shall do as I am told," she said, in a low voice.

He let Guy go and returned to her. He bent swiftly down over her and dropped a small key into her lap. "I leave you in charge of all that I possess," he said. "Good-bye!"

She looked up at him quickly. "Burke!" she stammered. "Burke! There is no—danger?"

"Probably not of the sort you mean," he answered. And then suddenly his arms were round her. He held her close and hard. For a second she felt the strong beat of his heart, and then forgot it in an overwhelming rush of emotion that so possessed her as almost to deprive her of her senses. For he kissed her—he kissed her—and his kiss was as the branding of a hot iron. It seemed to burn her to the soul.

The next moment she was free; the door closed behind him, and she was alone. She sank down over the table, quivering all over. Her pulses were racing, her nerves in a wild tumult. She believed that the memory of that scorching kiss would tingle upon her lips for ever. It was as if an electric current had suddenly entered her innermost being and now ran riot in every vein. And so wild was the tumult within her that she knew not whether dread or dismay or a frantic, surging, leaping thing that seemed to cry aloud for liberty were first in that mad race. She clasped her hands very tightly over her face, struggling to master those inner forces that fought within her. Never in her life had so fierce a conflict torn her. Soul and body, she seemed to be striving with an adversary who pierced her at every turn. He had kissed her thus; and in that unutterable moment he had opened her eyes, confronting her with an amazing truth from which she could not turn aside. Passion and a fierce and terrible jealousy had mingled in his kiss, anger also, and a menacing resentment that seemed to encompass her like a fiery ring, hedging her round.

But not love! There had been no love in his kiss. It had been an outrage of love, and it had wounded her to the heart. It had made her want to hide—to hide—till the first poignancy of the pain should be past. And yet—and yet—in all her anguish she knew that the way which Guy had so recklessly suggested was no way of escape for her. To flee from him was to court disaster— such disaster as would for ever wreck her chance of happiness It could but confirm the evil doubt he harboured and might lead to such a catastrophe as she would not even contemplate.

But yet some way of escape there must be, and desperately she sought it, striving in defence of that nameless thing that had sprung to such wild life within her under the burning pressure of his lips, that strange and untamed force that she could neither bind nor subdue, but which to suffer him to behold meant sacrilege to her shrinking soul— such sacrilege as she believed she could never face and live.

Gradually the turmoil subsided, but it left her weak, inert, impotent. The impulse to pray came to her, but the prayer that went up from her trembling heart was voiceless and wordless. She had no means of expression in which to cloak her utter need. Only the stark helplessness of her whole being cried dumbly for deliverance.

A long time passed. The bungalow was silent and empty. She was quite alone. She could hear the rising rush of the wind across the *veldt*, and it sounded to her like a thing hunted and fleeing. The sand of the desert whipped against the windows, and the gloom increased. She was not naturally nervous, but a sense of fear oppressed her. She had that fateful feeling, which sometimes comes even in the sunshine, of something about to happen, of turning a sharp corner in the road of life that must change the whole outlook and trend of existence. She was afraid to look forward. For the first time life had become terrible to her.

She roused herself to action at last and got up from the table. Something fell on the ground as she did so. It was the key that Burke had given into her care. She knew it for the key of his strong-box in which he kept his money and papers. His journeys to Brennerstadt were never frequent, and she knew that he usually kept a considerable sum by him. The box was kept on the floor of the cupboard in the wall of the room which Guy now occupied. It was very heavy, so heavy that Burke himself never lifted it, seldom moved it from its place, but opened and closed it as it stood. She wondered as she groped for the key why he had given it to her. That action of his pointed to but one conclusion. He expected to be going into danger. He would not have parted with it otherwise. Of that she was certain. He and Guy were both going into danger then, and she was left in utter solitude to endure her suspense as best she could.

She searched in vain for the key. It was small and made to fit a patent lock. The darkness of the room baffled her search, and at last she abandoned it and went to the pantry for a lamp. The Kaffirs had gone to their huts. She found the lamp empty and untrimmed in a corner, with two others in the same condition. The oil was kept in an outbuilding some distance from the bungalow, and there was none in hand. She diverted her search to candles, but these also were hard to find. She spent several minutes there in the darkness with the wind howling weirdly around like a lost thing seeking shelter, and the sand beating against the little window with a persistent rattle that worried her nerves with a strange bewilderment.

Eventually she found an empty candlestick, and after prolonged search an end of candle. Sand was everywhere. It ground under her feet, and made gritty everything she touched. Was it fancy that brought to her the smell of burning, recalling Burke's words? She found herself shivering violently as she went to her own room for matches.

It was while she was here that there came to her above the roar of the wind a sudden sound that made her start and listen. Someone was knocking violently, almost battering, at the door that led into the passage.

Her heart gave a wild leap within her. Somehow—she knew not wherefore—her thoughts went to Kieff. She had a curiously strong feeling that he was, if not actually at the door, not far away. Then, even while she stood with caught breath listening, the door burst open and a blast of wind and sand came hurling into the house. It banged shut again instantly, and there followed a tramping of feet as if a herd of cattle had entered. Then there came a voice.

"Damnation!" it said, with vigour. "Damnation! It's a hell of a country, and myself was the benighted fool ever to come near it at all. Whist to it now! Anyone would think the devil himself was trying for admittance."

Very strangely that voice reassured Sylvia though she had never heard it before in her life. It did more; it sent such a rush of relief through her that she nearly laughed aloud.

She groped her way out into the passage, feeling as if a great weight had been lifted from her. "Come in, whoever you are!" she said. "It is rather infernal certainly. I'll light a candle in a moment—as soon as I can find some matches."

She saw a dim, broad figure standing in front of her and heard a long, soft whistle of dismay.

"I beg your pardon, madam," said the voice that had spoken such hearty invective a few seconds before. "Sure, I had no idea I was overheard. And I hope that I'll not have prejudiced you at all with the violence of me language. But it's in the air of the country, so to speak. And we all come to it in time. If it's a match that you're wanting, I've got one in my pocket this minute which I'll hand over with all the good will in the world if you'll do me the favour to wait."

Sylvia waited. She knew the sort of face that went with that voice, and it did not surprise her when the red Irish visage and sandy brows beamed upon her above the flickering candle. The laugh she had repressed a moment before rose to her lips. There was something so comic in this man's appearance just when she had been strung up for tragedy.

He looked at her with the eyes of a child, smiling good-humouredly at her mirth. "Sure, you're putting the joke on me," he said. "They all do it. Where can I have strayed to? Is this a fairy palace suddenly sprung up in the desert, and you the Queen of No Man's Land come down from your mountain-top to give me shelter?"

She shook her head, still laughing. "No, I've never been to the mountain-top. I'm only a farmer's wife."

"A farmer's wife!" He regarded her with quizzical curiosity for a space. "Is it Burke's bride that you are?" he questioned. "And is it Burke Ranger's farm that I've blundered into after all?"

"I am Burke Ranger's wife," she told him. "But I left off being a bride a long time ago. We are all too busy out here to keep up sentimental nonsense of that sort."

"And isn't it the cynic that ye are entirely?" rejoined the visitor, broadly grinning. "Sure,

it's time I introduced myself to the lady of the
house.   I'm Donovan Kelly, late of His Majesty's
Imperial Yeomanry, and at present engaged in the
peaceful avocation of mining for diamonds under
the rubbish-heaps of Brennerstadt."

Sylvia held out her hand.   There could be no
standing upon ceremony with this man.   She
hailed him instinctively as a friend.   There are
some men in the world whom no woman can regard in any other light.

"I am very pleased to meet you," she said, with
simplicity.   "And I know Burke will be glad too
that you have managed to make your way over
here.   You haven't chosen a very nice day for your
visit.   What a ghastly ride you must have had!
What about your horse?"

"Sure, I'd given myself up for lost entirely,"
laughed Kelly.   "And I said to St. Peter—that's
my horse and the best animal bred out of Ireland
—'Pete,' I said to him, 'it's a hell of a country
and no place for ye at all.   But if ye put your back
into it, Pete, and get us out of this infernal sand-
pit, I'll give ye such a draught of ale as'll make ye
dance on your head with delight.'   He's got a
taste for the liquor, has Pete.   I've put him in a
cowshed I found round the corner, and, faith, he
fair laughed to be out of the blast.   He's a very

human creature, Mrs. Ranger, with the soul of a Christian, only a bit saintlier."

"I shall have to make his acquaintance," said Sylvia. "Now come in and have some refreshment! I am sure you must need it."

"And that's a true word," said Kelly, following her into the sitting-room. "My throat feels as if it were lined with sand-paper."

She rapidly cleared a place for him at the table, and ministered to his wants. His presence was so large and comforting that her own doubts and fears had sunk into the background. For a time, listening to his artless talk, she was scarcely aware of them, and she was thankful for the diversion. It had been a terrible afternoon.

He began to make enquiries regarding Burke's absence at length, and then she told him about the *veldt*-fires, and the menace to the land. Her distress returned somewhat as she did so, and he was quick to perceive the anxiety she sought to hide.

"Now don't you worry—don't you worry!" he said. "Burke wasn't made to go under. He's one in a million. He's the sort that'll win to the very top of the world. And why? Because he's sound."

"Ah!" Sylvia said. Somehow that phrase at such a moment sent an odd little pang through her. Would Burke indeed win to the top of the world, she wondered? It seemed so remote to her now—that palace of dreams which they had planned to share together. Did he ever think of it now? She wondered—she wondered!

"Don't you worry!" Kelly said again. "There's nothing in life more futile. Is young Guy still here, by the way? Has he gone out scotching *veldt*-fires too?"

She started and coloured. How much did he know about Guy? How much would it be wise to impart?

Perhaps he saw her embarrassment, for he hastened to enlighten her. "I know all about young Guy. Nobody's enemy but his own. I helped Burke dig him out of Hoffstein's several weeks back, and a tough job it was. How has he behaved himself lately? Been on the bust at all?"

Sylvia hesitated. She knew this man for a friend, and she trusted him without knowing why; but she could not speak with freedom to anyone of Guy and his sins.

But again the Irishman saw and closed the breach. His shrewd eyes smiled kindly comprehension. "Ah, but he's a difficult youngster," he said. "Maybe he'll mend his ways as he gets older. We do sometimes, Mrs. Ranger. Any-

how, with all his faults he's got the heart of a
gentleman. I've known him do things—decent
things—that only a gentleman would have thought
of doing. I've punched his head for him before now,
but I've always liked young Guy. It's the same
with Burke. You can't help liking the fellow."

"I don't think Burke likes him," Sylvia said
almost involuntarily.

"Then, begging your pardon, you're wrong,"
said Kelly. "Burke loves him like a brother. I
know that all right. No, he'll never say so. He's
not the sort. But it's the truth, all the same.
He's about the biggest disappointment in Burke's
life. He'd never have left him to sink if he hadn't
been afraid the boy would shoot himself if he did
anything else."

"Ah!" Sylvia said again, with a sharp catch in
her breath. "That was what he was afraid of."

"Sure, that was it," said Kelly cheerfully.
"You'll generally find that that good man of yours
has a pretty decent reason for everything he does.
It isn't often he loses his head—or his temper.
He's a fine chap to be friendly with, but a divil to
cross."

"Yes. I've heard that before," Sylvia said,
with a valiant little smile. "I should prefer to be
friendly with him myself."

"Ah, sure and you're right," said Kelly. "But is it yourself that could be anything else? Why, he worships the very ground under your feet. I saw that clear as daylight that time at Brennerstadt."

She felt her heart quicken a little. "How—clever of you!" she said.

He nodded with beaming appreciation of the compliment. "You'll find my conclusions are generally pretty near the mark," he said. "It isn't difficult to know what's in the minds of the people you're fond of. Now is it?"

She stifled a sigh. "I don't know. I'm not very good at thought-reading myself."

He chuckled like a merry child. "Ah, then you come to me, Mrs. Ranger!" he said. "I'll be proud to help ye any time."

"I expect you help most people," she said. "You are everybody's friend."

"I do my best," said Donovan Kelly modestly. "And, faith, a very pleasant occupation it is."

CHAPTER VI

THE HERO

THE wind went down somewhat at sunset and
Sylvia realized with relief that the worst was over.
She sat listening for the return of Burke and Guy
while her companion chatted cheerfully of a
thousand things which might have interested her
at any other time but to which now she gave but
fitful attention.

He was in the midst of telling her about the
draw for the great diamond at Brennerstadt and
how the tickets had been reduced from monkeys
to ponies because the monkeys were too shy, when
there came the sound for which she waited—a
hand upon the window-catch and the swirl of sand
blown in by the draught as it opened.

She was up in a moment, guarding the candle
and looking out over it with eager, half-dazzled
eyes. For an instant her look met Burke's as he
stood in the aperture, then swiftly travelled to the
man with him. Guy, with a ghastly face that
tried to smile, was hanging upon him for support.

Burke shut the window with decision and stood staring at Sylvia's companion.

Kelly at once proceeded with volubility to explain his presence. "Ah, yes, it's meself in the flesh, Burke, and very pleased to see ye. I've taken a holiday to come and do ye a good turn. And Mrs. Ranger has been entertaining me like a prince in your absence. So you've got young Guy with you! What's the matter with the boy?"

"I'm all right," said Guy, and quitted his hold upon Burke as if to demonstrate the fact.

But Burke took him by the arm and led him to a chair. "You sit down!" he commanded briefly. "Hullo, Donovan! Glad to see you! Have you had a drink?"

"Sure, I've had all that mortal man could desire and more to it," declared Kelly.

"Good," said Burke, and turned to Sylvia. "Get out the brandy, will you?"

She hastened to do his bidding. There was a blueness about Guy's lips that frightened her, and she saw that his hands were clenched.

Yet, as Burke bent over him a few moments later, he laughed with something of challenge in his eyes. "Ripping sport, old chap!" he said, and drank with a feverish eagerness.

Burke's hand was on his shoulder. She could

not read his expression, but she was aware of something unusual between them, something that was wholly outside her experience. Then he spoke, his voice very quiet and steady.

"Go slow, man! You've had a bit of a knockout."

Guy looked across at her, and there was triumph in his look. "It's been—sport," he said again. "Ripping sport!" It was so boyishly uttered, and his whole attitude was so reminiscent of the old days, that she felt herself thrill in answer. She moved quickly to him.

"What has been happening? Tell me!" she said.

He laughed again. "My dear girl, we've been fighting the devil in his own element, and we've beat him off the field." He sprang to his feet. "Here, give me another drink, or I shall die! My throat is a bed of live cinders."

Burke intervened. "No—no! Go slow, I tell you! Go slow! Get some tea, Sylvia! Where are those Kaffirs?"

"They haven't been near all day," Sylvia said. "I frightened Rosamond away this morning, and the others must have been afraid of the storm."

"I'll rout 'em out," said Kelly.

"No. You stay here! I'll go." Burke turned

to the door, but paused as he opened it and looked back. "Sylvia!" he said.

She went to him. He put his hand through her arm and drew her into the passage. "Don't let Guy have any more to drink!" he said. "Mind, I leave him to you."

He spoke with urgency; she looked at him in surprise.

"Yes, I mean it," he said. "You must prevent him somehow. I can't—nor Kelly either. You probably can—for a time anyhow."

"I'll do my best," she said.

His hand closed upon her. "If you fail, he'll go under. I know the signs. It's up to you to stop him. Go back and see to it!"

He almost pushed her from him with the words, and it came to her that for some reason Guy's welfare was uppermost with him just then. He had never betrayed any anxiety on his account before, and she wondered greatly at his attitude. But it was no time for questioning. Mutely she obeyed him and went back.

She found Guy in the act of filling a glass for Kelly. His own stood empty at his elbow. She went forward quickly, and laid her hand on his shoulder. "Guy, please!" she said.

He looked at her, the bottle in his hand. In his

22

eyes she saw again that dreadful leaping flame which made her think of some starved and desperate animal. "What is it?" he said.

An overwhelming sense of her own futility came upon her. She felt almost like a child standing there, attempting that of which Burke had declared himself to be incapable.

"What is it?" he said again.

She braced herself for conflict. "Please," she said gently. "I want you to wait and have some tea. It won't take long to get." Then, as the fever of his eyes seemed to burn her: "Please, Guy! Please!"

Kelly put aside his own drink untouched. "There's no refusing such a sweet appeal as that," he declared gallantly. "Guy, I move a postponement. Tea first!"

But Guy was as one who heard not. He was staring at Sylvia, and the wild fire in his eyes was leaping higher, ever higher. In that moment he saw her, and her alone. It was as if they two had suddenly met in a place that none other might enter. His words of the morning rushed back upon her—his passionate declaration that life was not long enough for sacrifice—that the future to which she looked was but a mirage which she would never reach.

It all flashed through her brain in a few short seconds, vivid, dazzling, overwhelming, and the memory of Kieff went with it—Kieff and his cold, sinister assertion that she held Guy's destiny between her hands.

Then, very softly, Guy spoke. "To please—you?" he said.

She answered him, but it was scarcely of her own volition. She was as one driven—"Yes—yes!"

He looked at her closely as if to make sure of her meaning. Then, with a quick, reckless movement, he turned and set down the bottle on the table.

"That settles that," he said boyishly. "Go ahead, Kelly! Drink! Don't mind me! I am—brandy-proof."

And Sylvia, throbbing from head to foot, knew she had conquered, knew she had saved him for a time at least from the threatening evil. But there was that within her which shrank from the thought of the victory. She had acted almost under compulsion, yet she felt that she had used a weapon which would ultimately pierce them both.

She scarcely knew what passed during the interval that followed before Burke's return. As in a dream she heard Kelly still talking about the Brennerstadt diamond, and Guy was asking him questions with a keenness of interest that seemed strange to her. She herself was waiting and watching for Burke, dreading his coming, yet in a fashion eager for it. For very curiously she had a feeling that she needed him. For the first time she wanted to lean upon his strength.

But when at length he came, her dread of him was uppermost and she felt she could not meet his look. It was with relief that she saw Guy was still his first thought. He had fetched Joe from the Kaffir huts, and the lamps were filled and lighted. He was carrying one as he entered, and the light flung upwards on his face showed it to her as the face of a strong man.

He set the lamp on the table and went straight to Guy. "Look here!" he said. "I'm going to put you to bed."

Guy, with his arms on the table, looked up at him and laughed. "Oh, rats! I'm all right. Can't you see I'm all right? Well, I must have some tea first anyway. I've been promised tea."

"I'll bring you your tea in bed," Burke said.

But Guy protested. "No, really, old chap. I must sit up a bit longer. I'll be very good. I want to hear all Kelly's news. I believe I shall have to go back to Brennerstadt with him to paint the town red. I'd like to have a shot at that diamond. You never know your luck when the devil's on your side."

"I know yours," said Burke drily. "And it's about as rotten as it can be. You've put too great a strain on it all your life."

Guy laughed again. He was in the wildest spirits. But suddenly in the midst of his mirth he began to cough with a dry, harsh sound like the rending of wood. He pushed his chair back from the table, and bent himself double, seeming to grope upon the floor. It was the most terrible paroxysm that Sylvia had ever witnessed, and she thought it would never end.

Several times he tried to straighten himself, but each effort seemed to renew the anguish that tore him, and in the end he subsided limply against Burke who supported him till at last the convulsive choking ceased.

He was completely exhausted by that time and offered no remonstrance when Burke and Kelly between them bore him to the former's room and laid him on the bed he had occupied for so long. Burke administered brandy again; there was no help for it. And then at Guy's whispered request he left him for a space to recover.

He drew Sylvia out of the room, and Kelly followed. "I'll go back to him later, and help him undress," he said. "But he will probably get on better alone for the present."

"What has been happening?" Sylvia asked him. "Tell me what has been happening!"

A fevered desire to know everything was upon her. She felt she must know.

Burke looked at her as if something in her eagerness struck him as unusual. But he made no comment upon it. He merely with his customary brevity proceeded to enlighten her.

"We went to Vreiboom's, and had a pretty hot time. Kieff was there too, by the way. The fire got a strong hold, and if the wind had held, we should probably have been driven out of it, and our own land would have gone too. As it was," he paused momentarily, "well, we have Guy to thank that it didn't."

"Guy!" said Sylvia quickly.

"Yes. He worked like a nigger—better. He's been among hot ashes and that infernal sand for hours. I couldn't get him out. He did the impossible." A curious tremor sounded in Burke's voice—"The impossible!" he said again.

"Sure, I always said there was grit in the boy," said Kelly. "You'll be making a man of him yet, Burke. You'll have to have a good try after this."

Burke was silent. His eyes, bloodshot but keen, were upon Sylvia's face.

It was some moments before with an effort she lifted her own to meet them. "So Guy is a hero!" she said, with a faint uncertain smile. "I'm glad of that."

"Let's drink to him," said Kelly, "now he isn't here to see! Burke, fill up! Mrs. Ranger!"

"No—no!" Sylvia said. "I am going to get the tea."

Yet she paused beside Burke, as if compelled. "What else did he do?" she said. "You haven't told us all."

"Not quite all," said Burke, and still his eyes searched hers with a probing intentness.

"Don't you want to tell me?" she said.

"Yes, I will tell you," he answered, "if you especially want to hear. He saved my life."

"Hooray!" yelled Kelly, the voice of one holloaing to hounds.

Sylvia said nothing for a moment. She had turned very pale. When she spoke it was with an effort. "How?"

He answered as if speaking to her alone. "One of Vreiboom's tumble-down old sheds fired while we were trying to clear it. The place collapsed and I got pinned inside. Piet Vreiboom didn't trouble himself, or Kieff, either. He wouldn't—naturally. Guy got me out."

"Ah!" she said. It was scarcely more than an intake of the breath. She could not utter another word, for that imprisoned thing within her seemed to be clawing at her heart, choking her. If Burke had died—if Burke had died! She turned herself quickly from the searching of his eyes, lest he should see—and understand. She could not—dared not—show him her soul just then. The memory of his kiss—that single, fiery kiss that had opened her own eyes—held her back. She went from him in silence. If Burke had died!

CHAPTER VII

THE NET

IT was not often that Sylvia lay awake, but that night her brain was in a turmoil, and for long she courted sleep in vain. For some time after she retired, the murmur of Burke's and Kelly's voices in the adjoining room kept her on the alert, but it was mainly the thoughts that crowded in upon her that would not let her rest. The thought of Guy troubled her most, this and the knowledge that Kieff was in the neighbourhood. She had an almost uncanny dread of this man. He seemed to stand in the path as a menace, an evil influence that she could neither avert nor withstand. Burke had barely mentioned him, yet his words had expressed the thought that had sprung instantly to her mind. He was an enemy to them all, most of all to Guy, and she feared him. She had a feeling that she would sooner or later have to fight him for Guy's soul, and she was sick with apprehension. For the only weapon at her disposal was that weapon she dare not wield.

The long night dragged away. She thought it would never end. When sleep came to her at last it was only to bring dreadful dreams in its train. Burke in danger! Burke imprisoned in a burning hut! Burke at the mercy of Kieff, the merciless!

She wrenched herself free from these nightmares in the very early morning while the stars were still in the sky, and went out on to the *stoep* to banish the evil illusions from her brain. It was still and cold and desolate. The guest-hut in which Kelly was sleeping was closed. There was no sign of life anywhere. A great longing to go out alone on to the *veldt* came to her. She felt as if the great solitude must soothe her spirit. And it would be good to realize her wish and to see the day break from that favourite *kopje* of hers.

She turned to re-enter her room for an extra wrap, and then started at sight of another figure standing at the corner of the bungalow. She thought it was Burke, and her heart gave a wild leap within her, but the next moment as it began to move noiselessly towards her, she recognized Guy.

He came to her on stealthy feet. "Hullo!" he whispered. "Can't you sleep?"

She held out her hand to him. "Guy! You ought to be in bed!"

He made an odd grimace, and bending, carried her hand to his lips. "I couldn't sleep either. I've been tormented with a fiery thirst all night long. What has been keeping you awake? Honestly now!"

He laughed into her eyes, and she was aware that he was trying to draw her nearer to him. There was about him at that moment a subtle allurement that was hard to resist. Old memories thrilled through her at his touch. For five years she had held herself as belonging to him. Could the spell be broken in as many months?

Yet she did resist him, turning her face away. "I can't tell you," she said, a quiver in her voice. "I had a good deal to think about. Guy, what is— Kieff doing at Piet Vreiboom's?"

Guy frowned. "Heaven knows. He is there for his own amusement, not mine."

"You didn't know he was there?" she said, looking at him again.

His frown deepened. "Yes, I knew. Of course I knew. Why?"

Her heart sank. "I don't like him," she said. "I know he is clever. I know he saved your life. But I never did like him. I—am afraid of him."

"Perhaps you would have rather he hadn't saved my life?" suggested Guy, with a twist of the lips. "It would have simplified matters considerably, wouldn't it?"

"Don't!" she said, and withdrew her hand. "You know how it hurts me—to hear you talk like that."

"Why should it hurt you?" said Guy.

She was silent, and he did not press for an answer. Instead, very softly he whistled the air of a song that he had been wont to sing to her half in jest in the old days.

> Love that hath us in the net
> Can he pass and we forget?

She made a little movement of flinching, but the next moment she turned back to him with absolute steadfastness. "Guy, you and I are friends, aren't we? We never could be anything else."

"Oh, couldn't we?" said Guy.

"No," she maintained resolutely. "Please let us remember that! Please let us build on that!"

He looked at her whimsically. "It's a shaky foundation," he said. "But we'll try. That is, we'll pretend if you like. Who knows? We may succeed."

"Don't put it like that!" she said. "Be a man, Guy! I know you can be. Only yesterday——"

"Yesterday? What happened yesterday?" said Guy. "I never remember the yesterdays."

"I think you do," she said. "You did a big thing yesterday. You saved Burke."

"Oh, that!" He uttered a low laugh. "My dear girl, don't canonize me on that account! I only did it because those swine wanted to see him burn."

She shuddered. "That is not true. You know it is not true. It pleases you to pretend you are callous. But you are not at heart. Burke knows that as well as I do."

"Oh, damn Burke!" he said airly. "He's no great oracle. I wonder what you'd have said if I had come back without him."

She clenched her hands hard to keep back another shudder. "I can't talk of that—can't think of it even. You don't know—you will never realize—all that Burke has done for me."

"Yes, I do know," Guy said. "But most men would have jumped at the chance to do the same. You take it all too seriously. It was no sacrifice to him. You don't owe him anything. He wouldn't have done it if he hadn't taken a fancy to you. And he didn't do it for nothing either. He's not such a philanthropist as that."

Somehow that hurt her intolerably. She looked

at him with a quick flash of anger in her eyes. "Do you want to make me hate you?" she said.

He turned instantly and with a most winning gesture. "No, darling. You couldn't if you tried," he said.

She went back a step, shaking her head. "I am not so sure," she said. "Why do you say these horrible things to me?"

He held out his hand to her. "I'm awfully sorry, dear," he said. "But it is for your good. I want you to see life as it is, not as your dear little imagination is pleased to paint it. You are so dreadfully serious always. Life isn't, you know. It really isn't. It's nothing but a stupid and rather vulgar farce."

She gave him her hand, for she could not deny him; but she gave no sign of yielding with it. "Oh, how I wish you would take it more seriously!" she said.

"Do you?" he said. "But what's the good? Who is it going to benefit if I do? Not myself. I should hate it. And not you. You are much too virtuous to have any use for me."

"Oh, Guy," she said. "Is it never worth while to play the game?"

His hand tightened upon hers. "Look here!" he said suddenly. "Suppose I did as you wish—

suppose I did pull up—play the game, as you call it? Suppose I clawed and grabbed for success like the rest of the world—and got it. Would you care?"

"I wasn't talking of success," she said.

"That's no answer." He swung her hand to and fro with vehement impatience. "Suppose you were free—yes, you've got to suppose it just for a moment—suppose you were free—and suppose I came to you with both hands full, and offered you myself and all I possessed—would you send me empty away? Would you? Would you?"

He spoke with a fevered insistence. His eyes were alight and eager. Just so had he spoken in the long ago when she had given him her girlish heart in full and happy surrender.

There was no surrender in her attitude now, but yet she could not, she could not, relentlessly send him from her. He appealed so strongly, with so intense an earnestness.

"I can't imagine these things, Guy," she said at last. "I only ask you—implore you—to do your best to keep straight. It is worth while, believe me. You will find that it is worth while."

"It might be—with you to make it so," he said. "Without you——"

She shook her head. "No—no! For other, better reasons. We have our duty to do. We must do it. It is the only way to be happy. I am sure of that."

"Have you found it so?" he said. "Are you happy?"

She hesitated.

He pressed his advantage instantly. "You are not. You know you are not. Do you think you can deceive me even though you may deceive yourself? We have known each other too long for that. You are not happy, Sylvia. You are afraid of life as it is—of life as it might be. You haven't pluck to take your fate into your own hands and hew out a way for yourself. You're the slave of circumstances and you're afraid to break free." He made as if he would release her, and then suddenly, unexpectedly, caught her hand up to his face. "All the same, you are mine— you are mine!" he told her hotly. "You belonged to me from the beginning, and nothing else counts or ever can count against that. I would have died to get out of your way. I tried to die. But you brought me back. And now, say what you like—say what you like—you are mine! I saw it in your eyes last night, and I defy every law that man ever made to take you from me. I defy the thing you call duty. You love me! You have always loved me! Deny it if you can!"

It was swift, it was almost overwhelming. At another moment it might have swept her off her feet. But a greater force was at work within her, and she stood her ground.

She drew her hand away. "Not like that, Guy," she said. "I love you. Yes, I love you. But only as a friend. You—you don't understand me. How should you? I have grown beyond all your knowledge of me. I was a girl in the old days—when we played at love together." A sharp sob rose in her throat, but she stifled it. "All that is over. I am a woman now. My eyes are open,—and—the romance is all gone."

He stiffened as if he had been struck, but only for a second. The next recklessly he laughed. "That is just your way of putting it," he said. "Love doesn't change—like that. It either goes out, or it remains—for good. It is you who don't understand yourself. You may turn your back on the truth, but you can't alter it. Those who have once been lovers—and lovers such as you and I—can never again be only friends. That, if you like, is the impossible. But—" He paused for a moment, with lifted shoulders, then abruptly turned to go. "Good-bye!" he said.

23

"You are going?" she questioned.

He swung on his heel as if irresolute. "Yes, I am going. I am going back to my cabin, back to my wallowing in the mire. Why not? Is there anyone who cares the toss of a halfpenny what I do?"

"Yes." Breathlessly she answered him; the words seemed to leap from her of their own accord, and surely it was hardly of her own volition that she followed and held his arm, detaining him. "Guy! You know we care. Burke cares. I care. Guy, please, dear, please! It's such a pity. Oh, it's such a pity! Won't you—can't you—fight against it? Won't you even—try? I know you could conquer, if only—if only you would try!" Her eyes were raised to his. She besought him with all the strength of her being. She clung to him as if she would hold him back by sheer physical force from the abyss at his feet. "Oh, Guy, it is worth while!" she pleaded. "Indeed—indeed it is worth while—whatever it costs. Guy,—I beseech—I implore you——"

She broke off, for with a lightning movement he had taken her face between his hands. "You can make it worth while," he said. "I will do it —for you."

He held her passionately close for an instant,

but he did not kiss her. She saw the impulse to do so in his eyes, and she saw him beat it fiercely back. That was the only comfort that remained to her when the next moment he sprang away and went so swiftly from her that he was lost to sight almost before she knew that he was gone.

CHAPTER VIII

THE SUMMONS

WHEN Kelly awoke that morning, it was some time later, and Burke was entering his hut with a steaming cup of cocoa. The Irishman stretched his large bulk and laughed up at his friend.

"Faith, it's the good host that ye are! I've slept like a top, my son, and never an evil dream. How's the lad this morning? And how's the land?"

"The land's all right so far," Burke said. "I'm just off to help them bring in the animals. The northern dam has failed."

Kelly leaped from his bed. "I'll come. That's just the job for me and St. Peter. Don't bring the missis along though! It's too much for her."

"I know that," Burke said shortly. "I've told her so. She is to take it easy for a bit. The climate is affecting her."

Kelly looked at him with his kindly, curious eyes. "Can't you get things fixed up here and bring her along to Brennerstadt for the races and the diamond gamble? It would do you both good to have a change."

Burke shook his head. "I doubt if she would care for it. And young Guy would want to come too. If he did, he would soon get up to mischief again. He has gone back to his hut this morning, cleared out early. I hope he is to be trusted to behave himself."

"Oh, leave the boy alone!" said Kelly. "He's got some decent feelings of his own, and it doesn't do to mother him too much. Give him his head for a bit! He's far less likely to bolt."

Burke shrugged his shoulders. "I can't hold him if he means to go, I quite admit. But I haven't much faith in his keeping on the straight, and that's a fact. I don't like his going back to the hut, and I'd have prevented it if I'd known. But I slept in the sitting-room last night, and I was dead beat. He cleared out early."

"Didn't anyone see him go?" queried Kelly keenly.

"Yes. My wife." Again Burke's tone was curt, repressive. "She couldn't stop him."

"She made him hold hard with the brandy-bottle last night," said Kelly. "I admired her for it. She's got a way with her, Burke. Sure, the devil himself couldn't have resisted her then."

Burke's faint smile showed for a moment; he said nothing.

"How you must worship her!" went on Kelly, with amiable effusion. "Some fellows have all the luck. Sure, you're never going to let that sweet angel languish here like that poor little Mrs. Merston! You wouldn't now! Come, you wouldn't!"

But Burke passed the matter by. He had pressing affairs on hand, and obviously it was not his intention to discuss his conduct towards his wife even with the worthy Kelly whose blundering goodness so often carried him over difficult ground that few others would have ventured to negotiate.

He left Kelly to dress, and went back to the bungalow where Sylvia was busy with a duster trying to get rid of some of the sand that thickly covered everything. He had scarcely spoken to her that morning except for news of Guy, but now he drew her aside.

"Look here!" he said. "Don't wear yourself out!"

She gave him a quick look. "Oh, I shan't do that. Work is good for me. Isn't this sand too awful for words?"

She spoke with a determined effort to assume

the old careless attitude towards him, but the nervous flush on her cheeks betrayed her.

He put his hand on her shoulder, and wheeled her round somewhat suddenly towards the light. "You didn't sleep last night," he said.

She tried to laugh, but she could not check the hot flush of embarrassment that raced into her pale cheeks under his look. "I couldn't help it," she said. "I was rather wound up yesterday. It —was an exciting day, wasn't it?"

He continued to look at her for several seconds, intently but not sternly. Then very quietly he spoke. "Sylvia, if things go wrong, if the servants upset you, come to me about it! Don't go to Guy!"

She understood the reference in a moment. The flush turned to flaming crimson that mounted in a wave to her forehead. She drew back from him, her head high.

"And if Schafen or any other man comes to you with offensive gossip regarding my behaviour, please kick him as he deserves—next time!" she said. "And then—if you think it necessary— come to me for an explanation!"

She spoke with supreme scorn, every word a challenge. She was more angry in that moment than she could remember that she had ever been before. How dared he hear Schafen's evidence against her, and then coolly take her thus to task? The memory of his kiss swept back upon her as she spoke, that kiss that had so cruelly wounded her, that kiss that had finally rent the veil away from her quivering heart. She stood before him with clenched hands. If he had attempted to kiss her then, she would have struck him.

But he did not move. He stood, looking at her, looking at her, till at last her wide eyes wavered and sank before his own. He spoke then, an odd inflection in his voice.

"Why are you so angry?"

Her two fists were pressed hard against her sides. She was aware of a weakening of her self-control, and she fought with all her strength to retain it. She could not speak for a second or two, but it was not fear that restrained her.

"Tell me!" he said. "Why are you angry?"

The colour was dying slowly out of her face; a curious chill had followed the sudden flame. "It is your own fault," she said.

"How—my fault?" Burke's voice was wholly free from any sort of emotion; but his question held insistence notwithstanding.

She answered it almost in spite of herself. "For making me hate you."

He made a slight movement as of one who shifts his hold upon some chafing creature to strengthen his grip. "How have I done that?" he said.

She answered him in a quick, breathless rush of words that betrayed her failing strength completely. "By doubting me—by being jealous and showing it—by—by—by insulting me!"

"What?" he said.

She turned from him sharply and walked away, battling with herself. "You know what I mean," she said tremulously. "You know quite well what I mean. You were angry yesterday—angry because Hans Schafen—a servant—had told you something that made you distrust me. And because you were angry, you—you—you insulted me!" She turned round upon him suddenly with eyes of burning accusation. She was fighting, fighting, with all her might, to hide from him that frightened, quivering thing that she herself had recognized but yesterday. If it had been a plague-spot, she could not have guarded it more jealously. Its presence scared her. Her every instinct was to screen it somehow, somehow, from those keen eyes. For he was so horribly strong, so shrewd, so merciless!

He came up to her as she wheeled. He took one of her quivering wrists, and held it, his fingers

closely pressed upon the leaping pulse. "Sylvia!"
he said, and this time there was an edge to his
voice that made her aware that he was putting
force upon himself. "I have never insulted you—
or distrusted you. Everything was against me
yesterday. But when I left you, I gave all I possessed into your keeping. It is in your keeping
still. Does that look like distrust?"

She gave a quick, involuntary start, but he
went on, scarcely pausing.

"When a man is going into possible danger, and
his wife is thinking of—other things, is he so greatly
to blame if he takes the quickest means at his disposal of waking her up?"

"Ah!" she said. Had he not waked her indeed? But yet—but yet— She looked at him
doubtfully.

"Listen!" he said. "We've been going round
in a circle lately. It's been like that infernal game
we used to play as children. 'Snail,' wasn't it
called? Where nobody ever got home and everybody always lost their tempers! Let's get out of
it, Sylvia! Let's leave Guy and Schafen to look
after things, and go to the top of the world by ourselves! I'll take great care of you. You'll be
happy, you know. You'll like it."

He spoke urgently, leaning towards her. There

was nothing terrible about him at that moment. All the mastery had gone from his attitude. He was even smiling a little.

Her heart gave a great throb. It was so long, so long, since he had spoken to her thus. And then, like a blasting wind, the memory of Guy's bitter words rushed across her. She seemed again to feel the sand of the desert blowing in her face, sand that was blended with ashes. Was it only a slave that he wanted after all? She hated herself for the thought, but she could not drive it out.

"Don't you like that idea?" he said.

Still she hesitated. "What of Guy?" she said. "We must think of him, Burke. We must."

"I'm thinking of him," he said. "A little responsibility would probably do him good."

"But to leave him—entirely—" She broke off. Someone was knocking at the outer door, and she was thankful for the interruption.

Burke turned away, and went to answer. He came back with a note in his hand.

"It's Merston's house-boy," he said. "I've sent him round to the kitchen to get a feed. Something's up there, I am afraid. Let's see what he has to say!"

He opened the letter while he was speaking, and there fell a short silence while he read. Sylvia took up her duster again. Her hands were trembling.

In a moment Burke spoke. "Yes, it's from Merston. The poor chap has had an accident, fallen from his horse and badly wrenched his back. His overseer is away, and he wants to know if I will go over and lend a hand. I must go of course." He turned round to her. "You'll be able to manage for a day or two?"

Her breathing came quickly, nervously. She felt oddly uncertain of herself, as if she had just come through a crisis that had bereft her of all her strength.

"Of course," she said, not looking at him. "Of course."

He stood for a moment or two, watching her. Then he moved to her side.

"I'm leaving you in charge," he said. "But you won't overdo it? Promise me!"

She laughed a little. The thought of his going was a vast relief to her at that moment. She yearned to be alone, to readjust her life somehow before she met him again. She wanted to rebuild her defences. She wanted to be quite sure of herself.

"Oh, I shall take great care of myself," she said. "I'm very good at that."

"I wonder," said Burke. And then he laid his

hand upon the flicking duster and stopped her quivering activity. "Are you still—hating me?" he said.

She stood motionless, and still her eyes avoided his. "I'll tell you," she said, "when we meet again."

"Does that mean that I am to go—unforgiven?" he said.

Against her will she looked at him. In spite of her, her lip trembled.

He put his arm round her. "Does it?" he said.

"No," she whispered back.

In that moment they were nearer than they had been through all the weeks of Guy's illness, nearer possibly than they had ever been before. It would have been so easy for Sylvia to lean upon that strong encircling arm, so easy that she wondered afterwards how she restrained the impulse to do so. But the moment passed so quickly, sped by the sound of Kelly's feet upon the *stoep*, and Burke's arm pressed her close and then fell away.

There was neither disappointment nor annoyance on his face as he turned to meet his guest. He was even smiling.

Sylvia recalled that smile afterwards—the memory of it went with her through all the bitter hours that followed.

CHAPTER IX

FOR THE SAKE OF THE OLD LOVE

KELLY accompanied Burke when, after hurried preparation and consultation with Schafen, he finally took the rough road that wound by the *kopje* on his way to the Merstons' farm. He had not intended to prolong his visit over two days, and he proposed to conclude it now; for his leisure was limited, and he had undertaken to be back in Brennerstadt for the occasion of the diamond draw which he himself had organized, and which was to take place at the end of the week. But at Burke's request, as they rode upon their way, he promised to return to Blue Hill Farm for that night and the next also if Burke could not return sooner. He did not mean to be absent for more than two nights. His own affairs could not be neglected for longer, though he might decide to send Schafen over to help the Merstons if necessary.

"My wife can't look after Guy single-handed," he said. "It's not a woman's job, and I can't risk it. I shall feel easier if you are there."

366

And Kelly professed himself proud to be of service in any capacity. If Mrs. Burke would put up with him for another night, sure, he'd be delighted to keep her company, and he'd see that the boy behaved himself too, though for his own part he didn't think that there was any vice about him just then.

They did not visit the hut on the sand whither Guy had betaken himself. The sun was getting high, and Burke, with the Kaffir boy who had brought the message running at his stirrup, would not linger on the road.

"He's probably having a rest," he said. "He won't be fit for much else to-day. You'll see him to-night, Donovan?"

And Donovan promised that he would. He was in fact rather proud of the confidence reposed in him. To treat him as a friend in need was the highest compliment that anyone could pay the kind-hearted Irishman. Cheerily he undertook to remain at Blue Hill Farm until Burke's return, always providing that Mrs. Burke didn't get tired of him and turn him out.

"She won't do that," said Burke. "You'll find she will be delighted to see you to-day when you get back. She hasn't been trained for solitude, and I fancy it gets on her nerves."

Perhaps it did. But on that occasion at least Sylvia was thankful to be left alone. She had her house to set in order, and at that very moment she was on her knees in the sitting-room, searching, searching in all directions for the key which she had dropped on the previous day during the dust-storm, before Kelly's arrival. Burke's reference to the matter had recalled it to her mind, and now with shamed self-reproach she sought in every cranny for the only thing of any importance which he had ever entrusted to her care.

She sought in vain. The sand was thick everywhere, but she searched every inch of the floor with her hands, and found nothing. The stifling heat of the day descended upon her as she searched. She felt sick in mind and body, sick with a growing hopelessness which she would not acknowledge. The thing could not be lost. She knew that Burke had slept in the room, and none of the servants had been alone in it since. So the key must be somewhere there, must have been kicked into some corner, or caught in a crack. She had felt so certain of finding it that she had not thought it necessary to tell Burke of her carelessness. But now she began to wish she had told him. Her anxiety was turning to a perfect fever of apprehension. The conviction was beginning to force itself upon her that someone must have found the key.

But who—who? No Kaffir, she was certain. No Kaffir had entered. And Burke had been there all night long. He had slept in the long chair, giving up his bed to the guest. And he had slept late, tired out after the violent exertions of the previous day.

He had slept late! Suddenly, there on her knees in the litter of sand, another thought flashed through her brain, the thought of her own sleeplessness, the thought of the early morning, the thought of Guy.

He had been up early. He generally rested till late in the morning. He too had been sleepless. But he had a remedy for that which she knew he would not scruple to take if he felt the need. His wild excitement of the night before rose up before her. His eager interest in Kelly's talk of the diamond, the strangeness of his attitude that morning. And then, with a lightning suddenness, came the memory of Kieff.

Guy was under Kieff's influence. She was certain of it. And Kieff? She shrank at the bare thought of the man, his subtle force, his callous strength of purpose, his almost uncanny intelligence. Yes, she was afraid of Kieff—she had always been afraid of Kieff.

The midday heat seemed to press upon her like a burning, crushing weight. It seemed to deprive her of the power to think, certainly of the power to reason. For what rational connection could there be between Kieff and the loss of Burke's key? Kieff was several miles away at the farm of Piet Vreiboom. And Guy—where was Guy? She wished he would come back. Surely he would come back soon! She would tell him of her loss, she yearned to tell someone; she would get him to help her in her search. For it could not be lost. It could not be really lost! They would find it somehow—somehow!

It was no actual reasoning but a blind instinct that moved her to get up at length and go to the room that Guy had occupied for so long, the room that was Burke's. It was just as Guy had left it that morning. She noted mechanically the disordered bed. The cupboard in the corner was closed as usual, but the key was in the lock. Burke kept his clothes on the higher shelves. The strong-box stood on the floor with some boots.

Her eyes went straight to it. Some magnetism seemed to be at work, compelling her. And then —she gave a gasp of wonder, and almost fell on to the sandy floor beside the box. The key was in the lock!

Was it all a dream then? Had it never been lost? Had she but imagined Burke's action in confiding it to her? She closed her eyes for a space, for her brain was swimming. The terrible, parching heat seemed to have turned into a wheel —a fiery wheel of torture that revolved behind her eyes, making her wince at every turn. The pain was intense; when she tried to move, it was excruciating. She sank down with her head almost on the iron box and waited in dumb endurance for relief.

A long time passed so, and she fancied later that she must have slept, for she dared not move while that awful pain lasted, and she was scarcely conscious of her surroundings. But it became less acute at last; she found herself sitting up with wide-open eyes, trying to collect her thoughts.

They evaded her for a while, and she dared not employ any very strenuous effort to capture them, lest that unspeakable suffering should return. But gradually—very gradually—the power to reason returned to her. She found herself gazing at the key that had cost her so much; and after a little, impelled by what seemed to be almost a new sense within her, she took it between her quivering fingers and turned it.

It went with an ease that surprised her, for she remembered—her brain was becoming every moment more strangely clear and alert—she remembered that Burke had said only a day or two before that it needed oiling. She opened the box, and with a fateful premonition looked within.

A few papers in a rubber band lay in the bottom of the box, and beside them, carelessly tossed aside, an envelope! There was no money at all.

She took up the envelope, feverishly searching. It contained a cigarette—one of her own—that had been half-smoked. She stared at it for a second or two in wonder, then like a stab came the memory of that night—so long ago—when he had taken the cigarette from between her lips, when he had been on the verge of speech, when she had stood waiting to hear . . . and Guy had come between.

Many seconds later she put the envelope back, and got up. Conviction had come irresistibly upon her; she knew now whose hand had oiled the lock, she knew beyond all doubting who had opened the box, and left it thus.

She was trembling no longer, but steady—firm as a rock. She must find Guy. Wherever he was, she must find him. That money—her own sacred charge—must be returned before she faced Burke again. Guy was mad. She must save him from his madness. This fight for Guy's soul—she had seen it coming. She realized it as a hand to hand fight with Kieff. But she would win. She was bound to win. So she told herself. No power of evil could possibly triumph ultimately, and she knew that deep in his inmost heart Guy acknowledged this. However wild and reckless his words, he did not really expect to see her waver. He might be the slave of evil himself, but he knew that she would never share his slavery. He knew it, and in spite of himself he honoured her. She believed he would always honour her. And this was the weapon on which she counted for his deliverance, this and the old sweet friendship between them that was infinitely more enduring than first love. She believed that her influence over him was greater than Kieff's. Otherwise she had not dared to pit her strength against that of the enemy. Otherwise she had waited to beg the help of Kelly, who always helped everyone.

The thought of Burke she put resolutely from her. Burke should never know, if she could prevent it, how low Guy had fallen. If only she could save Guy from that, she believed she might save him from all. When once his eyes were opened, when once she had beaten down Kieff's ascendancy, the battle would be won. But she must act immediately and with decision. There was not a moment to lose. If Guy were not checked now, at the very outset, there would be no saving him from the abyss. She must find him now, at once. And she must do it alone. There was no alternative to that. Only alone could she hope to influence him.

She stooped and locked the box once more, taking the key. Now that she knew the worst, her weakness was all gone. With the old steady fearlessness she went from the room. The battle was before her, but she knew no misgiving. She would win—she was bound to win—for the sake of the old love and in the strength of the new.

CHAPTER X

THE BEARER OF EVIL TIDINGS

It was late in the afternoon when Kelly returned to Blue Hill Farm. He had been riding round Merston's lands with Burke during a great part of the day, and he was comfortably tired. He looked forward to spending a congenial evening with his hostess, and he hoped that young Guy would not be of too lively a turn, for he was in a mood for peace.

The first chill of evening was creeping over the *veldt* as he ambled along the trail past the *kopje*. As he came within sight of the farm a wave of sentiment swept over him.

"Faith, it's a jolly little homestead!" he said, with a sigh. "Lucky devil—Burke!"

There was no one about, and he took his horse to the stable and gave him a rub-down and feed before entering. Then he made his way into the house from the back.

There was a light in the sitting-room, and he betook himself thither, picturing the homely scene of Sylvia knitting socks for her husband or engaged upon some housewifely task.

He announced himself with his customary, cheery garrulity as he entered.

"Ah, here I am again, Mrs. Burke! And it's good news I've got for ye. Merston's not so badly damaged after all, and your husband is hoping to be back by midday in the morning."

He stopped short. The room was not empty, but the figure that rose up with an easy, sinuous movement to meet him was not the figure he had expected to see.

"Good evening, Kelly!" said Saul Kieff.

"What the devil!" said Kelly.

Kieff smiled in a cold, detached fashion. "I came over to find Mr. Burke Ranger. But I gather he is away from home."

"What have you come for?" said Kelly.

He did not like Kieff though his nature was too kindly to entertain any active antipathy towards anyone. But no absence of intimacy could ever curb his curiosity, and he never missed any information for lack of investigation.

Kieff's motionless black eyes took him in with satirical comprehension. He certainly would never have made a confidant of such a man as Kelly unless it had suited his purpose. He took several moments for consideration before he made reply. "I presume you are aware," he said then, "that Mrs. Ranger has left for Brennerstadt?"

"What?" said Kelly.

Kieff did not repeat his question. He merely waited for it to sink in. A faint, subtle smile still hovered about his sallow features. It was obvious that he regarded his news in anything but a tragic light.

"Gone to Brennerstadt!" ejaculated Kelly at length. "But what the devil would she go there for? I was going myself to-morrow. I'd have taken her."

"She probably preferred to choose her own escort," said Kieff.

"What?" said Kelly again. "Man, is it the truth you're giving me?"

"Not much point in lying," said Kieff coldly, "when there is nothing to be gained by it! Mrs. Burke Ranger has gone to Brennerstadt by way of Ritzen, in the company of Guy Ranger. Piet Vreiboom will tell you the same thing if you ask him. He is going to Brennerstadt too to-morrow, and I with him. Perhaps we can travel together. We may overtake the amorous couple if we ride all the way."

Without any apparent movement, his smile in-

tensified at sight of the open consternation on
Kelly's red countenance.

"You seem surprised at something," he said.

"I don't believe a damn' word of it," said Kelly
bluntly. "You didn't see them."

"I saw them both," said Kieff, still smiling.
"Piet Vreiboom saw them also. But the lady
seemed to be in a great hurry, so we did not detain
them. They are probably at Ritzen by now, if
not beyond."

"Oh, damnation!" said Kelly tragically.

Kieff's smile slowly vanished. His eyes took on
a stony, remote look as though the matter had
ceased to interest him. And while Kelly tramped
impotently about the room, he leaned his shoulders
against the wall and stared into space.

"I am really rather glad to have met you," he
remarked presently. "Can you give me any tip
regarding this diamond of Wilbraham's? You
know its value to the tenth part of a farthing, I
have no doubt."

Kelly paused to glare at him distractedly. "Oh,
curse the diamond!" he said. "It's Mrs. Burke
I'm thinking of."

Kieff's thin lips curled contemptuously. "A
woman!" he said, and snapped his fingers. "A
woman who can be bought and sold again—for

far less than half its cost! My good Kelly! Are you serious?"

Kelly stamped an indignant foot. "You infernal, cold-blooded Kaffir!" he roared. "I'm human anyway, which is more than you are!"

Kieff's sneer deepened. It was Kelly's privilege always to speak his mind, and no one took offence however extravagantly he expressed himself. "Can't we have a drink?" he suggested, in the indulgent tone of one humouring a fractious child.

"Drink—with you!" fumed Kelly.

Kieff smiled again. "Of course you will drink with me! It's too good an excuse to miss. What is troubling you? Surely there is nothing very unusual in the fact that Mrs. Burke finds herself in need of a little change!"

Kelly groaned aloud. "I've got to go and tell Burke. That's the hell of it. Sure I'd give all the money I can lay hands on to be quit of that job."

"You are over-sensitive," remarked Kieff, showing a gleam of teeth between his colourless lips. "He will think far less of this than of disease in his cattle or crops. They were nothing to each other, nor ever could be. She and Guy Ranger have been lovers all through."

"Ah, faith then, I know better!" broke in Kelly. "He worships her from the crown of her head to the sole of her foot. He'll be fit to kill young Guy for this. By the saints above us, I could almost kill him myself."

"You needn't!" said Kieff with ironical humour. "And Burke needn't either. As for the woman —" he snapped his fingers again—"she'll come back like a homing dove, if he waits a little."

Kelly swore again furiously. "Ah, why did I ever lend myself to digging young Guy out of Hoffstein's? Only a blasted fool could have expected to bring anything but corruption out of that sink of evil. It was Burke's own doing, but I was a fool—I was a three times fool—to give in to him."

"Where is the worthy Burke?" questioned Kieff.

"Over at Merston's, doing the good Samaritan; been working like a nigger all day. And now!" There was actually a sound of tears in Kelly's voice. "I'd give me right hand," he vowed tremulously, "I'd give me soul—such as it is—to be out of this job."

"You want a drink," said Kieff.

Kelly sniffed and began a clumsy search for refreshment.

Kieff came forward kindly and helped him. It

was he who measured the drinks finally when they were produced, and even Kelly, who could stand a good deal, opened his eyes somewhat at the draught he prepared for himself.

"Dry weather!" remarked Kieff, as he tossed it down. "You're not going back to Merston's to-night, are you?"

"Must," said Kelly laconically.

"Why not wait till the morning?" suggested Kieff. "I shall be passing that way myself then. We could go together."

There was a gleam in his black eyes that made Kelly look at him hard. "And what would you want to be there for?" he demanded aggressively. "Isn't one bearer of evil tidings enough?"

Kieff smiled. "I wonder if the lady left any message behind," he suggested. "Possibly she has written a note to explain her own absence. How long did the good Burke propose to be away?"

"Two or three nights in the first place. But he is coming back to-morrow." A sudden idea flashed upon Kelly. "Ah, p'raps she's hoping to be back before he is! Maybe there's more to this than we understand! I'll not go over. I'll wait and see. She may be back in the morning, she and young Guy too. They're old friends. P'raps there's nothing in it but just a jaunt."

Kieff's laugh had a sound like the slipping of a stone in a slimy cave. "You always had ideas," he remarked. "But they will scarcely be back from Brennerstadt by the morning. Can't you devise some means of persuading Burke to extend his visit to the period originally intended? Then perhaps they might return in time."

Kelly looked at him sternly. That laugh was abominable in his ears. "Faith, I'll go now," he said. "And I'll go alone. You've done your part, and I'll not trouble you at all to help me do mine."

Kieff turned to go. "I always admired your sense of duty, Donovan," he said. "Let us hope it will bring you out on the right side,—and your friends the Rangers with you!"

He was gone with the words, silent as a shadow on the wall, and Kelly was left wondering why he had not seized the bearer of evil tidings and kicked the horrible laughter out of him.

"Faith, I'll do it when I get to Brennerstadt," he said to himself vindictively. "But it's friends first, eh, Burke, my lad?—Ah, Burke, my boy, friends first!"

CHAPTER XI

THE SHARP CORNER

WAS it only a few months since last she had looked out over the barren *veldt* from the railway at Ritzen? It seemed to Sylvia like half a lifetime.

In the dark of the early morning she sat in the southward-bound train on her way to Brennerstadt, and tried to recall her first impressions. There he had stood under the lamp waiting for her—the man whom she had taken for Guy. She saw herself springing to meet him with eager welcome on her lips and swift-growing misgiving at her heart. How good he had been to her! That thought came up above the rest, crowding out the memory of her first terrible dismay. He had surrounded her with a care as chivalrous as any of the friends of her former life could have displayed. He had sheltered her from the dreadful loneliness, and from the world upon the mercy of which she had been so completely thrown. He had not seemed to bestow, but she realized now how at every turn his goodness had provided, his strength had shielded. He had not suffered her to feel the obligation under which she was placed. He had treated her merely as a comrade in distress. He had given her freely the very best that a man could offer, and he had done it in a fashion that had made acceptance easy, almost inevitable.

Her thoughts travelled onwards till they came to her marriage. Again the memory of the man's unfailing chivalry came before all else. Again, how good he had been to her! And she had taken full advantage of his goodness. For the first time she wondered if she had been justified in so doing. She asked herself if she had behaved contemptibly. She had not been ready to make a full surrender, and he had not asked for it. But it seemed to her now that she had returned his gifts with a niggardliness which must have made her appear very small-minded. He had been great. He had subordinated his wishes to her. He had been patient; ah yes, perhaps too patient! Probably her utter dependence upon him had made him so.

Slowly her thoughts passed on to the coming of Guy. She realized that the rapid events that had succeeded his coming had rendered her impressions of Burke a little blurred. Through all those first stages of Guy's illness, she could scarcely recall him at all. Her mind was full of the image of Kieff, subtle, cruel, almost ghoulish, a man of deep cunning and incomprehensible motives. It had suited his whim to save Guy. She had often wondered why. She was certain that no impulse of affection had moved him or was capable of moving him. No pity, no sympathy, had ever complicated this man's aims or crippled his achievements. He had a clear, substantial reason for everything that he did. It had pleased him to bring Guy back to life, and so he had not scrupled as to the means he had employed to do so. He had practically forced her into a position which circumstances had combined to make her retain. He had probably, she reflected now, urged Guy upon every opportunity to play the traitor to his best friend. He had established over him an influence which she felt that it would take her utmost effort to overthrow. He had even forced him into the quagmire of crime. For that Guy had done this thing, or would ever have dreamed of doing it, on his own initiative she did not believe. And it was that certainty which had sent her from his empty hut on the sand in pursuit of him, daring all to win him back ere he had sunk too deep for deliverance. She had ridden to Ritzen by way of the Vreibooms' farm, half-expecting to find Guy there. But she had seen only Kieff and Piet Vreiboom. Her face burned still at the memory of the former's satirical assurance that Guy was but a few miles ahead of her and she would easily overtake him. He had translated this speech to Piet Vreiboom who had laughed, laughed with a sickening significance, at the joke. In her disgust she had ridden swiftly on without stopping to ascertain if Guy had gone to Ritzen or had decided to ride the whole forty miles to Brennerstadt.

The lateness of the hour, however, had decided her to make for the former place since she knew she could get a train there on the following morning and she could not face the long journey at night alone on the *veldt*. It had been late when she reached Ritzen, but she had thankfully found accommodation for the night at the by no means luxurious hotel in which she had slept on the night of her arrival so long ago.

Now in the early morning she was ready to start again, having regretfully left her horse, Diamond, in the hotel-stable to await her return.

If all went well, she counted upon being back, perhaps with Guy accompanying her, in the early afternoon. And then she would probably be at Blue Hill Farm again before Burke's return. She hoped with all her heart to accomplish this. For though it would be impossible to hide the fact of her journey from him, she did not want him to suspect the actual reason that had made it so urgent. Let him think that anxiety for Guy—their mutual charge—had sent her after him! But never, for Guy's sake, let him imagine the actual shameful facts of the case! She counted upon Burke's ignorance as the strongest weapon for Guy's persuasion. Let him but realize that a way of escape yet remained to him, and she believed that he would take it. For surely—ah, surely, if she knew him—he had begun already to repent in burning shame and self-loathing.

He must have ridden all the way to Brennerstadt, for he was not at Ritzen. Ritzen was not a place to hide in. Would she find him at Brennerstadt? There were only two hotels there, and Kieff had said he would stop at one of them. She did not trust Kieff for a moment, but some inner conviction told her that it was his intention that she should find Guy. He did not expect her influence to overcome his. That she fully realized. He was not afraid of being superseded. Perhaps he wanted to demonstrate to her her utter weakness. Perhaps he had deeper schemes. She did not stop to imagine what they were. She shrank

from the thought of them as purity shrinks instinctively from the contemplation of evil. She
believed that, if once she could meet Guy face to
face, she could defeat him. She counted upon
that understanding which had been between them
from the beginning and which had drawn them
to each other in spite of all opposition. She
counted upon that part of Guy which Kieff had
never known, those hidden qualities which vice
had overgrown like a fungus but which she knew
were still existent under the surface evil. Guy
had been generous and frank in the old days, a
lover of fair play, an impetuous follower of anything that appealed to him as great. She was
sure that these characteristics had been an essen-
tial part of his nature. He had failed through in-
stability, through self-indulgence and weakness of
purpose. But he was not fundamentally wicked.
She was sure that she could appeal to those good
impulses within him, and that she would not appeal in vain. She was sure that the power of good
would still be paramount over him if she held out
to him the helping hand which he so sorely needed.
She had the strength within her—strength that
was more than human—and she was certain of the
victory, if only she could find him quickly, quickly!

As she sat there waiting feverishly to start, her

whole being was in a passion of supplication that she might be in time. Even in her sleep she had prayed that one prayer with a fierce urging that had rendered actual repose an impossibility. She had never in her life prayed with so intense a force. It was as if she were staking the whole of her faith upon that one importunate plea, and though no answer came to her striving spirit, she told herself that it could not be in vain. In all her maddening anxiety and impatience she never for a moment dwelt upon the chance of failure. God could not suffer her to fail when she had fought so hard. Her very brain seemed on fire with the urgency of her mission, and again for a space the thought of Burke was crowded out. He occupied the back of her mind, but she would not voluntarily turn towards him. That would come later when her mission was fulfilled, when she could look him in the face again with no sense of a charge neglected, or trust betrayed. She must stand straight with Burke, but she must save Guy first, whatever the effort, whatever the cost. She felt she had forfeited the right to think of her own happiness till her negligence—and the terrible consequences thereof—had been remedied. Perhaps it was in a measure self-blame that inspired her frantic prayer, the feeling that the responsibility was hers, and therefore that she was a sharer of the guilt. That was another plea, less worthy perhaps; but one to which Guy could not refuse to listen. It could not be his intention to wreck her happiness. He could not know all that hung upon it. Her happiness! She shivered suddenly in the chill of the morning air. Could it be that happiness—the greatest of all—had been actually within her grasp, and she had let it slip unheeded? Sharply she turned her thoughts back. No, she must not—must not think of Burke just then.

The chance would come again. The chance must come again. But she must not suffer herself to contemplate it now. She had forfeited the right.

Time passed. She thought the train would never start. The long waiting had become almost a nightmare. She felt she would not be able to endure it much longer. The night had seemed endless too, a perpetual dozing and waking that had seemed to multiply the hours. Now and then she realized that she was very tired; but for the most part the fever of impatience that possessed her kept the consciousness of fatigue at bay. If only she could keep moving she felt that she could face anything.

The day broke over the *veldt* and the scattered open town, with a burning splendour like the kindling of a great fire. She watched the dawn-light spread till the northern hills shone with a celestial radiance. She leaned from the train to watch it; and as she watched, the whole world turned golden.

Burke's words flashed back upon her with a force irresistible. "Let us go to the top of the world by ourselves!" Her eyes filled with sudden tears, and as she sank down again in her seat the train began to move. It bore her relentlessly southwards, and the land of the early morning was left behind.

She reflected later that that journey must have been doomed to disaster from the very outset. It was begun an hour late, and all things seemed to conspire to hinder them. After many halts, the breaking of an engine-piston rendered them helpless, and the heat of the day found them in a desolate place among *kopjes* that seemed to crowd them in, cutting off every current of air, while the sun blazed mercilessly overhead and the sand-flies ceaselessly buzzed and tormented. It was the longest day that Sylvia had ever known, and she thought that the smell of Kaffirs would haunt her all her life. Of the few white men on the train she knew not one, and the desolation of despair entered into her.

By the afternoon, when she had hoped to be on her way back, tardy help arrived, and they crawled into Brennerstadt station, parched and dusty and half-starved, some three hours later.

Hope revived in her as at length she left the train. Anything was better than the awful inactivity of that well-nigh interminable journey. There was yet a chance—a slender one—that by an early start or possibly travelling by a night train she and Guy might yet be back at Blue Hill Farm by the following evening in time to meet Burke on his return.

Yes, the chance was there, and still she could not think that all this desperate effort of hers could be doomed to failure. If she could only find Guy quickly—oh, quickly! She almost ran out of the station in her haste.

She turned her steps instinctively towards the hotel in which she had stayed for her marriage. It was not far from the station, and it was the first place that occurred to her. The town was full of people, men for the most part, men it seemed to her, of all nationalities and colours. She heard Dutch and broken English all around her.

She went through the crowds, shrinking a little now and then from any especially coarse type, nervously intent upon avoiding contact with any. She found the hotel without difficulty, but when she found it she checked her progress for the first time. For she was afraid to enter.

The evening was drawing on. She felt the welcome chill of it on her burning face, and it kept her from yielding to the faintness that oppressed her. But still she could not enter, till a great, square-built Boer lounging near the doorway came up to her and looked into her eyes with an evil leer.

Then she summoned her strength, drew herself up, and passed him with open disgust.

She had to push her way through a crowd of men idling in the entrance, and one or two accosted her, but she went by them in stony unresponsiveness.

At the little office at the end she found a girl, sandy-haired and sandy-eyed, who looked up for a moment from a great book in front of her, and before she could speak, said briskly, "There's no more accommodation here. The place is full to overflowing. Better try at the Good Hope over the way."

She had returned to her occupation before the words were well uttered, but Sylvia stood motionless, a little giddy, leaning against the woodwork for support.

"I only want to know," she said, after a moment, speaking with an effort in a voice that sounded oddly muffled even to herself, "if Mr. Ranger is here."

"Who?" The girl looked up sharply. "Hullo!" she said. "What's the matter?"

"If Mr. Ranger—Mr. Ranger—is here," Sylvia repeated through a curious mist that had gathered unaccountably around her.

The girl got up and came to her. "Yes, he's here, I believe, or will be presently. He's engaged a room anyhow. I didn't see him myself. Look here, you'd better come and sit down a minute. I seem to remember you. You're Mrs. Ranger, aren't you?"

"Yes," said Sylvia.

She was past explanation just then, and that simple affirmative seemed her only course. She leaned thankfully upon the supporting arm, fighting blindly to retain her senses.

"Come and sit down!" the girl repeated. "I expect he'll be in before long. They're all mad about this diamond draw. The whole town is buzzing with it. The races aren't in it. Sit down and I'll get you something."

She drew Sylvia into a small inner sanctum and there left her, sitting exhausted in a wooden armchair. She returned presently with a tray which she set in front of her, observing practically, "That's what you're wanting. Have a good feed, and when you've done you'd better go up and lie down till he comes."

She went back to her office then, closing the door between, and Sylvia was left to recover as best she might. She forced herself after a time to eat and drink, reflecting that physical weakness would utterly unfit her for the task before her. She hoped with all her heart that Guy would come soon—soon. There was a night train back to Ritzen. She had ascertained that at the station. They might catch that. The diamond draw was still two days away. She prayed that he had not yet staked anything upon it, that when he came the money might be still in his possession.

She finished her meal and felt considerably revived. For a while she sat listening to the hubbub of strange voices without, then the fear that her presence might be forgotten by the busy occupant of the office moved her to rise and open the intervening door.

The girl was still there. She glanced round with the same alert expression. "That you, Mrs.

Ranger? He hasn't come in yet. But you go up and wait for him! It's quieter upstairs. I'll tell him you're here as soon as he comes in."

She did not want to comply, but certainly the little room adjoining the office was no place for private talk, and she dreaded the idea of meeting Guy before the curious eyes of strangers. He would be startled; he would be ashamed! None but herself must see him in that moment.

So, without protest, she allowed herself to be conducted upstairs to the room he had engaged, her friend in the office promising faithfully not to forget to send him up to her at once.

The room was at the top of the house, a bare apartment but not uncomfortable. It possessed a large window that looked across the wide street. She sat down beside it and listened to the tramping crowds below.

Her faintness had passed, but she was very tired, overwhelmingly so. Very soon her senses became dulled to the turmoil. She suffered herself to relax, certain that the first sound of a step outside would recall her. And so, as night spread over the town, she sank into sleep, lying back in the cane-chair like a worn-out child, her burnished hair vivid against the darkness beyond.

.   .   .   .

She did not wake at the sound of a step outside, or even at the opening of the door. It was no sound that aroused her hours later, but a sudden intense consciousness of expediency, as if she had come to a sharp corner that it needed all her wits to turn in safety. She started up with a gasp. "Guy!" she said. And then, as her dazzled eyes saw more clearly, a low, involuntary exclamation of dismay. "Ah!"

It was Burke who stood with his back against the closed door, looking at her, and his face had upon it in those first waking moments of bewilderment a look that appalled her. For it was to her as the face of a murderer.

CHAPTER XII

THE COST

HE did not speak in answer to her exclamation, merely stood there looking at her, almost as if he had never seen her before. His eyes were keen with a sort of icy fierceness. She thought she had never before realized the cruelty of his mouth.

It was she who spoke first. The silence seemed so impossible. "Burke!" she said. "What—is the matter?"

He came forward to her with an abruptness that was like the breaking of bonds. He stopped in front of her, looking closely into her face. "What are you doing here?" he said.

In spite of herself she shrank, so terrible was his look. But she was swift to master her weakness. She stood up to her full height, facing him. "I have come to find Guy," she said.

He threw a glance around; it was like the sweep of a rapier. "You are waiting for him— here?"

Again for a moment she was disconcerted. She

felt the quick blood rise to her forehead. "They told me he would come here," she said.

He passed on, almost as if she had not spoken, but his eyes were mercilessly upon her, marking her confusion. "What do you want with him?"

His words were like the snap of a steel rope. They made her flinch by their very ruthlessness. She had sprung from sleep with bewildered senses. She was not prepared to do battle in her own defence.

She hesitated, and immediately his hand closed upon her shoulder. It seemed to her that she had never known what anger could be like before this moment. All the force of the man seemed to be gathered together in one tremendous wave, menacing her.

"Tell me what you want with him!" he said.

She shuddered from head to foot as if she had been struck with a scourge. "Burke! What do you mean?" she cried out desperately. "You— you must be mad!"

"Answer me!" he said.

His hold was a grip. The ice in his eyes had turned to flame. Her heart leapt and quivered within her like a wild thing fighting to escape.

"I—don't know what you mean," she panted.

"I have done nothing wrong. I came after him to—to try and bring him back."

"Then why did you come secretly?" he said.

She shrank from the intolerable inquisition of his eyes. "I wanted to see him—alone," she said.

"Why?" Again it was like the merciless cut of a scourge. She caught her breath with a sharp sound that was almost a cry.

"Why?" he reiterated. "Answer me! Answer me!"

She did not answer him. She could not. And in the silence that followed, it seemed to her that something within her—something that had been vitally wounded—struggled and died.

"Look at me!" he said.

She lifted an ashen face. His eyes held hers, and the torture of his hell encompassed her also.

"Tell me the truth!" he said. "I shall know if you lie. When did you see him last?"

She shook her head. "A long while ago. Ages ago. Before you left the farm."

The memory of his going, his touch, his smile, went through her with the words. She had a sickening sensation as of having been struck over the heart.

"Where did you spend last night?" he said.

"At Ritzen." Her white lips seemed to speak

mechanically. She herself stood apart as it were, stunned beyond feeling.

"You came here by rail—alone?"

The voice of the inquisitor pierced her numbed sensibilities, compelling—almost dictating—her answer.

"Yes,—alone."

"You had arranged to meet here then?"

Still the scourging continued, and she marvelled at herself, that she felt so little. But feeling was coming back. She was waiting for it, dreading it.

She answered without conscious effort. "No—I came after him. He doesn't know I am here."

"And yet you are posing as his wife?"

She felt that. It cut through her apathy irresistibly. A sharp tremor went through her. "That," she said rather breathlessly, "was a mistake."

"It was," said Burke. "The greatest mistake of your life. It is a pity you took the trouble to lie to me. The truth would have served you better." He turned from her contemptuously with the words, setting her free.

For a moment the relief of his going was such that the intention that lay behind it did not so much as occur to her. Then suddenly it flashed upon her. He was going in search of Guy.

In an instant her passivity was gone. The necessity for action drove her forward. With a cry she sprang to the door before him, and set herself against it. She could not let him go with that look of the murderer in his eyes.

"Burke!" she gasped. "Burke! What—are you going to do?"

His lips parted a little, and she saw his teeth. "You shall hear what I have done—afterwards," he said. "Let me pass!"

But she barred his way. Her numbed senses were all awake now and quivering. The very fact of physical effort seemed to have restored to her the power to suffer. She stood before him, her bosom heaving with great sobs that brought no tears or relief of any sort to the anguish that tore her.

"You—you can't pass," she said. "Not—not —like this! Burke, listen! I swear to you—I swear——"

"You needn't," he broke in. "A woman's oath, when it is her last resource, is quite valueless. I will deal with you afterwards. Let me pass!"

The command was curt as a blow. But still she withstood him, striving to still her agitation, striving with all her desperate courage to face him and endure.

"I will not!" she said, and with the words she stood up to her full, slim height, thwarting him, making her last stand.

His expression changed as he realized her defiance. She was panting still, but there was no sign of yielding in her attitude. She was girt for resistance to the utmost.

There fell an awful pause—a silence which only her rapid breathing disturbed. Her eyes were fixed on his. She must have seen the change, but she dared it unflinching. There was no turning back for her now.

The man spoke at last, and his voice was absolutely quiet, dead level. "You had better let me go," he said.

She made a sharp movement, for there was that in the steel-cold voice that sent terror to her heart. Was this Burke—the man upon whose goodness she had leaned ever since she had come to this land of strangers? Surely she had never met him before that moment!

"Open that door!" he said.

A great tremor went through her. She turned, the instinct to obey urging her. But in the same instant the thought of Guy—Guy in mortal danger—flashed across her. She paused for a second, making a supreme effort, while every impulse fought in mad tumult within her, crying to her to yield. Then, with a lightning twist of the hand she turned the key and pulled it from the lock. For an instant she held it in her hand, then with a half-strangled sound she thrust it deep into her bosom.

Her eyes shone like flames in her white face as she turned back to him. "Perhaps you will believe me—now!" she said.

He took a single step forward and caught her by the wrists. "Woman!" he said. "Do you know what you are doing?"

The passion that blazed in his look appalled her. Yet some strange force within her awoke as it were in answer to her need. She flung fear aside. She had done the only thing possible, and she would not look back.

"You must believe me—now!" she panted. "You do believe me!"

His hold became a grip, merciless, fierce, tightening upon her like a closing trap. "Why should I believe you?" he said, and there was that in his voice that was harder to bear than his look. "Have I any special reason for believing you? Have you ever given me one?"

"You know me," she said, with a sinking heart.

He uttered a scoffing sound too bitter to be

called a laugh. "Do I know you? Have I ever been as near to you as this devil who has made himself notorious with Kaffir women for as long as he has been out here?"

She flinched momentarily from the stark cruelty of his words. But she faced him still, faced him though every instinct of her womanhood shrank with a dread unspeakable.

"You know me," she said again. "You may not know me very well, but you know me well enough for that."

It was bravely spoken, but as she ceased to speak she felt her strength begin to fail her. Her throat worked spasmodically, convulsively, and a terrible tremor went through her. She saw him as through a haze that blotted out all beside.

There fell a silence between them—a dreadful, interminable silence that seemed to stretch into eternities. And through it very strangely she heard the wild beating of her own heart, like the hoofs of a galloping horse, that seemed to die away. . . .

She did not know whether she fell, or whether he lifted her, but when the blinding mist cleared away again, she was lying in the wicker-chair by the window, and he was walking up and down the room with the ceaseless motion of a prowling animal. She sat up slowly and looked at him. She was shivering all over, as if stricken with cold.

At her movement he came and stood before her, but he did not speak. He seemed to be watching her. Or was he waiting for something?

She could not tell; neither, as he stood there, could she look up at him to see. Only, after a moment, she leaned forward. She found and held his hand.

"Burke!" she said.

His fingers closed as if they would crush her own. He did not utter a word.

She waited for a space, gathering her strength. Then, speaking almost under her breath, she went on. "I have—something to say to you. Please will you listen—till I have finished?"

"Go on!" he said.

Her head was bent. She went on tremulously. "You are quite right—when you say—that you don't know me—that I have given you no reason— no good reason—to believe in me. I have taken —a great deal from you. And I have given— nothing in return. I see that now. That is why you distrust me. I—have only myself to thank."

She paused a moment, but he waited in absolute silence, neither helping nor hindering.

With a painful effort she continued. "People

make mistakes—sometimes—without knowing it.
It comes to them afterwards—perhaps too late.
But—it isn't too late with me, Burke. I am
your partner—your wife. And—I never meant
to—defraud you. All I have—is yours. I—am
yours."

She stopped. Her head was bowed against his
hand. That dreadful sobbing threatened to overwhelm her again, but she fought it down. She
waited quivering for his answer.

But for many seconds Burke neither moved nor
spoke. The grasp of his hand was vicelike in its
rigidity. She had no key whatever to what was
passing in his mind.

Not till she had mastered herself and was sitting
in absolute stillness, did he stir. Then, very
quietly, with a decision that brooked no resistance,
he took her by the chin with his free hand and
turned her face up to his own. He looked deep
into her eyes. His own were no longer ablaze,
but a fitful light came and went in them like the
flare of a torch in the desert wind.

"So," he said, and his voice was curiously unsteady also; it vibrated as if he were not wholly
sure of himself, "you have made your choice—
and counted the cost?"

"Yes," she said.

He looked with greater intentness into her eyes, searching without mercy, as if he would force his way to her very soul. "And for whose sake this—sacrifice?" he said.

She shrank a little; for there was something intolerable in his words. Had she really counted the cost? Her eyelids fluttered under that unsparing look, fluttered and sank. "You will know —some day," she whispered.

"Ah! Some day!" he said.

Again his voice vibrated. It was as if some door that led to his innermost being had opened suddenly, releasing a savage, primitive force which till then he had held restrained.

And in that moment it came to her that the thing she valued most in life had been rudely torn from her. She saw that new, most precious gift of hers that had sprung to life in the wilderness and which she had striven so desperately to shield from harm—that holy thing which had become dearer to her than life itself—desecrated, broken, and lying in the dust. And it was Burke who had flung it there, Burke who now ruthlessly trampled it underfoot.

Her throat worked again painfully for a moment or two; and then with a great effort of the will she stilled it. This thing was beyond tears—a cataclysm wrecking the whole structure of existence. Neither tears nor laughter could ever be hers again. In silence she took the cup of bitterness, and drank it to the dregs.

PART IV

CHAPTER I

SAND OF THE DESERT

DONOVAN KELLY was out of temper. There was no denying it, though with him such a frame of mind was phenomenal. He leaned moodily against the door-post at the hotel-entrance, smoking a short pipe of very strong tobacco, and speaking to no one. He had been there for some time, and the girl in the office was watching him with eyes round with curiosity. For he had not even said "Good morning" to her. She wanted to accost him, but somehow the hunch of his shoulders was too discouraging even for her. So she contented herself with waiting developments.

There were plenty of men coming and going, but though several of them gave him greeting as they passed, Kelly responded to none. He seemed to be wrapped in a gloomy fog of meditation that cut him off completely from the outside world. He was alone with himself, and in that state he obviously intended to remain.

But the girl in the office had her own shrewd suspicions as to the reason of his waiting there, suspicions which after the lapse of nearly half an hour she triumphantly saw verified. For presently through the shifting, ever-changing crowd a square-shouldered man made his appearance, and without a glance to right or left went straight to the big Irishman lounging in the doorway, and took him by the shoulder.

Kelly started round with an instant smile of welcome. "Ah, and is it yourself at last? I've been waiting a devil of a time for ye, my son. Is all well?"

The girl in the office did not hear Burke's reply though she craned far forward to do so. She only saw his shoulders go up slightly, and the next moment the two men turned and entered the public dining-room together.

Kelly's ill-temper had gone like an early morning fog. He led the way to a table reserved in a corner, and they sat down.

"I was half afraid ye wouldn't have anything but a kick for Donovan this morning," he said, with a somewhat rueful smile.

Burke's own brief smile showed for a moment. "I shouldn't start on you anyway," he said. "You found young Guy?"

Kelly made an expressive gesture. "Oh yes, I found him, him and his master too. At Hoffstein's of course. Kieff was holding one of his opium shows, the damn' dirty skunk. I couldn't get the boy away, but I satisfied myself that he was innocent of this. He never engaged a room here or had any intention of coming here. What Kieff's intentions were I didn't enquire. But he had got the devil's own grip on Guy last night. He could have made him do—anything." Kelly ended with a few strong expressions which left no doubt as to the opinion he entertained of Kieff and all his works.

Burke ate his breakfast in an absorbed silence. Finally he looked up to enquire, "Have you any idea what has become of Guy this morning?"

Kelly shook his head. "Not the shadow of a notion. I shall look for him presently on the racecourse. He seems to have found some money to play with, for he told me he had taken two tickets for the diamond draw, one for himself and one for another. But he was just mad last night. The very devil had got into him. What will I do with him if I get him?"

Burke's eyes met his for a moment. "You can do—anything you like with him," he said.

"Ah, but he saved your life, Burke," said

the Irishman pleadingly. "It's only three days ago."

"I know what he did," said Burke briefly, "both before and after that episode. He may think himself lucky that I have no further use for him."

"But aren't you satisfied, Burke?" Kelly leaned forward impulsively. "I've told you the truth. Aren't you satisfied?"

Burke's face was grim as if hewn out of rock. "Not yet," he said. "You've told me the truth— what you know of it. But there's more to it. I've got to know—everything before I'm satisfied."

"Ah, but sure!" protested Kelly. "Women are very queer, you know. Ye can't tell what moves a woman. Often as not, it's something quite different from what you'd think."

Burke was silent, continuing his breakfast.

Kelly looked at him with eyes of pathetic persuasion. "I've been lambastin' meself all night," he burst forth suddenly, "for ever bringing ye out on such a chase. It was foul work. I see it now. She'd have come back to ye, Burke lad. She didn't mean any harm. Sure, she's as pure as the stars."

Burke's grey eyes, keen as the morning light, looked suddenly straight at him. Almost under his breath, Burke spoke. "Don't tell me—that!"

he said. "Just keep Guy out of my way! That's all."

Kelly sighed aloud. "And Guy'll go to perdition faster than if the devil had kicked him. He's on his way already."

"Let him go!" said Burke.

It was his last word on the subject. Having spoken it, he gave his attention to the meal before him, and concluded it with a deliberate disregard for Kelly's depressed countenance that an onlooker might have found somewhat brutal.

"What are you going to do?" asked Kelly meekly, as at length he pushed back his chair.

Burke's eyes came to him again. He smiled faintly at the woebegone visage before him. "Cheer up, Donovan!" he said. "You're all right. You've had a beastly job, but you've done it decently. I'm going back to my wife now. She breakfasted upstairs. We shall probably make tracks this evening."

"Ah!" groaned Kelly. "Your wife'll never speak to me again after this. And I thinking her the most charming woman in the world!"

Burke turned to go. "Don't fret yourself on that account!" he said. "My wife will treat my friends exactly as she would treat her own."

He spoke with a confidence that aroused Kelly's

admiration. "Sure, you know how to manage a woman, don't ye, Burke, me lad?" he said.

He watched the broad figure till it was out of sight, then got up and went out into the hot sunshine, intent upon another quest.

Burke went on steadily up the stairs till he reached the top story where he met a servant carrying a breakfast-tray with the meal practically untouched upon it. With a brief word Burke took the tray himself, and went on with the same air of absolute purpose to the door at the end of the passage.

Here, just for a moment he paused, standing in semi-darkness, listening. Then he knocked.

Sylvia's voice answered him, and he entered.

She was dressed and standing by the window. "Oh, please, Burke!" she said quickly, at sight of what he carried. "I can't eat anything more."

He set down the tray and looked at her. "Why did you get up?" he said.

Her face was flushed. There was unrest in every line of her. "I had to get up," she said feverishly. "I can't rest here. It is so noisy. I want to get out of this horrible place. I can't breathe here. Besides—besides——"

"Sit down!" said Burke.

"Oh, don't make me eat anything!" she pleaded. "I really can't.   I am sorry, but really——"

"Sit down!" he said again, and laid a steady hand upon her.

She yielded with obvious reluctance, avoiding his eyes.   "I am quite all right," she said.   "Don't bully me, partner!"

Her voice quivered suddenly, and she put her hand to her throat.   Burke was pouring milk into a cup.   She watched him, fighting with herself.

"Now," he said, "you can drink this anyway. It's what you're needing."   He gave her the cup, and she took it from him without a word.   He turned away, and stood at the window, waiting.

At the end of a full minute, he spoke.   "Has it gone?"

"Yes," she said.

He turned back and looked at her.   She met his eyes with an effort.

"I am quite all right," she said again.

"Ready to start back?" he said.

She leaned forward in her chair, her hands clasped very tightly in front of her.   "To-day?" she said in a low voice.

"I thought you wanted to get away," said Burke.

"Yes—yes, I do."   Her eyes suddenly fell before his. "I do," she said again. "But—but—I've got—something—to ask of you—first."

"Well?" said Burke.

Her breath came quickly; her fingers were straining against each other. "I—don't quite know—how to say it," she said.

Burke stood quite motionless, looking down at her. "Must it be said?" he asked.

"Yes." She sat for a moment or two, mustering her strength. Then, with an abrupt effort, she got up and faced him. "Burke, I think I have a right to your trust," she said.

He looked straight back at her with piercing, relentless eyes. "If we are going to talk of rights," he said, "I might claim a right to your confidence."

She drew back a little, involuntarily, but the next moment, quickly, she went to him and clasped his arm between her hands. "Please be generous, partner!" she said. "We won't talk of rights, either of us. You—are not—angry with me now, are you?"

He stiffened somewhat at her touch, but he did not repulse her. "I'm afraid you won't find me in a very yielding mood," he said.

She held his arm a little more tightly, albeit her hands were trembling. "Won't you listen to me?"

she said, in a voice that quivered. "Is there—no possibility of—of—coming to an understanding?"

He drew a slow hard breath. "We have a very long way to go first," he said.

"I know," she answered, and her voice was quick with pain. "I know. But—we can't go on—like this. It—just isn't bearable. If—even if you can't understand me—Burke, won't you— won't you try at least to give me—the benefit of the doubt?"

It was very winningly spoken, but as she spoke she leaned her head suddenly against the arm she held and stifled a sob. "For both our sakes!" she whispered.

But Burke stood, rigid as rock, staring straight before him into the glaring sunlight. She did not know what was passing in his mind; that was the trouble of it. But she felt his grim resistance like a wall of granite, blocking her way. And the brave heart of her sank in spite of all her courage.

He moved at last, but it was a movement of constraint. He laid his free hand on her shoulder. "Crying won't help," he said. "I think we had better be getting back."

And then, for the sake of the old love, she made her supreme effort. She lifted her face; it was white to the lips, but it bore no sign of tears. "I can't go," she said, "till—I have seen Guy."

He made a sharp gesture. "Ah!" he said. "I thought that was coming."

"Yes, you knew it! You knew it!" Passionately she uttered the words. "It's the one thing that's got to be settled between us—the only thing left that counts. Yes, you mean to refuse. I know that. But before you refuse—wait, please wait! I am asking it quite as much for your sake as for mine."

"And for his," said Burke, with a twist of the lips more bitter than the words.

But she caught them up unflinching. "Yes, and for his. We've set out to save him, you and I. And—we are not going to turn back. Burke, I ask you to help me—I implore you to help me—in this thing. You didn't refuse before."

"I wish to Heaven I had!" he said, "I might have known how it would end!"

"No—no! And you owe him your life too. Don't forget that! He saved you. Are you going to let him sink—after that?" She reached up and held him by the shoulders, imploring him with all her soul. "You can't do it! Oh, you can't do it!" she said. "It isn't—you."

He looked at her with a certain doggedness.

"Not your conception of me perhaps," he said, and suddenly his arms closed about her quivering form. "But—am I—the sort of man you have always taken me to be? Tell me! Am I?"

She turned her face aside, hiding it against his shoulder. "I know—what you can be," she said faintly.

"Yes." Grimly he answered her. "You've seen the ugly side of me at last, and it's that that you are up against now." He paused a moment, then very sombrely he ended. "I might force you to tell me the whole truth of this business, but I shall not—simply because I don't want to hear it now. I know very well he's been making love to you, tempting you. But I am going to put the infernal matter away, and forget it—as far as possible. We may never reach the top of the world now, but we'll get out of this vile slough at any cost. You won't find me hard to live with if you only play the game,—and put that damned scoundrel out of your mind for good."

"And do you think I shall ever be able to forgive you?" She lifted her head with an unexpectedness that was almost startling. Her eyes were alight, burning with a ruddy fire out of the whiteness of her face. She spoke as she had never spoken before. It was as if some strange force had entered into and possessed her. "Do you think I shall ever forget—even if you do? Perhaps I am not enough to you now to count in that way. You think—perhaps—that a slave is all you want, and that partnership, comradeship, friendship, doesn't count. You are willing to sacrifice all that now, and to sacrifice him with it. But how will it be—afterwards? Will a slave be any comfort to you when things go wrong—as they surely will? Will it satisfy you to feel that my body is yours when my soul is so utterly out of sympathy, out of touch, that I shall be in spirit a complete stranger to you? Ah yes," her voice rang on a deep note of conviction that could not be restrained—"you think you won't care. But you will—you will. A time will come when you will feel you would gladly give everything you possess to undo what you are doing to-day. You will be sick at heart, lonely, disillusioned, suspicious of me and of everybody. You will see the horrible emptiness of it all, and you will yearn for better things. But it will be too late then. What once we fling away never comes again to us. We shall be too far apart by that time, too hopelessly estranged, ever to be more to each other than what we are at this moment—master and slave.

Through all our lives we shall never be more than that."

She ceased to speak, and the fire went out of her eyes. She drooped in his hold as if all her strength had gone from her.

He turned and put her steadily down into the chair again. He had heard her out without a sign of emotion, and he betrayed none then. He did not speak a word. But his silence said more to her than speech. It was as the beginning of a silence which was to last between them for as long as they lived.

She sank back exhausted with closed eyes. The struggle—that long, fierce battle for Guy's soul—was over. And she had failed. Her prayers had been in vain. All her desperate effort had been fruitless, and nothing seemed to matter any more. She told herself that she would never be able to pray again. Her faith had died in the mortal combat. And there was nothing left to pray for. She was tired to the very soul of her, tired unto death; but she knew she would not die. For death was rest, and there could be no rest for her until the days of her slavery were accomplished. The sand of the desert would henceforth be her portion. The taste of it was in her mouth. The desolation of it encompassed her spirit.

Two scalding tears forced their way through her closed lids and ran down her white cheeks. She did not stir to wipe them away. She hoped he did not see them. They were the only tears she shed.

CHAPTER II

THE SKELETON TREE

"Ah, Mrs. Burke, and is it yourself that I see again? Sure, and it's a very great pleasure!" Kelly, his face crimson with embarrassment and good-will, took the hand Sylvia offered and held it hard. "A very great pleasure!" he reiterated impressively, before he let it go.

She smiled at him as one smiles at a shy child. "Thank you, Mr. Kelly," she said.

"Ah, but you'll call me Donovan," he said persuasively, "the same as everyone else! So you've come to Brennerstadt after all! And is it the diamond ye're after?"

She shook her head. They were standing on a balcony that led out of the public smoking-room, an awning over their heads and the open street at their feet. It was from the street that he had spied her, and the sight of her piteous, white face with its deeply shadowed eyes had gone straight to his impulsive Irish heart. "No," she said. "We are not bothering about the diamond. I think we shall probably start back to Ritzen to-night."

"Ah now, ye might stay one day longer and try your luck," wheedled the Irishman. "The Fates would be sure to favour ye. Where's himself?"

"I don't know." She spoke very wearily. "He left me here to rest. But it's so dusty—and airless—and noisy."

Kelly gave her a swift, keen look. "Come for a ride!" he said.

"A ride!" She raised her heavy eyes with a momentary eagerness, but it was gone instantly. "He—might not like me to go," she said. "Besides, I haven't a horse."

"That's soon remedied," said Kelly. "I've got a lamb of a horse to carry ye. And he wouldn't care what ye did in my company. He knows me. Leave him a note and come along! He'll understand. It's a good gallop that ye're wanting. Come along and get it!"

Kelly could be quite irresistible when he chose, and he had evidently made up his mind to comfort the girl's forlornness so far as in him lay. She yielded to him with the air of being too indifferent to do otherwise. But Kelly had seen that moment's eagerness, and he built on that.

A quarter of an hour later they met again in the

sweltering street, and he complimented her in true
Irish fashion upon the rose-flush in her cheeks. He
saw that she looked about uneasily as she mounted,
but with unusual tact he omitted to comment upon
the fact.

The sun was slanting towards the west as they
rode away. The streets were crowded, but Kelly
knew all the short cuts, and guided her unerringly
till they reached the edge of the open *veldt.*

Then, "Come along!" he cried. "Let's gallop!"

The sand flew out behind them, the parched air
rushed by, and the blood quickened in Sylvia's
veins. She felt as if she had left an overwhelming
burden behind her in the town. The great open
spaces drew her with their freedom and their vastness. She went with the flight of a bird. It was
like the awakening from a dreadful dream.

They drew rein in the shadow of a tall *kopje*
that rose abruptly from the plain like a guardian
of the solitudes. Kelly was laughing with a boy's
hearty merriment.

"Faith, but ye can ride!" he cried, with keen
appreciation. "Never saw a prettier spectacle in
me life. Was it born in the saddle ye were?"

She laughed in answer, but her heart gave a
quick throb of pain. It was the first real twinge
of homesickness she had known, and for a moment

it was almost intolerable. Ah, the fresh-turned earth and the shining furrows, and the sweet spring rain in her face! And the sun of the early morning that shone through a scud of clouds!

"My father and I used to ride to hounds," she said. "We loved it."

"I've done it meself in the old country," said Kelly. "But ye can ride farther here. There's more room before ye reach the horizon."

Sylvia stifled a quick sigh. "Yes, it's a fine country. At least it ought to be. Yet I sometimes feel as if there is something lacking. I don't know quite what it is, but it's the quality that makes one feel at home."

"That'll come," said Kelly, with confidence. "You wait till the spring! That gets into your veins like wine. Ye'll feel the magic of it then. It's life itself."

Sylvia turned her face up to the brazen sky. "I must wait for the spring then," she said, half to herself. And then very suddenly she became aware of the kindly curiosity of her companion's survey and met it with a slight heightening of colour.

There was a brief silence before, in a low voice, she said, "We can't—all of us—afford to wait."

"You can," said Kelly promptly.

She shook her head. "I don't think by the time the spring comes that there will be much left worth having."

"Ah, but ye don't know," said Kelly. "You say that because you can't see all the flowers that are hiding down below. But you might as well believe in 'em all the same, for they're there all right, and they'll come up quick enough when God gives the word."

Sylvia looked around her over the barren land. "Are there flowers here?" she said.

"Millions," said Kelly. "Millions and millions. Why, if you were to come along here in a few weeks' time ye'd be trampling them underfoot they'd be so thick, such flowers as only grow here, on the top of the world."

"The top of the world!" She looked at him as if startled. "Is that what you call—this place?"

He laughed. "Ye don't believe me! Well, wait—wait and see!"

She turned her horse's head, and began to walk round the *kopje*. Kelly kept pace beside her. He was not quite so talkative as usual, but it was with obvious effort that he restrained himself, for several times words sprang to his eager lips which he swallowed unuttered. He seemed determined that the next choice of a subject should be hers.

And after a few moments he was rewarded. Sylvia spoke.

"Mr. Kelly!"

"Sure, at your service—now and always!" he responded with a warmth that no amount of self-restraint could conceal.

She turned towards him. "You have been very kind to me, and I want—I should like—to tell you something. But it's something very, very private. Will you—will you promise me——"

"Sure and I will!" vowed the Irishman instantly. "I'll swear the solemn oath if it'll make ye any happier."

"No, you needn't do that." She held out her hand to him with a gesture that was girlishly impulsive. "I know I can trust you. And I feel you will understand. It's about—Guy."

"Ah, there now! Didn't I know it?" said Kelly. He held her hand tight for a moment, looking into her eyes, his own brimful of sympathy.

"Yes. You know—all about him." She spoke with some hesitation notwithstanding. "You know—just as I do—that he isn't—isn't really bad; only—only so hopelessly weak."

There was a little quiver in her voice as she said the words. She looked at him with appeal in her eyes.

"I know," said Kelly.

With a slight effort she went on. "He—Burke —thinks otherwise. And because of that, he won't let me see Guy again. He is very angry with me—I doubt if he will ever really forgive me—for following Guy to this place. But,—Mr. Kelly,—I had a reason—an urgent reason for doing this. I hoped to be back again before he found out; but everything was against me."

"Ah! Didn't I know it?" said Kelly. "It's the way of the world in an emergency. Nothing ever goes right of itself."

She smiled rather wanly. "Life can be—rather cruel," she said. "Something is working against me. I can feel it. I have forfeited all Burke's respect and his confidence at a stroke. He will never trust me again. And Guy—Guy will simply go under."

"No—no!" said Kelly. "Don't you believe it! He'll come round and lead a decent life after this; you'll see. There's nothing whatever to worry about over Guy. No real vice in him!"

It was a kindly lie, stoutly spoken; but it failed to convince. Sylvia shook her head even while he was speaking.

"You don't know all yet. I haven't told you. But I will tell you—if you will listen. Once when

Burke and I were talking of Guy—it was almost the first time—he said that he had done almost everything bad except one thing. He had never robbed him. And somehow I felt that so long as there was that one great exception he would not regard him as utterly beyond redemption. But now—but now—" her voice quivered again—"well, even that can't be said of him now," she said.

"What? He has taken money?" Kelly looked at her in swift dismay. "Ye don't mean that!" he said. And then quickly: "Are ye sure now it wasn't Kieff?"

"Yes." She spoke with dreary conviction. "I am fairly sure Kieff's at the back of it, but—it was Guy who did it, thanks to my carelessness."

"Yours!" Kelly's eyes bulged. "Ye don't mean that!" he said again.

"Yes, it's true." Drearily she answered him. "Burke left the key of the strong-box in my keeping on the day of the sand-storm. I dropped it in the dark. I was hunting for it when you came. Then—I forgot it. Afterwards, you remember, Burke and Guy came in together. He must have found it—somehow—then."

"He did!" said Kelly suddenly. "Faith, he did! Ye remember when he had that attack? He picked up something then—on the floor against his foot. I saw him do it, the fool that I am! He'd got it in his hand when we helped him up, and I never noticed,—never thought. The artful young devil!"

A hint of admiration sounded in his voice. Kelly the simple-minded had ever been an admirer of art.

Sylvia went on very wearily. "The box was kept in a cupboard in the room he was sleeping in. The rest was quite easy. He left the key behind him in the lock. I found it after you and Burke had gone to the Merstons'. I guessed what had happened of course. I went round to his hut, but it was all fastened up as usual. Then I went to Piet Vreiboom's." She shuddered suddenly. "I saw Kieff as well as Vreiboom. They seemed hugely amused at my appearance, and told me Guy was just ahead on the way to Brennerstadt. It was too late to ride the whole way, so I went to Ritzen, hoping to find him there. But I could get no news of him, so I came on by train in the morning. I ought to have got here long ago, but the engine broke down. We were held up for hours, and so I arrived—too late."

The utter dreariness of her speech went straight to Kelly's heart. "Ah, there now—there now!"

he said. "If I'd only known I'd have followed and helped ye that night."

"You see, I didn't know you were coming back," she said. "And anyhow I couldn't have waited. I had to start at once. It was—my job." She smiled faintly, a smile that was sadder than tears.

"And do ye know what happened?" said Kelly. "Did Burke tell ye what happened?"

She shook her head. "No. He told me very little. I suppose he concluded that we had run away together."

"Ah no! That wasn't his doing," said Kelly, paused a moment, then plunged valiantly at the truth. "That was mine. I thought so meself— foul swine as ye may very well call me. Kieff told me so—the liar; and I—like a blasted fool—believed it. At least, no, I didn't right at the heart of me, Mrs. Ranger. I knew what ye were, just the same as I know now. But I'd seen ye look into his eyes when ye begged him off the brandy-bottle, and I knew the friendship between ye wasn't just the ordinary style of thing; no more is it. But it was that devil Kieff that threw the mud. I found him waiting that night when I got back. He was waiting for Burke, he said; and his story was that he and Vreiboom had seen the pair of ye eloping. I nearly murdered him at the time.

Faith, I wish I had!" ended Kelly pathetically,
with tears in his eyes. "It would have stopped a
deal of mischief both now and hereafter."

"Never mind!" said Sylvia gently. "You
couldn't tell. You hadn't known me more than
a few hours."

"It was long enough!" vowed Kelly. "Anyway, Burke ought to have known better. He's
known you longer than that."

"He has never known me," she said quietly.
"Of course he believed the story."

"He doesn't believe it now," said Kelly quickly.

A little quiver went over her face. "Perhaps
not. I don't know what he believes, or what he
will believe when he finds the money gone. That
is what I want to prevent—if only I can prevent
it. It is Guy's only chance. What he did was
done wickedly enough, but it was at a time of
great excitement, when he was not altogether
master of himself. But unless it can be undone,
he will go right down—and never come up again.
Oh, don't you see—" a sudden throb sounded in
her tired voice—"that if once Burke knows of this,
Guy's fate is sealed? There is no one else to help
him. Besides,—it wasn't all his own doing. It
was Kieff's. And away from Kieff, he is so
different."

"Ah! But how to get him away from Kieff!" said Kelly. "The fellow's such a damn' blackguard. Once he takes hold, he never lets go till he's got his victim sucked dry."

Sylvia shuddered. "Can't you do anything?" she said.

Kelly looked at her with his honest kindly eyes. "If it were me, Mrs. Ranger," he said, "I should tell me husband the whole truth—and—let him deal with it."

She shook her head instantly. "It would be the end of everything for Guy. Even if Burke let him off, he could never come back to us. It would be as bad as sending him to prison—or even worse."

"Not it!" said Kelly. "You don't trust Burke. It's a pity. He's such a fine chap. But look here, I'll do me best, I'll get hold of young Guy and make him disgorge. How much did the young ruffian take?"

"I don't know. That's the hopeless part of it. That is why I must see him myself."

Kelly pursed his lips for a moment, but the next he smiled upon her. "All right. I'll manage somehow. But you mustn't go to-night. You tell Burke you're too tired. He'll understand."

"Do you know where Guy is?" she said.

"Oh yes, I can put me hand on the young divil
if I want him. You leave that to me! I'll do me
best all round. Now—suppose we have another
trot, and then go back!"

Sylvia turned her horse's head. "I'm—deeply
grateful to you, Mr. Kelly," she said.

"Donovan!" insinuated Kelly.

She smiled a little. She seemed almost more
piteous to him when she smiled. "Donovan,"
she said.

"Ah, that's better!" he declared. "That does
me good. To be a friend of both of ye is what I
want. Burke and you together! Ye're such a
fine pair, and just made for each other, faith, made
for each other. When I saw you, Mrs. Burke, I
didn't wonder that he'd fallen in love at last. I
give ye me word, I didn't. And I'll never forget
the look on his face when he thought he'd lost ye;
never as long as I live. It—it was as if he'd been
stabbed to the heart."

Tactless, clumsy, sentimental, he sought to
pour balm upon the wounded spirit of this girl
with her tragic eyes that should have held only
the glad sunshine of youth. It hurt him to see
her thus, hurt him unspeakably, and he knew himself powerless to comfort. Yet with that odd
womanly tenderness of his, he did his best.

He wondered what she was thinking of as she sat her horse, gazing out over the wide spaces, so wearily and yet so intently. She did not seem to have heard his last remarks, or was that merely the impression she desired to convey? A vague uneasiness took possession of him. He did not like her to look like that.

"Shall we move on?" he said gently.

She pointed suddenly across the *veldt*. "I want to ride as far as that skeleton tree," she said. "Don't come with me! I shall catch you up if you ride slowly."

"Right!" said Kelly, and watched her lift her bridle and ride away.

He would have done anything to oblige her just then; but his curiosity was whetted to a keen edge. For she rode swiftly, as one who had a definite aim in view. Straight as an arrow across the *veldt* she went to the skeleton tree with its stripped trunk and stark, outflung arms that seemed the very incarnation of the barrenness around.

Here she checked her animal, and sat for a moment with closed eyes, the evening sunlight pouring over her. Very strangely she was trembling from head to foot, as if in the presence of a vision upon which she dared not look. She had returned as she had always meant to return—but ah, the dreary

desert spaces and the cruel roughness of the road!
Her husband's words uttered only a few hours before came back upon her as she stood there. "We
may never reach the top of the world now." No,
they would never reach it. Had anyone ever
done so, she wondered drearily? But yet they
had been near it once—nearer than many. Did
that count for nothing?

It seemed to her that æons had passed over her
since last she had stood beneath that tree. She
had been a girl then, ardent and full of courage.
Now she was a woman, old and very tired, and
there was nothing left in life. It was almost as
if she had ceased to live.

But yet she had come back to the starting-
point, and here, as if standing beside a grave and
reading the inscription to one long dead, she
opened her eyes in the last glow of the sunshine to
read the words which Burke had cut into the bare
wood on the evening of his wedding-day. She
remembered how she had waited for him, the
tumult of doubt, of misgiving, in her soul, how
she had wished he would not linger in that desolate
place. Now, out of the midst of a desolation to
which this sandy waste was as nothing, she
searched with almost a feeling of awe as one about
to read a message from the dead.

The bare, bleached trunk of the tree shone strangely in the sinking sun, faintly tinted with rose. The world all around her was changing; slowly, imperceptibly, changing. A tender lilac glow was creeping over the *veldt*. A curious sensation came upon Sylvia, as if she were moving in a dream, as if she were stepping into a new world and the old had fallen from her. The bitterness had lifted from her spirit. Her heart beat faster. She was a treasure-seeker on the verge of a great discovery. Trembling, she lifted her eyes. . . .

There on the smooth wood, like a scroll upon a marble pillar, were words, rough-hewn but unmistakable—*Fide et Amore*. . . .

It was as if a voice had spoken in her soul, a clear, insistent voice, bidding her begone. She obeyed, scarcely knowing what she did. Back across the dusty *veldt* she rode, moving as one in a trance. She joined the Irishman waiting for her, but she looked at him with eyes that saw not.

"Well?" he said, frankly curious. "Did you find anything?"

She started a little, and came out of her dream. "I found what I was looking for," she said.

"What was it?" Kelly was keenly interested; there was no checking him now, he was like a hound on the scent.

She did not resent his questions. That was Kelly's privilege. But neither did she answer him as fully as he could have wished. "I found out," she said slowly, after a moment, "how to get to the top of the world."

"Ah, really now!" said Kelly, opening his eyes to their widest extent. "And are ye going to pack your bag and go?"

She smiled very faintly, looking straight before her. "No. It's too late now," she said. "I've missed the way. So has Burke."

"But ye'll try again—ye'll try again!" urged Kelly, eager as a child for the happy ending of a fairy-tale.

She shook her head. Her lips were quivering, but still she made them smile. "Not that way. I am afraid it's barred," she said, and with the words she touched her horse with her heel and rode quickly forward towards the town.

Donovan followed her with a rueful countenance. There were times when even he felt discouraged with the world.

CHAPTER III

THE PUNISHMENT

"GOOD evening, Mrs. Ranger!"

Sylvia started at the sound of a cool, detached voice as she re-entered the hotel. Two eyes, black as onyx and as expressionless, looked coldly into hers. A chill shudder ran through her. She glanced instinctively back at Kelly, who came forward instantly in his bulky, protective fashion.

"Hullo, Kieff! What are you doing here? Gambling for the diamond?"

"I?" said Kieff, with a stretching of his thin, colourless lips that was scarcely a smile. "I don't gamble for diamonds, my good Kelly. Well, Mrs. Ranger, I hope you had a pleasant journey here."

"He gambles for souls," was the thought in Sylvia's mind, as with a quick effort she controlled herself and passed on in icy silence. She would never voluntarily speak to Kieff again. He was an open enemy; and she turned from him with the same loathing that she would have shown for a reptile in her path.

His laugh—that horrible, slippery sound—followed her. He said something in Dutch to the man who lounged beside him, and at once another laugh — Piet Vreiboom's—bellowed forth like the blare of a bull. She flinched in spite of herself. Every nerve shrank. Yet the next moment, superbly, she wheeled and faced them. There was something intolerable in that laughter, something that stung her beyond endurance.

"Tell me," she commanded Kelly, "tell me what these—gentlemen—find about me to laugh at!"

Her face was white as death, but her eyes shone red as leaping flame. She was terrible in that moment—terrible as a lioness at bay—and the laughter died. Piet Vreiboom slunk a little back, his low brows working uneasily.

Kelly swallowed an oath in his throat; his hands were clenched. But Kieff, in a voice smooth as oil, made ready, mocking answer.

"Oh, not at you, madam! Heaven forbid! What could any man find to smile at in such a model of virtuous propriety as yourself?"

He was baiting her openly, and she knew it. An awful wave of anger surged through her brain, such anger as had never before possessed her. For the moment she felt sick, as if she had drunk of some overpowering drug. He meant to humiliate her publicly. She realized it in a flash. And she was powerless to prevent it. Whether she went or whether she stayed, he would accomplish his end. Among all the strange faces that stared at her, only Kelly's, worried and perplexed, betrayed the smallest concern upon her account. And he, since her unexpected action, had been obviously at a loss as to how to deal with the situation or with her. Single-handed, he would have faced the pack; but with her at his side he was hopelessly hampered, afraid of blundering and making matters worse.

"Ah, come away!" he muttered to her. "It's not the place for ye at all. They're hogs and swine, the lot of 'em. Don't ye be drawn by the likes of them!"

But she stood her ground, for there was hot blood in Sylvia and a fierce pride that would not tamely suffer outrage. Moreover, she had been wounded cruelly, and the desire for vengeance welled up furiously within her. Now that she stood in the presence of her enemy, the impulse to strike back, however futile the blow, urged her and would not be denied.

She confronted Saul Kieff with tense determination. "You will either repeat—and explain

—what you said to your friend regarding me just now," she said, in tones that rang fearlessly, echoing through the crowded place, "or you will admit yourself a contemptible coward for vilely slandering a woman whom you know to be defenceless!"

It was regally spoken. She stood splendidly erect, facing him, withering him from head to foot with the scorching fire of her scorn. A murmur of sympathy went through the rough crowd of men gathered before her. One or two cursed Kieff in a growling undertone. But Kieff himself remained absolutely unmoved. He was smoking a cigarette and he inhaled several deep breaths before he replied to her challenge. Then, with his basilisk eyes fixed immovably upon her, as it were clinging to her, he made his deadly answer: "I will certainly tell you what I said, madam, since you desire it. But the explanation is one which surely only you can give. I said to my friend,'There goes the wife of the Rangers.' Did I make a mistake?"

"Yes, you damned hound, you did!" The voice that uttered the words came from the door that led into the office. Burke Ranger swung suddenly out upon them, moving with a kind of massive force that carried purpose in every line. Men drew themselves together as he passed them with the instinctive impulse to leave his progress unimpeded; for this man would have forced his way past every obstacle at that moment. He went straight for his objective without a glance to right or left.

Sylvia started back at his coming. That which her enemy could not do was accomplished by her husband by neither word nor look. The regal poise went out of her bearing. She shrank against Kelly as if seeking refuge. For she had seen Burke's eyes, as she had seen them the night before; and they were glittering with the lust for blood. They were the eyes of a murderer.

Straight to Kieff he came, and Kieff waited for him, quite motionless, with thin lips drawn back, showing a snarling gleam of teeth. But just as Burke reached him he moved. His right arm shot forth with a serpentine ferocity, and in a flash the muzzle of a revolver gleamed between them.

"Hands up, if you please, Mr. Ranger!" he said smoothly. "We shall talk better that way."

But for once in his life he had made a miscalculation, and the next instant he realized it. He had reckoned without the blunderer Kelly. For a fierce oath broke from the Irishman at sight of the weapon, and in the same second he beat it

down with the stock of his riding-whip with a force
that struck it out of Kieff's grasp. It spun along
the floor to Sylvia's feet, and she stooped and
snatched it up.

Burke did not so much as glance round. He had
Kieff by the collar of his coat, and the fate of the
revolver was obviously a matter of no importance
to him. "Give me that horse-whip of yours,
Donovan!" he said.

Kelly complied with the childlike obedience he
invariably yielded to Burke. Then he fell back
to Sylvia, and very gently took the revolver out
of her clenched hand.

She looked at him, her eyes wide, terror-stricken.
"He will kill him!" she said, in a voiceless whisper.

"Not a bit of it," said Kelly, and put his arm
around her. "These poisonous vermin don't die
so easy. Pity they don't."

And then began the most terrible scene that
Sylvia had ever looked upon. No one intervened
between Burke and his victim. There was even a
look of brutal satisfaction upon some of the faces
around. Piet Vreiboom openly gloated, as if he
were gazing upon a spectacle of rare delight.

And Burke thrashed Kieff, thrashed him with
all the weight of his manhood's strength, forced
him staggering up and down the open space that

had been cleared for that awful reckoning, making a public show of him, displaying him to every man present as a crawling, contemptible thing that not one of them would have owned as friend. It was a ghastly chastisement, made deadly by the hatred that backed it. Kieff writhed this way and that, but he never escaped the swinging blows. They followed him mercilessly,—all the more mercilessly for his struggles. His coat tore out at the seams and was ripped to rags. And still Burke thrashed him, his face grim and terrible and his eyes shot red and gleaming—as the eyes of a murderer.

In the end Kieff stumbled and pitched forward upon his knees, his arms sprawling helplessly out before him. It was characteristic of the man that he had not uttered a sound; only as Burke stayed his hand his breathing came with a whistling noise through the tense silence, as of a wounded animal brought to earth. His face was grey.

Burke held him so for a few seconds, then deliberately dropped the horse-whip and grasped him with both hands, lifting him. Kieff's head was sunk forward. He looked as if he would faint. But inexorably Burke dragged him to his feet and turned him till he stood before Sylvia.

She was leaning against Kelly with her hands

over her face.   Relentlessly Burke's voice broke
the silence.

"Now," he said briefly, "you will apologize to
my wife for insulting her."

She uncovered her face and raised it.   There
was shrinking horror in her look.   "Oh, Burke!"
she said.   "Let him go!"

"You will—apologize," Burke said again very
insistently, with pitiless distinctness.

There was a dreadful pause.   Kieff's breathing was
less laboured, but it was painfully uneven and broken.
His lips twitched convulsively.   They seemed to
be trying to form words, but no words came.

Burke waited, and several seconds dragged
away.   Then suddenly from the door of the office
the girl who had received Sylvia the previous
evening emerged.

She carried a glass.   "Here you are!" she said
curtly.   "Give him this!"

There was neither pity nor horror in her look.
Her eyes dwelt upon Burke with undisguised
admiration.

"You've given him a good dose this time," she
remarked.   "Serve him right—the dirty hound!
Hope it'll be a lesson to the rest of 'em," and she
shot a glance at Piet Vreiboom which was more
eloquent than words.

She held the glass to Kieff's lips with a contemptuous air, and when he had drunk she emptied the dregs upon the floor and marched back into the office.

"Now," Burke said again, "you will apologize."

And so at last in a voice so low as to be barely audible, Saul Kieff, from whose sneer all women shrank as from the sting of a scorpion, made unreserved apology to the girl he had plotted to ruin. At Burke's behest he withdrew the vile calumny he had launched against her, and he expressed his formal regret for the malice that had prompted it.

When Burke let him go, no one attempted to offer him help. There was probably not a man present from whom he would have accepted it. He slunk away like a wounded beast, staggering, but obviously intent upon escape, and the gathering shadows of the coming night received him.

A murmur as of relief ran round the circle of spectators he left behind, and in a moment, as it were automatically, the general attention was turned upon Sylvia. She was still leaning against Kelly, her death-white face fixed and rigid. Her eyes were closed.

Burke went to her. "Come!" he said. "We will go up."

Her eyes opened. She looked straight at him,

29

seeing none beside. "Was that how you treated Guy?" she said.

He laid an imperative hand upon her. "Come!" he said again.

She made a movement as though to evade him, and then suddenly she faltered. Her eyes grew wide and dark. She threw out her hands with a groping gesture as if sticken blind, and fell straight forward.

Burke caught her, held her for a moment; then as she sank in his arms he lifted her, and bore her away.

CHAPTER IV

THE EVIL THING

WHEN Sylvia opened her eyes again she was lying in the chair by the open window where she had waited so long the previous evening. Her first impression was that she was alone, and then with a sudden stabbing sense of fear she realized Burke's presence.

He was standing slightly behind her, so that the air might reach her, but leaning forward, watching her intently. With a gasp she looked up into his eyes.

He put his hand instantly upon her, reassuring her. "All right. It's all right," he said.

Both tone and touch were absolutely gentle, but she shrank from him, shrank and quivered with a nervous repugnance that she was powerless to control. He took his hand away and turned aside.

She spoke then, her voice quick and agitated. "Don't go! Please don't go!"

He came and stood in front of her, and she saw

that his face was grim. "What is the matter?" he said. "Surely you don't object to a serpent like that getting his deserts for once!"

She met his look with an effort. "Oh, it's not that—not that!" she said.

"What then? You object to me being the executioner?" He spoke curtly, through lips that had a faintly cynical twist.

She could not answer him; only after a moment she sat up, holding to the arms of the chair. "Forgive me for being foolish!" she said. "I—you gave me—rather a fright, you know. I've never seen you—like that before. I felt—it was a horrible feeling—as if you were a stranger. But—of course—you are you—just the same. You are —really—you."

She faltered over the words, his look was so stern, so forbidding. She seemed to be trying to convince herself against her own judgment.

His eyes met hers relentlessly. "Yes, I am myself—and no one else," he said. "I fancy you have never quite realized me before. Possibly you have deliberately blinded yourself. But you know me now, and it is as well that you should. It is the only way to an ultimate understanding."

She blenched a little in spite of herself. "And you—and you—once—thrashed—Guy," she said, her voice very low, sunk almost to a whisper. "Was it—was it—was it like—that?"

He turned sharply away as if there were something intolerable in the question. He went to the window and stood there in silence. And very oddly at that moment the memory of Kelly's assurance went through her that he had been fond of Guy. She did not believe it, yet just for the moment it influenced her. It gave her strength. She got up, and went to his side.

"Burke," she said tremulously, "promise me—please promise me—that you will never do that again!"

He gave her a brief, piercing glance. "If he keeps out of my way, I shan't run after him," he said.

"No—no! But even if he doesn't—" she clasped her hands hard together—"Burke, even if he doesn't—and even though he has disappointed you—wronged you—oh, have you no pity? Can't you—possibly—forgive?"

He turned abruptly and faced her. "Forgive him for making love to you?" he said. "Is that what you are asking?"

She shivered at the question. "At least you won't—punish him like that—whatever he has done," she said.

He was looking full at her. "You want my promise on that?" he said.

"Yes, oh yes." Very earnestly she made reply though his eyes were as points of steel, keeping her back. "I know you will keep a promise. Please—promise me that!"

"Yes," he said drily. "I keep my promises. He can testify to that. So can you. But if I promise you this, you must make me a promise too."

"What is it?" she said.

"Simply that you will never have anything more to do with him without my knowledge—and consent." He uttered the words with the same pitiless distinctness as had characterized his speech when dictating to Kieff.

She drew sharply. "Oh, but why—why ask such a promise of me when you have only just proved your own belief in me?"

"How have I done that?" he said.

"By taking my part before all those horrible men downstairs." She suppressed a hard shudder. "By—defending my honour."

Burke's face remained immovable. "I was defending my own," he said. "I should have done that—in any case."

She made a little hopeless movement with her

hands and dropped them to her sides. "Oh, how hard you are!" she said. "How hard—and how cruel!"

He lifted his shoulders slightly, and turned away in silence. Perhaps there was more of forbearance in that silence than she realized.

He did not ask her where she had been with Kelly or comment upon the fact that she had been out at all. Only after a brief pause he told her that they would not leave till the following day as he had some business to attend to. Then to her relief he left her. At least he had promised that he would not go in search of Guy!

Later in the evening, a small packet was brought to her which she found to contain some money in notes wrapped in a slip of paper on which was scrawled a few words.

"I have done my best with young G., but he is rather out of hand for the present. I enclose the 'loan.' Just put it back, and don't worry any more. Yours, D. K."

She put the packet away with a great relief at her heart. That danger then, had been averted. There yet remained a chance for Guy. He was not—still he was not—quite beyond redemption. If only—ah, if only—she could have gone to Burke with the whole story! But Burke had become a stranger to her. She had begun to wonder if she had ever really known him. His implacability frightened her almost more than his terrible vindictiveness. She felt that she could never again turn to him with confidence.

That silence that lay between them was like an ever-widening gulf severing them ever more and more completely. She believed that they would remain strangers for the rest of their lives. Very curiously, those three words which she had read upon the tree served to strengthen this conviction. They were, indeed, to her as a message from the dead. The man who had written them had ceased to exist. Guy might have written them in the old days, but his likeness to Guy was no more. She saw them both now with a distinctness that was almost cruel—the utter weakness of the one, the merciless strength of the other. And in the bitterness of her soul she marvelled that either of them had ever managed to reach her heart.

That could never be so again, so she told herself. The power to love had been wrested from her. The object of her love had turned into a monstrous demon of jealousy from which now she shrank more and more—though she might never escape. Yes, she had loved them both, and still her compassion lingered pitifully around the thought of Guy. But for Burke she had only a shrinking that almost amounted to aversion. He had slain her love. She even believed she was beginning to hate him.

She dreaded the prospect of another long day spent at Brennerstadt. It was the day of the diamond draw, too. The place would be a seething tumult. She was so unutterably tired. She thought with a weary longing of Blue Hill Farm. At least she would find a measure of peace there, though healing were denied her. This place had become hateful to her, an inferno of vice and destruction. She yearned to leave it.

Something of this yearning she betrayed on the following morning when Burke told her that he was making arrangements to leave by the evening train for Ritzen.

"Can't we go sooner?" she said.

He looked at her as if surprised by the question. "There is a train at midday," he said. "But it is not a good time for travelling."

"Oh, let us take it!" she said feverishly. "Please let us take it! We might get back to the farm by to-night then."

He had sent his horse back to Ritzen the previous day in the care of a man he knew, so that both their animals would be waiting for them.

"Do you want to get back?" said Burke.

"Oh, yes—yes! Anything is better than this." She spoke rapidly, almost passionately. "Let us go! Do let us go!"

"Very well," said Burke. "If you wish it."

He paused at the door of the office a few minutes later, when they descended, to tell the girl there that they were leaving at noon.

She looked up at him sharply as he stood looking in. "Heard the latest?" she asked.

"What is the latest?" questioned Burke.

"That dirty dog you thrashed last night— Kieff; he's dead," she told him briefly. "Killed himself with an overdose of opium, died at Hoffstein's early this morning." She glanced beyond him at Sylvia who stood behind. "And a good job, too," she said vindictively. "He's ruined more people in this town than I'd like to be responsible for—the filthy parasite. He was the curse of the place."

Burke turned with a movement that was very deliberate. He also looked at Sylvia. For a long moment they stood so, in the man's eyes a growing hardness, in the woman's a horror undisguised. Then, with a very curious smile, Burke put his hand through his wife's arm and turned her towards the room where breakfast awaited them.

"Come and have something to eat, partner!"
he said, his voice very level and emotionless.

She went with him without a word; but her
whole being throbbed and quivered under his
touch as if it were torture to her. Stark and
hideous, the evil thing reared itself in her path,
and there was no turning aside. She saw him, as
she had seen him on the night of her arrival, as she
had seen him the night after, as she believed that
she would always see him for the rest of her life.
And the eyes that looked into hers—those eyes
that had held her, dominated her, charmed her—
were the eyes of a murderer. Go where she would,
there could be no escape for her for ever. The
evil thing had her enchained.

CHAPTER V

THE LAND OF BLASTED HOPES

THEY were still at breakfast when Kelly came
dashing in full of the news of the death of Kieff.
No one knew whether it had been accidental or
intentional, but he spoke—as the girl in the office
had spoken—as if a curse had been lifted from the
town. And Sylvia sat at the table and listened,
feeling as if her heart had been turned to ice. The
man had died by his own hand, but she could not
shake from her the feeling that she and Burke had
been the cause of his death.

She saw Kelly for a few minutes alone when the
meal was over, and whispered her thanks to him
for what he had done with regard to Guy. He
would scarcely listen to her, declaring it had been
a pleasure to serve her, that it had been the easiest
thing in the world, and that now it was done she
must not worry any more.

"But was it really easy?" she questioned.

"Yes—yes! He was glad enough of the chance
to give it back. He only acted on impulse, ye see,

and Kieff was pushing behind. He'd never have done it but for Kieff. Very likely he'll pull round now and lead a respectable life," said Kelly cheerily. "He's got the stuff in him, ye know, if he'd only let it grow."

She smiled wanly at his optimism. "Oh, do beg him to try!" she said.

"I'll do me best," promised Kelly. "Anyway, don't you worry! It's a sheer waste of time and never helped anybody yet."

His cheerful attitude helped her, small as was her hope for Guy's reformation. Moreover, she knew that Kelly would keep his word. He would certainly do his best for Guy.

He took his leave of her almost immediately, declaring it was the busiest day of his life, but assuring her that he would ride over to Blue Hill Farm to see her on the earliest opportunity with the greatest pleasure in the world.

She asked him somewhat nervously at parting if the death of Kieff were likely to hinder their return, but he laughed at the notion. Why, of course not! Burke hadn't killed the man. Such affairs as the one she had witnessed the night before were by no means unusual in Brennerstadt. Besides, it was a clear case of opium poisoning, and everyone had known that he would die of it

sooner or later. It was the greatest mercy he had
gone, and so she wasn't to worry about that! No
one would have any regrets for Kieff except the
people he had ruined.

And so with wholesome words of reassurance he
left her, and she went to prepare for her journey.

When Burke joined her again, they spoke only
of casual things, avoiding all mention of Guy or
Kieff by tacit consent. He was very considerate
for her, making every possible provision for her
comfort, but his manner was aloof, almost forbidding. There was no intimacy between them, no
confidence, no comradeship.

They reached Ritzen in the late afternoon.
Burke suggested spending the night there, but
she urged him to continue the journey. The heat
of the day was over; there was no reason for
lingering. So they found their horses, and started
on the long ride home.

They rode side by side along the dusty track
through a barren waste that made the eyes ache.
A heavy stillness hung over the land, making the
loneliness seem more immense. They scarcely
spoke at all, and it came to Sylvia that they were
stranger to each other now than they had been on
that day at the very beginning of their acquaintance when he had first brought her to Blue Hill

Farm.   She felt herself to be even more of an alien in this land of cruel desolation than when first she had set foot in it.   It was like a vast prison, she thought drearily, while the grim, unfriendly *kopjes* were the sentinels that guarded her, and the far blue mountains were a granite wall that none might pass.

The sun was low in the sky when they reached the watercourse.   It was quite dry with white stones that looked like the skeletons of the ages scattered along its bed.

"Shall we rest for a few minutes?" said Burke.

But she shook her head.   "No—no!   Not here.   It is getting late."

So they crossed the *spruit* and went on.

The sun went down in an opalescent glow of mauve and pink and pearl that spread far over the *veldt*, and she felt that the beauty of it was almost more than she could bear.   It hid so much that was terrible and cruel.

They came at length, when the light was nearly gone, to a branching track that led to the Merstons' farm.

Burke broke his silence again.   "I must go over and see Merston in the morning."

She felt the warm colour flood her face.   How much had the Merstons heard?   She murmured something in response, but she did not offer to accompany him.

A deep orange moon came up over the eastern hills and lighted the last few miles of their journey, casting a strange amber radiance around them, flinging mysterious shadows about the *kopjes*, shedding an unearthly splendour upon the endless *veldt*. It spread like an illimitable ocean in soundless billows out of which weird rocks stood up—a dream-world of fantastic possibilities, but petrified into stillness by the spell of its solitudes—a world that once surely had thrilled with magic and now was dead.

As they rode past the last *kopje*—her *kopje* that she had never yet climbed, they seemed to her to enter the innermost loneliness of all, to reach the very heart of the desert.

They arrived at Blue Hill Farm, and the sound of their horses' feet brought the Kaffirs buzzing from their huts, but the clatter that they made did not penetrate that great and desolate silence. The spell remained untouched.

Burke went with Joe to superintend the rubbing down and feeding of their animals, and Sylvia entered the place alone. Though it was exactly the same as when she had left it, she felt as if she were entering a ruin.

She went to her own room and washed away the dust of the journey.   The packet that Kelly had given her she locked away in her own box.   Burke might enter at any moment, and she did not dare to attempt to open the strong-box then.   She knew the money must be returned and speedily; she would not rest until she had returned it.   But she could not risk detection at that moment.   Her courage was worn down with physical fatigue. She lacked the nerve.

When Burke came in, he found her bringing in a hastily prepared supper.   He took the tray from her and made her sit down while he waited upon her.   Her weariness was too great to hide, and she yielded without demur, lacking the strength to do otherwise.

He made her eat and drink though she was almost too tired even for that, and when the meal was done he would not suffer her to rest in a chair but led her with a certain grim kindliness to the door of her room.

"Go to bed, child!" he said.   "And stay there till you feel better!"

She obeyed him, feeling that she had no choice, yet still too anxious to sleep.   He brought her a glass of hot milk when she was in bed, remarking that her supper had been a poor one, and she drank

30

in feverish haste, yearning to be left alone.   Then,
when he had gone, she tormented herself by wondering if he had noticed anything strange in her
manner, if he thought that she were going to be
ill and so would perhaps mount guard over her.

A chafing sense of impotence came upon her.
It would be terrible to fail now after all she had
undergone.   She lay listening, straining every
nerve.   He would be sure to smoke his pipe on the
stoep before turning in.   That was the opportunity
that she must seize.   She dared not leave it till
the morrow.   He might ask for the key of the
strong-box at any time.   But still she did not hear
him moving beyond the closed door, and she wondered if he could have fallen asleep in the sitting-
room.   A heavy drowsiness was beginning to creep
over her notwithstanding her uneasiness.   She
fought against it with all her strength, but it
gained ground in spite of her.   Her brain felt
clogged with weariness.

She began to doze, waking with violent starts
and listening, drifting back to slumber ever more
deeply, till at last actual sleep posssed her, and for
a space she lay in complete oblivion.

It must have been a full hour later that she became suddenly conscious again, with every faculty
on the alert, and remembered the task still un-

fulfilled.   It was almost as if a voice—Guy's voice —had called her, urging her to action.

The room was full of moonlight, and she could see every object in it as clearly as if it had been day.   The precious packet was under her pillow with the key of the strong-box.   She felt for and grasped them both almost instinctively before she looked round, and then, on the verge of raising herself, her newly awakened eyes lighted upon something which sent all the blood in a wild rush to her heart.   A man's figure was kneeling motionless at the foot of the bed.

She lay and gazed and gazed, hardly believing her senses, wondering if the moonlight could have tricked her.   He was so still, he might have been a figure wrought in marble.   His face was hidden on his arms, but there was that in his attitude that sent a stab of wonder through her.   Was it—was it Guy kneeling there in an abandonment of despair?   Had he followed her like a wandering outcast now that his master Kieff was gone?   If so, but no—but no!   Surely it was a dream.   Guy was far away.   This was but the fantasy of her own brain.   Guy could never have come to her thus.   And yet, was it not Guy's voice that had called her from her sleep?

A great quiver went through her.   What if Guy

had died in the night far away in Brennerstadt?
What if this were his spirit come to hold commune
with hers.   Was she not dearer to him than anyone else in the world?   Would he not surely seek
her before he passed on?

Trembling, she raised herself at last and spoke
his name.   "Guy, is that you?   Dear Guy, speak
to me!"

She saw an answering tremor pass through the
kneeling figure, but the face remained hidden.
The moonlight lay upon the dark head, and she
thought she saw streaks of white upon it.   It was
Guy in the flesh then.   It could be none other.   A
yearning tenderness thrilled through her.   He had
come back—in spite of all his sinning he had come
back.   And again through the years there came to
her the picture of the boy she had known and
loved—ah, how dearly! in the days of his inno-
cence.   It was so vivid that for the moment it
swept all else aside.   Oh, if he would but move and
show her once more the sparkling eager face of his
youth!   She longed with a passionate intensity
for one glimpse, however fleeting, of that which
once had filled her heart with rapture.   And in her
longing she herself was swept back for a few blind
seconds into the happy realms of girlhood.   She
forgot all the bitterness and the sorrow of this

land of strangers. She stretched out her arms to the golden-winged Romance that had taught her the ecstasy of first love.

"Oh, Guy—my own Guy—come to me!" she said.

It moved then, moved suddenly, even convulsively, as a wounded man might move. He lifted his head, and looked at her.

Her dream passed like the rending of a veil. His eyes pierced her, but she had to meet them, lacking power to do otherwise.

So for a space they looked at one another in the moonlight, saying no word, scarcely so much as breathing.

Then, at last he got to his feet with the heavy movements of a tired man, stood a while longer looking down at her, finally turned in utter silence and left her.

When Sylvia slept, many hours later, there came again to her for the third and last time the awful dream of two horsemen who galloped towards each other upon the same rocky path. She saw again the shock of collision and the awful hurtling fall. She went again down into the stony valley and searched for the man who she knew was dead. She found him in a deep place that no other living being had ever entered. He lay with his face upturned to the moonlight, and his eyes wide and glassy gazing upwards. She drew near, and stooped to close those eyes; but she could not. For they gazed straight into her own. They pierced her soul with the mute reproach of a silence that could never be broken again.

She turned and went away through a devastating loneliness. She knew now which of the two had galloped free and which had fallen, and she went as one without hope or comfort, wandering through the waste places of the earth.

Late in the morning she awoke and looked out upon a world of dreadful sunshine,—a parched and barren world that panted in vain for the healing of rain.

"It is a land of blasted hopes," she told herself drearily. "Everything in it is doomed."

CHAPTER VI

THE PARTING

SYLVIA entered the sitting-room that day with the feeling of one returning after a prolonged absence. She had been almost too tired to notice her surroundings the previous night upon arrival. Her limbs felt leaden still, but her brain was alive and throbbing with a painful intensity.

Mary Ann informed her that the big *baas* was out on the lands, and she received the news thankfully. Now was her chance! She took it, feeling like a traitor.

Once more she went to Burke's room. She opened the strong-box stealthily, listening intently for every sound. She slipped the packet of notes inside, and shut it again quickly with a queer little twist of the heart as she caught sight of the envelope containing the cigarette which once he had drawn from between her lips. Then with a start she heard the sound of hoofs outside the window, and she knew that Burke had returned.

She hurried from the room with the key in her

hand, meeting him in the passage. He had his back to the light, but she thought he looked very grim. The past weeks had aged and hardened him. She wondered if they had wrought a similar change in her.

He spoke to her at once, before she had time to formulate a greeting.

"Ah, here you are! Will you come in here? I want to speak to you."

She went into the sitting-room with a curious feeling of fatefulness that outweighed her embarrassment. There was no intimacy in his speech, and that helped her also. She saw that he would not touch upon that which had happened in the night.

He gave her a critical look as he entered. "Are you rested? Have you had breakfast?"

She answered him nervously. "Yes, I am quite all right to-day. Mary Ann brought me some breakfast in bed."

He nodded, dismissing the matter. "I have been over to see Merston. He is on his legs again, practically well. But she is not feeling up to the mark. She wants to know if you will go over. I told her I thought you would. But don't go if you would rather not!"

"Of course I will go," Sylvia said, "if I can do any good."

And then she looked at him with a sudden curious doubt. Had this suggestion originated with him. Did he feel, as she felt, that the present state of affairs was intolerable? Or was he, for her sake alone, offering her the only sanctuary in his power?

His face told her nothing. She had not the faintest idea as to whether he wished her to go or stay. But he accepted her decision at once.

"I will take you over in the cart this evening," he said. "I thought you would probably wish to go. They are more or less expecting you."

His tone was practical, wholly free from emotion. But the wonder still lingered in her mind. She spoke after a moment with slight hesitation.

"You—will be able to manage all right without me?"

"I shall try," said Burke.

There was no perceptible cynicism in his tone, yet she winced a little, for in some fashion it hurt her. Again she wondered, would it be a relief to him when she had gone? Ah, that terrible barrier of silence! If she could but have passed it then! But she lacked the strength.

"Very well," she said, and turned away. "I will be ready."

His voice arrested her at the door of her room. "May I have the key of the strong-box?"

She turned back.   Her face was burning.   He had taken her unawares.

"I have it here," she said, and gave it to him with a hand that shook uncontrollably.

"Thank you," he said, and put it in his pocket. "I should take it easy to-day if I were you.   You need a rest."

And that was all.   He went out again into the blazing sunshine, and a little later she heard him talking to Schafen as they crossed the yard to the sheep-pens.

She saw him again at the midday meal, but he ate in haste and seemed preoccupied, departing again at the earliest moment possible.   Though he did not discuss the matter with her, she knew that the cruel drought would become a catastrophe if it lasted much longer.   She prepared for departure with a heavy heart.

He came in again to tea, but went to his room to change and only emerged to swallow a hasty cup before they started.   Then, indeed, just at the last, as she rose to dress for the journey, she attempted shyly to penetrate the armour in which he had clad himself.

"Are you sure you want me to go?" she said.

He turned towards her, and for a moment her heart stood still.   "Don't you want to go?" he said.

She did not answer the question. Somehow she could not. Neither could she meet the direct gaze of the keen grey eyes upturned to hers.

"I feel almost as if I am deserting my post," she told him, with a rather piteous smile.

"Oh, you needn't feel that," he said quietly. "In any case you can come back whenever you want to. You won't be far away."

Not far away! Were they not poles asunder already—their partnership dissolved as if it had never been,—their good-fellowship—their friendship—crumbled to ashes? Her heart was beating again quickly, unevenly. She knew that the way was barred.

"Well, send for me if you want me at any time!" she said, and passed on to her room.

There was no need and small opportunity for talk during the drive, for Burke had his hands full with a pair of young horses who tried to bolt upon every conceivable occasion that offered, and he had to keep an iron control upon them throughout the journey.

So at length they came to the Merstons' farm, and with a mingling of relief and dissatisfaction Sylvia realized that any further discussion was out of the question.

Merston came out full of jovial welcome, to

meet them, and in a moment she was glad that she had come. For she saw that he was genuinely pleased to see her.

"It's most awfully good of you to come," he said, as he helped her down. "You've been having a strenuous time at Brennerstadt, I'm told. I wondered if you were going in for Kelly's diamond that he was so full of the other day. How the fellow did talk to be sure! He's a walking advertisement. I should think he must have filled Wilbraham's coffers for him. And you didn't hear who won it?"

It was Burke who answered. "No, we didn't stop for that. We wanted to get away."

Merston looked at Sylvia. "And you left young Guy behind? It was very sporting of you to go after him like that. Burke told me about it. I blame myself that he wasn't on the spot to help. I hope the journey wasn't very infernal?"

He spoke with so kindly an interest that but for Burke's presence she would have felt no embarrassment. He evidently thought that she had acted with commendable courage. She answered him without difficulty, though she could not restrain a quick flush at his words. It was thus then that Burke had defended her honour—and his own!

"It wasn't a very nice journey of course, but I

managed it all right. Mr. Kelly has promised to look after Guy."

"He'll do it then," said Merston reassuringly. "He's a grand chap is Kelly. A bit on the talkative side of course, but a real good sort. Come in now! Come and see my wife! Burke, get down! You must have a drink anyway before you start back."

But Burke shook his head. "Thanks, old chap! I won't wait. I've things to do, and it's getting late. If you can just get my wife's baggage out, I'll be off."

The last of the sunset light shone upon him as he sat there. Looking back at him, Sylvia saw him, brown, muscular, firm as a rock, and an odd little thrill went through her. There was a species of rugged magnificence about him that moved her strangely. The splendid physique of the man had never shown to fuller advantage. Perhaps the glory of the sunset intensified the impression, but he seemed to her great.

Merston was dragging forth her belongings. She went to help him. Burke kept his seat, the reins taut in his hands.

Merston abruptly gripped him by the knee. "Look here, old boy! You must have a drink! Wait where you are while I fetch it!"

He was gone with the words, and they were left alone. Sylvia bent over her suit-case, preparing to pick it up. A tumult of strange emotion had swept over her. She was quivering all over. The horses were stamping and chafing at their bits. He spoke to them with a brief command and they stood still.

Then, very suddenly, he spoke to her. "Good-bye!" he said.

She lifted her face. He was smiling faintly, but his smile hurt her inexplicably. It seemed to veil something that was tragic from her eyes.

He bent towards her. "Good-bye!" he said again.

She moved swiftly, seized by an impulse she could not pause to question. It was as if an unknown force compelled her. She mounted the wheel, and offered him her lips in farewell.

For a moment his arms encircled her with a close and quivering tension. He kissed her, and in that kiss for the first time she felt the call of the spirit.

Then she was free, and blindly feeling for the ground. As she reached it, she heard Merston returning, and without a backward look she took up her suit-case and turned to enter. There was a burning sensation as of tears in her throat, but she kept them from her eyes by sheer determination, and Merston noticed nothing.

"Go straight in!" he said to her with cheery hospitality. "You'll find my wife inside. She's cooking the supper. She'll be awfully pleased to see you."

If this were indeed the case, Mrs. Merston certainly concealed any excess of pleasure very effectually. She greeted her with a perfunctory smile, and told her it was very good of her to come but she would soon wish she hadn't. She was looking very worn and tired, but she assured Sylvia somewhat sardonically that she was not feeling any worse than usual. The heat and the drought had been very trying, and her husband's accident had given her more to do. She had fainted the evening before, and he had been frightened for once and made a fuss—quite unnecessarily. She was quite herself again, and she hoped Sylvia would not feel she had been summoned on false pretences.

Sylvia assured her that she would not, and declared it would do her good to make herself useful.

"Aren't you that at home?" said Mrs. Merston.

"Well, there are plenty of Kaffirs to do the work. I am not absolutely necessary to Burke's comfort," Sylvia explained.

"I thought you were," Matilda Merston's pale

eyes gave her a shrewd glance. "He was keen enough to run after you to Brennerstadt," she remarked. "How did you get on there?"

Sylvia hesitated. "We were only there a couple of nights," she said vaguely.

"So I gathered. Did you find Guy?"

"No. I didn't see him. But Mr. Kelly has promised to look after him."

"Ah, Donovan is a good sort," said Mrs. Merston. "He'd nursemaid anyone. So Kieff is dead!"

She said it abruptly, too intent upon the mixing of her cake to look up.

There came the sound of wheel and hoofs outside, and Sylvia paused to listen before she replied.

"Yes. Kieff is dead."

The sound died away in the distance, and there fell a silence.

Then, "Killed himself, did he?" asked Mrs. Merston.

"I was told so," said Sylvia.

"Don't you believe it?" Mrs. Merston looked across at her suddenly. "Did someone else have a try first? Did he have a row with Burke?"

There was no evading the questions though she would fain have avoided the whole subject. In a very low voice Sylvia spoke of the violent scene she had witnessed.

Mrs. Merston listened with interest, but with no great surprise. "Burke always was a savage," she commented. "But after all, Kieff had tried to kill him a day or two before. Guy prevented that, so Donovan told me. What made Guy go off in such a hurry?"

"I—can't tell you," Sylvia said.

Something in her reply struck Mrs. Merston. She became suddenly silent, and finished her task without another word.

Later, when she took Sylvia to the guest-room, which was no more than a corrugated iron lean-to lined with boarding, she unexpectedly drew the girl to her and kissed her. But still she did not say a word.

31

CHAPTER VII

PIET VREIBOOM

It was a strange friendship that developed between Sylvia and Matilda Merston during the days that followed; for they had little in common. The elder woman leaned upon the younger, and, perhaps in consequence of this, Sylvia's energy seemed inexhaustible. She amazed Bill Merston by her capacity for work. She lifted the burden that had pressed so heavily upon her friend, and manfully mastered every difficulty that arose. She insisted that her hostess should rest for a set time every day, and the effect of this unusual relaxation upon Matilda was surprising. Her husband marvelled at it, and frankly told her she was like another woman. For, partly from the lessening of the physical strain and partly from the influence of congenial companionship, the carping discontent that had so possessed her of late had begun to give way to a softer and infinitely more gracious frame of mind. The bond of their womanhood drew the two together, and the intimacy between them flourished in that desert place though probably in no other ground would it have taken root.

Work was as an anæsthetic to Sylvia in those days. She was thankful to occupy her mind and at night to sleep from sheer weariness. The sense of being useful to someone helped her also. She gave herself up to work as a respite from the torment of thought, resolutely refusing to look forward, striving so to become absorbed in the daily task as to crowd out even memory. She and Merston were fast friends also, and his wholesome masculine selfishness did her good. He was like a pleasant, rather spoilt child, unconventionally affectionate, and by no means difficult to manage. They called each other by their Christian names before she had been twenty-four hours at the farm, and chaffed each other with cheery inconsequence whenever they met. Sylvia sometimes marvelled at herself for that surface lightheartedness, but somehow it seemed to be in the atmosphere. Bill Merston's hearty laugh was irresistible to all but his wife.

It was but a brief respite. She knew it could not last, but its very transience made her the more ready to take advantage of it. And she was thankful for every day that carried her farther from

that terrible time at Brennerstadt. It had begun
to seem more like an evil dream to her now—a
nightmare happening that never could have taken
place in ordinary, normal existence.

Burke did not come over to see them again, nor
did he write. Evidently he was too busy to do
either. But one evening Merston announced his
intention of riding over to Blue Hill Farm, and
asked Sylvia if she would like to send a note by
him.

"You've got ten minutes to do it in," he gaily
told her. "So you'd better leave all the fond adjec-
tives till the end and put them in if you have time."

She thanked him carelessly enough for his ad-
vice, but when she reached her own room she found
herself confronted with a problem that baffled her.
How was she to write to Burke? What could she
say to him? She felt strangely confounded and
unsure of herself.

Eight of the allotted ten minutes had flown before she set pencil to paper. Then, hurriedly,
with trembling fingers, she scribbled a few sen-
tences. "I hope all is well with you. We are
very busy here. Matilda is better, and I am
quite fit and enjoying the work. Is Mary Ann
looking after you properly?" She paused there.
Somehow the thought of Burke with only the

Kaffir servants to minister to him sent an odd little pang through her. She had begun to accustom him to better things. She wondered if he were lonely—if he wanted her. Ought she to offer to go back?

Something cried out sharply within her at the thought. Her whole being shrank as the old nightmare horror swept back upon her. No—no! She could not face it—not yet. The memory of his implacability, his ruthlessness, arose like a menacing wave, shaking her to the soul.

Then, suddenly, the vision changed. She saw him as she had seen him on that last night, when she had awaked to find him kneeling by her bed. And again that swift pang went through her. She did not ask herself again if he wanted her.

The door of her room opened on to the yard. She heard Merston lead his horse up to the front of the bungalow and stand talking to his wife who was just inside. She knew that in a moment or two his cheery shout would come to her, calling for the note.

Hastily she resumed her task. "If there is any mending to be done, send it back by Bill."

Again she paused. Matilda was laughing at something her husband had said. It was only lately that she had begun to laugh.

Almost immediately came an answering shout of laughter from Merston, and then his boyish yell to her.

"Hi, Sylvia! How much longer are you going to keep me waiting for that precious love-letter?"

She called an answer to him, dashing off final words as she did so. "I feel I am doing some good here, but if you should specially wish it, of course I will come back at any time." For a second more she hesitated, then simply wrote her name.

Folding up the hurried scrawl, she was conscious of a strong sense of dissatisfaction, but she would not reopen it. There was nothing more to be said.

She went out with it to Bill Merston, and met his chaff with careless laughter.

"You haven't told him to come and fetch you away, I hope?" Matilda said, as he rode away.

And she smiled and answered, "No, not unless he specially needs me."

"You don't want to go?" Matilda asked abruptly.

"Not unless you are tired of me," Sylvia rejoined.

"Don't be silly!" said Matilda briefly.

Half an hour after Merston's departure there came the shambling trot of another horse, and

Piet Vreiboom, slouched like a sack in the saddle, rode up and rolled off at the door.

"Oh, bother the man!" said Matilda, "I shan't ask him in with Bill away."

The amiable Piet, however, did not wait to be asked. He fastened up his horse and rolled into the house with his hat on, where he gave her perfunctory greeting, grinned at Sylvia, and seated himself in the easiest chair he could find.

Matilda's face of unconcealed disgust nearly provoked Sylvia to uncontrolled laughter, but she checked herself in time, and went to get the unwelcome visitor a drink in the hope of speeding his departure.

Piet Vreiboom however was in no hurry, though they assured him repeatedly that Merston would probably not return for some hours. He sat squarely in his chair with his little greedy eyes fixed upon Sylvia, and merely grunted in response to all their efforts.

When he had refreshed himself and lighted his pipe, he began to search his mind for the few English words at his disposal and to arrange these in a fashion intelligible to the two very inferior beings who were listening to him. He told them in laboured language that he had come from Brennerstadt, that the races were over and the great Wil-

braham diamond was lost and won. Who had won
it? No one knew. Some said it was a lady. He
looked again at Sylvia who turned out the pockets
of her overall, and] assured him that she was
not the lucky one.

He looked as if he suspected ridicule behind her
mirth, and changed the subject. Guy Ranger
had disappeared, and no one knew what had become of him. Some people thought he was dead,
like Kieff. Again he looked searchingly at Sylvia,
but she did not joke over this information. She
began to peel some potatoes as if she had not heard
it. And Piet Vreiboom sat back in his chair and
stared at her, till the hot colour rose and spread
over her face and neck, and then he puffed forth
a cloud of vile smoke and laughed.

At that juncture Mrs. Merston came forward
with unusual briskness. "You had better go,"
she said, with great decision. "There is going to
be a storm."

He began to dispute the point, but meeting most
unexpected lightning in her pale eyes he thought
better of it, and after a few seconds for deliberation
and the due assertion of his masculine superiority,
he lumbered to his feet and prepared to depart.

Mrs. Merston followed him firmly to the door,
reiterating her belief in a coming change. Cer-

tainly the sky was overcast, but the clouds often came up thickly at night and dispersed again without shedding any rain. There had not been rain for months.

Very grimly Matilda Merston watched the departure of her unwelcome visitor, enduring the dust that rose from his horse's hoofs with the patience of inflexible determination. Then, when she had seen him go and the swirling dust had begun to settle again, she turned inwards and proceeded to wash the glass that the Boer had used with an expression of fixed disgust.

Suddenly she spoke. "I shouldn't believe anything that man said on oath."

"Neither should I," said Sylvia quietly. She did not look up from her task, and Matilda Merston said no more.

There was a brief silence, then Sylvia spoke again. "You are very good to me," she said.

"My dear!" said Matilda almost sharply.

Sylvia's hands were trembling a little, but she continued to occupy them. "You must sometimes wonder why Guy is so much to me," she said. "I think it has been very sweet of you never to ask. But I feel I should like to tell you about it."

"Of course; if you want to," said Matilda.

"I do want you to know," Sylvia said, with slight effort. "You have taken me so much on trust. And I never even told you how I came to meet—and marry—Burke."

"There was no necessity for you to tell me," said Matilda.

"Perhaps not. But you must have thought it rather sudden—rather strange." Sylvia's fingers moved a little more rapidly. "You see, I came out here engaged to marry Guy."

"Good gracious!" said Matilda.

Sylvia glanced up momentarily. "We had been engaged for years. We were engaged before he ever came here. We—loved each other. But—" Words failed her suddenly; she drew a short, hard breath and was silent.

"He let you down?" said Matilda.

She nodded.

Matilda's face hardened. "That was Burke's doing."

"No—no!" Sylvia found her voice again with an effort. "It isn't fair to say that. Burke tried to help him,—has tried—many times. He may have been harsh to him; he may have made mistakes. But I know he has tried to help him."

"Was that why he married you?" asked Matilda, with a bitter curl of the lip

Sylvia winced. "No. I—don't quite know what made him think of that. Perhaps—in a way —he felt he ought. I was thrown on his protection, and he never would believe that I was capable of fending for myself."

"Very chivalrous!" commented Matilda. "Men are like that."

Sylvia shivered. "Don't—please! He—has been very good to me."

"In his own way," said Matilda.

"No, in every way. I can't tell you how good till—till Guy came back. He brought him back to please me." Sylvia's voice was low and distressed. "That was when things began to go wrong," she said.

"There was nothing very magnanimous in that," commented Matilda. "He wanted you to see poor Guy when he was down. He wanted to give you a lesson so that you should realize your good luck in being married to him. He didn't count on the fact that you loved him. He expected you to be disgusted."

"Oh, don't!" Sylvia said quickly. "Really that isn't fair. That isn't—Burke. He did it against his judgment. He did it for my sake."

"You don't know much about men, do you?" said Matilda.

"Perhaps not. But I know that much about Burke. I know that he plays fair."

"Even if he kills his man," suggested Matilda cynically.

"He always plays fair." Sylvia spoke firmly. "But he doesn't know how to make allowances. He is hard."

"Have you found him so?" said Matilda.

"I?" Sylvia looked across at her.

Their eyes met. There was a certain compulsion in the elder woman's look.

"Yes, you," she said. "You personally. Has he been cruel to you, Sylvia? Has he? Ah no, you needn't tell me! I—know." She went suddenly to her, and put her arm around her.

Sylvia was trembling. "He didn't—understand," she whispered.

"Men never do," said Matilda very bitterly. "Love is beyond them. They are only capable of passion. I learnt that lesson long ago. It simplified life considerably, for I left off expecting anything else."

Sylvia clung to her for a moment. "I think you are wrong," she said. "I know you are wrong—somehow. But—I can't prove it to you."

"You're so young," said Matilda compassionately.

"No, no, I am not." Sylvia tried to smile as she disengaged herself. "I am getting older. I am learning. If—if only I felt happy about Guy, I believe I should get on much better. But—but —" the tears rose to her eyes in spite of her— "he haunts me. I can't rest because of him. I dream about him. I feel torn in two. For Burke —has given him up. But I—I can't."

"Of course you can't. You wouldn't." Matilda spoke with warmth. "Don't let Burke deprive you of your friends! Plenty of men imagine that when you have got a husband, you don't need anyone else. They little know."

Sylvia's eyes went out across the *veldt* to a faint, dim line of blue beyond, and dwelt upon it wistfully. "Don't you think it depends upon the husband?" she said.

CHAPTER VIII

OUT OF THE DEPTHS

THAT night the thunder rolled among the *kopjes*, and Sylvia lay in her hut wide-awake and listening. The lightning glanced and quivered about the distant hills and threw a weird and fitful radiance about her bed, extinguishing the dim light thrown by her night-lamp.

Bill Merston had brought her back a written message from her husband, and she lay with it gripped in her hand. For that message held a cry which had thrown her whole soul into tumult.

"I want you," he had written in a hand that might have been Guy's. "I can't get on without you. I am coming to-morrow to fetch you back— if you will come."

If she would come! In those last words she seemed to hear the appeal of a man's agony. What had he been through before he had brought himself to write those words? They hurt her unutterably, piercing her to the soul, when she remembered her own half-hearted offer to return.

Yet she would have given all she had for a few days' respite. The hot fierce longing that beat in those few words frightened her by its intensity. It made her think of one of those overwhelming *veldt* fires, consuming everything in its path, leaving behind it the blackness of desolation. Yes, he wanted her now because she had been denied to him. The flame of his desire had been fanned to a white heat. She seemed to feel it reaching out to her, scorching her, even as she lay. And she shrank with a desperate sense of impotence, feeling her fate to be sealed. For she knew that she must go to him. She must pass through the furnace anew. She must endure her fate. Afterwards—it might be—when it had burnt itself out, some spark of the Divine would be found kindled among the ashes to give her comfort.

And ever the thought of Guy waited at the back of her mind, Guy who had failed her so hopelessly, so repeatedly. Was she going to fail him now? Was she going to place herself so completely out of his reach that even if he called to her for help she would be powerless to stretch forth a hand to him? The thought tormented her. It was the one thing that she felt she could not face, the one point upon which she and Burke would be for ever at variance. Ah no! Whatever else she sur-

rendered, she could not yield to him in this.   She
could not, she would not, leave Guy to sink while
there remained the smallest chance of saving him.

So she told herself, lying there alone, while the
thunder rolled now near, now far, like a menacing
monster wandering hither and thither in search of
prey.   Earlier in the night she had tried to pray,
but it had brought her no relief. She had not
really prayed since that terrible journey to Brennerstadt when she had poured out her whole soul
in supplication and had met only failure. She
felt in a fashion cut off, forgotten in this land of
strangers. The very effort to bridge the gulf
seemed but to emphasize her utter impotence.
She had come to that barren part of the way where
even the most hopeful traveller sometimes feels
that God has forgotten to be gracious. She had
never felt more alone in all her life, and it was a
loneliness that frightened her.

Weirdly the lightning played about her bed.
She watched it with eyes that would not close.
She wondered if Burke were watching it also, and
shivered with the thought of the morrow, asking
herself for the first time why she had ever con-
sented to marry him, why she had not rather
shouldered her fate and gone back to her father.
She would have found work in England. He

would have helped her if she had only had the courage to return, the strength to be humble. Her thoughts lingered tenderly about him. They had been so much to each other once. Did he ever regret her? Did he ever wish her back?

A burning lump rose in her throat. She turned her head upon the pillow, clasping her hands tightly over her eyes. Ah, if she had but gone back to him! They had loved each other, and somehow love would have conquered. Did not love always conquer? What were those words that she had read cut deep in the trunk of a dead tree? They flashed through her brain more vividly than the glancing lightning—the key to every closed door—the balm for every wound—the ladder by which alone the top of the world is reached. *Fide et Amore!* By Faith and Love!

There came again to her that curious feeling of revelation. Looking back, she saw the man on horseback hewing those words while she waited. The words themselves shone in fiery letters across her closed eyelids. She asked herself suddenly, with an awed wonder if perchance her prayer had been answered after all, and she had suffered the message to pass her by. . . .

There came a crash of thunder nearer and more menacing than any that had gone before, startling her almost with a sense of doom, setting every pulse in her body beating. She uncovered her face and sat up.

Sullenly the echoes rolled away, yet they left behind a strange impresssion that possessed her with an uncanny force from which she could not shake herself free—a feeling that amounted to actual conviction that some presence lurked without in the storm, alert and stealthy, waiting for something.

The window was at the side of her bed. She had but to draw aside the curtain and look out. It was within reach of her hand. But for many breathless seconds she dared not.

What it was that stood outside she had no idea, but the thought of Kieff was in her mind—Kieff the vampire who was dead.

She felt herself grow cold all over. She had only to cross the narrow room and knock on the main wall of the bungalow to summon Merston. He would come at a moment's notice, she knew. But she felt powerless to move. Sheer terror bound her limbs.

The thunder slowly ceased, and there followed a brief stillness through which the beating of her heart clamoured wildly. Yet she was beginning to tell herself that it was no more than a nightmare panic that had caught her, when suddenly something knocked softly upon the closed window beneath which she lay.

She started violently and glanced across the room, measuring the distance to the further wall on which she herself would have to knock to summon help.

Then, while instinctively she debated the point, summoning her strength for the effort, there came another sound close to her—a low voice speaking her name.

"Sylvia! Sylvia! Wake up and let me in!"

She snatched back the curtain in a second. She knew that voice. By the shifting gleam of the lightning she saw him, looking in upon her. Her fear vanished.

Swiftly she sprang to do his bidding. Had she ever failed to answer any call of his? She drew back the bolts of her door, and in a moment they were together.

The thunder roared again behind him as he entered, but neither of them heard it. For he caught her in his arms with a hungry sound, and as she clung to him nearly fainting with relief, he kissed her, straining her to him gasping wild words of love.

The touch of those hot, devouring lips awoke

her. She had never felt the slightest fear of Guy
before that moment, but the fierceness of his hold
called a sharp warning in her soul. There was
about him an unrestraint, a lawlessness, that
turned her relief into misgiving. She put up a
quick hand, checking him.

"Guy—Guy, you are hurting me!"

He relaxed his hold then, looking at her, his
head back, the old boyish triumph shining in his
eyes. "Little sweetheart, I'm sorry. I couldn't
help it—just for the moment. The sight of you
and the touch of you together just turned my
head. But it's all right. Don't look so scared!
I wouldn't harm a single hair of your precious
little head." He gathered up the long plait of her
hair and kissed it passionately.

She laid a trembling hand against his shoulder.
"Guy, please! You mustn't. I had to let you
in. But not—not for this."

He uttered a low laugh that seemed to hold a
note of triumph. But he let her go.

"Of course you had to let me in! Were you
asleep? Did I frighten you?"

"You startled me just at first. I think the
thunder had set me on edge, for I wasn't asleep.
It's such a—savage sort of night, isn't it?"

Sylvia glanced forth again over the low *veldt*

where the flickering lightning leaped from cloud to cloud.

"Not so bad," said Guy. "It will serve our turn all right. Do you know what I have come for?"

She looked back at him quickly. There was no mistaking the exultation in his low voice. It amazed her, and again she was stabbed by that sense of insecurity.

"I thought you had come to—explain things," she made answer. "And to say—good-bye."

"To say—what?" He took her by the shoulders; his dark eyes flashed a laughing challenge into hers. "You're not in earnest!" he said.

She backed away from him. "But I am, Guy. I am." Her voice sounded strained even to herself, for she was strangely discomfited by his attitude. She had expected a broken man kneeling at her feet in an agony of contrition. His overweening confidence confounded her. "Have you no sense of right and wrong left?" she said.

He kept his hands upon her. "None whatever," he told her recklessly. "The only thing in life that counts is you—just you. Because we love each other, the whole world is ours for the taking. No, listen, darling! I'm not talking rot. Do you remember the last time we were together? How I swore I would conquer—for your sake? Well,—

I've done it. I have conquered. Now that that devil Kieff is dead, there is no reason why I shouldn't keep straight always. And so I have come to you —for my crown."

His voice sank. He stooped towards her.

But she drew back sharply. "Guy, don't forget—don't forget—I am married to Burke!" she said, speaking quickly, breathlessly.

His hands tightened upon her. "I am going to forget," he told her fiercely. "And so are you. You have no love for him. Your marriage is nothing but an empty bond."

"No—no!" Painfully she broke in upon him. "My marriage is—more than that. I am his wife —and the keeper of his honour. I am going back to him—to-morrow."

"You are not! You are not!" Hotly he contradicted her. "By to-morrow we shall be far away. Listen, Sylvia! I haven't told you all. I am rich. My luck has turned. You'll hardly believe it, but it's true. It was I who won the Wilbraham diamond. We've kept it secret, because I didn't want to be dogged by parasites. I've thought of you all through. And now—and now—" his voice vibrated again on that note of triumph—"I've come to take you away. Mine at last!"

He would have drawn her to him, but she resisted him. She pushed him from her. For the first time in her life she looked at him with condemnation in her eyes.

"Is this—true?" Her voice held a throb of anger.

He stared at her, his triumph slowly giving place to a half-formed doubt. "Of course it's true. I couldn't invent anything so stupendous as that."

She looked back at him mercilessly. "If it is true, how did you find the money for the gamble?"

The doubt on his face deepened to something that was almost shame. "Oh, that!" he said. "I —borrowed that."

"You borrowed it!" She repeated the words without pity. "You borrowed it from Burke's strong-box. Didn't you?"

The question was keen as the cut of a whip. It demanded an answer. Almost involuntarily, the answer came.

"Well—yes! But—I hoped to pay it back. I'm going to pay it back—now."

"Now!" she said, and almost laughed. Was it for this that she had staked everything—everything she had—and lost? There was bitter scorn in her next words. "You can pay it back to Donovan Kelly," she said. "He has replaced it on your behalf."

"What do you mean?" His hands were clenched. Behind his cloak of shame a fire was kindling. The glancing lightning seemed reflected in his eyes.

But Sylvia knew no fear, only an overwhelming contempt. "I mean," she said, "that to save you—to leave you a chance of getting back to solid ground—Donovan and I deceived Burke. He supplied the money, and I put it back."

"Great Jove!" said Guy. He was looking at her oddly, almost speculatively. "But Donovan never had any money to spare!" he said. "He sends it all home to his old mother."

"He gave it to me nevertheless." Sylvia's voice had a scathing note. "And—he pretended that it had come from you—that you had returned it."

"Very subtle of him!" said Guy. He considered the point for a moment or two, then swept it aside. "Well, I'll settle up with him. It'll be all right. I always pay my debts—sooner or later. So that's all right, isn't it? Say it's all right!"

He spoke imperiously, meeting her scorn with a dominating self-assurance. There followed a few moments that were tense with a mental conflict such as Sylvia had never deemed possible between them. Then in a very low voice she made answer.

"No. It is not all right. Nothing can ever make it so again. Please say good-bye—and go!"

He made a furious movement, and caught her suddenly and violently by the wrists. His eyes shone like the eyes of a starving animal. Before she had time to resist him, her hands were gripped behind her and she was fast locked in his arms.

He spoke, his face close to hers, his hot breath seeming to consume her, his words a mere whisper through lips that almost moved upon her own.

"Do you think I'm going—now? Do you think you can send me away with a word like that— fling me off like an old glove—you who have belonged to me all these years? No, don't speak! You'd better not speak! If you dare to deny your love for me now, I believe I shall kill you! If you had been any other woman, I wouldn't have stopped to argue. But—you are you. And— I—love you so."

His voice broke unexpectedly upon the words. For a moment—one sickening, awful moment— his lips were pressed upon hers, seeming to draw all the breath—the very life itself—out of her quivering body. Then there came a terrible sound—a rending sound like the tearing of dry wood—and the dreadful constriction of his hold was gone. She burst from it, gasping for air and freedom with the agonized relief of one who has barely escaped suffocation. She sprang for the door though her knees were doubling under her. She reached it, and threw it wide. Then she looked back. . . .

He was huddled against the wall, his head in his hands, writhing as if in the grip of some fiendish torturer. Broken sounds escaped him—sounds he fought frantically to repress. He seemed to be choking; and in a second her memory flashed back to that anguish she had witnessed weeks before when first she had seen Kieff's remedy and implored him to use it.

For seconds she stood, a helpless witness, too horrified to move. Then, her physical strength reviving, pity stirred within her, striving against what had been a sick and fearful loathing. Gradually her vision cleared. The evil shadow lifted from her brain. She saw him as he was—a man in desperate need of help.

She flung her repugnance from her, though it clung to her, dragging upon her as she moved like a tangible thing. She closed the door and went slowly back into the room, mastering her horror, fighting it at every step. She reached the struggling, convulsed figure, laid her hands upon it,— and her repulsion was gone.

"Sit down!" she said. "Sit down and let me help you!"

Blindly he surrendered to her guiding. She led him to the bed, and he sank upon it. She opened his shirt at the throat. She brought him water.

He could not drink at first, but after repeated effort he succeeded in swallowing a little. Then at length in a hoarse whisper, scarcely intelligible, he asked for the remedy which he always carried.

She felt in his pockets and found it, all ready for use. The lightning had begun to die down, and the light within the room was dim. She turned the lamp higher, moving it so that its ray fell upon Guy. And in that moment she saw Death in his face. . . .

She felt as if a quiet and very steady Hand had been laid upon her, checking all agitation. Calmly she bent over the bared arm he thrust forth to her. Unflinchingly she ran the needle into the white flesh, noting with a detached sort of pity his emaciation.

He put his other arm about her like a frightened, clinging child. "Stay with me! Don't leave me!" he muttered.

"All right," she made gentle answer. "Don't be afraid!"

He leaned against her, shuddering violently,
his dark head bowed, his spasmodic breathing
painful to hear. She waited beside him for the
relief that seemed so slow in coming. Kieff's
remedy did not act so quickly now.

Gradually at last the distress began to lessen.
She felt the tension of his crouched body relax, the
anguished breathing become less laboured. He
still clung to her, and her hand was on his head
though she did not remember putting it there.
The dull echoes of the thunder reverberated far
away among the distant hills. The night was
passing.

Out of a deep silence there came Guy's voice.
"I want—" he said restlessly—"I want——"

She bent over him. Her arm went round his
shoulders. Somehow she felt as if the furnace of
suffering through which he had come had purged
away all that was evil. His weakness cried aloud
to her; the rest was forgotten.

He turned his face up to her; and though the
stamp of his agony was still upon it, the eyes were
pure and free from all taint of passion.

"What do you want?" she asked him softly.

"I've been—horrible to you, Sylvia," he said,
speaking rather jerkily. "Sometimes I get a devil
inside me—and I don't know what I'm doing. I

believe it's Kieff. I never knew what hell meant till I met him. He taught me practically everything I know in that line. He was like an awful rotting disease. He ruined everyone he came near. Everything he touched went bad." He paused a moment. Then, with a sudden boyishness, "There, it's done with, darling," he said. "Will you forget it all—and let me start afresh? I've had such damnable luck always."

His eyes pleaded with her, yet they held confidence also. He knew that she would not refuse.

And because of that which the lamplight had revealed to her, Sylvia bent after a moment and kissed him on the forehead. She knew as she did it that the devil that had menaced her had been driven forth.

So for a space they remained in a union of the spirit that was curiously unlike anything that had ever before existed between them. Then Guy's arm began to slip away from her. There came from him a deep sigh.

She bent low over him, looking into his face. His eyes were closed, but his lips moved, murmuring words which she guessed rather than heard.

"Let me rest—just for a little! I shall be all right—afterwards."

She laid him back very gently upon the pillow,

and lifted his feet on to the bed. He thanked her almost inaudibly, and relaxed every muscle like a tired child. She turned the lamp from him and moved away.

She dressed in the dimness. Guy did not stir again. He lay shrouded in the peace of utter repose. She had watched those deep slumbers too often to fear any sudden awakening.

A few minutes later she went to the door, and softly opened it.

The sullen clouds were lifting; the night had gone. Very far away a faint orange light spread like the reflected glow from a mighty furnace somewhere behind those hills of mystery. The *veldt* lay wide and dumb like a vast and soundless sea.

She stood awed, as one who had risen out of the depths and scarcely yet believed in any deliverance. But the horror had passed from her like an evil dream. She stood in the first light of the dawning and waited in a great stillness for the coming of the day.

CHAPTER IX

THE MEETING

Joe, the Kaffir boy, bestirred himself to the sound of Mary Ann's shrill rating. The hour was still early, but the big *baas* was in a hurry and wanted his boots. Joe hastened to polish them to the tune of Mary Ann's repeated assurance that he would be wanting his whip next, while Fair Rosamond laid the table with a nervous speed that caused her to trip against every chair she passed. When Burke made his appearance, the whole bungalow was as seething with excitement as if it had been peopled by a horde of Kaffirs instead of only three.

He was scarcely aware of them in his desire to be gone, merely throwing an order here and there as he partook of a hasty breakfast, and then striding forth to their vast relief to mount into the Cape cart with its two skittish horses that awaited him beyond the *stoep*.

He departed in a cloud of dust, for still the rain did not fall, and immediately, like the casting of a

spell, the peace of a great somnolence descended
upon the bungalow. The Kaffirs strolled back to
their huts to resume their interrupted slumbers.
The dust slowly settled upon all things, and all was
quiet.

Down the rough track Burke jolted. The horses
were fresh, and he did not seek to check them. All
night long he had been picturing that swift journey
and the goal that awaited him, and he was in a
fever to accomplish it. Their highest speed was
not swift enough for him.

Through the heavy clouds behind him there
came the first break of the sunshine transforming
the *veldt*. It acted like a goad upon him. He
wanted to start back before the sun rose high.
The track that led to Bill Merston's farm was even
rougher than his own, but it did not daunt him.
He suffered the horses to take their own pace, and
they travelled superbly. They had scarcely slackened during the whole ten-mile journey.

He smiled faintly to himself as he sighted the
hideous iron building that was Bill Merston's
dwelling-place. He wondered how Sylvia appre-
ciated this form of life in the wilderness. He
slowed down the animals to a walk as he neared
it, peering about for some sign of its inhabitants.
The clouds had scattered, and the sun was shining

brilliantly behind him. He reflected that Merston
was probably out on the lands. His wife would
be superintending the preparation of breakfast.
And Sylvia——

Something jerked suddenly within him, and a
pulse awoke to a furious beating in his throat.
Sylvia was emerging at that very moment from
the doorway of the humble guest-chamber. The
sun was in her eyes, blinding her, and she did not
see him. Yet she paused a moment on the
threshold.

Burke dragged in his horses and sat watching
her across the yard. She looked pale and unspeakably weary in the searching morning light.
For a second or two she stood so, then, slightly
turning, she spoke into the room behind her ere
she closed the door:

"Stay here while I fetch you something to eat!
Then you shall go as soon as you like."

Clearly her voice came to him, and in it was that
throb of tenderness which he had heard once before when she had offered him her dreaming face
to kiss with the name of another man upon her
lips. He sat quite motionless as one transfixed
while she drew the door after her and stepped forth
into the sunshine. And still she did not see him
for the glory of the morning.

32

She went quickly round to the back of the bungalow and disappeared from his sight.

Two minutes later Burke Ranger strode across the yard with that in his face which made it more terrible than the face of a savage beast. He reached the closed door, opened it, and stepped within.

His movements were swift and wholly without stealth, but they did not make much sound. The man inside the room did not hear immediately.

He was seated on the edge of the bed adjusting the strap of one of his gaiters. Burke stood and watched him unobserved till he lifted his head. Then with a curt, "Now!" he turned and bolted the door behind him.

"Hullo!" said Guy, and got to his feet.

They stood face to face, alike yet unlike, men of the same breed, bearing the same ineradicable stamp, yet poles asunder.

The silence between them was as the appalling pause between the lightning and the thunder-clap. All the savagery of which the human heart is capable was pent within its brief bounds. Then Burke spoke through lips that were white and strangely twisted: "Have you anything at all to say for yourself?"

Guy threw a single glance around. "Not here," he said. "And not now. I'll meet you. Where shall I meet you?"

"Why not here—and now?" Burke's hands were at his sides, hard clenched, as if it took all his strength to keep them there. His eyes never stirred from Guy's face. They had the fixed and cruel look of a hawk about to pounce upon its prey and rend it to atoms.

But there was no fear about Guy, neither fear nor shame. Whatever his sins had been, he had never flinched from the consequences.

He answered without an instant's faltering: "Because we shall be interrupted. We don't want a pack of women howling round. Also, there are no weapons. You haven't even a *sjambok*." His eyes gleamed suddenly. "And there isn't space enough to use it if you had."

"I don't need even a *sjambok*," Burke said, "to kill a rat like you."

"No. And I shan't die so hard as a rat either. All the same," Guy spoke with quiet determination, "you can't do it here. Damn it, man! Are you afraid I shall run away?"

"No!" The answer came like a blow. "But I can't wait, you accursed blackguard! I've waited too long already."

"No, you haven't!" Guy straightened himself sharply, braced for violence, for Burke was close to him and there was something of the quality of a coiled spring in his attitude, a spring that a touch would release. "Wait a minute, Burke! Do you hear? Wait a minute? I'm everything you choose to call me. I'm a traitor, a thief, and a blackguard. But I'm another thing as well." His voice broke oddly and he continued in a lower key, rapidly, as if he feared his strength might not last. "I'm a failure. I haven't done this thing I tried to do. I never shall do it now. Because—your wife—is incorruptible. Her loyalty is greater than my—treachery."

Again there sounded that curious catch in his voice as if a remorseless hand were tightening upon his throat. But he fought against it with a fierce persistence. He faced Burke with livid, twitching lips.

"God knows," he said in a passionate whisper, "whether she loves you. But she will be true to you—as long as you live!"

His words went into silence—a silence so tense that it seemed as if it must end in furious action— as if a hurtling blow and a crashing, headlong fall could be the only outcome.

But neither came. After several rigid seconds Burke spoke, his voice dead level, without a hint of emotion.

"You expect me to believe that, do you?"

Guy made a sharp movement that had in it more of surprise than protest. His throat worked spasmodically for a moment or two ere he forced it to utterance.

"Don't you think," he said then, in a half-strangled undertone, "that it would be a million times easier for me to let you believe—otherwise?"

"Why?" said Burke briefly.

"Because—" savagely Guy flung back the answer—"I would rather be murdered for what I've done than despised for what I've failed to do."

"I see," Burke said. "Then why not let me believe the obvious without further argument?"

There was contempt in his voice, but it was a bitter self-contempt in which the man before him had no share. He had entered that room with murder in his heart. The lust was still there, but he knew now that it would go unsatisfied. He had been stopped, by what means he scarcely realized.

But Guy knew; and though it would have been infinitely easier, as he had said, to have endured that first mad fury than to have stayed it with a confession of failure, for some reason he forced himself to follow the path of humiliation that he had chosen.

"Because what you call the obvious chances

also to be the impossible," he said. "I'm not such a devil as to want to ruin her for the fun of the thing. I tell you she's straight—as straight as I am crooked. And you've got to believe in her—whether you want to or not. That—if you like—is the obvious." He broke off, breathing hard, yet in a fashion oddly triumphant, as if in vindicating the girl he had somehow vindicated himself also.

Burke looked at him fixedly for a few seconds longer. Then, abruptly, as if the words were hard to utter, he spoke: "I believe you."

Guy relaxed with what was almost a movement of exhaustion, but in a moment he braced himself again. "You shall have your satisfaction all the same," he said. "I owe you that. Where shall I meet you?"

Burke made a curt gesture as if dismissing a matter of but minor importance, and turned to go.

But in an instant, as if stung into action, Guy was before him. He gripped him by the shoulder. "Man! Don't give me any of your damned generosity!" He ground out the words between his teeth. "Name a place! Do you hear? Name a place and time!"

Burke stopped dead. His face was enigmatical as he looked at Guy. There was a remote gleam in his stern eyes that was neither of anger nor scorn. He stood for several seconds in silence, till the hand that clutched his shoulder gripped and feverishly shook it.

Then deliberately and with authority he spoke: "I'll meet you in my own time. You can go back to your old quarters and—wait for me there."

Guy's hand fell from him. He stood for a moment as if irresolute, then he moved aside. "All right. I shall go there to-day," he said.

And in silence Burke unbolted the door and went out.

CHAPTER X

THE TRUTH

WHEN Burke presented himself at the door of
the main bungalow he found it half-open. The
whirr of a sewing-machine came forth to him, but
it paused in answer to his knock, and Mrs. Merston's voice bade him enter.

He went in to find her seated at a plain wooden
table with grey flannel spread around her, her
hand poised on the wheel of her machine, which
she drove round vigorously as he entered. Her
light eyes surveyed him in momentary surprise,
and then fell straight upon her work. A slightly
deeper colour suffused her face.

"You've come early," she said.

"Good morning!" said Burke.

She nodded without speaking, absorbed in her
work.

He came to a stand on the opposite side of the
table, watching her. He was quite well aware
that Matilda Merston did not like him. She had
never scrupled to let him know it. The whirr of

the machine rose between them. She was work-
working fast and furiously.

He waited with absolute patience till she flung
him a word. "Sit down!"

He seated himself facing her.

Faster and faster spun the wheel. Matilda's
thin lips were compressed. Tiny beads appeared
on her forehead. She was breathing quickly. Suddenly there was a check, a sharp snap. She uttered
an impatient sound and stopped, looking across at
her visitor with undisguised hostility in her eyes.

"I didn't do it," said Burke.

She got up, not deigning a reply. "I suppose
you'd like a drink," she said. "Bill is out on the
lands."

His eyes comprehended her with a species of
grim amusement. "No. I won't have anything,
thanks. I have come for my wife. Can you tell
me where she is?"

"You're very early," Matilda remarked again.

He leaned his arms upon the table, looking up
at her. "Yes. I know. Isn't she up?"

She returned his look with obvious disfavour.
And yet Burke Ranger was no despicable figure
of manhood sitting there. He was broad, well-
knit, well-developed, clean of feature, with eyes
of piercing keenness.

He met her frown with a faint smile.   "Well?"
he said.

"Yes.   Of course she is up."   Grudgingly
Matilda made answer.   Somehow she resented
the clean-limbed health of these men who made
their living in the wilderness.   There was something almost aggressive about it.   Abruptly she
braced herself to give utterance to her thoughts.
"Why can't you leave her here a little longer?   She
doesn't want to go back."

"I think she must tell me that herself,"Burke said.

He betrayed no discomfiture.   She had never
seen him discomfited.   That was part of her
grievance against him.

" She won't do that," she said curtly.   "She has
old-fashioned ideas about duty.   But it doesn't
make her like it any the better."

"It wouldn't," said Burke.   A gleam that was
in no way connected with his smile shone for a
moment in his steady eyes, but it passed immediately.   He continued to contemplate the faded
woman before him very gravely, without animosity.   "You have got rather fond of Sylvia,
haven't you?" he said.

Matilda made an odd gesture that had in it
something of vehemence.   "I am very sorry for
her," she said bluntly.

"Yes?" said Burke.

"Yes." She repeated the word uncompromisingly, and closed her lips.

"You're not going to tell me why?" he suggested.

Her pale eyes grew suddenly hard and intensely bright. "Yes. I should like to tell you," she said.

He got up with a quiet movement. "Well, why?" he said.

Her eyes flashed fire. "Because," she spoke very quickly, scarcely pausing for breath, "you have turned her from a happy girl into a miserable woman. I knew it would come. I saw it coming. I knew—long before she did—that she had married the wrong man. And I knew what she would suffer when she found out. She tried hard not to find out; she did her best to blind herself. But she had to face it at last. You forced her to open her eyes. And now—she knows the truth. She will do her duty, because you are her husband and there is no escape. But it will be bondage to her as long as she lives. You have taken all the youth and the joy out of her life."

There was a fierce ring of passion in the words. For once Matilda Merston glowed with life. There was even something superb in her reckless denunciation of the man before her.

34

He heard it without stirring a muscle, his eyes fixed unwaveringly upon her, grim and cold as steel. When she ceased to speak, he still stood motionless, almost as if he were waiting for something.

She also waited, girt for battle, eager for the fray. But he showed no sign of anger, and gradually her enthusiasm began to wane. She bent, panting a little and began to smooth out a piece of the grey flannel with nervous exactitude.

Then Burke spoke. "So you think I am not the right man for her."

"I am quite sure of that," said Matilda without looking up.

"That means," Burke spoke slowly, with deliberate insistence, "that you know she loves another man better."

Matilda was silent.

He bent forward a little, looking straight into her downcast face. "Mrs. Merston," he said, "you are a woman; you ought to know. Do you believe—honestly—that she would have been any happier married to that other man?"

She looked at him then in answer to his unspoken desire. He had refused to do battle with her. That was her first thought, and she was conscious of a momentary sense of triumph. Then—

for she was a woman—her heart stirred oddly within her, and her triumph was gone. She met his quiet eyes with a sudden sharp misgiving. What had she done?

"Please answer me!" Burke said.

And, in a low voice, reluctantly, she made answer. "I am afraid I do."

"You know the man?" he said.

She nodded. "I believe—in time—she might have been his salvation. Everybody thought he was beyond redemption. I know that. But she —had faith. And they loved each other. That makes all the difference."

"Ah!" he said.

For the first time he looked away from her, looked out through the open door over the *veldt* to to that far-distant line of hills that bounded their world. His brown face was set in stern, unwavering lines.

Furtively Matilda watched him, still with that uneasy feeling at her heart. There was something enigmatical to her about this man's hard endurance, but she did not resent it any longer. It awed her.

Several seconds passed ere abruptly he turned and spoke. "I am going back. Will you tell Sylvia? Say I can manage all right without her

if she is—happier here!" The barely perceptible
pause before the word made Matilda avert her
eyes instinctively though his face never varied.
"I wish her to do exactly as she likes. Good-bye!"

He held out his hand to her suddenly, and she
was amazed by the warmth of his grasp. She
murmured something incoherent about hoping
she had not been very unpleasant. It was the
humblest moment she had ever known.

He smiled in reply—that faint, baffling smile.
"Oh, not in the least. I am grateful to you for
telling me the truth. I am sure you didn't enjoy
it."

No, to her own surprise, she had not enjoyed it.
She even watched him go with regret. There was
that about Burke Ranger at the moment which
made her wonder if possibly the harsh conception
she had formed of him were wholly justified.

As for Burke, he went straight out to his horses,
looking neither to right nor left, untied the reins,
and drove forth again into the *veldt* with the dust
of the desert rising all around him.

CHAPTER XI

THE STORM

HANS SCHAFEN met his master on the boundary of Blue Hill Farm with a drawn face. Things were going from bad to worse. The drought was killing the animals like flies. If the rain did not come soon, there would be none left. He made his report to Burke with a precision that did not hide his despair. Matters had never before looked so serious. The dearth of water had begun to spell disaster.

Burke listened with scarcely a comment. Blue Hill Farm was on rising ground, and there had always been this danger in view. But till this season it had never materialized to any alarming extent. His position had often enough been precarious, but his losses had never been overwhelming. The failure of the dam at Ritter Spruit had been a catastrophe more far reaching than at the time he had realized. It had crippled the resources of the farm, and flung him upon the chances of the weather. He was faced with ruin.

He heard Schafen out with no sign of consternation, and when he had ended he drove on to the farm and stabled his horses himself with his usual care. Then he went into his empty bungalow. . .

Slowly the long hours wore away. The sun rose in its strength, shining through a thick haze that was like the smoke from a furnace. The atmosphere grew close and suffocating. An intense stillness reigned without, broken occasionally by the despairing bleating of thirst-stricken sheep. The haze increased, seeming to press downwards upon the parched earth. The noonday was dark with gathering clouds.

At the hour of luncheon there came a slight stir in the bungalow. Mary Ann thrust her amazing visage round the door and rolled her eyes in frightened wonder at what she saw. The big *baas* was lying across the table, a prone, stricken figure, with his head upon his arms.

For a few seconds she stood in open-mouthed dismay, thinking him dead; for she had never seen him thus in life. Then she saw his shoulders heave convulsively, and promptly she turned and fled.

Again the bungalow was empty and still, the hours dragged on unheeded. Lower and lower pressed the threatening clouds. But the man who sat alone in the darkening room was blind to all outward things. He did not feel the pitiless, storm-laden heat of the day. He was consumed by the agony of his soul.

It was evening before the end came suddenly; a dancing flash that lighted the heavens from east to west and, crashing upon it, an explosion that seemed to rend the earth. It was a cataclysm of sound, drowning the faculties, stunning the senses, brimming up the void with awful tumult.

A great start ran through the man's bowed figure. He sat up dazed, stiffly opening his clenched hands. The world without seemed to be running with fire. The storm shrieked over the *veldt*. It was pandemonium.

Stiffly he straightened his cramped muscles. His heart was thumping in heavy, uneven strokes, obstructing his breathing. He fought for a few seconds to fill his lungs. The atmosphere was dense with sand. It came swirling in upon him, suffocating him. He stood up, and was astounded to feel his own weakness against that terrific onslaught. Grimly he forced his way to the open window. The *veldt* was alight with lurid, leaping flame. The far-off hills stood up like ramparts in the amazing glare, stabbed here and there with

molten swords of an unendurable brightness. He
had seen many a raging storm before, but never
a storm like this.

The sand blinded him and he dragged the
window shut, using all his strength. It beat upon
the glass with baffled fury. The thunder rolled
and echoed overhead like the chariot-wheels of
God, shaking the world. The clouds above the
lightning were black as night.

Suddenly far across the blazing *veldt* he saw a
sight that tightened every muscle, sending a wild
thrill through every nerve. It came from the
hills, a black, swift-moving pillar, seeming to trail
just above the ground, travelling straight forward
through the storm. Over rocks and past *kopjes* it
travelled, propelled by a force unseen, and ever as
it drew nearer it loomed more black and terrible.

He watched it with a grim elation, drawn irresistibly by its immensity, its awfulness. Straight
towards him it came, and the lightning was dulled
by its nearness and the thunder hushed. He
heard a swishing, whistling sound like the shriek
of a shell, and instinctively he gathered himself
together for the last great shock which no human
power could withstand, the shattering asunder
of soul and body, the swift amazing release of the
spirit.

Involuntarily he shut his eyes as the thing drew near; but he did not shrink, nor was there terror in his heart.

"Thank God I shall die like a man!" he said through his set teeth.

And then—while he waited tense and ready for the great revelation, while all that was mortal in him throbbed with anguished expectation—the monster of destruction swerved as if drawn by a giant hand and passed him by.

He opened his eyes upon a flicker of lightning and saw it whirling onwards, growing ever in volume, towards the *kopje* which Sylvia had never conquered. The blackness of the sky above was appalling. It hung so near, pressing earthwards through that mighty spout.

With bated breath he watched till the *kopje* was blotted from his sight, and the demons of the storm came shrieking back. Then suddenly there came a crash that shook the world and made the senses reel. He heard the rush and swish of water, water torrential that fell in a streaming mass, and as his understanding came staggering back he knew that the first, most menacing danger was past. The cloud had burst upon the *kopje*.

The thunder was drowned in the rush of the rain. It descended in a vast sheet through which the lightning leapt and quivered. The light of day was wholly gone.

The bungalow rocked on its foundations; the wrath of the tempest beat around it as if it would sweep it away. The noise of the falling rain was terrific. He wondered if the place would stand.

Gradually the first wild fury spent itself, and though the storm continued the sky seemed to lift somewhat, to recede as if the swollen clouds were being drawn upwards again. In the glimmering lightning the *veldt* shone like a sea. The water must be deep in the hollows, and he hoped none of the sheep had been caught. The fact that the farm was on rising ground, though it had been exposed to the full force of the storm, had been its salvation. He thought of the Kaffir huts, and dismissed the idea of any serious danger there. The stables, too, were safe for the same reason. It was only on the lower ground beyond the *kopje* that the flood could be formidable. He thought of the watercourse, dry for so many weeks, now without doubt a seething torrent. He thought with a sudden leap of memory of the hut on the sand above. . . .

"I shall go there to-day." How long was it since he had heard those words? Had they indeed been uttered only that morning? Or did they belong to an entirely different period of his life? He felt as if many empty and bitter years had passed over him since they had been spoken. Was it indeed but that morning that the boy's eyes with their fierce appeal had looked into his—and he had given him that stern command to await his coming?

His hand went up to the fastening of the window. He knew Guy. There was a strain of honour in his nature which nothing could ever change. He would keep that sort of appointment or die in the attempt. If he still lived—if that frightful cloudburst had not overwhelmed him—he was there waiting above the raging torrent.

The rain beat with a deafening rattle upon the roof of the *stoep*. It was falling perfectly straight now as if a million taps were running. And another memory flashed upon Burke as he stepped forth,—the memory of a girl who had clung to him in just such another downpour and begged him not to leave her. He heard the accents of her voice, felt again the slender youthfulness of her frame. He flung his arms wide with an anguished gesture.

Another voice, keen-edged and ruthless, was cutting its way through his soul, lacerating him, agonizing him. "And they loved each other. That made all the difference." Ah, God, the bitter difference that it made!

He went down the steps up which he had lifted her on that first day of her coming, and floundered into water that was half way to his knees. The rain rushed down upon him, beating upon his uncovered head. He was drenched to the skin in five seconds.

The lightning flashes were less frequent now, and the darkness in between less intense. He splashed his way cautiously round the bungalow to the stable.

A frightened whinnying greeted him. He heard the animals stamping in the sodden straw, but the water was not so deep here. It scarcely covered their hocks.

He spoke reassuringly to them as he made his way to Diamond, Sylvia's mount. Diamond had always been a favourite with him since the day she had laid her face against his nose, refusing to doubt him. By faith and love! By faith and love!

He saddled the horse more by feeling than sight, and led him out. The rain was still beating furiously down, but Diamond did not flinch with his master's hand upon him. He stood firm while Burke swung himself up. Then, with the lightning still flashing athwart the gloom and the thunder rolling in broken echoes all around them, they went down the track past the *kopje* to find the hut on the sand.

CHAPTER XII

THE SACRIFICE

THE sound of water, splashing, welling, over-flowing, was everywhere. It was difficult to keep the track, but Diamond trod warily. He knew the *veldt* by heart. Passing the *kopje*, the rush of the water was like the spouting of a thousand springs. It gurgled and raced over its scarred sides. The prickly pear bushes hung flattened over the rocks. By the fitful gleam of the lightning Burke saw these things. The storm was passing, though the rain still beat down mercilessly. It would probably rain for many hours; but a faint vague light far down on the unseen horizon told of a rising moon. It would not be completely dark again.

They splashed their way past the *kopje*, and immediately a loud roaring filled his ears. As he had guessed the dry watercourse had become a foaming torrent. Again a sharp anxiety assailed him. He spoke to Diamond, and they turned off the track.

The animal was nervous. He started and quiv-

535

ered at the unaccustomed sound. But in a moment or two he responded to Burke's insistence, and went down the sloping ground that led to the seething water.

Burke guided him with an unerring hand, holding him up firmly, for the way was difficult and uneven. A vivid flash of lightning gave him his direction, and by it he saw a marvellous picture. The spruit had become a wide, dashing river. The swirl and rush of the current sounded like a sea at high tide. The flood spread like an estuary over the *veldt* on the farther side, and he saw that the bank nearest to him was brimming.

The picture was gone in a moment, but it was registered indelibly upon his brain. And the hut —Guy's hut—was scarcely more than twenty yards from that swirling river which was rising with every second.

"He can't be there," he said aloud. But yet he knew that he could not turn back till he had satisfied himself on this point. So, with a word of encouragement to Diamond, he splashed onwards.

Again the lightning flared torchlike through the gloom, but the thunder of the torrent drowned the thunder overhead. He was nearing the hut now, and found that in places the rain had so beaten down the sandy surface of the ground that it sank and yielded like a quagmire. He knew that it was only a matter of minutes—possibly seconds—before the crumbling bank above the stream gave way.

He was close to the hut now, though still he assured himself that the place was empty. The roar of the water was deafening, seeming to numb the senses. He never knew afterwards whether a light suddenly kindled as he drew near behind the canvas that screened the hut-window, or if it had been there all along and the leaping elusive lightning had blinded him to it. But the light was there before him as he reached the place, and in a moment the knowledge flashed upon him beyond all questioning that he had not come upon a vain quest.

He knew also with that menacing roar below him and the streaming rain around that there was not a moment to be lost. He swung himself from Diamond's back and secured the bridle to a projecting piece of wood at the back of the hut. Then, floundering and slipping at every step, he made his way round to the door.

He groped for some seconds before he found it. It was closed and he knew that there was no handle on the outside. He battered upon it with his fist, shouting Guy's name.

There came no answer to his summons, but the

sound of the water seemed to swell in volume, filling the night. It drove him to a fierce impatience. If he had not seen the light he would scarcely have taken the risk. None but a fool would have remained in such a death-trap. But the presence of the light forced him on. He could not leave without satisfying himself. He set his shoulder against the closed door and flung the full weight of his body into one stupendous effort to force an entrance.

The wood cracked and splintered with the shock. He felt himself pitching forward and grabbed at the post to save himself. The door swung back upon its hinges, and he burst into the hut head-long.

The flame of a candle glimmered in his eyes, momentarily dazzling him. Then he heard a cry. A figure sprang towards him—a woman's figure with outstretched arms waving him back! Was he dreaming? Was he mad? It was Sylvia's face, white and agonized, that confronted him— Sylvia's voice, but so strained that he hardly recognized it, broken and beseeching, imploring him for mercy.

"Oh, Burke—for God's sake—don't kill him! Don't kill him! I will kill myself—I swear—if you do."

He caught the outflung hands, gripping them hard, assuring himself that this thing was no illusion. He looked into her eyes of wild appeal.

She attempted no further entreaty, but she flung herself against him, impeding him, holding him back. Over her shoulder he looked for Guy; and found him.

He was sitting crouched on a low trestle-bed at the further end of the hut with his head in his hands. Burke turned to the girl who stood palpitating, pressed against him, still seeking with all her strength to oppose his advance.

Her wide eyes met his. They were filled with a desperate fear. "He is ill," she said.

The roar of the rising water filled the place. The ground under their feet seemed to be shaking.

Burke looked down at the woman he held, and a deadly sensation arose and possessed him. For the moment he felt sick with an overpowering longing. The temptation to take her just as she was and go was almost more than human endurance could bear. He had undergone so much for her sake. He had suffered so fiery a torture. The evil impulse gripped and tore him like a living thing.

And then—was it the purity of those eyes upraised to his?—he was conscious of a change within him. It was as if a quieting touch had been laid upon him. He knew—quite suddenly he knew —what he would do. The temptation and the anguish went out together like an extinguished fire. He was his own master.

He bent to her and spoke, his words clear above the tumult: "Help me to save him! There is just a chance!"

He saw the swift change in her eyes. She bent with a sharp movement, and before he could stop her he felt her lips upon his hand. They thrilled him with a strange exaltation. The memory of that kiss would go with him to the very Gate of Death.

Then he had reached Guy, was bending over him, raising him with urgent hands. He saw the boy's face for a moment, ashen in the flickering candlelight, and he knew that the task before him was one which it would take his utmost strength to accomplish. But he exerted it and dragged him to his feet, half-supporting, half-carrying, him towards the open door, Sylvia helping on the other side. The thought went through him that this was the last act that they would perform in partnership. And somehow he knew that she would remember it later in the same way.

They reached the threshold. Guy was stum-

bling blindly. He seemed to be dazed, scarcely
conscious of his surroundings. The turmoil of the
water was terrific through the ceaseless rush of the
rain. With heads bent to the storm they forced
their way out into the tumult.

They found Diamond tramping and snorting
with fright at the back of the hut, but to Burke's
brief command and Sylvia's touch he stood still.

"Get up!" Burke said to the girl.

But she started and drew back. "Oh no—
no!" she cried back to him. "I will go on foot."

He said no more, merely turned and hoisted
Guy upwards. He landed in the saddle, instinctively gripping with his knees while Burke on one
side, Sylvia on the other, set his feet in the stir-
rups.

Then still in that utter silence Burke went back
to Sylvia. He had lifted her before she was aware,
and for one breathless moment he held her. Then
she also was up on the horse's back. He thrust
her hands away from him, pushing them into Guy's
belt with a mastery that would brook no resistance.

"Wake up!" he yelled to Guy, and smote him
on the thigh as he dragged the bridle free.

Then, slipping and sliding on the yielding
ground, he pulled the horse round, gave the rein
into Guy's clutching hand, and struck the animal

smartly on the flank. Diamond squealed and sprang forward bearing his double burden, and in a moment he was off, making for the higher ground and the track that led to the farm, terrified yet blindly following the instinct that does not err.

The sound of the scrambling, struggling hoofs was lost in the strife of waters, the swaying figures disappeared in the gloom, and the man who was left behind turned grimly and went back into the empty hut.

The candle still cast a flickering light over table and bed. He stood with his back to the raging night and stared at the unsteady flame. It was screened from extinction in the draught by a standing photograph-frame. The picture this contained was turned away from him. After a moment it caught his attention. He moved round the table. Though Death were swooping towards him, swift and certain, on the wings of the rising current, he was drawn as a needle to the magnet. Like a dying man, he reached for the last draught that should slake his thirst and give him peace in dying.

He leaned upon the table, that creaked and shook beneath his weight. He stretched forth his arms on each side of the candle, and drew the portrait close to the flame. Sylvia's face laughed at him through the shifting, uncertain light. She was standing on a wind-blown open space. Her lips were parted. He thought he heard her voice, calling him. And the love in her eyes—the love that shone through the laughter! It held him like a spell—even though it was not for him.

He gazed earnestly upon this thing that had been another man's treasure long before he had even seen her, and as he gazed, he forgot all beside. By that supreme sacrifice of self, he had wiped out all but his exceeding love for her. The spirit had triumphed over the flesh. Love the Immortal to which Death is but a small thing had lifted him up above the world. . . .

What was it that suddenly pierced him as he leaned there? No sound above that mighty tumult could possibly have reached him. No movement beyond that single flickering flame could have caught his vision. No touch was laid upon him. Yet suddenly he jerked upright with every nerve a-quiver—and beheld her!

She stood in the doorway, gasping for breath, clinging to the woodwork for support, with Death behind her, but no fear of Death in her eyes. They held instead a glory which he had never seen before.

He stood and gazed upon her, unbelieving,

afraid to move.   His lips formed her name.   And, as one who springs from tempest into safe shelter, Sylvia sprang to him.   Her arms were all about him before he knew that she was not a dream.

He clasped her then with such a rush of wonder and joy as nearly deprived him of the power to think.   And in that moment their lips met in a kiss that was close and sacred, uniting each to each beyond all severance—a soul communion.

Burke was trembling as she had never known him tremble before.   "Why—have you come back?" he said, as speech returned.

She answered him swiftly and passionately, clinging faster with the words: "Because—God knows—I would rather die with you—than—than live without you!   I love you so!   Oh, don't you understand?"

Yes, he understood, though all else were beyond his comprehension.   Never again would he question that amazing truth that had burst upon him here at the very Gate of Death, changing the whole world.

He looked down upon her as he held her, the light from the candle shining through her hair, her vivid face uplifted to his, her eyes wide and glowing, seeing him alone.   No, he needed no words to tell him that.

And then suddenly the roar without increased a hundredfold. A shrieking wind tore past, and in a moment the flickering light went out. They stood in darkness.

Her arms clasped his neck more closely. He felt the coming agony in her hold. She spoke again, her lips against his own. "Through the grave—and Gate of Death—" she said.

That aroused him. A strength that was titanic entered into him. Why should they wait here for Death? At least they would make a fight for it, however small their chance. He suddenly realized that mortal life had become desirable again—a thing worth fighting for—a precious gift.

He bent, as he had bent on that first night at the farm—how long ago!—and gathered her up into his arms.

A rush of water swirled about his knees as he made for the dim opening. The bank had gone. Yet the rise in the ground would give them a few seconds. He counted upon the chance. Out into the open he stumbled.

The water was up to his waist here. He floundered on the yielding ground.

"Don't carry me!" she said. "I can wade too. Let me hold your hand!"

But he would not let her go out of his arms. His

strength in that moment was as the strength of ten. He knew that unless the flood actually overwhelmed him, it would not fail.

So, slipping, struggling, fighting, he forced his way, and, like Diamond, he was guided by an instinct that could not err. Thirty seconds after they left it, the hut on the sand was swept away by the hungry waters, but those thirty seconds had been their salvation. They had reached the point where the ground began to rise towards the *kopje*, and though the water still washed around them the force of it was decreasing at every step.

As they reached the foot of the *kopje* itself, a stream of moonlight suddenly rushed down through the racing clouds, revealing the whole great waste of water like a picture flung upon a screen.

Burke's breath came thick and laboured; yet he spoke. "We are saved!" he said.

"Put me down now!" she urged. "Please put me down!"

But still he would not, till he had climbed above the seething flood, and could set her feet upon firm ground. And even then he clasped her still, as if he feared to let her go.

They stood in silence, holding fast to one another while the moonlight flickered in and out.

and Burke's heart gradually steadied again after the terrific struggle. The rain had almost ceased. Only the sound of the flood below and the gurgle of a hundred rivulets around filled the night.

Sylvia's arm pressed upon Burke's neck. "Shall we go—right to the top?" she said.

"The top of what?" He turned and looked into her eyes as she stood above him.

She bent to him swiftly, throbbing, human, alive. She held his face between her hands, looking straight back for a space. Then with a little quivering laugh, she bent lower and kissed him.

"I think you're right, partner," she said. "We don't need to go—any farther than this. We've—got there."

He caught her to him with a mastery that was dearer to her in that moment than any tenderness, swaying her to his will. "Yes—we've got there!" he said, and kissed her again with lips that trembled even while they compelled. "But oh, my soul—what a journey!"

She clung to him more closely, giving of her all in full and sweet surrender. "And oh, my soul," she laughed back softly—"what an arrival!"

And at that they laughed together, triumphant as those who have the world at their feet.

CHAPTER XIII

BY FAITH AND LOVE

THE flood went down in the morning, and behind it there sprang into being a new world of softest, tenderest green in place of the brown, parched desert that had been. Mary Ann stood at the door of her hut and looked at it with her goggle-eyes in which the fright of the storm was still very apparent.

Neither she nor her satellites would go near the house of the *baas* that morning, for a dread shadow lay upon it into which they dared not venture. The *baas* himself was there. He had driven her into the cooking-hut a little earlier and compelled her to prepare a hot meal under his stern supervision. But even the *baas* could not have forced her to enter the bungalow. For by some occult means Mary Ann knew that Death was waiting there, and the wrath of the gods was so recent that she had not courage left for this new disaster.

Diamond had brought his burden safely out of the storm, and was now comfortably sheltered in his own stable. But the man who had ridden him had been found hours later by the big *baas* face downwards on the *stoep*, and now he lay in the room in which he had lain for so long, with breathing that waxed and waned and sometimes stopped, and eyes that wandered vaguely round as though seeking something which they might never find.

What were they looking for? Sylvia longed to know. In the hush of that room with the light of the early morning breaking through, it seemed to her that those eyes were mutely waiting for a message from Beyond. They did not know her even when they rested upon her face.

She herself was worn out both physically and mentally, but she would not leave him. And so Burke had brought in the long chair for her and made her lie down while she watched. He brought her food also, and they ate together in the quiet room where the ever-changing breathing of the man upon the bed was the only sound.

He would have left them alone then, but she whispered to him to come back.

He came and bent over her. "I'll smoke on the *stoep*," he said. "You have only to raise your voice if you want me, and I shall hear."

She slipped her arms about his neck, and drew

him down to her. "I want you—all the time,"
she whispered.

He kissed her on lips and hair, but he would not
stay. She heard him pass out on to the *stoep*, and
there fell a deep silence.

It seemed to lap her round like a vast and soundless sea. Presently she was drifting upon it,
sometimes dipping under, sometimes bringing herself to the surface with a deliberate effort of the
will, lest Guy should come back and need her. She
was unutterably tired, and the rest was balm to
her weary soul, but still she fought against complete repose, until, like the falling of a mist, oblivion came at last very softly upon her, and she
sank into the deeps of slumber. . . .

It must have been some time later that something spoke within her, recalling her. She raised
herself quickly and looked at Guy to find his eyes
no longer roving but fixed upon her. She thought
his breathing must be easier, for he spoke without
effort.

"Fetch Burke!" he said.

She started up to obey. There was that about
Guy at the moment which she had never seen before, a curious look of knowledge, a strength new-
born that was purely spiritual. But ere she
reached the window, Burke was there. He came

straight in and went to Guy. And she knew that
the end was very near.

Instinctively she drew back as the two men met.
She had a strong feeling that her presence was not
needed, was almost an intrusion. Yet she could
not bring herself to go, till suddenly Burke turned
to her and drew her forward.

"He wants you to say good-bye to him," he
said, "and then—to go."

It was very tenderly spoken. His hand pressed
her shoulder, and the pressure was reassuring,
infinitely sustaining.

She bent over Guy. He looked straight up at
her, and though the mystery of Death was in his
eyes they held no fear. They even faintly smiled
upon her.

"Good-bye, darling!" he said softly. "Think of
me sometimes—when you've nothing better to do!"

She found and clasped his hand. "Often!"
she whispered. "Very often!"

His fingers pressed hers weakly. "I wish—I'd
made good," he said.

She bent lower over him. "Ah, never mind
now!" she said. "That is all over—forgiven long
ago."

His eyes still sought hers with that strange
intentness. "I never loved—anyone but you,

Sylvia," he said. "You'll remember that. It's
the only thing in all my life worth remembering.
Now go, darling! Go and rest! I've got—to
talk to Burke—alone."

She kissed him on the forehead, and then, a moment later, on the lips. She knew as she went
from him that she would never hear his voice
again on earth.

   .   .   .   .   .   .

She went to her own room and stood at the window gazing out upon that new green world that
but yesterday had been a desert. The thought of
her dream came upon her, but the bitterness and
the fears were all gone from her heart. The thing
she had dreaded so unspeakably had come and
passed. The struggle between the two men on
that path which could hold but one was at an end.
The greater love had triumphed over the lesser,
but even so the lesser had not perished. Dimly
she realized that Guy's broken life had not been
utterly cast away. It seemed to her that already
—there at the Gate of Death—he had risen again.
And she knew that her agonized prayer had found
an answer at last. Guy was safe.

   .   .   .   .   .   .

It was a long time before Burke came to her.
When he did, it was to find her in a chair by the

window with her head pillowed on the table, sunk
in sleep. But she awoke at his coming, looking at
him swiftly with a question in her eyes which his
as swiftly answered. He came and knelt beside
her, and gathered her into his arms.

She clung to him closely for a while in silence,
finding peace and great comfort in his hold. Then
at length, haltingly she spoke.

"Burke,—you—forgave him?"

"Yes," he said.

She lifted her face and kissed his neck. "Burke,
you understand—I—couldn't forsake him—
then?"

"I understand," he said, drawing her nearer.
"You couldn't forsake anyone in trouble."

"Oh, not just that," she said. "I loved him so.
I couldn't help it. I—had to love him."

He was silent for a few seconds, and the wonder
stirred within her if perhaps even now he could
misunderstand her. And then he spoke, his voice
very low, curiously uneven. "I know. I loved
him, too. That was—the hell of it—for me."

"Oh, Burke—darling!" she said.

He drew a hard breath, controlling himself with
an effort. "I'd have cut off my right hand to
save him, but it was no good. It came to me afterwards—that you were the one who might have

done it. But it was too late then. Besides—
besides—" he spoke as if something within him
battled fiercely for utterance—"I couldn't have
endured it—standing by. Not you—not you!"

She put up a hand, and stroked his face. "I
belonged to you from the first moment I saw you,"
she said.

"Sylvia!" He moved abruptly, taking her by
the shoulders so that he might look into her eyes.
"That is—the truth?" he said.

She met his look steadfastly. "Of course it is
the truth!" she said. "Could I tell you anything
else?"

He held her still. "But—Sylvia——"

Her hands were clasped against his breast. "It
is the truth," she said again. "I didn't realize it
myself at first. It came to me—quite suddenly—
that day of the sand-storm—the day Guy saved
your life."

"Ah!" he said.

She went on with less assurance. "It frightened
me—when I knew. I was so afraid you would
find out."

"But why?" he said. "Why?"

She shook her head, and suddenly her eyes fell
before his. She looked almost childishly ashamed.

"Won't you tell me why?" he said.

She made a small, impulsive movement of protest. "I didn't—quite—trust you," she said.

"But you knew I loved you!" he said.

She shook her head again with vehemence. "I didn't know—I didn't know! How could I? Why, you have never told me so—even now."

"Great heavens!" he said, as if aghast.

Very oddly his unexpected discomfiture restored her confidence. She faced him again. "It doesn't matter now," she said. "You needn't begin at this stage. I've found out for myself— as you might have done long ago if you hadn't been quite blind. But I'm rather glad, after all, that you didn't, because—you learnt to trust me without. It was dear of you to trust me, Burke. I don't know how you managed it."

"I would trust you to the world's end—blindfold," he said. "I know you."

"Yes, now. But you didn't then. When you found me in the hut—with Guy," her voice quivered a little—"you didn't know—then—that I was with him because he was too ill to be there alone."

"And to protect him from me," Burke said.

"Yes; that too." She laid her cheek suddenly against his hand. "Forgive me for that!" she said.

He drew her head back to his shoulder. "No —you had reason enough for fearing me," he said. "God alone knows what brought you back to me."

She leaned against him with a little sigh. "Yes, He knows," she said softly, "just as He knows what made you stay behind to die alone. It was the same reason with us both. Don't you understand?"

His arms grew close about her. His lips pressed her forehead. "Yes," he said. "Yes, I understand."

. . . .

They spoke later of Kieff and the evil influence he had exerted over Guy.

"The man was his evil genius," Burke said. "But I couldn't keep him away when the boy was damaged and there was no one else to help." He paused a moment. "He was the only man in the world I was ever afraid of," he said then. "He had an uncanny sort of strength that I couldn't cope with. And he was such a fiend. When he tried to get you into his toils—frankly, I was terrified. He had dragged down so many."

"And you think—Guy—might have been different but for him?" Sylvia questioned.

"Yes. I believe I could have kept him straight if it hadn't been for Kieff. He and Piet Vreiboom were thick as thieves, and between them the boy got pulled under. I was beat, and Kelly, too."

"Mr. Kelly!" Sylvia gave a slight start; that name reminded her. "Burke, do you know—I owe him money? I've got to tell you about that."

She paused in rather painful hesitation; it was hard to tell him even now what she had sacrificed so much to hide.

But he stopped her. "No. You needn't. I know all about it. I put Kelly up to the job. The money was mine."

"Burke!" She stared at him in astonishment. "You—knew!"

He nodded. "I guessed a little. And I made Donovan do the rest. You were so upset about it. Something had to be done."

"Oh, Burke!" she said again.

He went on. "Guy told me all about it too—only a little while ago. He made a clean breast of everything. He was—awfully penitent. Look here! We'll forget all that, won't we? Promise me you'll forget it!" He spoke rapidly, just as Guy would have spoken. She saw that he was deeply moved. "I was a devil ever to doubt you. I want to be sure—to be certain sure—that you'll never think of it again—that you'll forget it all—as if it had never been."

The earnest appeal in his eyes almost startled her. It brought the quick tears to her own. She gave him both her hands. "I shall only remember —one thing," she said. "And that is—your great goodness to me—from beginning to end."

He made a sound of dissent, but she would not hear.

"I am going to remember that always, for it is the biggest thing in my life. And now, Burke, please tell me—for I've got to know—are we quite ruined?"

He gave her an odd look. "What made you think of that?"

She coloured a little. "I don't know. I have been thinking about it a great deal lately. Anyhow," she met his look almost defiantly, "I've a right to think of it, haven't I? We're partners."

"You've a right to do anything that seems good to you," he said. "I am not absolutely down and out, but I'm pretty near it. There isn't much left.'

She squeezed his hands hard, hearing the news with no hint of dismay. Her eyes were shining with the old high courage. "Never mind, partner! We'll pull up again," she said. "We're a sound working proposition, aren't we?"

He drew her suddenly and closely into his arms. "My own brave girl!" he said.

.   .   .   .

Bill Merston came over in the evening, summoned by one of Burke's Kaffirs, and they buried Guy under the shadow of the *kopje* in what in a few more days would be a paradise of flowers. The sun was setting far away in an opalescent glow of mauve and pink and pearl. And the beauty of it went straight to Sylvia's heart.

She listened to the Burial Service, read by Merston in his simple sincere fashion, and she felt as if all grief or regret were utterly out of place. She and Burke, standing hand in hand, had been lifted above earthly things. And again there came to her the thrilling certainty that Guy was safe. She wondered if, in his own words, he had forgotten it all and started afresh.

Merston could not stay for the night. He looked at Sylvia rather questioningly at parting.

She smiled in answer as she gave him her hand. "Give my love to Matilda!" she said. "Say I am coming to see her soon!"

"Is that all?" he said.

She nodded. "Yes, that's all. No—one thing more!" She detained him a moment. "Thank her for all she has done for me, and tell her I have found the right mixture at last! She will understand, or—if she doesn't—I will give her the recipe when I come."

He frowned at her with masculine curiosity. "What is it for? A new kind of pickles?"

She turned from him. Her face was deeply flushed. "No. It's a thing called happiness. Don't forget to tell her! Good-bye!"

"Then in heaven's name, come soon!" said Merston, as he mounted his horse.

.   .   .   .

When he was gone, they mounted the *kopje* together, still hand in hand.

The way was steep, but they never rested till they reached the top. The evening light was passing, but the sky was full of stars. The *spruit* was a swift-flowing river below them. They heard the rush of its waters—a solemn music that seemed to fill the world.

Sylvia turned her face to the north, and the long, dim range of hills beyond the *veldt*.

"We will go beyond some day," Burke said.

She held his hand very fast. "I don't mind where we go, partner, so long as we go together," she said.

He drew something out of his pocket and held it out to her. "I've got to give you this," he said.

She looked at him in surprise. "Burke! What is it?"

"It's something Guy left to you," he said, "with his love. I promised to give it you to-night. Take it, won't you?"

She took it, a small object wrapped in paper, strangely heavy for its size. "What is it?" she said again.

"Open it!" he said.

She complied, trembling a little. "Oh— Burke!" she said.

It lay in her hand, a rough stone like a small crystal, oddly shaped. The last of the evening light caught it, and it gleamed as if with living fire.

"The diamond!" she whispered.

"Yes—the diamond." Burke spoke very quietly. "He gave it to me just before he died. 'Tell her she is not to keep it!' he said. 'She is to sell it. I won it for her, and she is to make use of it.'"

"But—it is yours really," Sylvia said.

"No. It is yours." Burke spoke with insistence. "But I think he is right. You had better sell it. Vreiboom and some of Hoffstein's gang are after it. They don't know yet who won it. Donovan covered Guy's tracks pretty cleverly. But they'll find out. It isn't a thing to keep."

She turned to him impulsively. "You take it, partner!" she said. "It was won with your money, and no one has a greater right to it."

"It is yours," he insisted.

She smiled. "Very well. If it's mine, I give it to you; and if it's yours you share it with me. We are partners, aren't we? Isn't that what Guy intended?"

He smiled also. "Well—perhaps."

She put it into his hand and closed his fingers over it. "There's no perhaps about it. We'll take it back to Donovan, and make him sell it. And when we've done that—" She paused.

"Yes?" he said.

She pushed her hand through his arm. "Would it bore you very much, partner, to take me back to England—just—for a little while? I want to see my daddy again and tell him how happy I am. He'll like to know."

"Of course I will take you," he said.

"Thank you." Her hand pressed his arm. "And then we'll come back here. I want to come back here, Burke. It isn't—a land of strangers to me any more. It's just—the top of the world. Shall I tell you—would you like me to tell you— how we managed to get here?"

His arm went round her. "I think I know."

She turned her face to his. "By faith—and love, my darling," she said. "There is—no other way. You taught me that."

He kissed her fervently, with lips that trembled. "I love you with my whole soul," he told her, with sudden passion. "God knows how I love you!"

She gave herself to him with a little quivering laugh. "Do you know, partner," she said, "I wanted you to tell me that? I've been wanting it—for ever so long."

And they were nearer to the stars above them in that moment than to the world that lay at their feet.

THE END